Why Dogs Chase Cars

SOUTHERN REVIVAL SERIES
Robert H. Brinkmeyer, Jr., Series Editor

Her Own Place, Dori Sanders
Why Dogs Chase Cars, George Singleton

WHY DOGS
CHASE CARS

Tales of a Beleaguered Boyhood

Expanded Edition

GEORGE SINGLETON

New Introduction by George Singleton

The University of South Carolina Press

PUBLISHED IN COOPERATION WITH THE INSTITUTE FOR
SOUTHERN STUDIES OF THE UNIVERSITY OF SOUTH CAROLINA

First edition published by Algonquin Books, 2004
Expanded edition published by the University of South Carolina Press,
2013, Columbia, South Carolina 29208

www.sc.edu/uscpress

Manufactured in the United States of America

22 21 20 19 18 17 16 15 14 13   10 9 8 7 6 5 4 3 2 1

The Library of Congress has cataloged the first edition as follows:

Singleton, George 1958–
Why dogs chase cars : tales of a beleaguered boyhood /
George Singleton.—1st ed.
p. cm.
"A Shannon Ravenel book."
ISBN 1-56512-404-9 (alk. paper)
1. Eccentrics and eccentricities—Fiction. 2. Fathers and sons—Fiction.
3. South Carolina—Fiction. 4. Boys—Fiction. I. Title.
PS3569.I5747W47 2004
813'.6—dc22   200404262

Expanded edition ISBN 978-1-61117-245-4

This book was printed on a recycled paper with 30 percent
postconsumer waste content.

For the bartenders and booksellers,
plus Shannon Ravenel for putting up with me

Contents

Southern Revivals, supported by the University of South Carolina Institute for Southern Studies's Robert E. McNair Fund, brings returns to print important works of literature by contemporary Southern writers. All selections in the series have enjoyed critical and commercial success. By returning these works to general circulation, we hope to deepen readers' understandings of, and appreciations for, not only specific authors but also the flourishing Southern literary landscape. Not too long ago, it was a fairly straightforward task to distinguish literature by Southerners, as most of their works focused on easily recognizable "Southern" themes, perspectives, and settings. Those days are long gone. Literature by Southerners is now quite literally all over the map, extending its reach from the coast of South Carolina to heart of West Africa, from the bayous of Louisiana to the rain forests of Brazil, from the mountains of Eastern Tennessee to the deserts of the Southwest. As our list of resurrected books grows, Southern Revivals will bring readers to many of these places, taking them on journeys into regions near and far away, journeys which attest to the astonishing diversity of contemporary Southern culture.

One of the initial two publications of the Southern Revivals series, George Singleton's *Why Dogs Chase Cars* was first published by Algonquin Books of Chapel Hill in 2004. This wickedly funny and dead-on serious collection of short stories is Singleton's "knock-you-upside-the-head" take on life in the rural South. Linking the stories is the voice of Mendal Dawes, an immensely likable and gifted oddball who quotes Schopenhauer as easily as *Hee Haw*, reflecting back on his even odder upbringing in the small upstate South Carolina town of Forty-Five. Singleton's South, the South of Forty-Five, is peopled with obsessive eccentrics, outrageous freaks who would make Flannery O'Connor blush. Or, as Mendal puts it, it's a place where the "gene pool [is] so shallow that it wouldn't take a Dr. Scholl's insert to keep one's soles dry." As the stories progress and Mendal comes of age, he becomes more aware of the humanity shimmering beneath the surface of the crackpot world of Forty-Five. Not that Mendal ever gives up on his idea of escaping Forty-Five. He knows that he shares something with all those dogs who chase cars (I'll not give the significance of the title away), and that the best way for him to understand his coming of age in Forty-Five is to see it from a great distance.

Why Dogs Chase Cars is Singleton's third collection of stories, following *These People Are Us* (2001) and *The Half-Mammals of Dixie* (2002) and coming before *Drowning in Gruel* (2006) and *Stray Decorum* (2012).

Besides these well-received collections, Singleton has published two novels, *Novel* (2005) and *Work Shirts for Madmen* (2007), together with a guide for writers, *Pep Talks, Warnings, and Screeds: Indispensable Wisdom and Cautionary Advice for Writers* (2008). Individual stories have appeared in a number of the nation's best magazines and journals, including *Atlantic Monthly, Harper's, Playboy, Georgia Review, Kenyon Review*, and *American Literary Review, Southern Review*, and *North American Review.* Almost all of Singleton's fiction takes the reader deep into the zany small-town world of upstate South Carolina, the area where Singleton now lives. Born in Anaheim, California, Singleton was raised in Greenville, South Carolina, and he currently teaches at the South Carolina Governor's School for the Arts and Humanities. Amongst his awards, he received a Guggenheim Fellowship in 2009 and won the Hillsdale Award for Fiction from the Fellowship of Southern Writers in 2011.

Singleton has been called "the unchallenged king of the comic southern short story" by the *Atlanta Journal-Constitution,* "a breakthrough writer you need to know" by *Book* magazine, and "a big-hearted evil genius who writes as if he were the love child of Alice Munro and Strom Thurman" by novelist Tony Earley. In the pages that follow, you'll find this praise to be well-deserved.

Robert H. Brinkmeyer, Jr.

Acknowledgments

I would like to thank Robert Brinkmeyer for including my work in the Southern Revival Series. Bob ranks high in southern culture, and I value his friendship and expertise. Also at the University of South Carolina Press I owe courageous and far-sighted director Jonathan Haupt, and Elizabeth Jones for her expertise in copyediting and gentle reminders about deadlines. Thank you Linda Fogle at the press, also.

It took nine years of writing before I jumped over from third-person narration to trying my hand (and luck, I hoped) at first-person. Then it took me another eleven years of writing before I discovered the outright deep psyche plunge a first-person retrospective-kind of story could offer. So I was forty or thereabouts when I wrote "Show and Tell," a story narrated by one Mendel Dawes, that ended up published in the *Atlantic Monthly*. Hot damn, I thought, maybe I should write some more of these types stories—ones wherein the narrator could be thirty-five or forty and speaking like an adult, looking back toward his odd and less-than-rational upbringing.

At the time I had finished up a collection called *The Half-Mammals of Dixie* and had it accepted for publication. For the year between acceptance and publication, I worked on a knot of stories that ended up being *Why Dogs Chase Cars*, all linked stories told from the point of view of Compton Lane, who happened to be Mendal Dawes's best friend in "Show and Tell."

Why didn't I just continue writing stories from Mendal Dawes's point of view from the get-go? Maybe I thought it would be cheating, I don't know. Hell, I feared writing in first person for those beginning nine years because I didn't want anyone reading a story and thinking "I" equaled "George." It took a granola-eating yoga enthusiast telling me that I never wrote in first person because I "couldn't share my emotions" that got me writing first-person narratives in the first place. I had thought, Oh yeah?—anger, hatred, envy, jealousy, and spite all seem to be emotions of which I'm pretty familiar—watch this. . .

Anyway, I got myself trudging onward with what became *Why Dogs Chase Cars*. Because there's not much to do in Dacusville, South Carolina where I live, I made up a little game for myself. I wanted the finished collection to come off as hourglass shaped. I wanted to start the stories with Compton Lane as an adult, and the first half of the linked stories would go backwards until, about midway, there would be a story about Comp's first memories. Then I'd go back upwards to his being forty or whatever age, married and divorced, and so on. The end.

I finished, I sent it to my agent, she sent it to Shannon Ravenel, and Shannon took it. She'd been the editor of *The Half-Mammals of Dixie*, too, and I understood that I could not have been in better hands. In the Top Row of Great Editors, Shannon stands smartly, believe me.

I had sent some of the stories out to magazines along the way, of course, and they appeared—in *Book, Georgia*

Review, Cincinnati Review, Shenandoah, New England Review, Atlanta magazine, *Yalobusha Review*, and *Greensboro Review*. They all had different titles. Way different titles.

On a side note, my agent's "assistant" at the time said she wanted to place the other six-plus stories. I said okay. About two months before the book came out she called me and said, "Do you want me to send any of those stories out yet?" I said, "What the hell are you talking about? You ain't been sending them out all along? I figured they'd been getting rejected." She said, "I was waiting for you to tell me that they were ready." I said, "Damn it to hell, the book had already been bought. Don't you think they were ready?" et cetera. There may have been more curse words on my part. To this day I have sent my own stories out, after this fiasco.

So. Shannon got ahold of the, say, 400+ page collection and starting a-cutting rightly. Compton got turned back into Mendal telling all of the stories, somehow, which was fine by me. (My memory's fuzzy on this—maybe she told me to do that long before I even started sending stories out. I do remember her saying something to the effect that Compton came off as mean-spirited at times, while Mendal was a more likeable narrator.) She cut out the stories wherein even Mendal wasn't all that nice. "I like your sweet stories," Shannon told me.

It's not easy for a man living in a town called Dacusville—surrounded by people who shoot *trees* on windy days—to accept "I like your sweet stories." But she was correct, per usual.

My hourglass shaped collection no longer existed. Maybe it wasn't the best idea in the first place.

So on 10/23/02 I received a proposed order of stories for *Nothing's Enough*, the original title of *Why Dogs Chase Cars*. I wouldn't remember any of this had I not kept, like some kind of weirdo pack rat likely to be on that *Hoarders* show, all the correspondence between editor and writer. Shannon had a proposed arrangement, and she had some new titles. Here they are, in the same order as what ended up being tertiary titles in the collection: How Dad Dealt with Loss, My Valentine, My First Win, My First Job, My First Girlfriend, My Last Night of Innocence, I Give Dad a Hand, Dad Explains how the World Works, My First Car, My First Dance, My First Real Job, What Dad Left Me "(cut this story at page 31, save the other half for another book)."

"No, no, no, no, no," I said to Shannon about these titles. It sounds like a Bobbsey Twins book." There's sweet, yes, and then there's flat-out wimpy." I might've used the P word. I hope I didn't. I love and respect Shannon Ravenel, and wouldn't want to say anything like that in her presence.

Maybe I thought, What if "My First Job" and "Giving Dad a Hand" somehow got transposed and rearranged somehow at the printer?

Shannon said something like, "Well, then come up with some titles that connect all these stories," and I'm sure she thought, You goofball rube wasting my time non-stop.

Understand that she probably wanted to shove this book off as a novel. If I remember correctly, it got sent off to that Barnes and Noble woman who's in charge of about Everything Published in America, and she let it be known that, for a novel, it didn't have much of a climax and denouement. The original Advanced Reading Copies didn't have "stories" down below the title, and it got changed—thankfully—soon thereafter before the "final" collection came out.

I sat down and looked at the stories. I thought to change *Nothing's Enough* to *Why Dogs Chase Cars* after first picking *When Dogs Chased Cars*. Then I thought about why a dog might—in his or her mind—try to catch a ride out of the town of Forty-Five, and so on. The secondary titles came into being, and that's what appeared—not totally to my liking, but I'm a curmudgeon and I'm never pleased—in the original collection.

So now we have one extra story, "Poetry," and the last pages of "After Women," which had been "What Dad Left Me," which had been "The Earth Rotates This Way."

There were others, I believe, but I don't know where they ended up. I tend to tend a large fire pit here in Dacusville, almost daily.

Why Dogs Chase Cars

Nearby Toxic Waste Dumps

I had to assume that my mother took the photographs of me standing near the alligator pit. The same goes for the ones of me standing next to Dad on the edge of Blowing Rock, and the ones in the cotton mill amid a thousand running looms. There's a curled black-and-white picture of me somewhere on the roadside near Cherokee, North Carolina, with my hand inside a black bear's cage. All of my childhood pictures had taken place in precarious situations: on my father's lap aboard a tractor cutting through cornstalks; at the rear end of a working cement truck's trough; held in my father's arms between two hot rods at the ready to race down Forty-Five's main drag. There were pictures taken of me sitting in a stroller on the roof of the house, bricks braking the wheels while Dad cleaned our gutters. I know that sometimes people think that they remember a situation when really they just recall hearing family stories ten thousand times, or they've seen the photographs and/or eight-millimeter home movies a million. For me, the occasions for these snapshots remained as vivid and recognizable as when I first teethed, took a step, or got potty-trained, except for who had held the Brownie camera. I wasn't three years old before I'd done about everything scary outside of flying upside down in a crop duster or shaking hands with Republicans. When the county fair came to town, my mother had evidently shot a series of photographs of me sitting on the laps of fat ladies, bearded ladies, geeks, Siamese twins, and knife swallowers—all people who could have kidnapped and made me part of their otherworld. I rode on the back of a two-headed calf. My father always stood nearby, usually only half his body in the frame, either smiling like a fool or as somber as any rebel soldier intent on being slain.

"Just because you're drowning in gasoline doesn't mean you should light a match to enhance evaporation," my father said when I asked him about the photos. I was seventeen, and full of myself, and although I remembered everything on a daily basis, this was the first time I'd seen those memories in monochromatic, two-dimensional splendor. These family photographs had remained in a shoe box tucked behind some pink insulation beneath a homemade safe in the attic. Now I needed to pick one out for some kind of Before-and-After thing Miss Ballard, the yearbook sponsor, wanted to try out.

I didn't know what my father meant by gas and evaporation, of course. "What're you talking about, man?" I said.

"Some things are best left alone. I was just trying to do what I thought best. Your mother had other ideas. If she'd've stuck around and had her way, you would've been brought up wearing safety boots and a helmet. I did the opposite. Sorry if you ended so messed up, son."

This was in mid-April of 1976, and the yearbook deadline approached. I already had a reputation for being some kind of loner hermit freak at Forty-Five High School because my father made me read all of Durkheim and Marx and recite it daily, because we didn't go to a church of any sort, because I could run two miles in ten minutes but wouldn't join the track team, because I planned on going to a college that didn't offer agriculture science, because I talked to and admired my female black friend, Shirley Ebo, because I listened to the Grateful Dead, because I accidentally laughed uncontrollably when our revered football coach died of a heart attack on the sidelines losing 72-0 midgame, because my father made me lure stray and feral dogs from the tree farm across from our house on Deadfall Road and keep them until we could get them properly fixed or neutered, because I didn't smoke cigarettes, because I knew early on that female genitalia wasn't known as "cock," though some of my idiotic redneck male counterparts called it that, because I could speak French perfectly without knowing what I said, because I wouldn't participate in the Pledge of Allegiance or daily prayer each morning, and because I probably won the countywide spelling bee six years earlier only by enunciating f-o-s-s-o-r-i-a-l without counting on my fingers.

I said to my father, "I'm not saying that I'm messed up, or that *you* messed up. I just need a picture of me when I was younger. We don't have a picture of me sitting on Santa's lap or anything like that? There's got to be a picture of me riding a tricycle, or opening Christmas presents. I remember Mom taking a picture of me holding that rat snake."

My father held the shoe box on his thighs. We sat at the kitchen table. He shook his head sideways. "Your mother might've stolen some pictures with her back then, I don't know. Your mother might've taken a lot of things from this house thirteen years ago or whenever, but I can't be responsible for all that. To hell with me. Here." He reached into the box and handed me a three-by-five photograph in which I stood beside a sign that bled off the left side of the frame. It only read IC UMP, and I wore a perfectly wonderful and crisp seersucker suit, plus a watch cap. My father's arm came out of the right side of the picture. Did the sign say TOXIC DUMP from top to bottom? Were we in Savannah, or Nevada? Was my father touching my shoulder gently, or pushing me toward the hole? I kind of remembered the day, but seeing as I couldn't read at the time, I wouldn't have known what the sign read. Maybe it said PUBIC LUMP and we stood near another one of those country fair sideshow people. Maybe it read SCENIC JUMP.

Or maybe the sign had read something else altogether, I didn't know. I said it would be good enough for Miss Ballard's yearbook, and got up from the kitchen table. I excused myself to go rig a garden hose from our car into the living room window, to rid our household of a probable degenerative disease passed on from father to son. My father said, "Make sure you come back in time for us to dig some holes in the backyard. I have a few more things to bury so you'll have something to unearth and sell later on after I die."

I told my father to hide my childhood photographs somewhere else so I wouldn't find them again, ever.

MY CHILDHOOD TOOK place a few miles outside of Forty-Five, South Carolina, which meant I lived a hundred miles from any town with a population of twenty thousand or more people. Charlotte, Greenville, Augusta, and Columbia were far away. In between were places like Level Land or Graniteville, Ninety Six or Doweltown, Putdown or Takeaway. Gruel. Between those towns stood plain *space*. Here—a mile up the gray, bumpy asphalt—was Rufus Price's Goat Wagon store, and down Deadfall Road slanted a series of shingle-sided shacks where people like Shirley Ebo lived. Over in Forty-Five stood three cotton mills, their requisite villages, and my high school on Highway 25. Between the town and my house was a flat, flat, barren expanse of red clay nothingness and uncultivated scrub pine ready for development by people like my father, maybe the only man in all of Forty-Five with the ability to look past tomorrow.

"I could take a photograph of some little child now and we could say it was you," my father said on the afternoon after I turned my mysterious IC UMP photograph in. "We've got some pictures of your momma's sisters' kids we could turn in and no one would know the difference. I've been upset all day thinking about what few relics I have of you growing up, and therefore what you have of yourself."

I said, "Miss Ballard said she liked the one of me standing in front of IC UMP. She asked me where we were, and I said California. I said we were somewhere on vacation in California."

My father put his hand on my shoulder—at this point I stood nearly as tall as he did—and said, "I'll tell you where we were if you promise not to tell anyone else. I mean, I'll let you in on a mean-ass joke I played, if you can keep your big barbecue pit doused."

I had a story to tell him, too. I'd gone by the Winn-Dixie on the way to homeroom, bought a jar of strained Gerber's pablum, taken off the label, then sworn to Miss Ballard later that I had been the child-baby actor who modeled for the picture. I said to my father, "Don't hit me."

He had that look on his face. My father had taken to walking with a hard, hard cane for no reason whatsoever, and he liked to slap me across the hamstrings with it in a similar fashion to what most people used to pat someone's shoulders.

"That picture your mother took of you was taken right

in the backyard there." He pointed out toward a field owned by a man named Few, one of Forty-Five's wealthier citizens, a man who kept land around because, over the generations, his kin had moved upstate from Charleston in order to escape heat and mosquitoes each summer. My father continued with, "I felt then and I feel now that, in time, that land will be sold to a land developer, and that that land developer will correctly begin making a subdivision out of it. You know for a fact that I would buy up the land if, and only if, I could sell it to land developers, but I don't want a subdivision on our back property."

I looked out the window of our sad cement-block house. I saw weeds, goldenrod, scattered four-foot pines, the small crosses I had fashioned over the last ten years when I'd buried dead wild dogs that had chased cars badly out in front of our house. I said, "No it wasn't. That picture was taken somewhere else. It doesn't even look like the same place."

My father hit me with his cane. "Landscapes change over fifteen years, fuzznuts. You're going to find out sooner or later, believe me. One day someone's going to start digging back there, and your property value for this house will drop dramatically. But you won't have a subdivision out the kitchen window. Those toxic-dump barrels will stop that little project." My father swiped at me again with his cane. "You won't ever remember this, though, seeing as you're not even listening."

My mother had snapped the photograph in the early 1960s. Out on the West Coast, entire cities of near-prefab houses were being developed. My father foresaw the groundswell moving to the southeastern United States— and although he never put it down on paper, he often liked to predict what would happen to places like Atlanta and Charlotte. My mother still lived with us then; my father went out and gathered, according to him right there in our kitchen, some hundred black fifty-five-gallon steel drums. He borrowed a backhoe and bought stencils and spray paint, supposedly. "Your momma helped me spray-paint TOXIC MATERIAL or TOXIC DUMP or TOXIC WASTE on every one of the barrels. I put them in the ground all over the place one Christmas week when I knew that old man Few wouldn't be over this way. He and his family always met down in the low country most of December and January, you know."

I said, "You've lost your mind. Did you have a dream last night? What're you talking about?"

"So then in years to come, long after I'm gone, somebody will buy up that land and set out to put down septic tanks. They'll unearth those drums and have no choice but to get scared and back out of the deal. I can't expect you to thank me now, but you and your wife will put flowers on my grave the day this all happens. Are you listening to me?"

I didn't say how I had a plan to move—if not out of America, out of the South. I didn't say how my entire life would not be worth living unless I got the hell out of South

Carolina, that I would find a way when traveling from, say, New York to Florida, to detour the state of my training in order not to buy gasoline and/or snacks. Even in 1976 the state sales tax went only to erecting roadside historical markers that described what pre–Civil War plantations stood nearby and how happy the slaves were there. I said, "Did you put anything in those barrels? What's in the barrels?"

I'll admit now that I wasn't listening, though. My mind wandered to some unknown woman I would meet in college, fall in love with, marry. My father said, "You don't think all those feral dogs just started chasing cars when you came along, do you?" He laughed hard, threw his head back, and pulled his cane back to hit me. I cringed and waited for the impact. When my father placed his cane on the kitchen table I went to get us beer out of the refrigerator and thought about how I had to get back my Gerber's label and replace it with the original photograph.

MISS BALLARD SAID, "I am proud of you, Mendal. I knew that you wasn't the model for the Gerber baby ad. I seen a magazine article one time about that baby. He ended up robbing banks for a living, and then moved off to Argentina where he's living amongst ex-Nazis." Miss Ballard taught dummy English when she wasn't trying to lay out the yearbook. She subscribed to and taught from the *National Enquirer*. The football players and cheerleaders were always talking about half-human, half-sheep children born in Alabama.

I said, "I want to go back to the old photo. It's the only one I got that isn't blurred. My mother took the picture. She wasn't much of a photographer."

Miss Ballard lowered her head. This was at 8:25, right before the homeroom bell. Presently a member of the Junior ROTC would say the Pledge of Allegiance over the intercom, then a prayer. The assistant principal would come on next and outline what car washes, candy bar drives, and PTA bake sales would take place in order to purchase new baseball bats, football helmets, basketball nets, track spikes, and orange cones for parallel parking in driver's ed. Our sad choir had robes so old and frayed that the altos might as well have stood there naked. They should've staged *Hair,* if anything. Miss Ballard said, "I heard your mother drank quite a bit. Maybe she shook bad, and that's why they blurred."

I said, "No, she wasn't a drunk, Miss Ballard. My mother left for Nashville to become a singer."

Miss Ballard shuffled through her manila envelope of photographs and found the torn Gerber's picture. I handed her the one of me standing next to the sign that said IC UMP. "Nashville," she said. "I understand that there's a problem with heroin in Nashville. And it's also the last sighting of Bigfoot east of the Mississippi." She took my three-by-five and said, "What does this mean?"

I looked at her scuffed metal bookcase with *National Enquirer*s stacked on top of each other working as bookends for the vertical stack of Dick and Jane classics, Bobbsey Twins, and search-a-word paperbacks. Her students would stay in Forty-Five, work for their own daddies, then marry each other and raise children. It was endless, and I knew it. I said, "Septic pump. We were at a water-treatment plant. Hey, Nashville has a large population of blind and deaf men. Maybe you should go visit there."

She didn't get it. Miss Ballard said, "I've been about everywhere I want to go in this life. I've been to Myrtle Beach. I can't imagine no other place to go for more fun. I don't like to be disappointed."

Her students filed in for homeroom. I looked over at Shirley Ebo and said, "Hey, Shirley." She popped her head up once, then set two or three books on the desk.

"What're you doing in here, Mendal Dawes?" she asked me.

I said, "Before-and-After."

Shirley said, "Too bad we didn't take a picture when you were a virgin, and one after. I guess they don't want to put a picture of you in the yearbook with your eyes closed both times all Chinesey. Like a moron or something."

Sergeant Penny Yingling—who would see her way out of Forty-Five via the military—got on the intercom and started the Pledge. I stood there bent over Miss Ballard's desk. I looked down her dress front, at first by accident. Miss Ballard stood up and chimed in about ". . . and to the public." I leaned closer to make sure that she said, ". . . un-der God, in the visible," and so on, like I knew she would. I looked back at Shirley Ebo, who, like me, didn't even try to mouth the words. Shirley stood up like everyone else, but stared at a poster of a cat and a pigeon sniffing each other's faces that Miss Ballard kept tacked on the wall.

I left my real photo on the desk and walked out during the Lord's Prayer. I knew that I had upwards of an hour be-fore my first-period class would start, that I could go out to the parking lot, get in my Jeep, drive to Rufus Price's Goat Wagon store, buy an eight-pack of Miller ponies, drink half of them, and get back in time to say *"Buenos dias"* to my new Spanish teacher, a woman named Senora Schulze who thought we should all take a field trip to *Brazil* one day to perfect our Spanish.

I would think, Ic ump, ic ump, ic ump, the entire morn-ing, and wonder if it meant anything in Latin.

Rufus Price was only three feet tall. He didn't have legs. He had stumps and had named his own little neighborhood store after the eight billy goats he liked to team up to trot him all over Highway 25 before, after, and during his hours of operation. Rufus Price's beard resembled his goats' faces— a long, long train of wild, wiry, grayish hair that came down in a point above his sternum. He wore a porkpie hat, al-ways, and sat in a wheelchair once his goats brought him back to the storefront. Unfortunately for my father, Mr. Price had sold off some fifty acres of his own land to Harley

Funeral Home, and they made a perpetual-care cemetery out of the place, behind the Goat Wagon, before anyone could plant fake toxic drums. I said, "Hey, Mr. Price," when I came in.

He said, "School not out again?"

I said, "Yessir," and walked past the cans of pork brains in milk gravy, Spam, Vienna sausages, Hormel Deviled Ham, and various other potted meats. I passed the penny gums and the pork rinds. I walked around a display of watchbands and another for Putnam Dyes. "I'm just taking a break before my first period."

"Running a special on day-old bread, Mendal. You can get you carbohydrates out of bread, day-old or not."

I was pretty sure that my father had asked Rufus Price to take care of me, but I didn't know for absolute sure. I said, "I'm getting something for Dad. I thought I might as well get it now than have to wait until after school. You might have a big rush between now and then."

He creaked his wheelchair forward. Out beside the shotgun-shack building, Rufus Price's goats bleated and shuffled and banged their horns against the wooden slat exterior. He said, "Your daddy might want some gum, too. He might want some gum or Life Savers. He ain't starting up a pulpwood business these days, is he? I won't sell to pulpwooders. You know why."

As I pulled out the eight-pack, I wondered if my friend Compton would show up like normally, but remembered how his art teacher had asked her students to come in early for an entire week so that they could go out on the football field and make a chalk collage of the history of Forty-Five Mills. The president of the place had promised to donate a picture book to the library about the history of textiles that he'd written and published himself.

I bought my beer, gum, and breath mints. Rufus shook his head at me. His beard swayed like a strange grandfather clock's pendulum. I said, "Ask my dad. This beer ain't for me."

Mr. Price wore his usual overalls, the legs folded up neatly to his stumps. He said, "You need a girlfriend who keeps you inside the hallways of school, son." He spat on his own floor. "You need a hobby. Don't end up like me. Don't end up like everyone around here. You smart, boy. Nothing's enough for some people. But nothing's a whole lot less than two minus one."

Mr. Price liked to show off that he was a graduate of Forty-Five High, too.

I'D BEEN KNOWN to dig holes in my father's backyard when I knew he'd be gone for more than an hour. And I acted thusly if, and only if, I'd awakened in the middle of the previous night to hear him grunting and cursing, burying something that he either foresaw would be valuable in the coming years—old metal gasoline-station signs seemed to be his forte—or that he thought was an eyesore. He seemed to have something against whatever Baptist preacher it was in Forty-Five who, plagiarizing roadside Burma-Shave ads, stuck BIRD ON A WIRE / BIRD ON A PERCH / FLY TOWARD HEAVEN / FIRST BAPTIST CHURCH up and down Deadfall Road, Powerhouse Road, Highway 25, and Calhoun Drive. I made a three A.M. note to myself as to where the sound emanated from so I could later find the pine straw covering the freshly dug clay and find out what it was that he deemed worthy of concealment.

Driving back to school from Rufus Price's Goat Wagon, I knew I'd get out a spade later in the afternoon, seeing as my dad would be somewhere over near the Savannah River all day trying to figure out what useless piece of land would later be bought up by the state for ten times its worth so a roadside park could be built, or a boat landing that dropped down to a fishless dammed lake. Maybe I would walk back to the acreage owned by the Few family trust and see if phony toxic barrels were actually standing upright beneath the surface.

"*Presente,*" I said to Senora Schulze when she called the roll.

Libby Belcher said, "I smell beer. I smell beer coming from Mendal's direction. Senora Schulze, I smell beer."

Senora Schulze said, "*Cerveza,* Libby. You smell *cerveza.*"

Well, ha ha ha ha ha, I thought. Libby had no way of knowing that I kept the other four beers in my backseat, that I kept the door unlocked so Senora Schulze could go

out there during her lunch break and down them. Libby
Belcher's head turned toward me in midspasm. I shot her a
peace sign, then curled my index finger away. Senora Schulze
turned on the overhead projector to reveal a slew of irregular verbs that we needed to know. I leaned over to the
left and whispered to Libby, "Why aren't you in Miss
Ballard's class with the rest of the cheerleaders and football
players? Why do you think you need to know a foreign language? Are you planning on having a Mexican baby or
something?"

Oh, I could be as mean as my father back then. And I'll
give Libby Belcher this: she grew up to get a doctorate in
education, then become a superintendent of schools. But she
didn't have the right answers on this particular day. She
said, "I'm taking Spanish because I'm taking home ec. I need
to know how to make tacos in an authentic manner." Then
she said, "I know you been drinking. And I saw your baby
picture from yearbook staff. When're you going to understand that you can't trick everybody, Mendal Dawes? You
can't. You been trying since first grade. We all know better.
We all know."

Senora Schulze said, "Oh, never mind," and cut off the
projector. "I doubt y'all will ever need to know these verbs.
It's been my experience that you only need to know a bunch
of nouns to get your idea across to foreigners."

When the bell sounded I walked to the gym, found Coach
Ware, and said I'd be willing to run track in May if he gave

me a note saying I needed to go home for the rest of the day. Forty-Five High couldn't afford to have its track team ride a bus to meets, but they splurged once a year and allowed us to take part in the regional meet. If anyone qualified for the Upstate, then his parents had to take him all the way up to Greenville—fifty-five miles away—in order to compete. I should mention that although no psychologist had invented attention deficit disorder in 1976, Coach Ware suffered from the malady. I went to him once a week and gave him my word about joining the track team, though he never took me up on it later.

Let me be the first to say that I felt bad whenever I drove home from school at midday. First off, Senora Schulze wouldn't get her *cerveza*—maybe the only word she really knew in Spanish. My biology teacher in second period wouldn't have anyone there to help him say "mitochondria," a word for which he never figured out the right syllable to stress. The third-period history teacher who never blinked, and always found a way to relate everything that ever happened in America to the invention of the cotton gin—in a way she was before her time, in relation to focus and specialization—would miss me. She should've become a college professor, and then maybe a full-out dean. When she experienced slight petit mal seizures, I was the one who always said something like, "Could you explain the connection between the Great Chicago Fire and the cotton gin?" Forget trigonometry—that teacher said "maff" when he wasn't undergoing coughing and/or sneezing attacks when someone asked for him to explain, again, how the notions of *sine* or *cosine* would be important to us later on in life.

And so on. But I got out of there. At this point I'd already gotten into a few colleges—the ag school that guidance counselor Mrs. McKnight made me apply to; all of South Carolina's state schools, including all-black S.C. State, just in case Shirley Ebo and I finally fell in love with each other; a liberal arts Baptist school my father said he'd let me go to if I didn't mind his daily visits with a firebrand to burn the place down; and an experimental place up in North Carolina founded by Unitarians, where I ended up going. It allowed students to double major in anthropology and basket weaving. Anthropology and pottery wheel. Anthropology and furniture making. Anthropology and metal casting. I knew to go into anthropology and geography, so I would know not to make a wrong turn and end up back in Forty-Five.

I should mention that Mrs. McKnight got some kind of yearly districtwide award for Miss Guidance, though she never understood the pun.

Anyway, I left Forty-Five High School and went back to Rufus Price's Goat Wagon. Rufus sat outside handing his goats the stale and expired products. When I got out of the Jeep he said, "School not out *again?*" He might've been kin to Coach Ware, for all I knew.

I said, "Hey, Mr. Price. I'll leave the money on your counter if you trust me."

He held out a piece of Little Debbie Snack Cake to three-horned Tripod, my favorite goat. "I don't trust anybody, son. The last man I trusted said the pulpwood truck wouldn't roll forward while I worked on its radiator." He dropped some oatmeal cake on his lap by accident, and Tripod gathered up the crumbs. Mr. Price leaned his head backwards.

I nodded. I said, "Yessir, I remember." I thought about doing anthropology and condemnation, mostly because my father had me read Schopenhauer when I finished those other books he ordered from publishing houses that never sent anything to our local library. But no one needed a minor in condemnation, I decided. Everyone in Forty-Five could brag about having a *major* in condemnation, whether they knew it or not.

BILLY GILLILAND HAD a photograph of himself sitting on a nice front porch while a Chihuahua licked his face. He wore what might've been knickers. Libby Belcher's picture had a fake background of Niagara Falls amid the Rocky Mountains. Timmy Stoddart stood in the middle of Ballantine Oldsmobile's car lot holding a car key in his hand, wearing a boat captain's hat. Helen Valentine wore a tutu. Glenn Flack looked angelically toward a wasps' nest. Bobby Coleman's red-topped head shone and shone as he looked straight at the camera from beside a land tortoise housed at the Forty-Five Petting Zoo. Bobby Williams—the king of calling a woman's nether parts "cock" later on— had a picture of himself with his diaper on backwards, his hands covering his nipples. Peter Human, Frank Funderburk, Mack McDowell, Vivian Hulsey, Eugenia Wimmer, and Patty Addy all had childhood photographs taken up in Ghost Town in the Sky, standing beside a wooden cutout figure of one of those Indian chiefs, or General Robert E. Lee, or Paul Bunyan, or the Marx Brothers, or Eisenhower.

My friend Shirley Ebo's picture was taken in front of Forty-Five Indoor Movie House, a place that still had a balcony where blacks had to sit. As a matter of fact, she was standing in front of the sign out on the sidewalk. At the left of the photograph you could see WHIT with an arrow before it. To the right of Shirley Ebo there was an arrow pointing upwards. Her little figure blocked the printing, though—all but OREDS.

I shuffled through all of the pictures like an idiot. Miss Ballard had either left altogether or was standing off in the smoking area. Me, I'd already been home, rifled through every drawer and safe in the house in case Dad had hid something new, found nothing special, drunk my beer, put on running clothes, covered six miles in thirty-six minutes *without* even sprinting toward the end, put some clothes in the washing machine, then come back to Forty-Five High School like I meant to attend one of the after-school clubs or meetings. Like I meant to care about Spanish Club, or Glee!

Club! Like I went to the Ecology Club meeting, whose members went out once a semester with convicts from the county detention center and always complained that they got bullied out of their cigarettes.

I am not proud of any of this, of course. I'm a buffoon, understand. I took those yearbook pictures home, spread them out on my father's kitchen table, and said things like, "Look, peckerhead, these are the kinds of pictures that get taken of children when they are children," et cetera. I accused my father of an abuse that wouldn't make the media for another decade.

"Listen," my father said. He rolled his neck in all kinds of directions. "I see your pictures here." He stared down at the kitchen table. It wasn't so much that I wanted to prove that everyone else had happy childhood photographs. No, I wanted *no one* to have them, I realized, even back then. Unfortunately, I wanted *no one* to have memories of happy days. "You have pictures of you *not* standing in front of a ditch, or poison ivy patch. *You just don't have those pictures in your possession,* fool," my father told me.

The telephone rang. As my father walked toward it, I believed that it was either my guidance counselor or my mother. My father said, "Yes . . . yeah . . . I understand. . . . We'll see that it doesn't happen again, I promise."

He hung up the phone and leaned on his cane. He didn't turn my way. I said, "That was Mrs. McKnight saying how I cut classes today, right?"

My father turned his head but not one bit of his torso. He said, "I believe you have something else to tell me, Mendal. Why are you acting up so much these days? I know I ain't done the best job raising you, but please, please understand that I've tried my best. Goddamn, son."

Hell, I thought he was going to cry. I went ahead and told him all about buying two eight-packs of tiny beers, of skipping classes, and how I used hot water when I washed clothes, even though he'd told me he read something somewhere about how cold water cleaned just as well and didn't run up the electric bill. I even went back a couple years and admitted that a stranger hadn't really driven by and shot our cement-block house with BBs, that in truth I'd found a three-wood and a sack of golf balls in a ditch over by the all-black Cokesbury Hills Country Club's nine-hole course and tried to tee off over our house on a dare from Compton.

My father turned his body almost imperceptibly and faced me. He said, "That was Mr. Lane. He called up to say how we used some inferior hooks on a trotline we laid out on Lake Between. They're all bent straight down, and unless there's some hundred-pound catfish on that lake, we probably cut corners too much."

I said, "There might be that big a catfish in Lake Between." Already I could feel his cane hitting my hamstrings, triceps, or side. It occurred to me that my father spoke cryptically on the telephone at all times, perhaps readying himself for a day such as this.

He lifted his arm, shifted his weight, and laughed. He said, "A firecracker's still a firecracker, lit or not."

I kept my eyes closed, waiting for him to strike me. I had no clue what he meant concerning pyrotechnics, and tried not to wonder about what a firecracker was after it exploded, outside of smoke and smell and nonflash.

I DIDN'T TAKE my classmates' baby photographs back to school the next day. My father had gotten up in the middle of the night and either buried or hid them somewhere. At the breakfast table—we ate grits every morning, with sausage balls to the side on special days—I asked, "Hey, I should take those pictures back. Where'd you put those pictures of everybody for their Before?"

My father tapped his cane on the linoleum. "That photograph of you was the only real picture. Where the heck do you see waterfalls around here?" He swung one arm. "I don't see any mountaingoddamntops. Give me a break. I knew I should've sent you to a private school. I'd've sent you to a private school if there was one around here that wasn't only a white-flight place. If there was one around here at all."

I pretended that there wasn't too much butter in the grits. I tried not to think about how my English teacher said how all southern novels had grits in them, or a grandmother who didn't want to go to Florida, and how grits and grandmothers were symbolic of Good. I said, "I like public school,

Dad. I like meeting people of different ilks in life." Well, maybe I just thought all of that later, like in college, when my new classmates all hailed from prep schools up and down the eastern seaboard.

My father got up from the table and opened the freezer door. He pulled out the manila envelope and tossed it like a Frisbee. "I was just playing with you. Go ahead and look through them if you want, make sure I didn't lose any of them."

I poured them out. I don't want to accuse my Forty-Five classmates of crawling from a gene pool so shallow that it wouldn't take a Dr. Scholl's insert to keep one's soles dry, but I have to tell you that they all, as babies, had held the same broad, high foreheads and eyes that floated a little too close to their noses. Except for Shirley Ebo, it looked as though the same child had posed in front of Santa, or the fake nature backgrounds, and so on.

My father had me recheck the pictures for a reason. I didn't find the one in which I stood in front of the fake toxic barrel, but there was a nice black-and-white of me with my mother. I'd not seen a picture of her since he'd either burned, buried, or otherwise destroyed every single document that proved she'd had a part in the short-lived marriage. I said, "This is Mom."

"I took that picture. Hell, it might be the only time I got the camera away from her. She was always a little shy about getting her photo taken. You'd think a woman like that, who ran off to Nashville, would want her picture taken a thousand times daily. Publicity photos and whatnot for her singing career. But not your mother."

I held it and pored over every square millimeter. My mother and I were standing in front of my father's old Buick. She wore a dress that seemed to have too many buttons. The neckline came halfway up her chin, like an old Puritan outfit. Shiny mother-of-pearl buttons clasped every inch down the front, all the way to the hem. Even in the black-and-white, I could see the bluish gray swirls of them. I imagined the dress in disuse, filleted out like a saltwater fish, those buttons off to one side like vertebrae.

She wasn't smiling. I wore some kind of ensemble made up of short pants and a jacket. I said, "I'd rather have my toxic-dump picture for the yearbook, Dad. This is too weird. They make enough fun of me over there."

He said, "But if you ever lose this picture, then you'll have it for keeps in the annual. I'd go with this one. Do it for me." He didn't tear up, or choke-voice. "Besides, I wasn't thinking right earlier. What if someone got real smart and saw that picture of you twenty, thirty years down the road, put two and two together, you know, and when the land developers started unearthing those barrels they thought you had a part in it all? You might go to prison for inciting a panic, or contributing to the delinquency of a businessman."

His speech sounded practiced. I knew that he'd sat up all night working on his words. I said, "Thanks. That's a good idea. Well, I better get going."

My father said, "When you're over at Rufus Price's Goat Wagon pick me up some pipe cleaners. I've been coming up with such good ideas, I might need to take up smoking some Captain Black."

I guess practicing words was a Dawes family trait: already I'd devised a way to explain to Miss Ballard how the photographs went missing originally, how I had accidentally picked them up off of her desk when I'd meant to pick up my Spanish project—a term paper detailing the life of architect Antonio Gaudí—and so on. I knew that Senora Schulze—bombed out of her mind—would back me up, seeing as she couldn't remember if or when her *muchachos* had special projects assigned or not. Then I could blame Miss Ballard for losing my research, and Senora Schulze would have no choice but to give me an A, and so on.

I drove east to school. The sunlight blinded me. All I could see were those buttons on my mother's dress. Later that day I would explain it all to Compton Lane. His mother had left his father, too, at about the same time. We always wondered if they ran off together, but this was a nice, naïve, quaint, and innocent time, before anyone knew about lesbians who finally figured things out between themselves and their bad marriages. I wasn't even sure that all of the Nixon Watergate stuff made it into the local weekly newspaper. The Forty-Five Indoor Movie House had been showing *Mary* fucking *Poppins* for an entire year.

• • •

Miss Ballard had called in sick, evidently. I stood in her homeroom, waiting. Shirley Ebo said, "Mendal Dawes, what you think you are, some kind of teacher now? You can do better than that."

I said, "Where's Miss Ballard?"

Shirley said, "Drinking beer with your Spanish teacher, out in your Jeep. I saw them driving around the parking lot, tooting the horn." She got up from her desk. "Let me see those pictures of yours."

Shirley lived on an island more deserted than mine. She was the only black girl preintegration at Forty-Five Elementary, and when integration occurred she was shunned by her black counterparts. Shirley survived six years of white kids mesmerized by her white palms and feet, then six years of white kids who no longer found her exotic and black kids who didn't trust her surrounded-by-whiteys past.

I said, "That's a good one of you, Shirley. If we had a Xerox machine at this school I might go copy some of these pictures and put them on my wall back home."

Shirley said, "A *what?*" Everyone else in the room looked at me as if they'd heard me speak Russian. None of them knew of any copiers besides those mimeograph machines that produced purplish-blue inky facsimiles. Not much earlier—maybe in the 1960s—according to my father, Forty-Five High employed *monks* to handwrite duplicates.

Shirley slid out the photos and spread them on Miss Ballard's desk. No one in the homeroom got up to inspect them, which I thought to be odd later on. Were they so respectful of rules that they wouldn't get out of their desks until they were told to do so? Did they have no curiosity whatsoever? Had one of the dozen P.E. teachers told them that they should conserve energy in order to live a long, long life?

Shirley picked up the one of my mother and me. She said, "This is your momma?"

I said, "You didn't really see Miss Ballard and Senora Schulze driving around in my Jeep, did you? You made that up, right?"

Shirley turned the photograph ten or twenty degrees to the left and right, which made those buttons shine more so. I made a point not to look down Shirley's worn cotton dress front. Her nipples poked out like little fried-clam strips I'd eaten at a Red Lobster up in Greenville. She said, "I seen these buttons before. These are buttons a person remembers."

Then she put the photograph down on top of the picture of Charles Dunn wearing his mother's high-heeled shoes and wig, walking around the den. I said, "They're buttons."

Shirley leaned toward me and whispered, "I can take you to a place that has these buttons, Mendal Dawes. You want to see your mother's buttons, I know where they is. But you can't call it a date. We ain't going out on a date or nothing like that."

Sergeant Penny Yingling came on and said, "The Pledge of Allegiance. I pledge allegiance, to the flag," as if someone had shot her with a tranquilizer dart. Everyone in the absent Miss Ballard's class stood up and acted accordingly. I said to Shirley, "Did my father give your mother this dress?"

It wasn't unlikely. My father and Mr. Ebo were friends. Sometimes Shirley came to school wearing T-shirts that I'd once worn. On those days she made a point not to make eye contact with me. One time she showed up wearing a watch cap I once owned, and another time some pointy wingtips. She said, "I don't know nothing about the dress. But I know these buttons. Over in the old slave graveyard."

I said, "Don't mess with me, Shirley. That ain't funny."

She said, "*Ain't* ain't a word. You think you so smart. You can ask Miss Ballard when she comes back from driving around your car."

Sergeant Yingling finished up the Pledge and went into prayer. I sat down in Miss Ballard's chair and put my hands out on her desk, the spilled Before photographs within reach. Mr. Botts, the assistant principal, came on the intercom and said, "Good morning. Miss Ballard won't be in today or tomorrow. Anyone in Miss Ballard's classes needs to report to the cafeteria for study hall today and tomorrow. If you are on the annual staff, Miss Ballard wants to know if someone picked up her pictures by accident."

Shirley looked at me wide-eyed and put her right hand over her mouth. She said, "You stole Miss Ballard's pictures, and she didn't come in today, I bet, 'cause she's having a nervous breakdown at home."

Mr. Botts said, "The Forty-Five High Home Ec Club will be selling handmade crocheted doilies so money can go to the football team's new jerseys," and then he went on and on. No one seemed to notice that he pronounced it "crotch-it-ed."

I said to Shirley, "Just tell me where the graveyard is. I can go by myself."

"You can if you want to get killed by the spirits there," she said.

The bell rang and Miss Ballard's homeroom class ventured off to whatever home ec, shop, or vocational class they needed to attend next. Shirley walked back to her desk and picked up her books. I said, "You want to meet me after school or something?"

She shook her head no. "You leaving Forty-Five for good, ain't you?"

I said, "Do you mean am I going to college somewhere far from here? Uh-huh."

"I can't take you to the slave graveyard until I know that you won't be coming back. My daddy says I shouldn't take no one back there in the first place. And I don't want to make any judgment or nothing, but I don't think you'll be able to take what you're going to see there, Mendal Dawes. I got family back there and it's tough enough. But what you got back there's going to drive you over the edge, boy."

She swished out of the room. I gathered up all of the Before photographs, put them in the envelope, and waited for the hallway to clear. Then I snuck inside the girls' restroom and set the envelope on top of the Kotex dispenser. I went to Spanish class on time and said "*Presente*" like any native of Madrid. Later in the period Senora Schulze came over to me and put her hand on my forehead. She said, "*Calliente*, Mendal. Are you sick, or have you been thinking too hard?"

I MISSED MY final three weeks of high school. Fortunately the Forty-Five school system worked on a weighted absentee basis, and seeing as I'd not officially missed but a couple days between first and twelfth grade—we were allowed five absences per semester—I had built up something like a hundred permitted unexcused absences. If I'd've known any of this—like if I had had a sixth-grade mathematics teacher worth a simple equation—I wouldn't have shown up most of my final semester, or at least not after I'd gotten accepted by a college. I didn't go to my own graduation. I wasn't present to pick up my Spanish, English, or history awards. I wasn't the valedictorian, seeing as I'd made a B in calculus. Libby Belcher chose to skip a second course in math and made an A in chorus.

I sat at home, then took to realizing how I wasn't sick, then went with my father wherever he thought it necessary to go. We went fishing. We drove up past the South Carolina–North Carolina border and looked at tracts of land he thought might be worthy of buying. We stopped at Stuckey's and ate pecan logs. I tried not to think about how when I went off to college he'd either be horrendously alone or show up often at my dormitory unexpected.

On the day that I finally got brave I said, "Do you know anything about a slave graveyard somewhere in Forty-Five, maybe over by the Ebos' land?" We were on our way to a place called Hickory Tavern, where my father felt sure a superhighway would intersect one day.

My father let up on the accelerator. He said, "I'm sure there are slave graveyards all over the state, Mendal. Why do you ask?"

I thought to myself, You know why I'm asking. "Shirley said something about a slave graveyard. I'd kind of like to see one. I'd kind of like to know. She said that a bunch of her relatives are buried there, and that they don't have tombstones or anything."

Dad resumed his reckless driving, dodging potholes like a professional slalom skier. "I don't have much to do with graveyards. I don't think there's enough money in them, really. It's a dead business, ha ha." He pulled down his visor, then stuck it back up. "I tell you one thing, though. When the graveyards get all filled up up north, it might be a good thing to start a cemetery and charge a couple thousand bucks a plot. Now you're thinking, son."

I didn't say how I hadn't thought it up whatsoever. I said, "Okay. Forget it."

"There's enough to learn from the living, Mendal. Don't

go get all obsessed with graveyards and tombstones. The only thing you can learn in an old graveyard, if you ask me, is how hard the granite carver had to work." My father pulled over into some weeds and checked a piece of paper he'd written directions on. In the field to our right, a field-stone chimney leaned alone, surrounded by honeysuckle. Three others stood off in the distance. "You want to know about graveyards—word is an entire family lived here back around 1870. They all got killed by a tornado that skipped from one house to the next. Land's been passed down from family member to family member until now, and they're ready to sell it for a hundred dollars an acre."

I said, "Maybe it's cursed," because—although my father's odd business acumen hadn't failed to my knowledge—I never saw how any scrubland could end up a golf course, subdivision, or recreational development.

My father walked through beggar-lice fifty yards into the parcel, then took out his compass. He slashed at sweet grass with his cane. I followed him, wary of copperheads. The sun beat down on this parched, cracked red land. We might as well have been tredding across Mars. "Sooner or later Duke Power will want to dam up the Saluda River," he pointed northwest, "or the Reedy." He pointed west. "And if this doesn't become lakefront property, it'll be close enough for people to want to build bait shacks and boat dealerships. Hell, boy, you might even want to build your first house down here one day, just to get away from the rat race. It would make a nice place for a nursery. This land's got to be arable by now, doomed and cursed or not."

I didn't say, "What rat race?" or "Oh, maybe I forgot to tell you that I won't be returning to South Carolina anytime soon." I said, "It would make a nice spot for a brick factory. You wouldn't even need a kiln."

My father raised his cane. He turned to me and said, "If I ever catch wind that you and Shirley Ebo go off to that slave graveyard, believe me when I say that I'll disinherit you faster than a bitch dog its runt of the litter." He had a look in his eye that I'd not seen in real life before, though I'd once found a book in the public library on abnormal psychology that had a series of pictures of a full-fledged schizophrenic who, according to a panel of experts, could change from Betty Boop to Hitler's unknown mean brother in a matter of seconds.

"Okay. Okay. I was only asking. Sometimes Shirley Ebo tells me things that she made up in the first place."

"Like what?" my father asked. He brushed past me on his way back to the car.

I didn't say, "That you were brought up by wolves in the tree farm across the street from our house."

On the way back home I kind of wished that I still sat in Senora Schulze's class. She liked to start off each day telling us about the importance of siestas. Senora Schulze said that if we'd had Spanish class in the afternoon, right after lunch, we'd have had a little thirty-minute nap planned each period. My father and I didn't speak. I remembered an article I'd read somewhere about how children who hear, "Don't ever smoke a cigarette," or "Don't drink booze," or "Don't ever smoke marijuana, seeing as it'll lead straight to heroin," are six million times more likely to disregard their parents' admonitions.

I SHOULD MENTION that a yearbook normally takes more than a month to reproduce. Staff members had already taken pictures of the athletic teams and cheerleaders, and a professional photographer had come in early in the fall term so we could wear our bow ties and/or best dresses while seated in front of a Forty-Five High Speed Fire Ants banner. The Before-and-After collage was a new feature, an insert only, something that had come to Miss Ballard in a dream. Our principal decided to use what leftover money he had at the end of the school year for Miss Ballard's project instead of buying new books for the library.

"Are you feeling any better?" Miss Ballard called to ask during the last week of regular classes. "Senora Schulze and I are worried about you, Mendal."

I said, "I think I'm fine."

"Our inserts came in for the yearbook. Do you think you feel up to coming by school this afternoon and helping us slide them into the front of each book?"

I said, "Oh, what the hell. Okay." I pointed to my friend

Compton to go get me another beer out of the refrigerator. It was nearly three o'clock in the afternoon. He'd talked his father into letting him get sick for the final two weeks of school, also. Mostly we sat around at either his house or mine, or got stuck driving around with our fathers, both of whom were intent on telling their life stories over and over. On two occasions Mr. Lane and my father swapped sons— which I thought was a little weird even back then. On this particular day, they had gone to Charlotte, supposedly looking for cheap farm equipment to resell, but as Comp and I had found matchbooks from a Charlotte strip joint in both our fathers' pants pockets more than once, we weren't convinced. I said to Miss Ballard, "Compton isn't doing anything this afternoon. Can he come help?"

She paused. She said, "I tell you what. Why don't we do this over at my house. Why don't y'all stop by the store and bring some beer, and we can make a little party of it all." I heard Senora Schulze in the background, making noises as if she had asthma. "Miss Schulze says you can bring anything stronger, if you want, you know. If you know what I mean."

I hung up the telephone and looked at Comp. I said, "We got us a couple teachers who want to smoke a joint with us. Are you game?"

Like we had any weed. Comp said, "Hey. They went to college over in Graywood. They won't know any better." He opened my father's cupboards, found the Lipton's tea bags, and grabbed a handful.

We could only purchase Zig-Zag rolling papers at Rufus Price's Goat Wagon, and we knew that he'd tell on us. Fortunately, though, Rufus Price sold apples, and I had learned how to make a portable pipe out of a cored apple and a scrap of tinfoil a few years earlier, when my father forced me to go to some kind of live-off-the-land summer camp up on Skyuka Mountain, a place that attracted rich kids from all over who had parents drop them off on their way to Florida.

Compton and I walked all high-kneed into the Goat Wagon, and I went straight to the fruit and vegetable bin. Comp picked up two eight-packs of Miller ponies and yelled from back there, "I'm really eighteen now, Mr. Price." Comp had about a pound of loose tea leaves in his front pocket; we didn't think about using a baggy or anything.

I bought two apples, a roll of Reynolds Wrap, and a thin cardboard sleeve of sewing needles. At the counter Rufus Price wheeled up to the register, eyed our products, and said, "You boys fools." He jerked his thumb backwards. "Rolling papers don't cost much of nothing, but if you want to go this route, don't let me be a road map in your way."

"Yeah. Yeah. We don't need a road map in our way," Comp said. Me, I thought I would pee in my pants, I was so nervous. "You don't sell rubbers by any chance, do you Mr. Price?" Comp said, looking behind the counter at blue jars of VapoRub, squeeze bottles of Unguentine, and boxes of headache powders.

Rufus Price pointed over toward a small section where he

kept cheap toys: squirt guns, bouncy balls, pinwheels, and the like. He said, "I got a pack of balloons over there might work for you boys. They work on my goat peckers. I don't want to have no more kids around here, my age."

Compton turned around and walked to retrieve them. I didn't say anything one way or the other. We were both complete fools.

Outside the store Compton said, "We should ask Mr. Price if he has any of his goats' horns laying around somewhere. They're supposed to work as aphrodisiacs. We might should chew on some goat horn before we go over there."

I got in the Jeep. I didn't respond. It's not as though I feared having sex for the second time in my life—and maybe for the first time with a woman who wouldn't make fun of me—but I kept thinking about those Before-and-After pictures that awaited. And then I started thinking about my mother's mother-of-pearl buttons and that hidden mysterious graveyard that I knew I'd visit before leaving Forty-Five, led by Shirley Ebo on a disastrous pilgrimage that could only scar and disconcert me forever.

SENORA SCHULZE SHOULD'VE gone by "Senorita" in the strict world of Spanish language. She introduced herself as Senora Schulze on the first day of class, though, and back then no one knew the difference. She could've called herself "Frau" or "Madame" and we wouldn't have known the difference. Back in mid-1970s South Carolina there were no migrant workers. Back then there were enough recently released ex-convicts who'd pick peaches, plus a variety of Shirley Ebo's relatives, who'd not been taught that Abraham Lincoln wrote a big old proclamation some hundred years earlier.

Unlike most Forty-Fivers, Senora Schulze's life wasn't fulfilled merely by her job. Teaching high-school students was only a way to pay her bills. Senora Schulze's life depended on earning starring roles in each Forty-Five Little Theatre production. "When it gets to the point where my name's not listed at least third on the cast of characters, I'll know it's time to move to a smaller town," she once told me out in the Forty-Five High parking lot. But maybe she was telling it to God. She didn't make eye contact, and kind of held her head upwards to the sky. She said, "Drinking was a vice held by many of my favorite actresses, Mendal. So don't judge me. Just think of me as another Judy Garland!"

Comp and I drove over to Miss Ballard's house on the corner of Durst and Powerhouse Road, which might as well have been two states away from our homes. Comp said, "I want to be with Miss Ballard. If it all comes down to us not having a choice in the matter, okay. But if we do, I want Miss Ballard."

I pulled into the driveway and parked behind Senora Schulze's Datsun. She liked to tell us that Liza Minnelli drove the same kind of car up in New York, on her way to Broadway plays. I had no choice but to tell Comp, "If mine starts singing show tunes, I'm out of there."

Comp and I argued a while out there on the gravel driveway, and then we flipped a coin. He said that some show tunes weren't all that bad, and I told him I was going to mention his love of *The Sound of Music*—which played at Forty-Five Indoor Movie House for an entire year, too—to anyone who would listen. We did eenie-meenie-miney-moe. We played rock/paper/scissors/dynamite. In the end, we realized that we would let the teachers decide, and that we would follow their lead.

Oh, we had everything figured out until the door opened and Shirley Ebo stood there, all smiles and crazy pigtails. "Hello, Comp. Hello, Mendal," she said. Shirley closed the door behind her and doubled halfway over. She slapped her ashy gray knees. "Y'all got any Mad Dog in that bag there? These women only seem to like Skrawberry Ripple."

By the time we made it onto the porch we could hear Senora Schulze in the background belting out "Que Sera, Sera" without any accompaniment. I said, "What're you doing here, Shirley Ebo?"

She said, "Miss Ballard made me the editor. She said that in the history of Forty-Five High there ain't been no girl editor, and she wanted to make a statement." Shirley looked down at Comp's pocketful of tea and said, "What you got in there, boy?"

Senora Schulze kept singing. She rearranged the lyrics; what I'm saying is, she seemed to know all the words, just not in order. That goofball song would stick in my head for another six to ten years: *Whatever will be, will be. When I was just a little girl*. I said, "How'd you get over here? You don't know how to drive, Shirley Ebo."

"I rode with them. I rode with Miss Ballard. Y'all come on in and see what I done with the pictures." She reached behind and grabbed the doorknob. "Bring that beer inside. I wouldn't mind me a cold, frosty beverage about right now." She said that last part in white-voice. It sounded like my father talking.

I don't know if Compton started sweating, but I distinctly smelled tea brewing from his pants pocket. I said, "Okay," to Shirley and stepped into the den first.

Senora Schulze and Miss Ballard were waltzing—together. It was more than I could take. I didn't drop my bag of beer, sewing needles, apples, and tinfoil or anything. I looked back at Comp, though, and I could tell he was thinking exactly like I was—that either these two teachers were mercilessly making fun of us, or that they, too, would soon be leaving Forty-Five for Nashville, Memphis, New Orleans, or any of those other cities that welcomed female crooners. Compton Lane reached in his pocket to extract the faux pot, and proceeded to spill it all over Miss Ballard's wooden floor.

Here's what Senora Schulze said to me, "Oh my God!— do y'all smoke the marijuana?!"

I said, "Miss Ballard said she wanted something stronger. If I knew what she meant."

Miss Ballard let go of Senora Schulze and said, "*Like wine*. Something stronger like wine, or maybe some *vodka,* Mendal."

Shirley Ebo sat down on the floor, picked up some tea between her thumb and forefinger, and said, "This ain't weed. They was going to trick y'all and say you was smoking the real thing, Miss Ballard. They was going to sell y'all bag tea." Shirley pointed at my face and said, "That was tea you brought over to my house last year, wasn't it, Mendal?"

I shook my head. I promised it wasn't. It wasn't. I'd brought over some dried-up okra leaves from my father's garden. Shirley and I pretended to smoke them in her daddy's corncob pipe.

"I'm glad y'all quit coming to school, both of y'all'ses," Senora Schulze said. "You should be ashamed. We thought we were doing you a favor asking you over here. How many teachers allow their students in their homes? Not many. And there's a reason, obviously." Senora Schulze tried to grasp Miss Ballard's hand again—the senora had led—but Miss Ballard stepped back.

Shirley Ebo said, "I guess I'mo have to stick these inserts in every yearbook all by myself. White boys. Y'all mess up everything."

This all took place in about a minute, I should mention. My knees couldn't tell whether to bend or not. I said, "Well, I guess I won't have to share this booze," which I would say more often than I would want, later on in life, when people threw me out of their parties, arenas, stadiums.

Shirley walked into the kitchen. Comp and I backed out of the house, got in the Jeep, and took off. About a mile down the road he said, "They're just mad because we figured out a way not to have to go to school anymore." He dug out some tea leaves jammed under his fingernails. I swerved away from two chow-mix dogs standing at the edge of someone's yard, both perched as if on starting blocks, ready to follow my hubcaps down Powerhouse Road.

Comp said, "You know why dogs around here chase cars?"

I'd heard it before. "They can't form a noose without opposable thumbs. They don't know how to turn on the gas in a kitchen. It's impossible for them to slit their wrists. They don't have trigger fingers."

SHIRLEY EBO SHOWED up at my house an hour before dusk and said we had just enough time to make it to the graveyard. She looked stoned. I'd never known her to partake of anything except for one time when my father left a quart bottle of malt liquor over at her daddy's house and another time when she and I snuck cans from a Fourth of July party in her backyard. Maybe a couple other times. I said, "Did y'all get all those baby pictures in the yearbook?"

Shirley's hair stood out in a giant wedge. Since I'd known

her she'd always had her scalp carved into anywhere from six to twenty pigtails, which hovered above her head like scattered question marks. She walked me to the end of my narrow gravel-and-clay driveway. "It might be important for your father not to be around, Mendal. Your daddy ain't home, is he?"

We crossed Deadfall Road onto a path that wound through pines. Shirley and I walked past the foundations of what had been a couple old cabins. We passed the sad indentions of dried springs and the creek beds those springs once fed. There were the thickets of honeysuckle and blackberry, there were the pine trunks I'd notched with a folding Kut-Master to mark places where I'd seen copperheads. I wore a backpack in case I needed to hike something out. Shirley walked with swinging arms and otherwise seemed flatter than usual, barely three-dimensional.

We passed a place where she and I, maybe at the age of ten, had once played veterinarian, where she and I dropped our pants and looked to see if we had the same things our ex–stray dogs owned. I didn't look when we got to the place—maybe a quarter mile from my house—where my father once took me long ago to bury the china my parents had gotten for a wedding present.

Shirley walked with purpose; she strode out in a way that I always thought she should've done when someone told a racist joke right there in front of her. A stilt-walker couldn't have strode as fast and meaningful. She said, "We finished.

Me and those teachers finished. Though I did most of the work. Which don't surprise me none."

I pulled off the path. I placed my hands on my knees to catch my breath. Shirley didn't stop. She didn't turn around and acknowledge my request. Shirley kept striding on, long-legged as a Dinka on the hunt. "I can't believe you ain't ever followed this path all the way to our graves," she called over her shoulder. "You white boys don't have much sense of adventure."

I didn't know about the rest of the white-boy race, but I knew for a fact that I didn't ever want to come up on bubbling Forty-Five Creek, which separated the Earth as far as I was concerned. I'd been on those banks before and then run home nonstop after witnessing the half-mammal, half-amphibians that lounged on its banks. This wasn't a dream: there were ape-animals with skink bodies, and salamanders with hairy, muscled arms living in the area. The place possessed a flat-out primordial landscape with all of the amenities. I had come upon these creatures one day in midsummer some ten years earlier, and then when I studied Darwin by pure accident I felt like maybe I was the only person on the planet who could snigger and feel special about how the Galápagos Islands had nothing on my hometown.

Shirley strode onward, and luckily when we got to the creek the water was down and the animals were either still hibernating or had left altogether for more hospitable climates and societies, like maybe in south Georgia. I'd gotten to the point where I had forgotten the whole reason why we undertook the trek. I trotted behind Shirley, thinking all about going off to Miss Ballard's house, how Senora Schulze had sung and danced there, and so on. I thought about Compton ready to roll Lipton's, about Rufus Price's goats staring at me with their slashed pupils, tap dancing their hooves.

How could anyone live in a large town like Charlotte or Atlanta and keep his or her sanity?

"Just jump the damn thing, Mendal," Shirley said. "It ain't like water got arms." She was standing on the other side. I hadn't paid attention when she crossed over, and for all I knew she'd walked on the water.

I said, "I want to go up that way and see if there's a log, or a group of rocks." I looked at Shirley's shoes, her socks, her ankles. She showed no signs of being wet anywhere, and Forty-Five Creek had to be ten yards across. If she'd jumped it, then she deserved to be on Coach Ware's track team.

And there were no footprints on the other side, either. I need to mention all of this—the banks were as forgiving as soft-serve ice cream. I looked and saw no indentions where Shirley Ebo might've plopped. She summoned me with one arm as slowly as she might've asked a ghost to join her.

Later on in my life I would look back at this day and remember that my feet, too—my goofy tennis shoes—didn't get wet. I would remember that I matched Shirley Ebo stride for stride for the rest of the way, that we sprang across the pine-straw path in leaps as yet unknown to antelopes. We covered another mile in less than four minutes and only slowed when she needed to turn her head left and right at undetectable crossroads. And then Shirley Ebo took my hand, kept her face lowered, and said, "You can't tell my daddy or any other of my people about this place."

I didn't nod. I didn't shake my head sideways. Either my heart had quit beating, or it was rattling so hard that it wasn't discernible.

MY FATHER HAD told me early on about how some members of various Indian tribes planted the placentas of their children right after the birthing process. He'd read it somewhere. My father had sat drunk in his lounge chair when I was nine or ten, and imparted this knowledge. It all got started because I was up to the Gs in the dictionary and encyclopedia. He said, "You know—I don't know— it might've been the Cherokees, but I'm thinking more like it was the Hopis, or Navahos, or Sioux, who went out and buried the placenta of newborns out in the ground to be closer to the world. Or for good luck, I forget which one. Maybe it was just to get the thing away from the living space. I don't think it was the original Cherokees. Their land was a little rocky up there in North Carolina. Maybe Chippewas." He repeated "Chippewas" over and over, dragging out that last syllable.

I had asked my father about Gorky and what it meant to

write an unfinished cycle of novels—what I'd read about, nothing more. Somehow he'd made a connection. I said, "Huh. What's a placenta?"

My father kept staring at the ceiling. He'd barely taken me to the Sunken Gardens Lounge, or any other drinking establishment at that point, much less explained the birthing process. I asked him again.

He explained everything. He went from courtship to marriage, erection to penetration, seed to egg. My father tried to explain DNA—which I'd come across in the dictionary and encyclopedia—and romance, which I'd not. He said, "And in some cultures the father goes out with a big shovel to plant the thing in the ground."

I said, "That's the oddest thing I've ever heard," which was true. "It can't grow *into* something out there, can it?" I didn't want to ever come across a fruit-bearing placenta tree, at least from the image he'd conjured.

My father looked me in the eye. He said, "I don't know what the Eskimos do, seeing as it's all ice up there. We didn't do the same thing for you, but we did for your brother."

Again, it was the middle of the Vietnam War but before the Summer of Love. Up until that point I had never heard the term "brother" in our house—my father had none, and my mother was long gone by then. I said, "Say all that again?"

"Your momma and me had another boy before you were born. I been meaning to tell you when the time was right.

You mentioned Gorky, that led to placenta, and I remembered that your mother and I were going to name the child Gordon."

My father had gotten out of his chair and taken me by the hand. We walked outside our cement-block house to the backyard, where he had just begun storing pallets of heartpine lumber that he'd made me help him collect "so you'll have something to build on later in life, ha ha ha." I said, "Gordon. My brother's name was Gordon?"

Dad sat down on some nice Bermuda grass. "It was your mother's idea, I forget why. It must've been someone in her family. His name was Sam until he showed up dead. Then she said she wanted to name him Gordon. Maybe she thought of it as 'gored on.'"

In a few decades I would think about how most sane people wouldn't have told this story, at least not in this manner, to anyone under the age of twenty-one. I said, "Sam."

"Anyway, he had a placenta and we planted the thing over there." He pointed behind him, past the house and over toward the trees across Deadfall Road. "I thought you might want to know."

My father had gotten up and gone back inside the house as if he'd just told me what a particular center fielder batted the previous year. I wouldn't get to the S sections for quite a while—thus knew nothing of *symbiosis, synchronicity, symbolism,* and the like—and followed him saying, "What about mine, what about mine?"

"Your what?" he asked. My father walked to the refrigerator and extracted a can of Schlitz. He closed the door, reopened it, and handed me one.

I said, "What about my placenta?" I don't want to say that I was confused by the entire situation, but in my mind a placenta looked exactly like a piñata, especially after his explanation—all the bursting and spilling forth and falling out.

My father put his large hand on my narrow shoulder and led me back into the den. *Hee Haw* came on presently. "Your momma buried your placenta in the backyard there, but after she left us alone I went out and dug it up. Then I drove you and me down to the beach. We rented a boat, and I threw your placenta out into the middle of the Atlantic Ocean. I'm figuring some little fishes ate yours up, and then larger fish ate those things, and then those fish got caught by fishermen and sold to the public. If you think about it, I'm thinking that every person on this planet has been eating a little of you all along the way. What do you think about that?"

He smiled in the same way that most fathers smile as their sons open up a wrapped bicycle or go-cart. I said, "Maybe I just sank to the bottom."

"No. No, I saw sharks come up and swarm the whole thing. It was still all blobby and red—I'd sealed it up tightly before burying it the first time, so dogs wouldn't get to you. Anyway, you were on the deck, but you were little. And looking off at a school of jellyfish on the port side." My dad and I were standing in front of the console TV, a commercial went off, and the *Hee Haw* theme song started. I could feel my eyes squinting in disbelief, my head cocking to the left. "I'm sorry you had to learn about all of this so early," my father said. "Hey, sit down next to me and let me tell you how I used to play baseball for the Yankees in the summer, football for the Packers each winter, and the Olympics every four years before you came around."

I said how I needed to take something to show-and-tell the next day. My father held up his palm and said he had a variety of things for me to take, all of which would surprise and delight my teacher and classmates.

WHEN SHIRLEY EBO tiptoed, I did, too. We crept out of a copse of tulip poplars. Her daddy's three-room shack poked out of the clearing, and in the distance we saw Mr. Ebo with his back to us, gazing at his tomatoes and okra. Even I knew not to speak in a normal voice. I said quietly, "This is no cemetery, Shirley Ebo."

We slunk thirty steps south, always facing her father, then returned to the woods. We walked through unkempt honeysuckle and briars over a football field's length, then turned toward a circular clearing no bigger than a flying saucer. There were a dozen sandstone rocks the size of Sunbeam bread packages propped up haphazardly, spread apart from each other in a uniform manner.

Then off to the side stood a jug, and even from where I stood I recognized on it the buttons that had once clasped my mother's dress front. Shirley said, "They it is," and pointed.

"Can I walk across here?" I asked. I looked straight up at the darkening sky, through the hole formed by missing trees. "I don't like walking on people's burial spots, man." Shirley led me around the outer edge of the graves toward the jug.

More than buttons covered this earthen, gallon-sized vessel, too: paper clips, a metal fingernail file, pieces of thread, hair, two barrettes, a couple of false eyelashes, a shoehorn, what appeared to be tiny glints of diamond, the cap to an aspirin bottle, and a compass had been glued on it. Shirley Ebo said, "My daddy said it just showed up one day. He said I could look at it all I wanted, but not to disturb it. He calls it a memory jug some days, and a whatnot jar others. My daddy says a long time ago sometimes these worked the same as headstones for the dead."

I didn't touch the jar. On my hands and knees I looked into the mouth, hoping not to find ashes—or another photograph of me, standing at attention beside my mother's sharp hips. I said, "My mother's not buried here, Shirley. Take it back. I know for a fact that my mother's not buried here. She used to call me up. My mother used to call me up from Nashville, and New Orleans. She called from St. Louis one time, and another time from Las Vegas." I turned my head and squinted one eye, but the day's sunlight in these woods had disappeared already.

Shirley stood up. "I took a flashlight one time and looked in there, but there ain't nothing. Don't worry. It's empty." She pulled her cotton dress halfway up her thigh and scratched at a bite.

I remained crouched. "My father wouldn't lie to me about this. He couldn't. He'd end up getting drunk and telling me the truth."

Shirley said, "Now's the time if when you sing 'Amazing Grace' or 'The Battle Hymn of the Republic' you can hear the dead sing along. I don't know the words but my daddy do."

By the time I quit staring at the jar—by the time the mother-of-pearl buttons quit reflecting what light remained in the sky—Shirley Ebo had vanished from the circle.

In later years I would say that I walked out of there calm as a wealthy man's cat. I would say that Shirley must've played a trick on me and that I followed the same path out that we took in, that I saw Shirley and her father sitting on their stoop drinking iced tea and that I hollered over to them, "Thanks, Shirley! Good night!" But that wasn't the case. Once that goddamn "Battle Hymn of the Republic" tune came into my head and I felt an urge to vocalize, I took off running blindly through a land I'd never explored. And within about fifteen seconds I reached Deadfall Road, maybe a quarter mile up from my house. Shirley and I had cut a giant fishhook-shaped path through those woods, and the slave graveyard, in actuality, rested a cheap BB gun's arced shot away from where we'd begun.

Marching home, slowly, I caught myself whispering *"Glory, glory hallelujah."* I didn't hear any choir providing backup, though.

My father wasn't home, and because I noticed a new pack of matches from Gruel's All-U-Can-Eat BBQ on the kitchen table, I knew that he'd been there, then home, during my little excursion with Shirley. So I got in the Jeep and drove straight to the Sunken Gardens Lounge. My father and Mr. Lane sat straight up at the bar, across from bartender Red Edwards. From outside the plate-glass window I watched my father in midstory, holding his hands a couple feet in front of his face, palms upward, jerking them back and forth. It looked as though he was shoving an imaginary watermelon to his mouth.

I walked in and said to Mr. Red Edwards, "A draft beer and a shot of bourbon, please," like I knew what I was doing. Like I wasn't the kind of high school–skipping teenager who tried to sell his teachers unpacked tea leaves for pot. Like my misspelled name rightly derived from the eastern Semitic word *Mendel,* meaning, "A man who gains knowledge by experience and study."

My father swiveled somewhat and yelled out, "Mendal! My son, Mendal! Hotdamn, boy, grab yourself a seat over here." He patted the red-vinyl stool on the other side of him.

Mr. Red Edwards said, "You want that straight up or on the rocks? House bourbon okay, or are you celebrating something, boy?"

I knew what "on the rocks" meant, but didn't cotton to drinking anything Red Edwards bottled on the premises. I said, "I want it straight up, and I want something that's not house bourbon."

Mr. Lane said, "Where's Comp? How come my son ain't with you?"

I said, "I was with him earlier, but he didn't have to go find out where his mother ended up being dead," trying to be all cryptic and telling. "So he went on home to have a peaceful night."

Mr. Red Edwards slid my beer over to the other side of my father's space. He handed me the shot of bourbon across the bar. My father said, "Mr. Lane and I just came back from Charlotte. Boy-oh-boy, we had us some business dealings up there." He lifted his bottle, as did Comp's daddy.

I didn't have the patience to wait for a perfect time to bring up what I thought I knew: that my father had murdered his wife, buried her in a slave graveyard, and used some kind of clay jug for a pathetic marker; that he told me over and over how his wife ran off to Nashville to become another Patsy Cline who wanted to croon in a way that would make men and women alike break down; that he hired some mysterious woman to call me up periodically on the telephone—or send sporadic birthday, Valentine's Day, and Christmas cards—to say how much she missed me.

I said, "You haven't been to Charlotte. You've been to Gruel's All-U-Can-Eat BBQ." I said, "I know how you killed Mom and buried her over by Mr. Ebo's farm."

To our left, at the end of the bar, Dunny Dunlap urged the pinball machine from his wheelchair. His father stood behind him, feet pressed hard against the wheels so his son wouldn't roll backwards. The boy would graduate with my class, even though he only got to go to school because his rich Forty-Five National Bank–owning father had paid off the school superintendent somewhere down the line. Dunny's IQ couldn't have been much more than those of any of the feral dogs I'd ever encountered, but all of us knew that he'd end up running that bank once his father died off. Dunny performed with the high-school marching band, in his own way. The back of his wheelchair had been designed to hold a snare drum, and Nelson Townes paradiddled away in the rear, while shoving Dunny through the routines—the band members just had to stand together, start an off-key song, then walk to their spots to make a big 45 in the middle of the football field. Because our football team always lost, and because no girl from Forty-Five High would ever date either of us, Comp Lane and I usually sat in the short wooden stands on the visitors' side, hoping to make time with girls from Greenville, Aiken, McCormick, Ninety Six, Batesburg, Laurens, or Clinton. During the halftime show, from our vantage point, our band looked like it was spelling out s4, which seemed appropriate.

My father said, "Boy, I hope you think you're only dreaming. Pain doesn't hurt as much in dreams."

Mr. Lane got up and walked to the men's room. I said,

"Shirley Ebo took me to the graveyard, and I saw that jug you put down for Mom's tombstone, and I saw all the buttons on it from that picture."

My father's eyes looked exactly like those of the copperheads I'd seen before in the woods. He had his head turned funny, and I could tell that he had sobered immediately. He said, "You stupid son of a bitch."

I said, "I saw what I saw," threw back my bourbon shot, and proceeded to cough it right back out. My father hit my back until I quit. "I saw what I saw, and then I figured out what I figured out."

Dunny Dunlap yelled out, "Neeee! Neeee! Neeee!" His father looked at the machine's back glass and tapped his son's head over and over.

My father looked at Mr. Red Edwards and nodded once. I drank half of my beer, cleared my throat, and coughed for five more minutes. "Is Shirley Ebo your girlfriend, Mendal?"

I said, "No sir. No."

"Is Shirley your friend, like her papa's my friend?"

I didn't get where he was going. "I guess."

"That's right."

Comp's father returned and said, "There's a good one written in the bathroom now. Someone wrote, 'I'd rather have a beer than a lobotomy.' No, that's not right. It went something like that. It's funny. Some them college boys must've come in here recently."

My father grabbed my forearm so I couldn't leave. He said to Mr. Lane, "I'm glad you're back. You remember when you took that pottery class up in Greenville, and you gave me that big old jug you made with the handle on it?"

"Uh-huh," Mr. Lane said. "Why are y'all making fun of me?" He spoke quietly and measured his words out. His eyes sliced over to Red Edwards.

My father looked back at me. "When about was that?"

Mr. Lane shook his head like he couldn't believe that someone would call him on trying to better himself, that his attempt at bettering himself or finding a new trade would end up in humiliation. The jukebox came on, playing "Sixty-Minute Man." Dunny Dunlap's father walked off to greet a woman he'd been waiting for, evidently—a woman I knew to be a teller at his bank.

Compton Lane's father said, "I know exactly. It was nineteen sixty-six."

My father turned to me and said, "Your mother left before then. There you go. Goddamn this reminds me of how your mother was. You burn my testes sometimes. I was having a perfectly good day, and then you come in and step on my high."

I nodded when Mr. Red Edwards asked if I'd like another beer, and shook my head when he asked if I wanted another bourbon. Someone in the back room yelled out, "You're up, Lee!" and my father and Mr. Lane got up to play pool. My father said, "Maybe I just wanted to put to rest her memory.

Did it have those ugly goddamn fake eyelashes on it? Or the stones from the engagement ring I gave her that she left on our kitchen table? Did it have that nail file she spent more time looking down at than my feet that hurt from working sixteen hours a day so she could buy what she wanted? What about the compass—was that on the jug? She left that compass on our door when she left, and a note that she'd be anywhere from northwest to southeast, which only left out California, and for me to not come looking. Did you find the hair I swept out of the bathroom so I wouldn't have to look at it anymore?"

Another song came on the jukebox, Johnny Cash singing about walking a line. My father went on and on. He mentioned some things that I didn't find on the jug: a pack of Picayune cigarettes he found in the fireplace flue, a tube of ruby red lipstick he'd never seen adorn my mother's face, and an Elvis Presley 45-rpm record of a song my father never heard played in our house. I said, "Yessir. I found some of those things. I apologize, Dad. I'm sorry."

"You damn right." My father got up to find a cue stick that wasn't warped.

I didn't stare at myself in the mirror behind Mr. Red Edwards. I looked at the packs of salted peanuts, the jarred pickled eggs and sausage. Would I ever come to a point where I believed my own father? Could I ever get to the point of telling him that it was possible that he and Mr. Lane had practiced this routine beforehand, over the years? What would it take for me to convince myself that my dad didn't have a vengeful side, and how could I ever look a woman in the face and say how I came from a long line of functional, understanding people?

Mr. Lane yelled, "I want to say right now that we don't have chalk or sticks around here that's worth a crap. If we lose, I call foul. The chalk's dry, and the sticks're warped. It's like Forty-Five sex. We all need to go out yonder and see what's going on in the rest of the country, I swear. It can't be like this everywhere, can it?"

I watched Dunny Dunlap peripherally, grunting in front of the pinball machine. His father walked off to a booth with the teller. I got up, stuck a quarter in the slot, and pushed the drummer's helper forward. I stuck my right foot forward hard, looked down to my pants leg, and noticed all of the beggar-lice still stuck there from my adventure in the woods. It looked like any wild dog's scruff. "I saw you chasing your father down the road once, Dunny. You had this wheelchair rolling. I'm thinking you probably shouldn't do that."

My father broke in the back room. I watched him until I realized that he was keeping his face turned from me all the time, even if it meant inventing awkward and difficult bank shots that rarely fell in.

UNEMPLOYMENT

My second-grade teacher didn't think ahead when she agreed to let us sing that "Name Game" song the last hour of Valentine's Day class. Because— as Miss Dupre even admitted—her homemade heart-shaped cookies turned out warped into looking more like bananas, it seemed almost necessary to sing. My friend Compton Lane had suggested everything, seeing as we no longer took music classes weekly; the chorus teacher had quit during Christmas break, saying she couldn't distinguish an on-key student in all of Forty-Five Elementary.

I didn't quite understand the implications of Compton's request, didn't realize what lyrics would occur in a class that, oddly, included two Chucks, a boy named Lucky, another named Tucker, and an unfortunate girl—unless later on in life she had gathered work in a Nevada brothel— whose parents tabbed her Bucky.

"Okay," Miss Dupre said. "We'll sing the song starting with Compton. Then, Comp, you point to whoever's next." She went on to say how we would hand out our cheap

Valentine's cards to each other afterwards and eat her mis-baked cookies that, once she realized hadn't come out heart-shaped, were iced yellow with HAPPY VALENTINE'S DAY painted in red.

As years went on, I remembered those cookies as reading only HAPPY V.D., but maybe my memory turns that way because twenty-three-year-old Miss Dupre had gotten fired soon after handing them out.

The class stood in a circle, surrounded by four cork-boards that stressed personal hygiene, poisonous plants, things to do on rainy days, and how to crouch during both natural and unnatural disasters. Compton pointed at me when his name was done, only because we were best friends who both had crazy runaway mothers. We went, "Mendal, Mendal bo bendal—banana fanna fo fendal," et cetera, and the whole while Comp jerked his head for me to call on Tucker. I pointed toward Tucker next, not knowing—this was second grade in a town where people gossiped when someone said "darn" or "heckfire" after falling from a roof—that our song would have a term I'd heard only once, when my father stepped on a nail.

Miss Dupre didn't even know the bad word, at least from the expression on her face. Later on I figured that she'd been trained thusly, in her education classes, in some course like "Psychology of Pranksters" or whatever.

Tucker pointed at one of the Chucks. Chuck pointed at the other, and then that Chuck chose Bucky, in succession.

From down the second-grade hallway I'm sure it sounded like a shipload of merchant marines were holding a sing-along.

I know this because our principal, a stern, unamused man named Mr. Uldrick, happened to be taking a group of state legislators on a tour of Forty-Five Elementary at the time, hopeful that we'd get more funding to at least reroof the place so there wouldn't be doves nesting in every classroom's ceiling and attracting hunters during season, which subsequently made it difficult to comprehend Miss Dupre over the shotgun blasts.

Uldrick motioned for us to stop, then took our teacher outside the door. I made out, "See me in my office after school," and then Miss Dupre said, "My cookies came out funny. I didn't take any home-ec classes in a South Carolina state-supported college."

Compton held his shoulders almost to his ears and his eyebrows toward the doves' nests. Glenn Flack said, "I heard my daddy say those bad words one time to my mom. He was talking about the Korean War."

Miss Dupre walked back in slower than she normally moved. Her red-and-white-polka-dot skirt didn't swish. "I think we're going to have to stop now, class. I think y'all did a wonderful job. But Mr. Uldrick says it's very important that we have no fun until three o'clock. It's officially quiet time. Y'all can pass out your cards to one another and come get two each of my cookies. But we can't make noise. I'm sorry."

I didn't know at the time that presently we would have a new teacher who'd start each day singing a hymn, that Miss Dupre would quit and never teach again. But I swear I studied her face and noticed the same thing I would later see on my own wife's face and on the faces of both men and women in a textile town gone bust during the Reagan and Bush administrations.

We tiptoed across our linoleum floor and handed out those "Be Mine," "I'm All Yours," and "You're Special" nonfolding cards. Shirley Ebo, the only black girl stuck in an otherwise nonintegrated school, gave me a card that must've been a reject or a second. Instead of "Let's Be Friends" it read only, "Let's Fend." She hadn't signed it.

I said, "Thanks, Shirley Ebo."

She said, "Does your name stand for something else, Mendal? I mean, is it short for something?"

I said, "I don't know. Men-doll. I doubt it."

Comp came over and said, "My mother says my name means 'free,' but she didn't want to name me that." Comp was my best friend from birth onward. In college, he would tell women that his name was short for Complimentary, Compulsive, Compatible, and Complex.

Shirley said, "My last name means something in Africa. I'm a warrior."

I said, "Uh-huh," and took more cards from my classmates. Miss Dupre sat at her desk, opened the drawer, and stared down. I had completely forgotten to sign a card for her and had no other choice but to approach the desk and hand Miss Dupre what Shirley Ebo had given to me earlier. " 'Let's Fend,' " my teacher said aloud. "That's funny, Mendal. Let's fend. I agree with that."

And then she stood up, walked around her desk, took my face in her young hands, and kissed me on the forehead. When she hugged me, the side of my face wedged directly into her cleavage. My classmates let out an "ooh" in a way none of us could perform in music class. I blushed, almost cried, and then the bell rang.

On my way out of school that day I passed Mr. Uldrick's office. My teacher sat across from him, her face turned away. I stood there and watched the principal wave his arms. Then he leaned back in his chair and spread his feet on the desk. Miss Dupre stood up, pointed at him, then looked at me standing by the door.

Years later I would say that she blew a kiss, mouthed "Thank you," and waved to me in a manner that meant for me to get away and keep going.

Every country boy on our Little League team could hit that knuckleball during practice. We had no choice. Coach D. R. Pope and both of his assistants had worked in the cotton mill, and all three of them had undergone tragic digit loss due to spinning frames, looms, and/or pneumatic presses of one sort or the other. D. R. pitched batting practice most of the time with his right hand, which had only a thumb and a little finger. So the baseball always lolled toward the plate without as much as one rotation between his grasp and the Louisville Slugger. Our own pitcher during games—a farm boy named Yancey Allison—must've thought that the knuckleball was some kind of Forty-Five, South Carolina, miracle, for he'd perfected it, too. Yancey let his nails grow out an inch beyond his fingertips, he dug them into the ball's seams, and even with the arm movement of a catapult, the ball crossed the plate at maybe twenty miles an hour. Our foes regularly hit Yancey's pitches a good hundred feet past the outfield fences. Meanwhile, all the rest of us stood stock-still when the opponents' pitchers threw fastballs, sliders, changeups, and curves in our direction. I wasn't the only player to take a mighty swing *after* the ball reached the catcher's mitt and he threw back to his pitcher. One time I actually got two strikes called on me by the umpire because I stood there and watched for strike one, then fouled off a ball as the catcher threw back and I finally swung.

Let me make it clear that the grounds on which we played needed regular tending before each game, for hunters would steal onto the field at night, regardless of legal hunting season, and deposit salt blocks and mounds of sweet corn to attract deer. If anyone decided to sleep in the bleachers overnight, like my friend Compton Lane and I did once, he'd be awoken an hour before dawn by camouflaged men sporting anything from .410 shotguns to thirty-aught-sixes. D.R. and his assistant coaches sent us out like boys with metal detectors to scour the rye grass between the infield and the cheap outfield signs advertising 45 OFFICE SUPPLY, 45 EXTERMINA-TION, 45 FLORISTS, 45 LUMBER, 45 GRAVEL AND ASPHALT, 45 MEN'S WEAR, 45 DEBS AND BRIDES, 45 JEANS, the *FORTY-FIVE PLATTER* newspaper, 45 TRASH PICK-UP, 45 RECORDS, 45 MODERN BARBERS (who sponsored our Little League team, the Flattops), SUNKEN GARDENS LOUNGE (which *used* to sponsor our team before Mr. Red Edwards decided he couldn't afford a losing team's destruction of his reputation), and RUFUS PRICE'S GOAT WAGON store. We took wheelbarrows out with us while the opposing team got to stretch, run wind sprints, take infield practice, and get ready to raise their collective batting averages.

"Just do the best you can, Mendal," my father always said as we pulled into the parking lot of the Forty-Five rec center. "I'll talk to D. R. and see if we can't get you playing first base, or left field." More than once he'd said something about how Bennie Frewer didn't really have head lice, and that it was okay for us to touch the baseball after Bennie threw it in from right field on those odd occasions when somebody from the other team didn't hit the ball over the fence and Bennie would gather it up and throw it to first or second base.

"I don't like being catcher," I said to my dad. "I'm a faster runner than anyone else. Why's D. R. have me be Yancey's catcher? A slow fat guy usually plays catcher. I've seen it on TV." Me, I crouched every game, waiting for Yancey to throw one of his knuckleballs. I waved my arm back and forth like a windshield wiper in hopes of only touching the ball coming my way. A blind boy could've caught for Yancey just as well.

My father never answered. Years later, I would think that for some reason he knew it would be best for me to hear what went on in the stands, right behind me, as I crouched, eyes closed, while the slow projectiles came my way.

"Hey, Mendal, you might want to get two catcher's masks," Coach D. R. Pope said more than once. "Find a way to fashion one over your privates."

"Yessir," I always squeaked out. D. R. held up his right hand with that thumb and little finger poked out like the biggest peace sign ever, like a big-time Texas Longhorns fan, like a deaf man saying he loved me, like—I would learn later—a man trying to approximate the length of his pecker.

"We don't want to set no records as to the worst team in Little League baseball, Mendal. You a smart boy. Can't you not figure out nothing to say back there to avert the batter none?"

I'd think, This is some kind of double- or triple- or quadruple-negative trick on me. And then I'd crouch, and close my eyes, and smile with glee about every tenth time, when I'd actually catch a ball thrown by Yancey that didn't either get thrown in the dirt or smacked straight over the 45 FEED AND SEED COMPANY sign in center field.

I sat in front of the umpire two days a week for an entire summer and listened to him bark "Ball!" unless our opponent's batter blasted a pitch out of the park. A lot of times I missed catching it completely, of course, and the umpire's shin stopped the ball. He said often, "Goddamn you, Dawes, I'mo send your daddy my doctor's bill for bruises."

And I always said, "A man with his leg stuck hard on the ground isn't going to go far in life," like my father told me to say, which wasn't the smartest thing, of course. Or I thought, A man with his leg stuck hard on the ground will never learn how to fly no matter how hard he flaps his arms. Invariably the umpire was one who'd worked at the cotton mill at one time or another and was missing digits, too.

COACH D. R. POPE wouldn't get his wish in regard to the team not setting a losing-streak record. Our team had lost all of its games for the three years before I could play and went on to lose until D. R. quit the mill and moved down to Myrtle Beach less than a year later. He got a job, I found out, as the maître d' at a fancy shellfish restaurant in Murrells Inlet. He had always talked about his dreams and goals and ambitions after we lost games by enormous margins, but I thought he talked big like that so that we would play harder the next game, *maybe win,* and not chance losing him for a coach who popped his players' hamstrings after every strikeout or error.

"My wife's cousin Sandy married into a rich family down there at the beach. They made they money paving driveways with seashells, you know. And then they thought, Hey, why don't we open up a big old restaurant, and we can get our clam and oyster and scallop shells for free every night? So that's what they done. And Sandy's husband, Claude—he's no account, and the family just flat-out give him his place to manage called Sandy Claude's—he said I'd be perfect for greeting eaters, when the time was right."

D. R. Pope told me his little story after everyone else left the players' bench, while I tried to stuff my mask, glove, shin guards, and chest protector into an old duffel bag.

"You know what's keeping him from going down to that restaurant today?" my father asked me as we drove home maybe midway through the 1968 season. This was a time before some touchy-feely psychologist figured out that losing kids would feel better about themselves if a game plain ended when one team was behind by ten runs at the end of the third inning or whenever. We'd lost this particular massacre 49-0. I remember only because their coach kept yelling at D. R., "Hey, we done scored seven touchdowns and every extra point after!"

To my father I said, "Coach doesn't want to go on to Myrtle Beach until we finally win a game, I guess."

My father honked the horn at nothing and laughed. "He'd never get to go to Myrtle Beach if he waited for that." He laughed and laughed. "That's a good one, Mendal."

I said, "I ain't trying to be funny and you know it. Why's he waiting, then?"

My father pulled into the Dixie Drive-In so we could get milkshakes. "The mill pays those boys a thousand dollars for every missing digit. It's something like five thousand dollars for an arm from the elbow down. Times get tough, a man like D. R. Pope just grits his teeth and sticks his arm in a machine. I'm thinking that his cousin-in-law wants D. R. to go ahead and lose the matching fingers on his left hand so he'll look more like a lobster. Or crab. Or any of those other things with pincers. Like a scorpion. And I bet D. R. needs three more thousand dollars in order to make the move, you know. If he puts his other three grand in a bank account, that's a pretty nice little jump start."

I ordered a plain vanilla when the carhop woman showed

up. I always got plain vanilla. My father ordered weird things, like strawberry with a glob of peanut butter whisked through it, but I think he just did this in order to shock people. "He doesn't put his hand in any of those spinning frames," I said. "Anybody that crazy doesn't care about coaching baseball."

My father turned the radio dial to some man singing opera. "Anybody that crazy doesn't want to hang out around kids who can't hit a baseball. Ask him. Or ask those other two coaches helping out. You make a buck-sixty an hour after a number of years and feel your lungs turning inside out, you'll about do anything to move away. If you're smart. D. R. Pope's a smart man, son. His daddy was a smart man. Why you think he's named D. R.? It's so when he got a checking account it looked like 'Dr. Pope.' People treat him with respect when he writes out a check. Dr. Pope. You can't be a surgeon with all those missing fingers, of course. But you can be a dermatologist. Or an English professor."

My father went on to list a number of doctors, from allergists to zoologists. He didn't say, "Gynecologist." The carhop returned with our extra-large milkshakes and said, "I ain't never heard no one order a strawberry peanut butter milkshake. What's it taste like?"

My father pulled out his straw, turned it toward the woman, and said, "Stick this in your mouth and give me your opinion."

I didn't pay much attention to what was going on over on that side of the Buick. I sucked.

"Hey, did you ever work over at Forty-Five Cotton?" my father asked the carhop. She wore a paper hat.

"Both my parents do. I made a pact with myself, though. I said I wanted to get out of high school and do better for myself. My momma and daddy never got a tip on *their* jobs."

My father nodded. He said, "What's your name?"

"Emmie Gunnells." She pointed at a name tag half-hidden beneath her collar.

"Emmie Gunnells, I want you to help my boy and me with a little argument we're having. Did your folks ever have any tough times financially? I'm talking, like, back when gasoline prices went up to thirty-five cents a gallon?"

Emmie leaned down and looked at me closer. She said, "Y'all ain't union organizers are you? We've already had the union organizers over to the house."

I shook my head. My face felt like an hourglass, that's how thick the vanilla milkshake was. My father said, "Hell no, we ain't no organizers. I'm only trying to prove a point with Mendal here."

"I don't know," Emmie Gunnells said.

My father said, "How many fingers has your father lost at this point in time?"

Emmie Gunnells slapped her hip with the tray she was holding. "Law!" she said. "How'd you know?" She stooped back down to look at me. "Y'all are from the fair, I bet. Y'all are those people who can guess ages and weights and family trees."

My father said, "How many?"

Emmie Gunnells said, "He's got six left. It's enough for him to drive his Cadillac."

SEEING AS THERE was little else to do in Forty-Five, everyone came out to the games. If a mastermind thief ever traveled through, he could've broken in to about every house in the entire town on early-dusk nights. And he might've gotten gold watches and pearl earrings from those doffers and weavers who'd jammed their hands into machines. Here's what I heard from behind the plate every game: "Y'all are an embarrassment to Forty-Five"; "Hey, Bennie Frewer, see if you can get knocked in the head with the ball so no one will touch it and you can run around the diamond"; "Nice reflexes, boy. Remind me not to let you in on my driver's ed class in six years"; "You boys must all think you're famous, standing there like statues"; "I thought y'all'ses were the Flattops, not the Heart Stops."

I couldn't *not* listen to what went on. I mean, I was prepared to hear "Ball!" four times in a row from the umpire, or "Hotdamn, I hope NASA ain't sent up a mission—that ball might hit one them astronauts up there," when Yancey Allison offered up a slow melon with no movement on it.

But I never was prepared to hear Compton Lane's father

say something like, "This is going to be a long game. Do y'all have anything back there that's got arsenic in it?" from the concession stand. Midway through the season I heard my own father's voice. He tried to whisper, but I could tell that he had sat down next to Emmie Gunnells. "I thought me up another concoction," he said. "Banana and liver pudding. You know what liver pudding does for a man, don't you? And, hey, I thought of another concoction. You and me."

The concession stand was owned and operated by Danny Clements's father, and for some reason it occurred to me that he must've been in cahoots with D. R. Pope. Games lasted sometimes five hours, and probably each sad, sunburned, tired spectator averaged a Coke an hour, a couple hot dogs, maybe some potato chips. These were brown-bagging days, too, so every player's father might've put away *two* Cokes an hour to go with his Old Crow or Rebel Yell or Southern Comfort. Forgetful mothers loaded up on zinc oxide. Bored little kids inevitably started a game of tag or hide-and-go-seek or kick-the-can in the gravel parking lot, fell down, and required Band-Aids sold by Mr. Clements.

During one particular game against Calhoun Falls—a town that later got mostly submerged by shallow and algae-ridden Strom Thurmond Lake—the Calhoun Falls team batted around three times in one inning. I heard the parents of our shortstop, Bev Lagroon, get in such a fight that they vowed to end the marriage. Then they went off to the concession stand separately—she ordered chili tater tots, a Dr

Pepper, and some Juicy Fruit gum; he, two Cokes to go with his Jim Beam, a corn dog, and pork rinds—before finally settling back down just before a six-foot-two-inch fourth grader from Calhoun Falls hit a ball that went through the 45 DRUGS sign in left field right where it read COSMETICS! The umpire said to me, "We better call the fire department and make sure that ball's not smoldering back there on Leonard Self's dry land."

Mr. Lagroon said to his wife, "I didn't mean nothing by all that. Let's you and me go down to Myrtle Beach and renew our vows."

I called time-out and walked to the pitcher's mound. The bases were empty and there were no outs. I called the infield in and kept my back to D.R. Pope. Bev Lagroon came in pounding his fist to his glove. I said, "Okay. We're getting smeared. But not all's bad. Bev's parents are going to Myrtle Beach next week for some kind of second honeymoon. I'll steal some of my father's beer, and, Yancey, you steal some of your father's peach-bounce moonshine, and we'll all meet at Bev's. That okay with you, Bev?"

He faced the stands. "Shirley Ebo's waving at us up there."

Comp said, "Hey. When this games over, let's all beat these boys up. Let's get in a big fight and kick them in the nuts instead of shaking hands."

I turned around and looked at their bench. I said, "No. No way. The only thing we got going for us is knowing that the best thing those boys got going for them is moving to Forty-Five, getting jobs at the mill, and losing their fingers on purpose. Let's just let them beat us silly."

It's what I said. My father had given me a pep talk of his own before this particular game. He said that the funny thing about Emmie Gunnells thinking he was a union organizer was that he really was one, in his own way. My father had said, "Down here, if they was called *rebel* organizers we'd have a lot better chance. All them mill workers would have the same chance in life as D. R. Pope's lucky marriage into a crab joint–owning family. But let us learn to live the way we live, and do the best that we can. Let us be strong and proud and forward-looking."

I said, "Amen."

He whapped me a little too hard upside the head. "Amen? What the hell are you talking about, boy? I thought I taught you better than that." Luckily I was wearing my catcher's mask already.

I said, "I wasn't thinking. I'm sorry."

My father opened the car door for me. I threw my duffel bag on the backseat. He said, "You're not sorry. Your *team* is sorry, but you're not sorry, son. You're the best goddamn thing that's ever happened to Forty-Five. What you need to do is get out of here and tell everyone about it."

I said, "I'm not doing so great in English."

He said something about how stand-up comedians don't need to write things for print. He said that archaeologists and anthropologists didn't either, what with the advent of the television documentary.

THE SEASON DRAGGED ON, and I continued listening to all the conversations that went on behind the backstop. I caught wind of people making plans, breaking promises, speculating who'd be the first dead Forty-Fiver sent back from Vietnam. People made bets as to who would be the first player on my team to foul a ball off, actually get a hit, or knock himself out plowing into one of the outfield signs. They made bets as to what time the seventh-inning stretch would take place, when the game would end, and who would be the first batter to throw his bat toward the opposing team's bench. Coach D. R. Pope smiled throughout our long, long losing season. He clapped his hands to make puttering muffler sounds. Grover Henderson, the local dermatologist, salivated in the bleachers, for he knew that skin cancer was growing on the nine of us in the field and the couple hundred local spectators.

"We gone be leaving Forty-Five within the next year for Myrtle Beach," I heard D. R. Pope's wife say one extended first inning. Mrs. Pope sat with Danny Clements's mother. "I know I give him a little bit of Hades, but he'd do about anything for me. He's promising another three thousand dollars before September. Then we ready. I'm thinking I might could get a job down at that hammock factory, what with my skill before a loom. D. R.'s got a fancy job lined up, due to my family connections."

This was the first inning of the last game against the team from Graywood. Yancey Allison threw a knuckleball that came closer to our third baseman than it did the plate. I tried to point my ears in another direction. I tried to listen to Shirley Ebo and her daddy talking about how they might invest in some horses, seeing as horsehide got so worn out at our Little League games, et cetera. But I couldn't get it out of my mind, my coach sticking his hand in a spinning frame just so he could wear a shiny suit at the entrance of a place that probably prided itself on its homemade cocktail sauce. I heard Mrs. Pope say, "If I don't get a job at the hammock place, then I might see if D. R. can bring some oyster shells home. I had a dream one time about putting those little plastic wiggle-eyes on shells and selling them as ashtrays."

"Time out, please," I said to the umpire.

I walked to the mound and motioned for the infield. Yancey said, "That last pitch slipped from my hand." He showed me his index finger. "I broke off half the nail trying to pry off some old nasty bathroom tile my daddy said had hidden treasure behind. It didn't."

I said, "Coach D. R.'s planning on cutting more fingers off."

One of the assistant coaches yelled out, "Watch the runner at first," even though there was no one on base, seeing as their lead-off batter was still standing there with a 3-0 count.

"There's got to be a better way to spend the summer," I said. My father had started me reading Kierkegaard.

I looked out at Bennie Frewer in right field and it came to me as if God had tapped me on the forehead to think harder. Without even looking back to our coach, I yelled out so that the opposing team on its bench could hear—and everyone on our team and the people in the stands—"Bennie's got head lice real bad! Let's have him pitch!" I motioned for Bennie to come in. He pointed at his own chest just like in a sitcom, like in a cartoon, and I sent Yancey out to right field. *"Head Lice is going to pitch!"* I yelled. "Come on down here, Head Lice."

Bennie could throw in a straight line, I knew that much. He didn't have much range or velocity, but that didn't matter. Coach D. R. came out to the mound at the same time as the umpire to get things going. The umpire said, "Y'all know that these games already last longer than a Pentecostal Sunday. Come on. I got things to do tonight. I promised my wife we'd play Yahtzee later."

D. R. Pope said, "Yancey's our pitcher, Mendal. You kind of stepping on my authority." He held his deformed hand out like a manta ray.

I might've been four-foot-six back then, but I said, "We'd kind of like to make a showing, once."

My father yelled from the stands, "I told you reading that Danish fellow would get you thinking right!"

The coach went back to the bench. I sent the infield back out to their positions. Yancey started crying until I said that I had a feeling that the Graywood team's left-handers might start hitting the ball toward right field, and only Yancey could run a ball down and catch it. I said to Bennie Frewer—a boy who looked as if he'd been whipped every day since he'd starred in an educational television-produced documentary about the myths and realities of head lice—"You can lob up pitches softball-style for all I care. Just leave it to me. I'll talk to the batters."

Like I said, Graywood's lead-off batter had a 3-0 count. I crouched back behind the plate and said, "This old boy Bennie Frewer's got lice so bad I'm afraid if he scratches his scalp and touches the ball, it might look like sparks coming off our way."

Bennie threw his first pitch overhand, but it came up in a loop the likes of a top-heavy bottle rocket. The umpire hesitated before saying, "Strike one?" The batter practically ran back toward the on-deck circle.

Danny Clements's father understood what was going on. He yelled from his concession stand, "Somebody get me another pot to boil 'dogs in, boys!"

The Graywood players jumped back from each pitch as if it was soaked in toxic waste. They regularly struck out

watching, as if they played for Forty-Five. And our players—me included—did about the same at bat, seeing as we
couldn't hit a pitch whatsoever. This continued. Somewhere
between the twelfth and thirteenth inning Coach D. R. Pope
came up to me in the dugout, gripped my neck like a
C-clamp, and said, "You a different kind of boy living down
here. How come you didn't figure this out about game number two?" I shrugged. "This game might last ten days. They's
got to be some kind of record for the longest Little League
game ever in the history of boyhood."

"Maybe you won't have to cut off the rest of your fingers
and go down there to the beach," I said. "Maybe you can
get on television."

The umpire yelled out, "Play ball!" again, the score tied
nothing to nothing. Bennie Frewer, our hero, came to the
plate. Evidently Graywood's team had a boy with something
like my ability to figure out ways to win. Their pitcher hit
Bennie right in the head with a fastball that must've clocked
in at seventy miles an hour. Bennie went down. The Graywood catcher ran away from the batter's box.

IT DIDN'T TAKE a second for me to figure out what
to do next, I swear. I'm not sure if it was reading Kierkegaard, or if my father was beaming ESP into my brain from
his vantage point behind the backstop. I said to the coach,
"If we use a pinch runner for Bennie, he can't go back in.

Let's just set him down on first. The next two batters are going to strike out anyway."

Coach D. R. Pope gave me a thumbs-up. He gave me a pinkie-up, too, of course. Glenn Flack and little Johnny Scott came up next, and stood there to watch their three balls zip straight over the plate. Bennie sat on first base with his head turned backwards, probably trying to regain his senses. Coach Pope said, "What're we going to do now, smarty-pants?"

Smarty-pants! I envisioned him working at Sandy Claude's and saying, "Where do you want to sit, smarty-pants?" or "Would you like a menu or the buffet, smarty-pants?" I was that way—looking into the future—even back then. I said, "I'll pitch. Bennie Frewer will play second base, but really let him just stand there by me on the mound. Go get . . . I don't know," I looked down the bench for who might be able to play catcher. I looked up to the stands at Shirley Ebo, who shook her head no. I said, "It doesn't matter. You pick someone."

Coach Pope gave a death-ray point toward Blink Harvel—a little fat kid with the IQ of a doorknob—and said, "You catching, boy." Harvel spent most games finding a way to sneak off the bench to scour beneath the bleachers and retrieve the outside paper wrappers of Doublemint, Juicy Fruit, and Fruit Stripe gum he used to make chains and necklaces.

Blink Harvel said, "Okay, Coach," and dropped his paper chain. He would've said the same thing if the coach asked him to pull off his pants and run down the third-base line.

When we got to the field I motioned for Blink to approach me at the mound. I said, "This won't be hard. I'm going to throw the ball to you just like playing catch. You don't worry any."

Blink said, "How'm I supposed to know if it's a ball or a strike? I've never called balls and strikes." Blink went on to get a doctorate in administrative studies, and got a job with the Department of Education as a grief-therapy expert. He got interviewed on the local news whenever a tornado hit some trailer park where children lived, or a fourth grader shot another fourth grader, or when Clemson lost a football game and no little redneck kid felt like living anymore.

I explained to him that it was the umpire's job. I said, "Just catch the ball and throw it back to me. That's it."

Blink Harvel nodded his head around, wearing my catcher's mask.

I jerked my head to Bennie Frewer, who lolled around near second base. He wandered my way and said, for no apparent reason, "This *itches,* y'all."

I said, "Uh-huh." Oh, he'd have trouble in his later years—maybe rob a couple of banks or whatever—and try to say to both judge and jury that his damaged frontal lobe had caused it all. I said, "Take off your hat and just stand beside me. Right here."

Graywood's first batter came up and held the bat like Carl Yastrzemski. I held the ball in my mitt, rubbed my hand on Bennie Frewer's head as if his head were a lucky piece, then threw toward home. Yastrzemski stepped back twice, and the umpire yelled, "Strike one!" Blink Harvel handed the ball to the umpire, who acted like he didn't want to touch it, then told Blink, "Throw it on back to the pitcher, son."

And so it went. I rubbed Bennie's head, the Graywood batters thought head lice was still coming their way, I struck out three batters in a row each time, and we—the Forty-Five Flattops, sponsored by 45 Modern Barbers—came in at the bottom of the inning to act likewise.

We didn't win. But we didn't lose, either. It was the end of the season, and there was no way to make up the game later. About an hour after dark, it seemed, the umpire motioned both managers to the field and explained how he had to call the game. I was glad, because my palm was burning from rubbing Bennie Frewer's head so much. It was the twenty-sixth inning. Probably a record, everyone said. For the first time in my life I knew what it was like to be Bennie Frewer, for when both teams lined up to shake hands, no one would touch me. No one touched Blink Harvel, and no one shook hands with Bennie.

On the drive home my father said, "This worked out exactly as I wanted it to work out, son. Did you learn anything about life today?" He laughed and looked at his watch. "I mean, today and tonight?"

I nodded. To be honest, I didn't get it.

We went to the Dixie Drive-In and barely got there before it closed. A new woman took our orders. My father asked about Emmie Gunnells. The new carhop said that Emmie had quit, that she left without notice, but word was she had hitchhiked down to Myrtle Beach and gotten a job as a third-shift desk clerk at the Anchored Sloop hotel. My father said, "I'll be damned," and I heard the sadness of loss in his voice.

We didn't talk after we got our milkshakes. He rubbed my head a couple times in the same way I had rubbed Bennie Frewer's. My father and I both came down with head lice within the week, maybe from Blink's borrowing my catcher's mask. But we didn't tremble around the house. My father and I scrubbed our scalps, washed our bedsheets. We furrowed our hair with those special nit combs. My father promised a weekend of camping out in the Forty-Five rec center bleachers, where we could point a flashlight and look for what deer were staring back, either mesmerized or transformed, not knowing whether to jump the fence or not.

A Wheelchair's Too Slow

Because my father believed that there was some kind of inherent and inexorable value in understanding what other people lived without, he procured— without warning or father-son discussion—a suspect, paying, part-time job for me down at a former elementary school turned nursing home. I was to perform whatever duties my boss, Mr. Wylie Alexander, asked of me, and my father promised that I would probably only empty wastebaskets, sweep tile floors, and take residents on short jaunts around the perimeter of Forty-Five Longterm Care, pushing their wheelchairs around the playground. There were still eight-foot-high basketball hoops, tetherball poles, and faded hopscotch outlines. A quarter-mile cinder track encircled the area, and Wylie Alexander said that I might help organize a field day of sorts, should the nursing home residents gain my trust. I said that maybe I should lower the basketball goals another four feet. My boss handed me a time sheet to fill out and said I'd do fine, more than likely, if I remained nothing but honest.

"We might have to build a higher fence around the track," Wylie said. "For the most part you get the ambulatory going in a circle, they'll keep it up until the next meal. Every once in a while, though, one'll make a break for it. I remember one day we had three ladies snagged to the fence, what with their gowns getting caught."

My father said that I would be getting paid under the table, because I wasn't old enough for a social security card. I told my friend Compton Lane, "I only have to work Wednesday nights and Sundays, and all I do is pick up peas and forks from the floor. And then I'll get paid under the table."

"You better wear a rubber suit," Compton said. "They're going to be peeing on you all the time. Especially those old men." He shook his head, then squinted toward the sun. We sat atop a new load of torn-down barn wood my father stacked in the front yard for—at the time—unknown purposes. "Don't ever say to those old-timers that you want them to eat every bean and pea on their plates. They might hear you wrong."

I punched his arm. The only thing Compton got paid for at this point was riding around with his daddy, pretending to be helpful and needed. He would live his teenage years without ever having to fill out a job application, though Mr. Lane did make him partake in some questionable activities for which Compton got money. Sometimes I did, too. One time Compton's father had invested money in a dent-and-fender man's shop, and then Compton got paid to go out with a roofer's hammer and ding just about everybody's car hoods and roofs and trunks, just as though a nighttime hailstorm had traveled through.

I didn't help him out that night. It was ten days after the Duke Power meter reader came through, and—as always—I had to help my father jerk out our pronged meter, turn it upside down, and run our electricity bill backwards for a while. A couple weeks later we'd unplug it again, shove it in right side up, then wait for the meter reader to come by. He'd write down the number and drive away wondering how we lived off four bucks' worth of heat and light, I imagine.

Let me say that, although Compton Lane was my same age, I believed about everything that he said. He wasn't bigger and didn't hold his mouth half-open like my classmates and their parents, and he wasn't any smarter than I was. But he could flat-out tell lies. Compton could look George Washington in the face and convince him that George *hadn't* chopped down the cherry tree, after all. So you can't blame me for showing up to retrieve slung vegetables and fallen silverware wearing a big yellow rain suit and galoshes, Playtex rubber gloves, and a pair of work goggles my father wore when he dealt with car batteries and chain saws.

Mr. Alexander said, "Well, Mendal, I'm happy that you showed up early. Why exactly are you dressed such?" He looked outside. "It ain't raining, is it?"

This was 3:30 on a Wednesday. I'd taken my outfit with me to school, changed in the boys' bathroom, then ridden my bicycle the three miles out to the nursing home. I got there as residents rolled into the dining hall—it still had a LUNCH ROOM sign on the door from the old days. Man, I felt like a regular breadwinning adult. I said, "My father doesn't want me messing up my good clothes," as if I had any.

"Huh," said Wylie Alexander. "Well. I'm no psychologist or anything, but I'd be willing to bet that that cap and goggles might confuse some of the older residents here. You kind of look like the Morton Salt Girl's crazy brother, son."

He held out his hand. He said he'd put my unneeded belongings in the ex-janitor's office, beside the nurse's handbag. Then he told me to fetch Mr. Self and push his wheelchair as slowly as possible in any direction until I saw a property stob. Mr. Self, I soon learned, was prone to stealing food from anyone not paying attention.

I'M NOT SURE what a regular, square elementary classroom's dimensions might be—at least forty by forty—but the Forty-Five Longterm Care facility, which was once known as Forty-Five Black School, had been refurbished in such a way that the entrance to any classroom turned hard left, then three pie-shaped rooms shot off to the side. The first room always held a chalkboard. When viewed from above, if there had been no roof, it would've looked as if a warped hard-boiled-egg cutter had come down and inserted walls. Forty-Five Black was a one-story L-shaped elementary school, as opposed to the one-level U-shaped old Forty-Five White, first through sixth. When Forty-Five Black became a nursing home, for what reason I didn't understand until much later, no white man would place his mother or father there unless a certified medical doctor admitted that the parent's condition had gone past any capability of recognizing family. Oddly enough, the Forty-Five Longterm Care facility may have been the only bastion of nonracist thought or action in town, if not in all of South Carolina.

The dozen chalkboard rooms were given to men. My father said it was due to notch-on-bedpost mentality, and that the chalkboard's presence helped preserve their sense of manliness. Yellow sticks of chalk even stayed on the shelves, which I thought wasn't all that smart a move when asthmatics moved in. Maybe it was done intentionally. The male patients did seem to die off faster.

I pushed wheelchairs and emptied trash cans. I learned to grasp the hands of old men and women who stretched their arms out when I walked in. On Wednesday nights—churchgoing nights in the rest of Forty-Five—I helped people turn the pages of their useless hymnals in what used to be Forty-Five Black's sad, poor auditorium, which wasn't anything more than two classrooms without a partition in between.

I did my work a few good Wednesday/Sunday stints before

Mr. Self said, "You know they using you. I hope you smart enough to know how you smarter than any doctor they bring rambling through here to check us once a week. I can tell."

We had circled the playground and gone past the track on our way to a yellow metal property stob south of the home. Up to this point Mr. Self had only rattled on about things like how cotton didn't loom like it used to in the mills he once owned, or how a nurse named Glorene shuffled his balls a little roughly while giving him sponge baths. I said, "I'm supposed to keep you out of the way until all those old women get done eating. It's corn-dog night, from what I understand. They have you figured out." Wylie Alexander had taught me how to hard-lean a wheelchair back in case Mr. Self or anyone else looked like he was about to conjure up some leg muscles.

"If you're smart as I think you are, then I think you know how I'm not touched in the head. And I'm not that old, either. At least not as old as a man should be to be put in a nursing home." He started hacking like an ex–chicken plucker. "On my honor," he forced out.

"I'm just doing what I'm told," I said, which was true. What else could I say? "I'm doing what I'm told, and they ain't paying me under the table like they said they would."

Mr. Self kicked his legs in the air like a tar-stuck yellow jacket. "Snot-nose," he said. "I'm telling you, boy. I'm telling you. They're paying another fellow twice as much to push me around nights you're not here. I'll ask him for the exact amount tomorrow and get back to you on all this."

I could only look at my watch, see that it was past five o'clock, and say, "Yessir." I put Mr. Self's front wheels down and started rolling him back toward home. I said, "People might get paid more than I do, but they have taxes taken out. I get flat-paid money Mr. Alexander says I make."

Mr. Self opened his eyes wide. "That right? Well I'll take note of that. Do you know what I did before my kids slapped me in here, boy? I'll tell you. I was an accountant. I was an accountant, and I was an IRS agent. A T-man they call it. I worked with the mafia. My brother and I cracked the code so we didn't have to stay in the war as long as people thought we'd be—the war the mafia got that country to start up with us."

I pushed, knowing better. These were the kinds of stories I had hoped to hear from these folks all along. I dodged gravel. I knew what Mr. Self really had done for a living and wondered how his mind contorted fabric- and yarn-making into the world of bookkeeping and espionage. I said, "Y'all had something to do with the atomic bomb?"

"*World War I!*" he yelled. If his back hadn't been fused together like beef jerky, he would've turned in his wheelchair and walloped me across the face. "Foxholes and nerve gas, little boy."

We approached the nursing home's back patio. The ambulatory patients walked toward the cinder track. A black coworker named Mr. Perlotte was hovering behind them like a good herding dog. I called out to him, "Is the cafeteria open?"

He nodded. "Ain't no food left for Mr. Self in the kitchen, though. Sorry."

He had said the same thing every other time I worked. Mr. Self stuck out the wrong finger—his ring finger—and said, "Up yours, Honeypot."

Mr. Perlotte laughed. He clucked his tongue toward his charge, as one might to a horse. "We ain't in your cotton mill no more, is we, Leonard Self? Un-uh."

Mr. Self said to me, "And then when I figured out how to get us all out of the Depression, I took over for my daddy at the mill. Do you appreciate the shirt you're wearing, son? Well, do you? Sometimes you taint my blood, what with your inconsideration. All of you and your people."

I pushed him into the cafeteria, went past tables, and left him in front of the ice dispenser. I said, "I'll be right back. I need to go into your room and rifle through your belongings." It's what I always said. It was a way to get Mr. Self to clear out his air passages before meals, which allowed him to swallow easier, which kept any of us from having to stick our fingers down his throat in search of lodged corn bread, biscuits, and so on. At least that's what my boss told me.

In reality, Mr. Self owned nothing at the facility. His relatives had made sure of that. On the chalkboard in his room I printed out, POUR SALT ON SLUGS, not because Wylie

Alexander had said I looked like the crazy brother of the Morton Salt Girl, I don't think, but because my father told me this every morning when I got up to get the newspaper.

Later on, after I left my part-time job, I would learn that pouring salt meant a number of things.

THE RESIDENTS TOOK to me like grids on a waffle iron, no lie. Whenever I walked in—after I'd parked my bicycle straight up in azalea bushes out front—every wheelchair-confined invalid scooted toward the front door, propelling themselves with their standard-issue house slippers, until it looked like one giant demolition-derby clog. Everybody's hubs got stuck in someone else's spokes, and my first job, always, was to back them out one at a time, pushing them to their own quarters, or the TV room, or the cafeteria. I pushed them wherever I thought was best, and told them they'd have dinner soon.

Alzheimer's hadn't been invented at this point, of course. I let men and women alike call me "son," "wife," "husband," "daughter," "doctor," "waiter," "car mechanic," "house-painter," "teacher," "ship captain," "Fuller Brush man," "Avon lady," "veterinarian," or "maid." One man was so old he thought I was his *slave,* and he threatened to take me back behind the tobacco barn in his mind and whip me silly for juking with the white girls. I could only think, Man, please let me get to the same point before I'm thirty. I thought, I want to be able to say anything I like, all the time.

But after I rolled the shovees into the cafeteria, I always went straight back to Leonard Self, took him outside no matter the weather, and inched along until I knew that, back inside, the last lima bean had been slurped up and gnashed into nothingness. "Other boys getting paid union wages," Mr. Self said a month before I quit for good, seeing as I had a B in math. "They getting upwards of three dollars an hour."

There were no unions in South Carolina, and Mr. Self had fought hard against them for most of his life, according to my dad. My father also kept me apprised daily of the evils of capitalism in general and Republican leaders in particular, and let me know early on that I'd be better off running a truck farm off Highway 25 during drought than upper management at one of the cotton mills.

I said to Mr. Self, "I don't care. I'm fine getting what I get. And there aren't any unions, by the way, in case you've forgotten."

"There's a *town* called Union, so that's where you're wrong. I own a mill in Union. Almost wanted to have the name of the town changed before we built it there."

"There's a town," I said. This was late October. The leaves had turned somewhat, even though it was still eighty degrees outside going toward dusk. I should've been thinking about what I'd wear on Halloween, but instead I felt confident enough to argue with a man whose family made entirely too much money off the labors of Forty-Fivers. "I thought you meant labor unions. You got me."

Understand that I'd about gotten to know everything about Leonard Self—he kind of repeated his stories—outside of the subject of his adult diapers. Mr. Self looked forward as I pushed him uphill on the asphalt walkway between the fifth- and sixth-grade wing and the cinder track. "Let's you and me go beyond the line this afternoon," he said. He reached into his pajamas and produced an old-timey tweed riding cap. "Let's see what's on the other side of those trees."

We went slowly. I said, "I don't know."

"You afraid that when we don't get back in time Wylie Alexander will call the sheriff's department and they'll get you for kidnapping a tycoon?"

"Yessir. That's exactly what I'm afraid of." My father had taught me never to trust anyone who'd had more than one person working for him, ever.

Mr. Self reached back in his pajamas and pulled out a fifty-dollar bill. "I can't imagine bail being more than this. Here. Take this money. Show me where other people live. I won't even tell on you about how you're sticking Mexican jumping beans beneath old Blindman Martin's bed, driving him crazy. I won't do that."

I said, "What? I don't stick anything beneath his bed."

Mr. Self laughed. His thin white hair stood up like a poor, deranged Mohawk. "I can do or say anything I want around here. Like always. Who do you think owns this place?"

I could not call my father for advice. There were no pay

phones on the edge of Forty-Five Longterm Care, and this was a thousand years before cell phones. I'd never seen a fifty-dollar bill, although I'd heard that they existed in exotic faraway places like Atlanta, Charleston, and Nashville. My father and Compton's daddy didn't know I was standing on the other side of a door once, when Mr. Lane said he drove up to Charlotte to a titty bar and gave a strange woman a fifty-dollar bill to do something I couldn't quite envision. This little act of eavesdropping occurred not long after my own mother had skipped town, and Mr. Lane evidently tried to talk my father into going on the next excursion. For a half-year after this incident I would check my father's pockets at night, hoping to find a pack of matches with a naked woman pictured on front. But for the longest time I found nothing worthwhile and quit searching altogether after my dad—who somehow became aware of my nosiness—stuck safety razors in each pocket, then waited for me to come wake him up as my sliced index finger bled between the yellow, curled kitchen linoleum where he'd left his dirty clothes and the brown, curled linoleum where he slept, always, on Mom's old side of the bed. He didn't take me to the hospital—which looked similar to Forty-Five Longterm Care. My father took me into the bathroom, poured plain isopropyl in a metal bucket, forced my hand in, and said, "It looks like Kool-Aid, don't it?" as my blood mixed in. "I'm going to put a butterfly stitch on this. And then maybe every time you see a monarch flit by you'll remember not to rifle through my clothes looking for money. Don't be like your momma, boy."

I said, "I'm not stealing your money." I screamed. The bucket turned redder, and my filleted finger throbbed. "I promise. I was looking for naked-women pictures."

My father released my hand. "Goddamn it to hell, I told you not to be like your mother. Do I need to get your hearing checked?" He reached in the drawer and pulled out a circular tin of white adhesive tape. "Give me your finger."

I did. Oh, I gave him my finger from then on out.

I pushed Mr. Self faster by accident and saw the property line ahead, the trees beyond it, and the path that led into some woods where the kitchen crew went occasionally to drink beer on breaks. Self held that fifty-dollar bill up and said, "Fitty, fitty, fitty, fitty, fitty. Just take me to the other side, son. I want to see what's on the other side. I'm betting that it's changed since when my brother and I used to come down here with girls my daddy would've killed us for seeing."

Even back then I thought of that greener grass cliché. Because my father wasn't a churchgoer, thus making me the same, I didn't know how the other side could mean anything else.

LEONARD SELF FEIGNED death thirty minutes past the kitchen help's secret hobo jungle. I stopped the wheelchair there for a couple minutes, and we looked at four plastic chairs stolen from the cafeteria, a mound of malt-liquor bottles, an IV stand that the doctor brought over to the home one day in case anyone got dehydrated, and a still-smoking, half-buried campfire of fat lighter, paper plates, old flower arrangements, and lobby magazines donated by an auxiliary of women way over in Columbia who felt guilty about being married to rich doctors and lawyers.

There at the heap—and I'm sure he had in mind his fake death by this point—Mr. Self said, "This used to be a place where I hunted arrowheads as a child. I can't remember for sure, but I believe I got my first kiss here, way before I made my money. Long before I realized there are people who *want* to be held down."

Even I, at this age, wondered if I'd heard him right. "No one wants to be held down, according to my dad. The only man wants to be held down either finds his way to prison on purpose, or moves to South Carolina on purpose from elsewhere. According to my father."

Mr. Self stared straight ahead. His hair waved around slower than a sea anemone stuck in doldrums. "Well. I was born in the nineteenth century. I might be wrong, nowadays, boy. Both my parents were born before the Industrial Revolution." Mr. Self pointed toward one tendril of smoke. "I always wanted to be a potter, to tell you the truth. Dirt lasts forever, you know." He stuck out his hand like a referee calling first down.

Let me say here that Mr. Self didn't display exactly the

same dementia that most of our residents did, but he tended toward non sequitur and flat-out mean lies. This particular fifty-dollar ride—and I had not touched the money by this time—showed him to be a contrite, sad, and vulnerable ex-mill president. I said, "Dirt and cockroaches. I've heard say that at the end of the world the only things left will be dirt, cockroaches, and duct tape." I pushed him through the woods and looked at the scar on my finger.

We made it to a clearing and a slight bluff overlooking the Saluda River below Lake Between's pitiful dam. A handful of men and women held cane poles and fished the water. They stood beside drywall buckets. I thought to ask Mr. Self if he wanted to join these folks, maybe see if they had an extra pole. I thought to say how we could go no further safely.

I said, "Maybe tomorrow we can head out in the other direction. There's a nice hill overlooking the county landfill. We can watch the seagulls. You can tell me about what you used to find in the dump way back when you were my age."

I'd gotten outright giddy, and startlingly brave. Maybe I was feeling the preliminary twinges of false power one receives from newfound wealth. It would take thirty years before I would regain such a feeling. I popped old man Self's crown to get a response. And I got one—when he slumped straight out of his wheelchair onto the red clay that sloped down to the river.

"Hey. Hey, hey!" I said. Whatever jazzy kind of song had

been running through my head—saxophones, clarinets, and trumpets—stopped.

Unfortunately one of the river people saw Mr. Self fall out and pointed us out to his fellow anglers. They dropped their poles and trudged up the incline as I tried to shove Mr. Self back into his chair. Just as this was a time before cell phones, it was a time before wheelchairs had good and trustworthy brakes.

The fifty-dollar bill must've flown off. I hate to admit it, but the closer the fisherpeople came, the more concerned I was with shoving fifty dollars into my pocket as opposed to getting Leonard Self in an upright position.

"He dead," one of the men said. It was, luckily, a black friend of my father's, one of Shirley Ebo's uncles. "Mr. Self, he dead."

Although it seemed like the most trivial and obvious pronouncement at the time, later I would have nightmares, from college Intro to Literature onward. I said, "I didn't do anything. He wanted me to show him the river. He said he wanted to see the other side."

A woman said, "He finally got to see for hisself what we got to do for food, that sad money he pay at Forty-Five Cotton Mill."

We got him into the wheelchair. Shirley Ebo's uncle said, "Wha'chew gone do now, pusher-man?" He said, "You ought to look through his pajamas, see what money he got wrapped around his belly. All them Selfs wrap they money around they belly. People think they fat. But it money."

It seemed like Wylie Alexander or someone would've come looking for us. It had been a good hour since the last shovee had finished her plate of gray and yellow food. I said, "I guess take him back and tell them what happened is all I can do."

"Let us look under his pajamas first," the woman said. "Come on. I know you. You Lee Dawes's boy, right? I know Mr. Lee."

Mr. Self's wrinkled clothes were full of clay. His hat brim was bent mercilessly. There was blood on the blade of his nose, and for some reason I could only worry about how he'd soon crap in his pants like dead people always did in the stories Compton and I told each other. I said, "That's not right."

My onlookers backed off. One of the men said, "You want all that money for yourself, I bet. You should be ashamed, boy. Just 'cause he's a white man don't mean you got claim to everything."

I began the long Forty-Five Longterm Care push homeward, and listened for followers.

Now it doesn't matter that I took dead Leonard Self back to the kitchen workers' hideout, that we waited there until an hour after the sun set, that no one seemed alarmed. I pushed Mr. Self toward the still-smoking fire pit, found stray branches and twigs, and heaped them atop what burnt-edged magazines lay frayed on the outskirts of the pit. It doesn't matter that I considered looking for a sewn-in secret pocket down at the bottom of Leonard Self's pajama bottoms, imagining crisp fifty-dollar bills that I could shove into my own socks. I sat across from him on an upright oak stump, held my head in my hands, and cried in a way I'd not even done when my mother left for good.

I'd not even been to a funeral yet, at this time. I'd never witnessed a dead person. But that's not what made me undergo my first of many near–nervous breakdowns. I didn't think of all the spinners, doffers, loom fixers, or supervisors that Mr. Self had killed off in his own way to amass the millions of dollars his heirs would squander over the next few generations. It wasn't the poor relatives of my classmate Shirley Ebo having to stick doughballs on hooks so they could make catfish stew to eat over a three-day period.

"I tried to give him CPR," I told Wylie Alexander. "It didn't work," I said when I finally got up the courage to push Leonard Self back to the nursing home. "He held his heart and let out a gasp. Then I got him out of the chair and performed mouth-to-mouth. I must've spent an hour beating his chest. He wouldn't come back."

Wylie Alexander put his soft hand on my shoulder. "You done the best you could, Mendal. I don't know what else you could've done." He turned his head toward the nurse's station and said, "Ain't that right, Lee?"

My father popped out from behind the counter. I began crying again. "I didn't mean to be late for supper," I said. My father had come looking for me, certainly, like any good single parent might.

"This is all my fault," he said. "Hell, this would've been too mean if we'd've done it on Halloween *proper* like we first planned."

Mr. Self expelled a ton of air and said, "Try shallow-breathing for two hours! Someone owes me corn-dog suppers until the end of the year." He looked at Dad and said, "You got you a top-notch son, Lee. Some of that stuff about beating my chest for an hour might be an exaggeration, but he didn't try to steal my money. And he wouldn't let anyone else do it either." If Mr. Self had walked away from his wheelchair I would've gone home, swiped my father's thirty-aught-six, returned to the nursing home, and killed everyone involved. Mr. Self looked at me and said, "You got you some strange politics going on in your head, boy, but you all right with me." He stuck out his hand to shake.

My bicycle still stood wedged inside the azalea bushes. I had no headlight or reflectors. For all I knew, my father and Wylie Alexander and Mr. Self had concocted this scam years earlier, to test my abilities to shun temptation. I almost hoped so.

But I didn't say anything when I went back inside to get

my galoshes, hat, and yellow slicker. In the distance, a late-autumn thunderstorm neared, the smell of rain in the air. I said nothing to the three laughing men in Forty-Five Long-term Care's lobby, and rode off into a darkness I had never known before. I could keep straight A's, I knew, and never return to my part-time job.

The rain began a half mile toward home. What had I said to Mr. Self over our time together? I tried to remember, pedaling hard. What secrets had I divulged? Would those men have considered me a better worker had I chosen to steal money, a better Forty-Fiver in the tradition of our cheating, lying, and stealing business and civic leaders?

Water shot off my front and back fenderless tires, soaking my pants. I rode slower and slower and couldn't believe that I didn't plain topple over during each weak motion. Lightning struck nearby. If it had been winter, and below forty degrees, the road crews would've been out throwing salt on all two-lane bridges. That would be perfect, I thought. I realized later that if lightning had come down from God to me—for whatever wrongs I'd accrued—my rubber suit might have helped ease the sting.

Duration the Summer of Monkeys and Anacondas I tutored Shirley Ebo in English, because Mr. Ebo and my father were friends and I was one of only two Forty-Five Junior High School students who'd scored above average in reading and comprehension. I liked Shirley enough at the time but had no idea how to teach, or even how to get her to speak. Over the years, our white teachers had called on Shirley regularly during the first six-weeks grading period, then given up altogether when she went from shaking her head no to plain staring them down. I never saw any of Shirley's report cards, but couldn't imagine her passing. Every August I felt surprised to see her in my same grade, always sitting in a desk as far from the door as possible.

"Tutor her for money?" I asked my father. This was June between seventh and eighth grade. "How much is Mr. Ebo paying?"

The Summer of Monkeys and Anacondas came at the

end of the Fall, Winter, then Spring of Monkeys and Anacondas. A rumor started that the last county fair and freak
show's traveling zoo had somehow become unlocked and
that a dozen spider monkeys took off out of there. Of course
every Forty-Five child and half their parents couldn't think
of anything better than to trap a spider monkey and bring it
home as the family pet. Over at the Dixie Drive-In, I heard
Glenn Flack's father tell somebody that there wasn't a better coon dog than a spider monkey.

At some point during all this, a rational person in our
midst realized that Forty-Five children might actually *catch*
a monkey and contract rabies. What would keep kids from
wandering around our near-flat countryside in search of the
kind of mammals that looked so cute on that *Mutual of
Omaha's Wild Kingdom* show?

Anacondas.

So word went out that the freak snake lady's two big anacondas—and we'd seen her up close wearing a two-piece
bathing suit with forty feet of snakes around her body—
had escaped, too. What did snakes eat?

Monkeys and children, nothing else.

All in all, it didn't matter that exactly zero monkeys or
snakes had escaped. Later on I learned that a local bird lover
had worried about all of us BB-gun-toting kids killing off
jays, crows, grackles, cardinals, mockingbirds, and spar-
rows, and believed that whatever it took to keep us inside
our houses would help in ornithological ways we would

never comprehend. Bird Lover had anonymously started the monkey escapade.

My father punched me in the chest half as hard as he had the time I asked him if Mom was a whore with my best friend's momma, Mrs. Lane, up in Nashville. This time my father pulled back somewhat. "Mr. Ebo ain't got money to pay for Shirley's tutoring, peckerhead. When're you going to learn that not everything's about money? Sometimes you scald my scrotum."

I said nothing. I didn't say how my dad tore down heart-pine barns because he knew he could sell wood to rich folks in need of authentic flooring in the coming years. It wasn't possible, without near-fatal retribution, to point out how my own father found odd ways to scam unworthy men out of things once thought priceless or miserable, like baseball cards and Edsels.

I wanted to say, "Shirley Ebo's black, and everybody'll think I'm her boyfriend." I knew no better at the time. I said, "How'm I supposed to teach English? I don't know how to teach English."

My father and I stood in the backyard, planting tomatoes a month too late. "Listen, boy. You think *we* ain't got nothing? Try the Ebos. Go on over there and see what they got. How many times have we eaten *grass soup* for supper? Never. The Ebos eat grass soup when they can't catch catfish down on the Saluda. Or when Mr. Ebo can't veer just right and take out one of those suicidal strays chasing his truck."

I'd grown old enough to know not to ask if my mother whored around but not enough to know not to say, "Grass soup? They eat grass soup and dead dogs?" My father found a tomato stake that could've been used in the Kentucky Derby and whipped me like a gelding wanting to turn around in the middle of the second turn. He snapped my hamstrings until I made my way out of the garden. I might've said, "Hey, you son of a bitch, that hurts like hell." Or I might've said, "Hey. Hey, stop, sir, please. Hey, hey, ouch."

It doesn't matter. My father said, "You'll find a way for Shirley Ebo to read, you understand me, son? There's no question about any of this. You'll find a way to change Shirley Ebo."

SHIRLEY NEVER SPOKE in class because she had what I learned some years later was called "dialect interference." That would've been a nice and bland term to explain Shirley's speech. No wonder she only stared straight ahead when called upon by our teachers.

My father drove me over to the Ebos' house, a mile away from mine, let me out, and drove away. Mr. Ebo answered my knock. He said, "Mendal Dawes. I forgot total." It was noon. He worked midnight to eight over at Forty-Five Cotton; Mrs. Ebo worked there first shift as a secretary for one of the purchasing agents.

I said, "I brought along a couple books. I thought we might just start reading a couple books."

Mr. Ebo stepped back and yelled, "Shirley Ebo! Mendal here to teach you," as if she might've been lounging around at the far end of the Biltmore Estate. The Ebos' square, shingle-sided home wasn't any larger than a classroom, and was divided into three rooms. An add-on toilet/shower installation stuck out from the living room.

Shirley slumped out of her bedroom as if she was facing two bushels of hickory nuts to crack. She barely held up one hand toward me, I supposed in greeting, and her white palm glistened. I said, "Hey, Shirley. I brought along a couple books. I thought we might just start reading a couple books."

I didn't make fun of Shirley Ebo then, and I don't want to now, but she said, exactly, "They weren't no monkeys on the *skreet*? How you get here? Anaconda's *skrong,* knock you off your bike."

I said, "I could've ridden my bike. My father was going by this way so he brought me over." I patted down my wonderfully new and mostly maroon plaid short-sleeved shirt.

Mr. Ebo left the house. He said, "I got to go to the doctor, babydoll. I'll be back before your momma."

I said good-bye, Mr. Ebo drove off in his old pickup, and Shirley sat down on a love seat. "Daddy's heart's hurting. He got to have a skress test."

I stood there like a dumbskruck white boy in a black family's house for the first time. But this wasn't the case, really. My father, in an attempt to make me know that people lived differently than we did, went out of his way to find albinos, one-armed men, burn victims, waterheads, and vegetarians for me to meet. He drove me all the way over to Augusta, Georgia, the previous summer to shake hands with Siamese twins joined at the chest. So I'd been in houses owned by members of the African-American community, but I'd never been alone with a girl whom I may or may not have secretly desired to kiss, feel up, and see what other parts of her body faded away from the dark-dark skin of Shirley Ebo's face, arms, and legs.

I said, "Have you had a good summer so far?"

Shirley rolled her eyes. She wore a thin, thin, cotton dress, mostly pink, that seemed to be see-through in my mind. Shirley said, "Well, I guess. It only been three days, Mendal. I ain't seen no movies or nothing."

The Ebos' house smelled different than anything I'd experienced nasally before. Its scent was a grand mixture of collard greens, pomade, boiled sweetmeats, fatback, and maybe witch hazel. The word *permeate* did no justice to what the heavy gray air that filled Shirley's home did. I looked at my own arms to see what kind of odd plaster cast had formed on my skin as I still stood in the middle of the room, within a couple yardsticks' reach of a console TV, a ceramic sculpture of a donkey, a ceramic sculpture of a black man wearing overalls and a straw hat, two ladderback chairs, and Shirley in the love seat. Four or five steps away stood a metal-legged table, an old-timey Hoosier cabinet, and a chest-high refrigerator with a chalkware sculpture of an African queen on top. Two hot plates stood on either side of a double-drainboard white enamel sink. I said, "Yeah. Yeah. Me either."

Thank God Shirley got up and went toward the table. She pulled out a chair for herself and said, "We can read here. I got growing pains and need to skretch my legs 'bout every ten minutes."

In a movie there would've been a close-up of my face, open-mouthed and wide-eyed, and a *boy-yoi-yoi-yoing* sound effect would've taken over.

But at the time, no movie companies chose to film in Forty-Five, South Carolina, instead of on Hollywood lots. I said, "I brought a book called *The Strapping Stray Dogs of Street and Stream*," as a joke. At least that's how I remember it, and the reason she held up her open palm as if to slap me.

DAD PICKED ME up ninety minutes after our agreed-upon time. I hadn't been supposed to teach English to Shirley Ebo for but an hour. Her father never showed up, either. Shirley and I got through half of some book I brought along about a little boy who complained and whined because no one liked his artworks, and in the end he found out that everybody in town outside of him was a genius—including the one man who liked the boy's paintings. And that man was blind. I think my father had found the old, worn story and given it to me as some kind of lesson to stay away from all those whiney "misunderstood" artists.

Shirley and I read a couple pages of the second book, about a white dog that ran loose and attacked the main character, who "skruck it and skruck it with a skraight, hard skick," according to Shirley Ebo.

I said, "I don't know how to tell you this, Shirley, but you have some kind of weird speech impediment. Say 'string.'"

"Skring."

"Do you hear that? Can you hear the difference? You're making a *K* sound when it should be a *T* sound. Say this." I had to think a minute. I had to exhale the dull, thick air. "My father doesn't want to have a stroke."

She said, "Skroke." But she smiled and slapped her bony knee. "Daggum. I hear it! Hey, I also say 'ax' instead of 'ax,' like 'Ax me a question.'"

I said, "Uh-huh. I was going to wait on that one. We were going to get to that one, too."

She shrugged. She stood up, sat down, and performed a side-to-side stretch when the growing pains came on. Shirley said, "My momma made some brownies for us to eat. I guess we better eat them."

It was obvious that she hadn't planned to offer me these homemade brownies ever, but with my father so late she had little choice. We dug in. Shirley took a serrated knife, split the pan into quarters, and shoved her delicate fingers in. Listen. I've thought about the next part of this story almost daily for thirty years. It doesn't even make sense, logically, stylistically, or oratorically.

With her mouth full of brownie mix, Shirley Ebo said, "My momma says this goes straight to your butt. It makes me feel stronger, though."

If we'd've taken a French class at Forty-Five Junior High I might've screamed out "Voilà!" If we'd've known more about anything else outside of South Carolina, from Greece to Gold Rush, I would've yelled "Eureka!" I took Shirley's hand, took her out on the porch, looked around, then walked her out into the middle of Deadfall Road. I'd been taught well enough by my tardy father never to curse inside anyone's house against whose walls curses might never have reverberated previously. I said, "Goddamn, Shirley, can't you hear yourself? When you have something stuck inside your mouth, you end up speaking perfectly."

I'll admit that I wouldn't figure out until about my sophomore year in college how I could've taken advantage of the situation.

Shirley swallowed. "Quit yelling out here, man. You crazy? Get back in the house and quit skrutting around." In a high, piercing voice she squealed, "I don't want no one seeing me out here with no fool white boy."

Listen, this would be a good time to go fill the roof of your mouth with anything from Cheez-whiz to white bread.

Go say the word "strumpet." Notice how it comes out more like "skrumpet," and wonder how Miss Shirley Ebo maneuvered backwards through this whole process.

Well, anyway that's what I did after my father finally showed up. I said to him, "Where the hell have you been?"

My father tooted the horn at no one in particular, and drove in the wrong direction for our pathetic cinder-block house. He said, "Wait'll you hear what I just discovered." I could smell his breath across the front seat. "If you urinate Pabst Blue Ribbon on fire ant mounds and molehills, they leave. Don't think I'm not thinking about calling the patent office in Washington right before I call the people at PBR."

I slumped deep down in our front seat holding my two books. I smelled my index and middle fingers, only because my friend Compton Lane had told me a joke one time. "What?" I said.

"There ain't no mole can't live nowhere when I'm out pissing," my father said. "Beat *that,* English professor. Another *quadruple* negative I've designed."

I looked out the window and laughed. "A zebra has skripes," I said. "Skripes. What did Darwin think about that?"

My father floored it. He didn't say how he wished he'd never bought me a set of encyclopedias. "How'd it go with Shirley Ebo?"

I turned in my seat. "She can speak right with her mouth full, but can't otherwise. She'd be fine reading out loud in school when the teacher asks, if the teacher would let her eat about ten pieces of taffy right before."

My father eased off the gas. He turned left on Northside Drive. "Obviously I wasn't the best husband ever, and that might be why I don't know what's better—a woman who can't speak closed-mouth, or a woman who can rattle on while holding a banana in her mouth." My father flipped the radio on. I didn't follow what he'd said. "Hell, maybe either both are good or neither's good, I don't know."

I didn't know what he was talking about and figured— as usual—that he was continuing some imaginary conversation he'd been having with himself earlier. I said, "Next week we're going to concenkrate on verbs."

THIS WAS EITHER selfish or all-out mean, but I started taking my set of encyclopedias to Shirley Ebo's house, and I didn't start with the A–B volume. No, I went straight to the S volume of a New Standard Encylopedia and jumped to the *str-* section. I'm talking we started off with *strabismus,* and we ended with *strychnine.* In between we learned all about *stroboscopes, Strindberg,* four or five different *Strausses,* and *Stratford-on-Avon,* among other things. We learned that Shirley couldn't pronounce a *str-* word correctly with an empty and hollow soft palate, but she could enunciate like any anal-retentive spelling bee champion when she shoved marshmallows, pimento cheese, or homemade white bread way up there in the cavern—the dome—I couldn't see without dental and/or caving instruments.

"We never heard her talk funny or different than us," Mrs. Ebo said one afternoon when she'd gotten half a day off on the Fourth of July. "'Cause I guess every time we talk to her, it's with her mouth full. Dinner and breakfast."

I said, "My father thinks maybe an orthodontist might have some kind of contraption to shove up Shirley's mouth roof, kind of like a retainer. I'm going to get braces in August up in Greenville and I'll ask."

Mrs. Ebo sliced pork shoulder on the countertop, then minced it. On one of the hot plates she simmered a concoction of vinegar, mustard, scallions, ramps, and hot peppers. "We'll make do with something, Mendal. Don't you worry. But I can tell you right now, we ain't got the money for no fancy dentist." She walked over to the tiny refrigerator and pulled off an oven mitt she'd stuck there with duct tape.

I thought to volunteer my dad but knew that he didn't have the money to get braces for even me, really. He had agreed to trade out free installed flooring in the orthodontist's house, plus he would spend a weekend or two painting the doctor's place of work, both inside and out. I said, "Maybe my father can invent something. He's always inventing devices and cures." I didn't go into what he thought was patentable.

The whole time I spoke with Mrs. Ebo, watching her hand flake pig, then knead sauce into it, Shirley sat on the love seat, drumming and tapping her fingers on a one-by-six piece of pine maybe eighteen inches long. Every half minute she said, "Ding."

I looked behind me and said, "What're you doing, Shirley Ebo?"

She raised her white palms. "Momma taught me how to type. I'm practicing."

"When she gets good enough I'mo let her sneak in the mill and work on mine. Best a black girl can do in South Carolina these days's work as a secretary," Mrs. Ebo said. In that high, whining, barely audible voice her daughter always used on me when things seemed wrongheaded, Mrs. Ebo said, "Harder to trace a threatening letter or ransom note typed up on a Royal."

Shirley stopped. "Do Mendal and his daddy have to stay? I don't want them staying here. It's a holiday."

"Shirley," Mrs. Ebo said. "You apologize, girl. Mr. Dawes is bringing over all the fireworks. You want fireworks, don't you? It's Independence Day."

I stared off at a space on the brown kitchen wall. I couldn't look at Shirley or her mother, and wished that Mr. Ebo would show up. At the time, I didn't know that he was with my father, looking for the cheapest beer in a two-county area. And I don't know what made me all of a sudden realize that it was one southern man, Lyndon B. Johnson, who understood—and later on only Jimmy Carter and Bill Clinton understood, above all else—how things weren't right.

Sitting there as poor Shirley pecked on a plank of wood, I wondered how and why she and hers ever celebrated independence. I said, "You ain't got to apologize, Shirley."

She said, "I don't care 'bout shooting off bottle rockets or screamers."

I looked at her mouth to see if she meant *streamers*. She was eating nothing, but meant what she said.

Shirley continued her fake typing. Mrs. Ebo said, "I can tell that y'all's reading's helping. Shirley been reading to me better at night."

"Momma can't read," Shirley said without looking up. "She know the ABCs, but she can't read yet."

I was young, understand. I said, "How can you work as a secretary if you can't read?"

Mrs. Ebo held her hands up out of the meat. "The man writes up what to type, and I find the letters. I ain't blind." She washed her hands, opened the refrigerator, and pulled out a head of cabbage.

Shirley Ebo said, "I want me some more that skrawberry pie."

I WON'T SAY that I officially fell in love with Shirley Ebo on the Fourth of July. My father and Mr. Ebo returned in Dad's weird DeSoto he'd bought for nothing and planned to fix up, as always, and indeed they brought bottle rockets, strings of Black Cats, a couple boxes of sparklers, and cherry bombs. They had M8os, whistling chasers—which most white people called something else, but none of us did on this day—smoke bombs, and assorted cones that sprayed various fizzing colors.

And my father brought case after case of beer. Shirley and I didn't know that a large-scale party had been planned without our knowledge or approval. About every black family living on Deadfall Road showed up by four o'clock, and then a slew of Ebo uncles, aunts, and cousins. My father's best friend, Mr. Lane, and my best friend, Compton Lane, showed up, and that was it for white folks, outside of a squirrelly albino second cousin of Shirley's named White Clay, a boy I'd met some time before while driving around with my dad meeting afflicted people.

My father walked up to Shirley and me at the back of the Ebo property as we tried to hide from everybody. "Y'all aren't stashing beer away back here for a little celebration of your own, are y'all?"

Shirley shook her head sideways. I said, "No, sir. We're going through some verb conjugations. Show Dad, Shirley."

She smiled. "I come, you come, he/she/it comes; we come, you come, they come."

My father said, "Well all right, then. That's pretty good, Shirley Ebo."

Neither Shirley nor I got up from the ground because, sure enough, we had snuck four cans of beer and a church key and stashed them within the root system of an untamed wisteria behind us. I had already shared one of them with

Shirley, and, although I thought myself unaffected, I said, "So, Dad, you're always bragging about how handy you are with tools and whatnot. When're you going to invent some kind of mouthpiece for Shirley so she can say her words right?"

My father looked up at a bottle rocket stuck and hissing in an oak tree behind him. It popped and showered sparks down on top of White Clay, who yelled how the doctor said he wasn't allowed to get burned. "What you say, son?"

I made Shirley say some words, then I told her to stick a hot dog in her mouth and say them again. She conjugated "strap," "strip," and "stray." Shirley swallowed and, for some reason, decided it necessary to say, "My momma's got a cousin in Charlotte who works at a skrip-tease club."

I said, "I told you, Dad."

Mr. Ebo walked up and said, "I hope y'all ain't out here planning no wedding. I ain't got the money for no church service right now. Shirley, you and Mendal have my blessing to elope." He was all haw-haw-haw-ain't-our-childrens-innocent-at-this-age about it. He let his gold tooth shine.

My father took Shirley's chin and edged her head back. He stared in. "I can grind out a nice small piece of pine. Later on tonight let me pull out my tape measure and micrometer. I can get something in there that'll help you out. This'll be a challenge. I'm betting we can fix you up nicely."

Shirley started to talk, stopped, bit into her hot dog, and

said, "Mendal, you got to give me a string of pearls before I say 'I do.'"

Compton Lane walked into the backyard. He watched us all and said, "Hey, Mr. Ebo. Mr. Dawes. Lookit what I got." He held up a six-pack. "Put these with the ones y'all hid, Mendal. Has Shirley loosened up any for you yet?"

My father said, "I can mold a piece of pine. You ain't allergic to pine, are you Shirley?"

Somebody lit a cherry bomb. Mrs. Ebo yelled out how she had more barbecue and cole slaw ready. Shirley hiccupped. I knew that I'd lost my goodwill volunteer job tutoring at that moment.

THE TOWN OF Forty-Five somehow held on to the Forty-Five Indoor Movie House running over the years. I didn't realize until I moved away years later that most of the films we saw had already been seen by the rest of America six to ten years earlier. For all that most of my hometown knew, I'm willing to bet, World War II had occurred between about 1951 and 1955 or thereabouts, what with those newsreels.

The Forty-Five Indoor was the tallest building in town, for it had a balcony. Black people were forced to sit up there. They had their own line going in, too, through a side door. Not to sound weird or liberal, but as a child I wanted to watch a movie from upstairs more than anything else. It seemed to me that *Son of Flubber* would be bouncier, *Cleopatra* sexier, when viewed from above.

Outside of masquerading in blackface, there was no chance that I could go up there, though. Once or twice Compton and I stood in the black line, but we never made it to the ticket booth, seeing as we got the feeling that we weren't wanted by our queue-mates up top.

Right before the school year started, Comp and I rode our bicycles into town—still on the lookout for monkeys and anacondas—to see *Cool Hand Luke*. We sat in the middle of the lower level, kind of confused about the parking meters at the beginning of the movie, as neither of us had ever seen one. Paul Newman walked around that town wrenching and clipping the heads off. I whispered to Comp, "I don't think it's his job," like Luke was an employee of the city or something. Ten years later I would sign up for a film studies course taught by a Marxist-feminist-Freudian professor. She believed that Cool Hand Luke's actions replicated circumcision, and that he was crying out for a return to the womb—a place where no one could instill capitalistic values in him.

Compton and I watched that movie slightly disappointed. Both his father and mine had eaten fifty hard-boiled eggs at one sitting, easy. We had all kinds of kinfolk and family friends who had escaped from prison at one time or another. Eating cockroaches wasn't that big of a deal—I'd eaten a salt-covered slug once, on a dare from Comp, and he'd bitten the head off a female praying mantis right after reading about what they do to their mates.

During one of those chain-gang scenes, I felt something wet hit the top of my head. I put my hand up there and felt water, then looked at the ceiling for a leak. Within a minute—Cool Hand Luke had just run off with that other guy with the fake southern accent—my head got spattered again. I turned and looked at Glenn Flack behind me, but his plastic black-rimmed glasses only reflected the screen.

I looked up at the balcony and saw Shirley Ebo.

She was sitting in the front row, her popcorn box and Coke resting on the long banister that kept Forty-Five's black population from spilling onto the rest of us. Shirley had her feet up—maybe she was undergoing growing pains—so that her face was framed between shoe soles.

She spit again.

Shirley Ebo took the wooden hockey puck that my father had carved out of her mouth and threw it down hard. This mouthpiece glanced off Glenn Flack's head and landed three or four rows ahead of me. On the screen, dogs bayed crazy, looking for their prey.

"You ain't as nice as you think, Mendal. You ain't as cool as you think, either."

I mean, she yelled this out. Every white person on the lower level of the Forty-Five Indoor Movie House turned and looked upwards. Compton Lane said, "Your girlfriend's calling you."

Glenn Flack from behind me said, "You're in trouble, Mendal Dawes." He held his head, and kept looking at his palm to see if blood showed yet.

Shirley Ebo went into her high-whining voice and said things about how white people thought they knew everything, how white people didn't know what really went on in the world, how white people were the poison of the earth. She yelled, "Mendal sits down there now, but he wants to be up here with me." She said, "What's it matter what a woman sounds like talking, as long as you know what she means?"

Cool Hand Luke got shot in church. His best friend yelled out and tried to attack the sniper.

Everyone filed out of the separate sides once the movie was over. Those of us who were kids, we would study history, government, and biology for real, soon. We would try to understand the outside world better, or as best we could without much warning as to what was ahead of us in terms of cause and effect. My hometown's adults would leave, walking in straight lines, humming whatever easy songs evolved in their heads.

ASPHALT'S BETTER THAN CINDER

Even though he starred in this stupid educational documentary about parasites on his scalp, Bennie Frewer probably didn't really have head lice. I'll tell you what—and I know it's flat-out mean—but whenever one of the prettier girls in our class looked like she doubted Bennie's affliction, either Compton Lane or I would mention seeing Bennie's nit comb poking from his back pocket or the barber flapping his CLOSED sign upon viewing Bennie Frewer and his father trudging up Montague Street to get themselves dual flattops.

Those were competitive days, when we all knew inherently how difficult it might be to escape Forty-Five, and that a pretty girlfriend or wife for the rest of our days in a town best known for its "Widest Main Street in the World!" and "Second Largest Population of Albino Squirrels!" might be the best we could ever do while working at Forty-Five Cotton Mill in a midlevel management position.

Later on in life I would read some French philosopher's notion that every society needed a madman so that we could all feel better about ourselves. The same went for small South Carolina communities: we needed our freaks, goof-balls, pinheads, schizophrenics, dwarves, losers, adulterers, freckled children, Peeping Toms, exhibitionists, near-gays, and has-beens in order to feel like we all lived upstanding, fulfilled, committed lives. In the sixth through twelfth grades Bennie Frewer participated as our one-boy caste of untouchables. Without him, I supposed even back then, it would've been me. My chin's size and shape were unlike anything this side of half a loaf of white bread.

"Your friend Bennie's coming over later to spend the night in the backyard with you," my father said one Friday in September. I'd planned on riding my bike over to Forty-Five High School to watch the Forty-Five High Speed Fire Ant team get smeared by the Ninety Six Wildcats. Compton and I liked to walk around the cinder track nonstop—as did about another fifty sixth- and seventh-grade boys. We stuck our right hands in our front pockets with our middle fingers out when we walked past the visitors' bleachers, lap after lap, during the entire game. On the home side we slowed down to watch the cheerleaders and pretended like we knew things about sex that we wouldn't understand until our junior years in college. "Mr. Frewer's a friend, and his boy needs one."

I made a face. "Bennie Frewer's got head lice, Dad. I can't have him over here. Comp and I are going to the football game."

"Well, Comp and you and Bennie can go to the game. But afterwards, Bennie and you will camp out in the backyard. Comp can, too, if he wants. If you think that you're going to get head lice from Bennie—and you won't, by the way—consider it as living dangerously."

My father wouldn't make eye contact with me. I figured he must've owed Mr. Frewer some money or—this was later on, too—that he had had an affair with Bennie's mother. I will admit that I kind of whined out, "Dad," in the way that Bennie Frewer had on finding out that he had head lice in his ETV-supported television documentary.

"I have the pup tent all ready," my father said. "I have a place for y'all to build a bonfire and roast marshmallows and weenies."

This is the weird part: I actually said, "I think Bennie doesn't eat meat. He's turned himself into a vegetarian, so I'm willing to bet that he doesn't want anything to do with wieners."

"Look, son. There are times in life when you have to do some things for other people. That's just the end of that." When my father said, "That's just the end of that," it meant that the monologue might go on for half a day. "I've been trying to teach you that there are other people from other stations in life. Evidently you're not getting it. Get it, boy. What I'm trying to teach you is that there are some people out here in the world that ain't got it as good as you. There're some people, you know?" My father went into the kitchen and picked up a yardstick from Snead's Builder Supply, which he'd used to hit me on the hamstrings before. He slicked his black, black hair back, then wiped the Brylcreem off on his blue work pants. "Goddamn, sometimes you sear my sack."

Dad held that yardstick like a saber. This is no lie: I wondered if a metric stick would hurt more or less, if the extra few inches caused more of a whiplash pain, or less. I said, "Yessir. Okay. I'll do it."

My father said, "I can dig a hole out back, fill it with ice, and stick beer out there."

I said, "Yessir."

My father began twirling his yardstick in a way that didn't make me comfortable. It's not like I thought he'd *hit* me anymore—no, I worried that he had some kind of majorette tendencies. "You're now, what—twelve, thirteen years old?"

"Yeah. You're in the right vicinity."

"I know I gave you a beer back in the third grade. And I've kept track of what beer I kept in the fridge, by the way, so I know you know."

I didn't know. I thought my father couldn't even count, since he always told complete strangers that exactly zero wives—my mother—had left him in his whole life.

I tried to think of what I could talk to Bennie Frewer about in a pup tent. My father spent more time out there at night either pining about his wife, my mother, leaving, or digging these deep oblong holes he tended to dig in order to bury whatever he needed to conceal, things I pretended not to know about.

I said, "That tent smells like an old sock. It smells like bad cheese, like dirty wet towels, like a river-swimming dog, like a basement bag of flood-ridden Bibles, like a Persian rug left outside during monsoon season." We'd been studying similes in our weird sixth-grade class. I kind of got into it. I said, "That pup tent smells kind of like an ashtray filled with junebugs."

My father stuck his yardstick through one of his belt loops. He looked at the ceiling. "And I'll throw in a half-pint of peach bounce," he said.

WHEN WE GOT past the visitors' side—at the fourth curve of the track toward Forty-Five's cheerleaders—Bennie Frewer took one look at beautiful Ferrell Waldrep and said, "I would flip her over to the B-side and see what *that* song sounded like."

Comp wasn't with us. When he found out that Bennie Frewer would be tagging along he called up and said, "Y'all go on without me. What's your father trying to do to you, man? You're going to end up just like Bennie if people see you with him."

To Bennie I said, "What're you talking about?" I held a stack of wax Coke cups that, when stomped correctly, sounded like shotgun blasts. Bennie held another twenty or thereabouts.

Bennie smiled and nodded his head up and down as fast as a skittering metal toy frog. "*You* know. I'd do her from behind."

Let me say here that my father had offered me zero sex talks—another reason I figured he couldn't count—and, although I could come up with something like sixty similes in a minute, I knew nothing about human relationships beyond scratching a dog's side until she thumped a leg crazy. Oh, my father had tried once a few years earlier, but he happened to be drunk, and I pretty much guessed that he'd made things up, about seeds and eggs and placenta. I said to Bennie, "Yeah. I'd do that to her, too."

We walked past the cheerleaders real cool and didn't look up at the parents, high-school students, and ex–Forty-Five football players who made up the crowd in the stands. I tried to either walk six steps ahead of Bennie or lag behind and search the cinder track for arrowheads. We made it past Ferrell, Bunny Barnett, and Julie Sizemore—Forty-Five could only afford three cheerleaders, and if there was ever a vote for Most Spectacular Pyramid Formation in the History of High School Cheerleading, my future school would come in dead last. The cheerleaders were finishing up that ubiquitous, "Unh, ungowah—you know we got the power" cheer as Bennie brushed up against Julie Sizemore. He said, "You got you a nice B-side, too."

She held her pom-poms down against her thighs. "Get away from me, Head Lice."

I took off running for a good twenty yards, which was okay, seeing as a Ninety Six halfback was going down the sidelines and it looked like I just wanted to keep up and watch better. When he ran out of bounds I stopped and began my slow amble again. I didn't turn to see if Bennie Frewer had caught up with me. When he did, at the first turn around the track, I said, "Hey, let's go get a seat over on the visitors' side and pop these Coke cups."

Bennie said, "I know all of our cheerleaders' phone numbers. You know how I can keep track of them all? By using either pro football players' numbers, or stock car drivers' numbers. It's easy. Everyone in Forty-Five has the first FO, you know. And then there's a nine for everyone. Then it's like this: Johnny Unitas, Don Meredith. That comes out to FO-nine-one-nine-one-seven. Or your number: FO-nine, Richard Petty, David Pearson. Ferrell Waldrep's is FO-nine, Bob Hayes, Fran Tarkenton. It's easy."

We made it around the second turn of the track. Ninety Six scored for the third time in the first quarter. I said, "I use a phone book when I want to find out someone's number."

Bennie Frewer scratched his head and veered off toward the wooden bleachers. I think he might've mumbled, "You would," like that, but I wasn't sure. He said, louder, "These cups aren't going to make the same kind of noise on wood that they would over on the cement stands."

We sat down away from the hundred or so people who'd traveled the fourteen miles between Ninety Six and Forty-Five, both towns named for an Indian maiden who ran that many miles to warn settlers of the invading British. I thought, What am I going to do in a pup tent with Bennie Frewer for the rest of the night? I thought, What did he mean by what he wanted to do to Ferrell Waldrep's B-side? "I wish they sold Milk Duds at the concession stand," I said.

We looked out at the field. For some reason Ninety Six decided to perform an onside kick, and they recovered it easily. Bennie said, "They're out for revenge, Mendal. Oh, they want to take us over. Last year they only beat us forty-eight to nothing. It was an upset, my father said. Some of the parlay-card people lost some money on that one. Ninety Six was supposed to win by sixty points."

I didn't ask Bennie what "parlay card" meant. What did this poor guy think about between eight-thirty and three o'clock every day, seated two rows from everyone else because of his head lice, while the rest of us tried to think up similes and memorize the birth dates of John C. Calhoun, Francis Marion, and Strom Thurmond? I wanted the halftime show to include a display of some of Forty-Five High School's track and field stars. I wanted a pole vaulter to have his bamboo stick to shatter, for the shards to blind me. I wanted a javelin thrower to screw up and toss his spear through my brain.

I looked forward, and didn't feel the wooden bleacher plank bounce as Shirley Ebo—still the only black girl in our class—stepped our way. She said, "Hey, Mendal. When did you and Bennie Frewer 'come friends?"

I said, "Shirley!" and scooted over. "Come sit down right here. Why're you over on the visitors' side? Come sit down." I patted the bleacher and got a splinter.

Shirley shook her head no. She wore a thin black and gold cotton dress, the colors of the Ninety Six team. "Daddy and I sit over here every game. He says we got to pull for everyone else, he says. He says the best offense is a good defense, he says."

Bennie Frewer didn't look up at Shirley. He kept his eyes on the field. "My dad says the same thing. Hey, Shirley— you want to come over to Mendal's house tonight? We're camping out in the backyard. We're going to have some beer and a fire."

Shirley looked back in the stands for her people. "I might can come by there."

Bennie said, "You're number's FO-nine, Willie Mays, Joe Willie Namath, Willie Mays."

I wanted a shotputter to show up and land twelve pounds of iron on the crown of my head, a discus thrower to take me out between the eyes.

WE POPPED OUR CUPS. No one noticed. Ninety Six recovered fumbles and ran them back for touchdowns. One cornerback intercepted three passes in the second quarter. At halftime the score was fifty-six to nothing. Shirley went back up to sit with her mother and father. I said to Bennie, "Let's you and me go on back to my house. My father won't be there yet. He's playing cards with Comp's father. We can maybe find his stash of beer and add it to what we already have, you know. We can make some prank phone calls, seeing as you know all the numbers."

Bennie stood up. "I don't have head lice. Everybody thinks I have lice, but I was just an actor in a documentary. No one in this town seems to understand. There's no real Godzilla, either, by the way. No matter how far people stretch, they're not going to find the truth they're looking for."

I could've told Bennie that he shouldn't end a sentence with a preposition. I had no clue what he meant, seeing as he had the word "truth" in his statement, something everyone else in Forty-Five never puzzled over, either. I said, "Uh-huh," and looked back for Shirley. She stood up, clapping and dancing as the Ninety Six band came out playing a selection that may or may not have come from *The Sound of Music*.

I said, "My dad says that my mother didn't keep him on a short leash as much as he just kept running around the stob until his neck was right up against it. He says it a lot. He promises it's the truth."

We rode our bicycles back home. Me, I had only a spider bike one-speed, but Bennie had this thing that looked like a dirt bike, put out by somebody better than Schwinn and with this three-speed toggle switch in the middle. I was pretty sure that he got it from the money he made starring in that ETV-produced documentary. We zigged and zagged past each other up Powerhouse Road, and turned on Deadfall Road, neither of us with headlights or reflectors. Because the entire town was at the football game we didn't pass a car in either direction.

At my driveway I said, "I hope my father put some batteries in the flashlight."

"I hope he had some money left over," Bennie said. "My dad says that your dad owes him some money. For something. My dad's playing cards with your daddy and Mr. Lane, too. I guess that's it."

I didn't look at Bennie. I didn't say, "Well, I figured that out a long time ago, seeing as Dad made us be friends for the night." I said, "Probably."

We found a pit of ice holding a six-pack of PBRs. The canvas tent had five regular aluminum spikes holding it down, plus this one long thick metal stob. A fire pit two steps from the ice hole burned slowly, and a bag of marshmallows and Valleydale hot dogs were set right inside the tent's entrance. My own sad, red cotton sleeping bag had been rolled out next to Bennie's goose-down mummy bag. Bennie said, "I thought you said your father said we'd have some peach bounce."

I walked around the tent and found a half-pint of homemade whiskey strung up from a pine branch, like a piñata. I said, "My father lies at times."

Bennie said, "Yeah, tell me about it. My father's the same. And my father says your father lies all the time."

Of course I wanted to punch him in the face hard, and I would've, had I not thought that I'd get lice on my fist. A few years later I would feel the same way when I realized how I could make fun of South Carolina, but if anyone from elsewhere came down and said something like, "Hey, this state's got a collective IQ of something like eighty-eight"— which might have been true—I would start off with head butts and end with kicks to the crotch.

I said, "My father's many things, but he ain't a liar, Head Lice."

Bennie crouched down next to the fire. He held his hands out. "It's going to be a long life for both of us. You'll see what I mean."

We were twelve or thirteen at the time, understand. How did Bennie Frewer become so cosmopolitan and philosophical and worldly? Would he become a man who would later change the world in regard to cancer and/or world peace? Or would he become another pathetic loser running the South Carolina Student Loan Corporation? I said, "Don't call my father a liar. You have to take that back." I stood up, like I would fight—something I learned to love doing later on in life, unfortunately.

Bennie said, "I was only talking. Nothing. I'm sorry if I insinuated anything."

I was trying to figure out what "insinuated" meant when Bennie pulled down his pants right there outside the tent and said, "My big brother taught me how to do this. It feels good."

I thought he was trying to pull off his pecker, that's what I thought. I won't lie and say I didn't watch. When it looked like Bennie Frewer had started peeing, though, I ran inside my father's house. At that moment I realized all the things Bennie wouldn't be in life.

He yelled at me, "Come on, try this! Try it, Mendal! This is a feeling you ain't had in your life!"

I had never thought of myself as a prude, but even back then I knew that I could only put my hands to me ears and hum "Camptown Races," and pray for the first time that my father would come home way earlier than he normally came home on poker nights. I yelled back toward the backyard, "No! No! No! I think I need to be in here in case Dad calls and needs a ride back home!" It's not like it hadn't happened before.

MY FATHER KNEW POKER. He taught me early on that a straight flush beat four of a kind, and so on. I knew from the age of seven that three of a kind beat two pair. I don't want to sound like I got brought up in a den filled only with statistics and probability—I also knew how to make a variety of omelets—but that's how it went. I learned poker early on. We didn't have dog racing in South Carolina officially, or I would've learned how to bet those things, I'm sure.

"What do you think the odds are that Shirley will come by here after her folks go to bed?" Bennie Frewer asked me after I came back outside. I sat about twenty feet away from him, on the other side of the fire. I didn't want to chance his springing another leak or eruption.

"I kind of like Shirley," I said. "I know she's black and all, but I think she's the prettiest girl at school."

Bennie laughed and scratched his head with his left hand. "I kind of think of her as my girlfriend, too. She won't talk to me, though. She don't talk to hardly anyone, as far as I can tell."

I said, "She comes over here sometimes. I'm betting that she'll come over. Hey, you want to pitch pennies or something?"

Bennie shook his head. "My brother says that I'll last longer now for beating myself earlier. I wonder if Shirley might be interested in my playing her A-side. I'm thinking her A-side might sound better than her B-side. She's got a nice face and all."

I stared at Bennie Frewer like a good cat stares down a snake. I wasn't sure what he meant—he might as well have been speaking in tongues—but it didn't sound like he wanted to treat my friend Shirley in a way befitting a sad, sad girl who didn't want to hang out with white people all the time.

"Don't talk like that," I said. In my mind I went through how three of a kind beats two pair, a straight beats three of a kind, a full house beats a flush, and so on. This is funny—when I finally got a real girlfriend in college I ran these options through my head while making love and almost made it all the way to royal flush one time.

Bennie bent over and got a can of beer out of the ice. "I know you make all A's in school, bubba, but you aren't all that smart when it comes to the ways of women, are you? I can tell. Man, when I was making the documentary I learned all kinds of things from my TV mom. She used to be a model. She almost made it up in New York on one them soap operas."

I said, "You lie."

I could hear gravel crunching on the driveway. Both Bennie and I stood up and looked to the side of the house. Shirley Ebo ambled up as if she was waiting for a late bus. "Y'all ain't drunk, is you?" she said.

Bennie Frewer said, "Would you please tell Mendal what it means to play a girl's A-side and B-side? He doesn't even know. I told him that I would play your A-side, Shirley. That's a real compliment."

Shirley walked to the fire and stuck her toe on a piece of molten pine. She stepped over and picked up a beer. "What?"

Bennie spread his hands out and sighed. "What am I doing in Forty-Five?" he said. "I got to get my parents to move us to a place where people know some things. Like Florida. Shirley, get in this tent with me and let me show you some things. I'll give you a dollar."

I think it was my second punch that made him lose his balance and fall into the fire. Shirley yelled out for me to stop. Bennie's head fell right onto a smoldering log, and the only thing I could think about was how a head louse would probably pop in the same way a swollen tick did. I pulled Bennie from the fire and pushed him toward the ice pit. There was an audible sizzle and the smell of burning hair.

Bennie pushed himself off the ground and said, "I'mo tell on you. I'mo kill you," which is the same thing I would've said and done, I know.

"I didn't like the way you talked to her," I said, pointing to Shirley. "It's also not good to go over to someone's house and pull your pecker out. I read it somewhere. In one of the advice columns."

Shirley stepped back twice and said, "Y'all gross. Y'all too weird for me."

Bennie Frewer pulled his sleeping bag out of the tent, rolled it up haphazardly, and got on his bike. He rolled away awkward as an escaped hubcap. I yelled, "I didn't mean for you to land in the fire," which was true.

"I was trying to show you something that felt good! Maybe you don't want to feel good ever, for the rest of your life! I hope you don't!" Bennie screamed over his shoulder.

Shirley Ebo said, "What did he mean? What did he mean, Mendal?"

I couldn't tell her that I didn't know. My new male ego wouldn't allow for it. I walked behind the tent, reached up, and got the half-pint down from its noose. At the time I didn't know that this entire incident pretty much shut up

Bennie for the rest of his days in Forty-Five; we'd be in some of the same classes, but I would never hear him really speak again.

Nowadays I wish I could've patented whatever happened, bottled it, and learned to shut up about everyone else.

MY FATHER LATER told me that he almost hit Bennie Frewer, that the stupid kid was riding his bicycle in the middle of Deadfall Road with his sleeping bag unzipped and slung all the way down his body. Dad said that it looked like a giant blue cocoon coming up the macadam. Shirley and I remained in the backyard, coughing on peach bounce like fools. We roasted marshmallows, and then the hot dogs. Shirley said that she didn't know the final score of the football game, seeing as the scoreboard didn't go past ninety-nine.

We were drunk, drunk by the time my father returned all smiles. He said, "What did you do to Bennie?"

"Mendal saved my life, Mr. Dawes," Shirley said. "We ain't real sure what ever happened, but we think that Bennie had some ideas."

I said, "Go ahead and get the yardstick out. I know you're not going to believe me. Go ahead and hit me right here in front of Shirley Ebo."

My father toed the fire. "Bennie's having a rough time of it as of late, son. His daddy told me that he ain't got no friends, for one. If y'all kids ain't accusing him of having head lice, then y'all're accusing him of being some hotshot TV star. Is that true?"

I said, "Is this really homemade peach bounce or did someone pee-pee in the jar?"

Shirley laughed and slapped her ashy kneecap. "Oh, it home brew. I had my daddy's peach bounce before." She slid on the ground toward me and put her hand on my bicep. "Mendal my hero tonight. That Bennie kept talking about doing something to my B-hind."

My father crouched down. He stood on both knees and pulled his pockets inside out. They were empty. He said, "In case you want to know how I did tonight, I won. I took everyone's money. And we were playing high stakes, son. We played dollar ante, twenty-dollar limit."

My father took the last beer out of the ice pit and opened it. I said, "Where's your money, then?"

"I owed. I owed some to Mr. Frewer, you know. If your mother ever calls up and asks how I'm taking care of you, please don't tell her that at times I lose money and then I have to make up for it. That's all I ask." My dad reached over and tousled my hair. He pulled on one of Shirley's thousand pigtails. He looked at his watch and said, "Man. It's almost midnight. Shirley, do you want me to drive you over to your house, or do you want me to call up your daddy and say you're safe here for the night."

Shirley shrugged. "I might need to sit here make sure Mendal don't get sick to his stomach. You got more beer inside?"

I'd like to say that a shooting star streaked across the sky like some kind of omen. I stretched out on the ground and put the back of my head, plus my hurt fist, in the ice pit. I looked upward, started to count stars, then fell asleep.

Nowadays I like to tell people that my father went inside to call Shirley's father, and Bennie's father, that Shirley struggled me up and put me atop my sleeping bag. I tell people that she unzipped the shell, splayed it out, and when we woke up in the morning I was on my stomach, she on her back.

I tell people that I knew exactly what Bennie Frewer meant about the two sides of a woman, but it doesn't have to do with his A- and B-side versions: it has to do with kindness and patience, or patience and tolerance, or giving and forgiving. It has to do with respect and capabilities, with capabilities and truth.

But really, I woke up alone—which also happened more often than not later on in life—with my bike moved right outside the pup tent's entrance, leaned fully on its kickstand. There was a piece of paper folded up and jammed into the grip of my handlebars, with "I owe" written on it, barely, in charcoal. She wrote, "FO, Willie Mays, Joe Willie Namath, Willie Mays."

Like I said, Bennie Frewer never really spoke much to me again. I think that somewhere in that period my father broke Mr. Frewer's jaw for cursing at him. Shirley Ebo, though, spoke with me daily for the rest of my life, if only through her eyes, her swishing down school hallways, her wagging finger and smile, the shake of her wild head.

In Need of Better Hobbies

Coach Adair prided himself on transforming boxwoods into topiary figures without the use of hedge clippers. According to him, our seventh-grade coach, he could stare down and persuade a wisteria into becoming one of the Seven Dwarves, or a redbud into a groundhog at full roadside attention. Of course he couldn't, but we never challenged our insane coach's ability to control his own plants, bushes, trees, or lawn. Adair shied from regular topiary figures: stallions, Disney characters, grazing sheep, historical figures. Instead, the coach trained his personal botanical treasures into giant cobras — our junior high's unlikely mascot. Right there in class, Coach Adair swore on the Bible that he had only to stare down a plant in order to make it permanently flange out a hood, then sway east and west. When we look back on things, maybe it didn't take that much mental telepathy to bend a rose of Sharon or Leyland cypress into an erect, hooded viper.

We did our sit-ups, squat-thrusts, push-ups, pull-ups, and hurdler's stretches there on the hardwood gymnasium floor third period, and we ran those stupid things called suicides that ruined our tennis shoes. On occasion, Coach Adair took us outside to play dodgeball, using unripe peaches that he gathered from a tree in his backyard, which, he said, would one day grow into the biggest cobra north of Panama.

We said, "Hey there, Coach Adair," when we passed him in the halls.

He said, "A-dare," like that. He wore short gray coach's pants every day, and a Clemson University T-shirt. Black-rubber-soled shoes and white tube socks. Adair was the offensive line coach for football each fall, assistant basketball coach in winter, and golf coach each spring. Our golf team consisted of a half-dozen white boys whose daddies worked in Forty-Five Cotton Mill management. When he didn't coach P.E. he taught a course in South Carolina history for students who hadn't quite passed it in first, third, or fifth grades. From what I understood, Coach Adair skipped over people like John C. Calhoun and General Francis Marion, the entire Fort Sumter Civil War episode, and Dixiecrats, in order to focus on various questionable horticulture experiments going on at state-supported agriculture colleges—namely Clemson—ranging from edible kudzu to seedless fruits. From what I heard, he spent most of his time explaining how South Carolina's chief crops—tobacco, cotton, and soybeans—could probably be coaxed into lifelike topiaries, which could only aid in the tourist industry.

One time in the middle of P.E. class he even piped out,

"Y'all boys get in good shape maybe you can get jobs on golf courses down Myrtle Beach, Hilton Head, Charleston. Tourism's the quintessexual job future for me and you."

I couldn't make these things up.

Coach Adair's best—we learned later that it was his only—friend at Forty-Five Junior High was the shop teacher, a man named Mr. Finger, who made everyone build caskets to be used down at the county farm for prisoners buried in a potter's field out back. I didn't take shop, but I heard boys in the smoking area laugh about how Mr. Finger would start every day off by saying, "Fingers is important, boys. They the second best friend a girl can have, you'll learn later in life. So don't cut y'all'ses off."

And I should mention that, although the school budget got cut something like 50 percent every year after the nearby bomb factory laid off workers as Vietnam slowed down, the Forty-Five Junior High football team always had enough booster club money to buy new uniforms, pads, helmets, grass seed, and chalk. This went unnoticed by every Forty-Five resident, probably, outside of a good, serious science teacher named Lanky Jenkins, who tried to run his class without Bunsen burners, petri dishes, test tubes, beakers, dissection frogs, tongs, goggles, and scalpels.

Mr. Lane, my friend Compton's father, drank with Lanky Jenkins on Wednesday nights, when the rest of Forty-Five attended Baptist church services. According to my father, Mr. Lane was a communist and the only other person in town who seemed to understand the need for unions. Mr. Lane got tabbed an instigator only because he sold some land in a white neighborhood to a black funeral home director richer than 99 percent of the town. Over time, the story turned into how Comp's daddy actually had given the two acres away just to upset longtime residents still worried over particular stations in life.

Maybe he had. I only know that Comp and I got paid good money to sneak onto Coach Adair's property one Wednesday night—when no one would be around whatsoever, seeing as they sang the doxology and those other hymns in their weird churches—armed with scythes, limb cutters, machetes, and sling blades to cut Coach Adair's cobras down.

WE DIDN'T KNOW that Mr. Lane believed that pathetic Forty-Five would one day shrink to become a town of even simpler-minded misfits unless a slew of teachers either got fired or quit and a whole new batch replaced them. Whenever I was over at Compton's house—usually drinking bad cans of cheap beer right in front of Mr. Lane, seeing as he handed them over like most Forty-Five fathers handed over shotgun shells to their sons—I bet I heard his daddy say "zeitgeist" at least once per visit. I thought maybe he had sneezed or had heard one of us do so. When I was a sophomore in college, one of my professors used the term and I pretty much jerked straight up in my seat. The professor had said, "Spirit of the time!" like that, staring at the ceiling, his little pencil-thin moustache winging out like a tiny, tiny turkey vulture in midglide.

I remember that it was a mandatory course in art history, and we had talked about Marcel Duchamp.

"My father needs to talk to you," Comp said to me, walking from P.E. to fourth period English on a Thursday in mid-October.

I said, "What did I do?" What I had done was sneak a six-pack of PBR from Mr. Lane's garage on my way out the night before. It wasn't like Compton didn't do the same from mine, always.

We carried our books carelessly. "He wants us both to be there, man. I told him how you didn't have anything to do on Friday, seeing as you never have anything to do. He wants to talk to you and me both. Seven o'clock."

Added together, Comp and I already stood twelve feet tall and didn't weigh much more than two-forty. But we didn't have acne. Mr. Lane said to me once, "You'll find drunks with scarred-up faces, Mendal, but they only started drinking *afterward*s. To forget about their acne. Oh, it's a fine and mysterious line."

I couldn't think of an excuse not to meet Mr. Lane. I said, "Okay." We passed the president of the glee club, but she looked the other way.

Comp tapped his book against his hip. "Did you read this Mark Twain stuff? God-o-mighty. Getting somebody else to paint a fence doesn't seem like that big a scam to me. That old boy would've never made it around here. I've about had it. My cousin Dale's thinking about going up to Alaska to work on some kind of oil pipeline. Let's you and me go. There's nothing but money, oil, and women in Alaska, according to Dale. Money, oil, and women mix."

It's what he said. We were thirteen years old. I remember it vividly. We walked down the B Wing's checkered linoleum hallway toward our English class. We passed the star golfer on Coach Adair's team, who was struggling to remember his locker combination. Not that I'm one of those guys who can only remember what happened in school— whenever I returned to Forty-Five, more often than not some pinhead son-of-a-banker who became another banker would say something like, "You 'member that time when I dropped a pencil on the floor in maff class and looked up Vivian's dress?"—but this day stood out because it would change our lives.

I said, "I'm not going to Alaska. What's in Alaska? I'll get out of town somehow. But there's Florida, Kentucky, and Ohio. There's Delaware."

Comp shrugged. "Well, I promised Dad you'd come over. He thinks you're the only friend I have who can keep his mouth shut and his testicles swinging. That's what he said, word for word, I swear to God."

We passed Libby Belcher, one of the cheerleaders. I said, "Hey, Libby," but she didn't hear me. To Comp I said, "I'm your *only* friend, idiot. And your father's crazier than mine. But I'll be there. I'll show up on time." As we walked into the classroom I kept saying, "I'll be there, I'll be there," like some kind of retard. I wouldn't think about this moment again until studying *The Waste Land* and that "Hurry up please, it's time" part.

Comp sat down in his desk. He said, "Our sea of excuses doesn't seem to have enough waves anymore." I told him to shut up.

"Y'ALL MAY GROW up to be the types of men who won't even cut the grass, seeing as you think it hurts a living thing," Mr. Lane told us. He wore brown pants and a blue work shirt. His hair bristled as thick as a boot scraper. "I've talked to your daddy, Mendal, and he's a hundred percent behind what I'm going to have y'all do for good reason. As a matter of fact he told me personally just yesterday that if he had fifty extra bucks he'd hire you and Compton here his self."

I sat in what had always been Mr. Lane's chair. Comp sat on the den floor cross-legged. The television wasn't on. Mr. Lane stood above us half-hunched, as if he didn't know whether to call a huddle or work up some gas. I said, "Yessir."

"Now, Mendal, I've taught my boy here all there is to know about cause-and-effect. And I'm fully aware that most parents don't have time to even come close to such high-minded thinking. Your father's my friend, and I'm sure he's done a good job. But I'm sure that every other man in Forty-Five's pretty much said wipe your butt, tie your shoes, drive a car, and wear a rubber. I'm not making any comments on how to barbecue, understand. Everybody's got a favorite, time-tested recipe, right?"

I already felt drunk and he'd not opened his special refrigerator yet. "I guess so," I said, though I didn't follow his monologue.

"Show off some cause-and-effect, son," Mr. Lane said to Comp.

My buddy didn't pause. He stood up. "Men quit cutting grass. Grass grows high. Venomous snakes have a place to hide. Dogs run out and get bitten by snakes. Dogs die in high grass and rot. Buzzards come down and eat like all get-out. Men have to shoot buzzards. Buzzards are protected by the law, so men go to jail. There are no fathers left in America. The grass keeps growing, letting off useful gasses. We live in a cleaner, less-polluted environment."

"You got that right," Mr. Lane said. He slapped Compton twice hard on his pate. "See, Mendal, that's good cause-and-effect. It's what your daddy and I were talking."

Comp sat back down. I said, "I need to go home."

"So here's what we're going to do," Mr. Lane said. "We're going to make it so every Forty-Five student has a chance to get a perfect score on those college tests y'all have to take in a few years. Then you'll go off to a top-notch school. Then you'll come back to South Carolina and live more productive lives. Get it?"

Comp said—and later I would give him two dollars for saying it—"We might understand it better if you'd share some of your latest investment, Dad."

Mr. Lane's eyebrows, oddly enough, looked soft, and kind of moved like a stand of sea oats. "If I give you a beer each, I might go to jail. If y'all mess up and tell on me. On us." Then, like his son, he went from unkempt lawns to clean air. Mr. Lane walked into the kitchen. He said, "So none of us should ever feel bad or guilty. Y'all's Coach Adair might get unemployed, but he'll be all that much healthier in the long run."

It would've been a good time to kick back the La-Z-Boy and swing my legs upward in celebration. I didn't. Later on I would tell this rite-of-passage story to my wife, friends, and colleagues. I would exaggerate and say how I shimmied my hands in the air like a vaudevillian dance troupe member. To Mr. Lane I said, "Coach Adair says we won't get an A unless we shoot forty-five free throws in a row, sink a putt from forty-five feet, or run the mile in less than four forty-five. We can't get him any madder than he already is."

Mr. Lane handed me a can of Olympia he'd gotten shipped in from Washington state. "I have some frosted glasses in the freezer. You want a frosted glass, Mendal?"

"No sir," I said. My father was exactly like Mr. Lane, except for the frosted glasses thing.

"If Adair goes nuts do you think his replacement's going to want the same thing?" Mr. Lane asked me. "No." He held his eyebrows arched upward and his mouth in an O. One time I saw a documentary on Russian male ballet dancers, and they displayed similar facial expressions.

Comp stood up. He took from his beer, then lifted the can toward me in salute. "To our missing moms."

Mr. Lane jerked his head. "Do you think Adair's ways are going to help you get into college later on, Mendal? Do you think you'll ever have to sink forty-five free throws to pass a final exam in philosophy, or anthropology? You'll be taking those kinds of courses, believe me. I can tell. I know. And my son."

One time Comp and I played a game of H-O-R-S-E that lasted two days. Neither one of us could make a shot. I said, "Maybe I'd have to sink free throws in math." I said, "I don't know." Mr. Lane bobbed his head up and down like a windup toy. He said for me to trust him.

Comp said, "If Mendal had a date tonight, then he'd have a hard-on. If he had a hard-on, then he'd mess his pants. If he messed his pants then he'd go to a dry cleaner, learn how much dry cleaners make for a living, then aim his sights on being a plain dry cleaner for the rest of his life."

"Good work, son," Mr. Lane said. "Now let me go get tools out of the shed to make sure you little weenies will know how to use them next Wednesday night. *Zeitgeist!*"

I said, "Bless you, sir."

MAYBE I SHOULD mention again that my own father hung out with Mr. Lane and Lanky Jenkins, the science teacher, Wednesday nights while everyone else in Forty-Five underwent midweek prayer meetings. I don't think my father was a full-fledged red-card-carrying communist at this point, but he knew enough to hate my mother's father once Mom took off without warning; my father realized he had to quit working for his father-in-law and start up any kind of business that would contradict his in-law family's means of sustenance.

Maybe I should mention how most Wednesday nights these three men drove aimlessly around the small town of Forty-Five, through the "Widest Main Street in America" with its six or eight shops on both sides of what was really only a major railroad confluence. These men commented on how it would be easy to break into houses and steal what pathetic belongings these people held within their walls. "If anyone knew art outside of laminated plastic Norman Rockwell place mats, we could release ourselves to places between Miami and Minneapolis," my father once said to me as he burned hamburger patties, right before a Little League game where I'd get bruised up trying to catch Yancey Allison's knuckleball. "We could go to Memphis and eat real chopped barbecue nightly. We wouldn't have to drive all the way over to Gruel BBQ."

These men drove three abreast in Mr. Lane's Cadillac, with a cooler in back. If there had been reliable local cops in

Forty-Five they wouldn't have pulled Comp's father over, seeing as he either owned their rental houses or sold them trailer land cheap. My dad and his friends cruised, from what I understood, doing what a teenager would think of as unplanned scouring.

Comp and I acted similarly soon thereafter, and I would be surprised that we never got caught, maybe weaving up Deadfall Road, our pockets filled with loose Lipton's tea, pretending to have marijuana that we sold to the two smartest female Forty-Five classmates, who later went to the College of William and Mary and Wake Forest. Not to mention what we nearly sold to our high-school Spanish teacher. But this particular Wednesday night was five years before smart women entered our doomed weekends.

"Dad says they'll be right around the corner if we get in trouble. If for some reason the churches let out early," Comp said.

We stood in the middle of Coach Adair's front yard, like idiots, holding farm and garden implements of destruction. This was eerie—cobras loomed above us from all angles. I was the first one to whisper, "There's no way we're not going to get caught doing this."

Comp watched his father's taillights fade down Edgefield Street. He said, "I'd rather get caught by the police than by Hey-There, A-Dare. He'd kill us. He'd beat us with a pitching wedge."

And then we went to work. I took a machete and knocked

down a stray Japanese plum tree as if it were goldenrod. I walked five feet over to a nice, full, bowed and persuaded persimmon tree and hacked it six inches from its root ball. Comp laughed and laughed, then whacked every cobra cypress, cobra red tip, and cobra spruce. Me, I looked up at the sky and noticed how no God's face appeared in the stars, no matter how hard I tried to connect the dots.

We hewed Coach Adair's yard. We harvested faster than Comp's father thought we could've. If there was a *Guinness World Records* category for turning topiary into wasteland, then Comp and Mendal would've ranked first and only, is what I'm saying.

We never spoke to each other. We looked back at the deciduous destruction we'd leveled, and I still don't know how Comp felt, but I knew deep down what we did was wrong, no matter what the long-term effects his father had rationalized. "Fifty dollars each won't be too bad," my best friend said. "You need to say 'thank you' to Dad when he comes back, you know."

I said, "I will," even though I didn't feel good about what we'd done. Most fathers received vicarious pleasure from their sons shooting par or better. Why was it that our dads wanted only for us to prove ourselves as swindle-worthy as they?

"This'll work out better than you think, Mendal. I know what's going to happen afterwards."

I stood on spongy ground surrounded by sad, felled cobras.

In the distance I thought I could hear my father hoot out the open passenger window. Both Compton and I wore black watch caps at his father's insistence.

When our fathers returned with the man who would teach us how to dissect a regular local toad using box cutters and chopsticks, they piled out of the Brougham better than European secret agents. Lanky Jenkins pulled three signs from the trunk, then held the wooden spikes as my father hammered them into the ground. Mr. Lane took a can of spray paint and went to work on poor Coach Adair's front-porch windows. Comp and I threw our garden tools in the open trunk before getting in the backseat with the cooler between us. I said, "They seem to have thought this out over a long period of time."

Comp lifted the Styrofoam lid. "You don't even know, man. My father's been talking about this night since you and me got stuck in Adair's stupid class."

"Goddamn," I said. I didn't mention how maybe Comp's daddy was insane, too. Later on I would watch daytime talk shows concerning obsessed human beings and understand that Mr. Lane could've been elected president of any obsessive organization, that he would've been self-nominated over and over and over until everyone else wore out.

The men executed their part of the job and returned to their front-seat positions. Comp's father motioned not to close the doors, and we drove out of Coach Adair's driveway without headlights for a good mile down the road.

"Pass up a few cans, boys," Lanky Jenkins finally said, half-turning his face. "Y'all know not to mention any of this back at school."

Comp said, "We kind of figured that out."

I said, "Thank you, Mr. Lane. Thanks."

My own father said, "You boys don't even tell your mothers what we done, should they ever get back into your lives. They ain't getting back in touch with y'all, are they? Mendal, you're not holding out on me, right?"

I said, "What were those signs? I couldn't read them in the dark."

Mr. Lane hit the horn and bucked his head forward twice. " 'Forty-Five Sucks, Forty-Five Sucks,' " and " 'Ninety Six Rules.' "

Ninety Six's elementary, junior, and high schools regularly beat Forty-Five in any sport. This'll tell you about our area of South Carolina: an Indian maiden crossed forty-five creeks to tell pioneers how the British were advancing on their settlement back in 1776. That same maiden crossed ninety-six creeks to warn settlers in what later became Ninety Six, only fourteen miles away. One time Lanky Jenkins took his science class on a three-day walking field trip, and they forded eight streams between the two towns.

Or: an Indian maiden ran forty-five miles, et cetera, then ninety-six miles—as if Indian maidens kept odometers on their ankles. Whatever, no one seemed to question why the British ever encamped forty-five or ninety-six or, hell, two hundred miles from our pathetic crust of red-clay piedmont. Did they need indigo?

I said, "Coach Adair will think all this was done by Ninety Six pranksters."

"Cause-and-effect, Mendal." Mr. Lane leaned forward to look past Lanky Jenkins and said to my father, "Good job, Heart Pine. Good parenting."

We drove twenty miles an hour, not going toward any-one's house. My father, whose name was Lee, told Mr. Lane not to call him Heart Pine. I said, again, "Thank you, Mr. Lane. Thanks for the money," though we'd not received it yet.

I COULDN'T LOOK Coach Adair in the face Thursday third period. And Coach Adair didn't seem intent on teaching us the intricacies of throwing medicine balls to one another like he'd promised a day earlier. Even when we passed him in the morning before homeroom and said, "Hey there, Coach Adair," he stared forward, the only sound coming out of him the squeak of his rubber-soled coach's shoes on linoleum. In the middle of our class three hours later he plain wandered off.

In fourth-period English class I reached over to Comp and said, "I'm glad we're over with Tom Sawyer and Huck Finn. What were we supposed to read last night?"

Mrs. Herndon came in wearing a pink pantsuit. She said, "I know this will make y'all sad, but we're going to have an unscheduled assembly this period. We have to go to the cafeteria."

Our stupid and slight principal, Mr. Knox, stood in front of the mashed-potato lady and held his hands up for us to sit down. "I know some of y'all have friends or cousins over in Ninety Six. And I know how important our game is with them tonight. But some them fans come over here last night and cut down all Coach Adair's cobras." There was a clear, loud chorus of "oohs" and "aahs" and a couple of "those bastards," just like in a bad teen movie shown mostly at the Forty-Five Drive-In. Coach Adair's cobras had attracted people from all over—at Christmas he put *lights* on them. I didn't look over at Comp; I looked for Coach Adair, but he wasn't in attendance.

The assistant principal, Mr. White—who made Knox look like a genius—said, "If any of y'all'ses know names, you need to give them up. This is a federal offense."

A federal offense! I thought for about two seconds before I realized that maybe he didn't know the law. All of my Forty-Five Junior High classmates shook their heads sideways, like they would've if we'd had a tennis team for Coach Adair to supervise.

Libby Belcher stood on a lunchroom table, lifted her arms, performed a split, and yelled, "What do we need, what do we need?"

"Forty-Five Cobra poison!" my moron classmates yelled, outside of Comp and me and some of the special kids who got pushed in from their portables out back of the L-shaped building.

"Kill those Ninety-Sixers—uh-huh, uh-huh, uh-huh!"

Later on I wondered if dyslexic students from Ninety Six got real popular with members of the opposite sex. But I didn't think any of this inside the cafeteria. I felt my face redden, afraid I'd get caught.

I sat at the table where I always ate lima beans, canned peaches, mashed potatoes, and meat loaf. I sat and made a point of keeping eye contact with the principal, a man who would later duct tape a garden hose to his muffler and off himself just because the football team went 0-10 three years in a row, which caused Forty-Five High to go 0-10 three years in a row subsequently, seeing as the same players were playing, which caused people to write editorials in the *Forty-Five Platter* asking what had happened to our school system. I didn't look peripherally and ignored Libby Belcher's pleas concerning the upcoming game.

I thought of my father, and Comp's father. I tried not to think about how I would eventually learn biology from a man who leaned toward promoting anarchy.

I remembered a time when Coach Adair took all of us in his P.E. class outside, how he had found a spectacular ant-hill, and how—for fifty minutes—we watched ants work back and forth, some carrying food into the mound, others leaving on missions of some sort. Coach Adair had said, "Teamwork. I want y'all to understand teamwork."

Maybe we listened closer than he ever thought we would.

My FATHER AND his friends got their way. As it ended up, while we listened to Knox and White blather on, slaughtering the English language and offering up illogical, useless, too obvious "epiphanies," Coach Adair was loading up on gasoline cans and Ohio Blue Tip matches. That afternoon he burned down the entire Ninety Six field, the wooden bleachers, two school buses, and their gym. He got caught within an hour. The local paper ran a long article about the disaster, then a short item three pages later about the culprit. Word was he just yelled, "They only jealous, they only jealous," on his way to jail. He didn't return to school, but we received mimeographed statements before the year was out saying how Coach Adair was sorry for his actions, and how none of us should follow in his footsteps, and how we should all pray for him. Coach Adair wrote an open letter to the *Forty-Five Platter* about how we should look toward South Carolinian Joel Poinsett, inventor of the poinsettia, as a leader.

And then he somehow got shipped away somewhere in the manner that only guilty, half-insane schoolteachers do. He didn't go to prison. But he was never far from a padded cell, from what we understood.

When I ran a mile in 4:44 one year later—an age-group state record—I thought of Coach Adair. While I ran, though, I could only zip those "blank is to blank, as blank is to blank" propositions through my head, so I would end up with a better SAT score, as if "blank is to blank" mattered whatsoever. I ran and ran my four laps, and hunched my shoulders waiting for a second wind, and blew my nose using thumb to nostrils like my father taught me.

I never took up golf. I didn't play basketball in a way that would get me placed on a foul line. Coach Adair finally moved to the small town of Gig, South Carolina, once released from the mental institution in Columbia. He got a job teaching, too—at Gig Junior High, where their mascot was, of course, a frog. The Gig Frogs. I tried to imagine wild rosebushes transformed into leaping, water-thriving amphibians.

Compton and I never again brought up Coach Adair's name. We couldn't. Our fathers had us focused on a man teaching history named Mr. Case who thought God made America biggest of all the continents on purpose, a man who believed dates didn't matter except for Jesus' birthday and Easter. He didn't have plants out in his front yard, though. He had no obvious hobbies worthy of destruction. Some mornings I woke up to find my father and Mr. Lane together at the kitchen table, drinking coffee before dawn. I understood that they were scheming ways to persuade Mr. Case from teaching, and that somehow Comp and I would be their assistants, earning money to fund our own way out of town.

No Fear of God or Hell

I learned early on that psychiatrists and dentists don't care about their patients being cured. Why would a therapist want a client to stop having neuroses, nightmares, or delusions? Why would a dentist promote a brushing technique that would eradicate cavities forever?

My father took the time to let me in on a number of the mysteries of capitalism: how lawn care men had no choice but to spread fertilizers *and* weed spores sporadically; how no doctor cared about a cure for the common cold, red or German measles, migraine headaches, acne, or arthritis; how fishmongers, butchers, and farmers didn't want the government to develop a long-lasting preservative. Way before anything made it to the newspapers, my father predicted that tobacco corporations had included addictive ingredients on par with heroin and vagina—his words and theory—to cigarettes.

I came to understand how entomologists had developed a chemical that kept termites away from wooden building materials, but that the lumber industry paid them off to keep it a secret. Oil companies didn't give us their best. Although the United States Patent Office might have another inventor's name down on the list, in reality it was a lawyer who thought up the foam-rubber neck brace and the term "whiplash." Stockbrokers never gave up their best tips, seeing as their clients would get rich, retire, and stop investing. Insurance agents hadn't been mentioned in Dante's circles of Hell only because they didn't exist back then. There were razor blades out there in the laboratories of America that never needed sharpening, batteries that never died, light bulbs that didn't fizzle, clothes that didn't wear or fade, asphalt that didn't succumb to potholes, and reusable ice cubes. There were oak trees that never lost their leaves, but the rake manufacturers didn't want that secret out. Veterinarians just plain made up canine and feline diseases in order to shoot up domestic pets with spurious vaccines and antidotes.

I heard it all. My father should've invested some money in a muckraking, yellow-journalism rag to sell at annual meetings for the disenfranchised, skeptical, and out of touch. Oddly, my father believed that man had landed on the moon instead of somewhere in the Mojave Desert. Unfortunately, he also believed that we'd already put a series of daredevil secret soldiers on Mars and on all of Jupiter's moons, and that there was a hole in the ocean that went all the way through, guarded by bivalve mollusks on both sides at the two-and-a-half-mile depth mark. When I asked him what was in between the Atlantic and Indian Oceans he said, "You don't want to know. Well, I can tell you what it's *not*—there ain't no Hell in between. And there ain't no scuba divers brave enough to swim through."

So it didn't come as a surprise when I came home from school one day to be met at the door with, "I got a letter today from some peckerhead environmentalist telling me how trees are valuable, and how we shouldn't be cutting them down. Do you believe that? Do you get it? Have you any concept about what's going on here, Mendal?"

I got the concept that the mail must've been delivered really early that day, because my father had built up enough blood pressure to run a steam engine. Like any other day in my upbringing, I'd spent the prior thirty minutes thinking up excuses in case I got accused of anything I might've done. Every time I accidentally left the water hose on out back from filling the dog bowls or drenching tomato and pepper plants, I only had to say, "I bet it's those damn meter readers. They drive around all day turning on people's spigots when they see nobody's home." It always worked, I promise. I had a harder time convincing my dad that the Duke Power people actually broke into our home and turned on all the lights, plus two eyes on the electric stove.

"Shirley Ebo wanted to see the inside of the cement truck's drum, then she panicked, and I had to go in after her," I blurted out. It's the excuse I'd been working on since Algebra I class at eight thirty that morning. My father had bought a man's land, and then—for reasons unknown to anyone on Deadfall Road—took over the guy's 1955 cement truck. He parked it right in our front yard and left it there. I don't remember why I thought it necessary to get Shirley Ebo and me inside the giant drum, for us to discover each other's nakedness there, unless it was so that later on in our respective lives no mattress would seem as exciting as the cold metal and rough, cement-boogered walls. We unlatched each other's snaps and buttons; we sweated profusely. When Shirley finally grabbed at my hopeful erection she said, "Mighty small gearshift for such a big truck." She, too, had practiced lines long before she got to use them, I figured out later.

Me, I had only hoped that my father wouldn't come home drunk and decide it would be a good time to take the truck out on a joyride, or—worse—flip the switch.

My father said, "What're you talking, boy? Black Shirley Ebo's caught in the cement truck?" He looked out the window. On his face I read how he was thinking up excuses to give Mr. Ebo, how he would honestly make a plea that we were white folks who didn't cotton to such acts of mock violence and/or imprisonment.

I said, "Well, there's no *White* Shirley Ebo that I know of, first off. And, no, she got out of there all right. We didn't do anything wrong or mess up your truck. What do you think—she and I are going to lose our virginity with each other in the back end of a cement mixer when we could come inside and use a bed?"

This was a hot, hot, end-of-the-school-year afternoon. My father was wearing a blue cotton jumpsuit. The sweat stains between his armpits and neckline met in a way that looked like three waves on a cartoon ocean. He shook his head quickly, as a man with petit mal seizures might, and closed his eyes. "I don't know what the hell you're talking about," he said, which allowed me to breathe again.

"I don't know what you're talking about, either."

"Paper's made of trees. Are they not teaching you anything at Forty-Five High? Goddamn. This is called *logic.* You got people out there yelling about saving *trees,* and they're sending *letters* to tell you about it. No one knows nothing no more."

I didn't correct his speech because I thought it might be a ploy to hit me on the hamstrings. I said, "Shirley Ebo got some scrapes on her knees and butt and elbows, but nothing else. And I got some on my knees and elbows, trying to get her out."

My father didn't listen. He picked up the telephone and started calling people to see if they had gotten the same kind of mail. I thought about how things would be different if my mother hadn't run away from home. No wife would allow her husband to obsess over junk mail. Then again, no good mother would allow for a cement truck parked in the front yard, a giant, empty, inviting hole making up most of its being.

• • •

I'D BEEN TAUGHT that life was relatively meaningless, too. I had been taught that no matter how good or bad a man happened to be, when he died—in time and eventually—he would be forgotten for what good he did or forgiven for what bad he did. My father said the same for women, I should mention. No matter what good a woman did—say Madame Curie—she would be forgotten with time. Animals fell into the same categories as men and women. No matter how many laughs Mr. Ed had brought on, or how many tears Rin Tin Tin, Lassie, and Old Yeller, they would die off after a meaningless life, and the rest of us would trudge on for no apparent reason.

Oh, man, listen: our home teemed with optimism.

If we had lived in an entirely conservative Jewish neighborhood, my father would have sent me out every Saturday morning to work hard publicly. But we didn't, and he and I lived in a predominantly Baptist setting, a verifiable Christian area, and although I pretended to be proud of our refutation of those tall tales in the Bible, it embarrassed me to go out Sunday mornings to cut the grass between ten and twelve thirty, or to clean out the gutters, or dig out built-up silt from the drainage ditch and throw it onto the nearby macadam.

"This can wait until next Saturday," I always said.

"There's no time like the present for doing something that won't matter anyways for people living a life that doesn't matter in the first place," he always said. It didn't take an advanced degree in existentialism to understand my father's paradox. By the time I conjured up enough vocabulary to verbalize my skepticism, though, he had already begun using a cane. It took one strike on my hamstrings to remind me that, as a species on Earth, we were supposed to shy from pain as much as possible. I didn't know anything about hedonism, really—back then, at least—but I soon learned that any supposed comfort was still better than outright pain.

So on Sundays my father sent me out to do meaningless chores that may or may not have needed doing. I pulled his car or pickup truck down to the end of the driveway and changed the oil; I cut grass; I crawled around looking for dandelions, and sprayed the boundaries of our land with a homemade insecticide made up of Dad-pee and cheap beer—which meant it was basically just Dad-pee. I burned leaves in a fifty-five-gallon drum; I followed mole holes to nowhere. Every Sunday I went out to do something and stayed out there until somebody came to tell me how the Lord made Sundays for rest.

It was almost always Marvin Childress who bestowed this knowledge upon me.

Marvin Childress was one of a number of town fools, but he was known as the official one. None of us ever used that term around him, of course. How could we? Marvin made everyone in Forty-Five feel better about themselves. He wasn't a drunk, and his IQ might've been quite high in regard to psychological standards. He was forty-five years old, always, according to him. Marvin tended to walk into social settings and blurt out stuff like, "I must go now— I have an important lecture to give at the University of Moscow," or "When I was at the Sorbonne, I ate many, many snails. I don't do that anymore, though. I'm forty-five!" He stood five feet tall, had graduated from Anders College when it was still a religious institution, and came from a prominent Forty-Five family that had somehow thrived outside of the cotton mill community. Marvin bought one vitamin daily down at Durst Drugs from a pharmacist named Byrd who could cluck his tongue and make it sound like a cello. Marvin Childress kept a paperback world atlas in his back pocket, pulled it out often, and when out shopping said things like, "Potenza, Modenda, Lacenza, Grosseto—I've been there. Oh, I've been there. Don't you think that I haven't been there. I'm forty-five! Ciao!" and then he'd take off swishy as an Olympic walker. Sometimes it was "Segovia, Palencia, Villa Real—I've been there. Oh, I've been there. Don't you think that I haven't been there. I'm forty-five! Adios!" and so on. A couple times Marvin cited Canadian cities and said, "Au revoir" and "Ta-ta" before exiting.

It's necessary to understand that as much as my father distrusted everyone, and downright hated most people, he taught me not to make fun of Marvin Childress. He told me just to agree with whatever Mr. Childress said, especially if it had anything to do with religion or science, no matter what I thought was incorrect. "It don't matter none winning arguments with a fool," my father said more than once. "What matters is not getting swell-chested or big-headed after walking away from a man like Mr. Childress. Who wants to have WON ARGUMENT AGAINST IDIOT on his tombstone? Not me. It don't matter. You remember to be nice to that old boy, Mendal. That's more important than being correct."

All of this does have to do with my father getting that letter from the environmentalists saying how he should be more careful with cutting down trees, by the way. Hold on.

Forty-five-year-old Marvin Childress—for all of his supposed IQ and awareness—went to church every Sunday at the Forty-Five Three Holy Trinity Ten Commandment Church, which was the only other cement structure on Deadfall Road. Anytime one of my teachers asked what church we attended and someone mentioned Forty-Five Three/Ten, I thought of pro-football quarterbacks calling a play. From the first grade on, my father told me to say that I went to the Sixty-Nine Church of Sacred Lips, and for me to come home and say which teachers laughed and nodded and caught on. I did. They didn't.

Anyway, Marvin's church of choice—for me—was a regular mathematics problem, and he rode his old one-speed Schwinn bicycle right past our cement-block house on Deadfall Road one-seventh of every week. The Sunday after I told my father about Shirley and me, I was standing out there

painting the cement truck a variety of swirling colors because Dad had read an interesting article on hallucinogens,
thought he might throw a big southern Woodstock one day,
and wanted to turn the drum around to make people say
"Far out, man." Marvin Childress came up as per custom,
except he was carrying a beehive. He carried the entire
white box atop his bicycle seat as he rolled it toward Forty-
Five Three Holy Trinity Ten Commandment, the queen bee
inside, workers zipping all around his uncovered face. I said,
"Hey, Mr. Childress."

He stepped down his kickstand, but held on to the hive.
"You ain't supposed to be working on Sunday, monsieur,"
he said.

I said, "Yessir," because my father made me. If it'd been
the mayor, or anyone who worked high up in the cotton
mill, my response was supposed to be, "Is there anything in
the Bible about taking a vow of silence? Why don't you just
goddamn shut up." And then I was supposed to run away
toward the front door.

Marvin Childress had eyes that would've made a shark's
seem penetrable. He had the eyes of a molester, but the mind
of sweetgrass. "I got my bees in this box," he said. "I'm taking them to the church. The good people there can put their
jars down and get them the best honey this side of Tupelo,
Mississippi. I've been there! I attended the University of
Mississippi. You want some of God's sweet Truth nectar,
you come on up to the church." Those bees flew into his

eyes. They lit in his tear ducts, but Marvin Childress didn't swat once.

I had made a wide swath of swirled red going down my father's cement truck and had used half the blue paint. It was going to be a patriotic, hallucinogenic, twirling thing that I would later paint two big tits on and call the "Red, White, and Boobs" when I drove it around town. I said to Marvin Childress, "Yessir."

He didn't move. The church sermon will start in ten minutes, I thought. He needed to get along to pour his slow honey for not-allergic-to-bee-stings parishioners. "God wants us to preserve and take care of His inventions, son. That's what He wants. He wants us to take care of what animals grew up in the Garden of Eden, and of what trees He blessed with petals."

I looked at Mr. Childress's wooden beehive and said, "Somebody chopped down a tree for you to make that hive." I pointed at the Bible in his hand. "Bible's made of paper. Paper made of wood. Wood from a tree. Tree from God. You're a sinner."

What was I—fourteen, fifteen—old enough to know that I'd always have more questions than answers, that maybe I should've taken a vow of silence myself. I lived. People had lived before. Something bigger than us had made the universe. My father would beat me with a stick if he heard that I'd questioned a simple man.

"God made everything, but He wouldn't be upset with a

Bible," Marvin Childress said. "Oh, He'd be upset with about everything else we've done with His creation. I studied up on these things when I was over at the University of Tokyo, teaching classes on economics and agriculture." He handed me a sushi-bar menu tucked inside his Bible, right about in the Mark section. Who ate sushi in Forty-Five, South Carolina?

I said, "This menu is made of paper. It's from a tree. God made the tree, right?"

"Jesus was a fisherman," Marvin Childress said. "You can look it up. It's in the third chapter, second verse, of Warren."

My father came outside about this time and yelled. He pointed at the cement truck. My father waved his cane in the air as if swatting at Marvin Childress's stray bees. I said, "I'm working, I'm working."

Thirty seconds later Mr. Childress picked up a rock the size of a baseball and hit me in the back of the head. Right before I went down I heard him say something about how any prophet with a chisel could etch out the eleventh commandment on a good-sized stone.

MY FATHER DIDN'T press charges against Mr. Childress, and didn't even tell the police that he wanted one of those don't-come-within-five-hundred-yards injunctions. "It's your own damn fault, Mendal," my father said at the emergency room. "I told you, never taunt an idiot. I have a good mind to take this hospital bill out of your allowance."

The back of my head didn't require stitches, but I'd been knocked unconscious for a few minutes, and my father worried. It wasn't the first time I woke up on the ground yelling out, "What day is it, what day is it?" Not that I was a clumsy child and teenager, but my head had a propensity for finding hard objects, from cement floors to hickory trees. On this occasion, I had looked up at the red and half-blue cement truck and thought I'd been run over somehow.

Dr. Wiggins came in and said, "Hey, Mendal, how you feeling?" He grabbed my knee. Dr. Wiggins had been my pediatrician since birth and had treated my father for gout, migraines, boils, snakebite, and food poisoning. Forty-Five wasn't the kind of town for specialists.

I said, "Fine. I got hit in the head with a rock by crazy Marvin Childress."

"Fine? Then what the hell did I bring you all the way over here for, son?" my father yelled. Someone on the other side of the curtain kept screaming about how he'd gone blind. "You didn't feel so fine all blubbering in the front yard." My father pulled a tongue depressor out of its dispenser, broke it lengthwise, and started cleaning his fingernails.

The doctor shined a light in my pupils and asked me to follow his finger. He felt my skull and said, "I don't have any experience with phrenology, really. Have you always had these knots on your head?" Dr. Wiggins had said the same thing every other time I got knocked out.

I didn't have time to answer. My father said, "That's from

his mother's side of the family. They're a bunch of knot-heads from way back." It's what he always said, too.

Dr. Wiggins didn't laugh. My father didn't say, "That was a little joke."

"I'm of the belief that you'll be okay. You need to stay away from whoever threw the rock at you, though, or at least keep him in front of you at all times," the doctor said. "Anything else?"

My father nodded up and down. And I never have figured out what secret sign language he and Dr. Wiggins knew, but before I could say anything, the doctor pulled out a special foot-long cotton swab. He reached for a rubber mallet normally used for testing reflexes. "The boy says he had sex with a girl in the back end of my cement truck. While we're here, you want to go ahead and test him for the VDs?"

Years later I would figure out that my father had *paid* Marvin Childress to hit me in the head, so then I'd have to go to the doctor, so then I'd learn my lesson about unprotected sex. I figured out that my father bought the cement truck so I'd have a dark place to take girls, and he took the truck in payment on purpose, and so on. The chain of events was monumental, well planned, and far-reaching. On the butcher-paper-covered examination table, though, I didn't understand all of this, how this cause-and-effect went all the way back to God, really. When the doctor told me to drop my pants, I could only blurt out, "I didn't really have sex with Shirley Ebo, Dad. I promise. I was only talking big. It was a joke. I made it all up."

The blindman on the other side of the curtain laughed and laughed. He said, "I didn't really splash battery acid in my eyes, either."

The doctor dropped the mallet on the floor and put his middle and index fingers to my jugular. He said, "I believe he's lying to us now, Lee. His pulse is too rapid for honesty."

"Uh-huh," my father said. "Maybe I should get both Shirley Ebo and her daddy in here to clear this up."

"Whoa. You should feel his heart beating now, boy. Everybody stand back—I think Mendal's fixing to explode."

I said, "No I'm not," but just sat there.

"Where's ye erection now, boy?" the blindman on the other side of the partition yelled out. "That'd get your blood slowed down in the neck area."

I paid attention to the voice, finally. It could've been my high-school principal. It could've been the man who gave my father the cement truck. Hell, it might've been my mother.

A TOWN WITHOUT whores must invent its celebrities. Ours was a man named Sonny Pearman who visited the schools on a bimonthly basis. Mr. Pearman had a passion for mimickry and deceit, and worked, for whatever reason, as a special guest speaker of sorts. I had known Mr. Pear-man in real life—he worked as a housefather at the local orphanage, ran a plant nursery, and walked around Forty-Five swinging an empty watch chain. He tipped his hat to passersby, and spoke in foreign accents. He wore fake facial hair of one kind or another, always.

On the day after my syphilis/gonorrhea exam I went to Coach Tappy Pinson's first period P.E. and found a slightly familiar-looking man sitting at the locker room's desk. Coach Pinson said, "Boys, we have a real treat today. This here's a real, live ex–major league baseball player who's come to talk to y'all today. I want all of you to listen close. This is Mr. Eli McClintock, the old center fielder for the St. Louis Cardinals. He has some things he wants to talk to y'all about." As soon as he said that I figured out it was re-ally Sonny Pearman, wearing a perfect handlebar mous-tache.

Coach Tappy Pinson wasn't but a step up from being a waterboy for the junior varsity football team, but he took himself seriously and seemed to know a little bit about foot and ankle injuries when one of us tripped while running up the bleachers every morning. This Eli McClintock was also the famed world-bounding travel writer who came into my English class the previous nine weeks. The year before, he was a famous good-hearted medical doctor who worked in Uganda and talked to my biology class about the dangers of an unhygienic lifestyle. When I was in the seventh grade Mr.

Pearman showed up to my Civics class as a purported descendent of Stonewall Jackson.

"Howdy, fellows," the fake center fielder said. "How many of y'all like the game of baseball? How many of y'all like football, baseball, basketball, and a good fight song?" We raised our hands because our parents had told us to be polite. Mr. Eli McClintock's moustache danced like electrons around Sonny Pearman's face. He smiled sideways and had that faraway look in his eyes that let me in on the fact that he'd given this speech before, beneath a giant evangelical tent erected beside a country store on par with Rufus Price's Goat Wagon down on Highway 25. Sonny Pearman used the lilting melodic voice of a hypnotist or animal-control specialist.

He also owned the voice of the blinded man next to me at the emergency room.

I should mention that Sonny Pearman—no matter what historical or made-up expert he chose to be—ended every session, no matter what the topic, by getting students to join him in prayer and to recognize that there was no peace without Jesus Christ in their lives. He meant well. I didn't care. Later on, after I finally escaped my hometown, Sonny Pearman pretended to be Hal Holbrook pretending to be Mark Twain at the Forty-Five Little Theatre. It got rave reviews in the *Forty-Five Platter*.

Anyway, we sat there in our short gym pants, our tube socks, and our T-shirts that all read 45. Fake Eli McClintock said, "I want to tell you about the time I hit for the cycle two games in a row. Y'all know what a cycle is, don't you?"

My friend Compton Lane said, "It's the best time not to get a girl pregnant."

Glenn Flack yelled out, "My daddy used to have a motorcycle back when he fought in the Korean War."

Sonny Pearman didn't veer off. "It's a single, double, triple, and *home run* in one game. It don't have to be in that order, but you have to get all of them."

Coach Pinson said, "The odds are against it happening. One time I got two singles in a row playing church league softball, but that was it."

I wanted to go outside and run around the cinder track until I got rubber legs and fell down face first. I wanted to walk over to the home ec class and stick my hand beneath the sewing machine needle. Compton Lane hit my bare leg and whispered, "Ask Coach Pinson if they were single men or single women."

Sonny Pearman droned on and on about his fake major league career, and then finally said, "And we have no other recourse but to be proud that God invented a pastime such as baseball."

Don't ask me why I raised my hand when Eli McClintock asked if we had any questions prior to our obligatory prayer, or why I wanted to prolong our special get-right-with-God-and-you-can-do-anything pep talk. I said, "Mr. Pearman, are you of the belief that all of God's creatures are splendid and special?" like I'd heard him say when he was pretending to be a hundred other people.

He said, "Son, I'm Eli McClintock, the world-famous center fielder from the St. Louis Cardinals."

I said, "Uh-huh." And then, for no reason outside of hardheaded meanness, I said, "To play baseball, God made trees, then trees get cut down and made into bats. God made horses, then horses get slaughtered so their hides can make balls. Gloves made from cows. Rosin bag made from rosin." I kept going. I went into bleachers, and popcorn boxes, and hot dog wrappers.

Compton said, "Foul ball, foul ball, foul ball," with each of my examples.

Coach Pinson said, "Hey, that'll be enough, Mendal. That's enough."

Before Sonny Pearman led us in prayer as Eli McClintock, he said, "That's right. God gives up horses, cows, and trees so we can enjoy our nation's pastime. Isn't God wonderful?"

To me Coach Pinson said, "You think about that when you're burning in Hell." Then he gave me two demerits for talking back.

I MADE IT through the remainder of the school day without dropping my lunch tray, and without Melissa Beasley or Libby Belcher raising their hands to tell a teacher that I didn't go to church on Sundays, that my father didn't have a real job, or that my mother traveled with a pack of gypsies. I got home, though, to find Sonny Pearman waiting on the front porch. My father was off looking for cheap land to buy up at one-tenth its true value once some land developer decided to make a golf course subdivision there.

I said, "Hey, Mr. Pearman."

"Hey you own goddamn self, boy," he said. He didn't wear his St. Louis Cardinals uniform anymore, even though he held a thirty-four-ounce wooden Louisville Slugger. "You go and try to make a fool of me one more time in public and I'll beat your face in. You do it in private, and I'll see to it that you dead."

I could actually feel my knees knocking together. I thought for sure my cling peaches, corn bread, mashed potatoes, lima beans, and sloppy joe sandwich would find their way out of my body one way or the other. I said, "My father told me to say all that. He just got a thing in the mail from some environmentalists saying we should care about the trees. I guess I had it on my mind."

Mr. Pearman's hair was perfectly greased back in swirly Vitalis waves. I couldn't help but picture tiny men surfing down his forehead and temples. "You got hit in the head yesterday by a man with the IQ of a desk clerk's bell. I know your daddy told you not to question Marvin Childress, ever. And now today. Don't you learn? I thought you was smart. I got boys at the orphanage who don't stick their hands in a rat trap twice. I got plants at my nursery that don't let aphids bother them none."

My brain worked way ahead of itself trying to think of excuses. I didn't say, "How in the world would you know about Marvin Childress popping my head with a rock unless my father planned some grand scheme that involved your hanging out next to my emergency room bed?" I said, "Was Eli McClintock a real baseball player? I thought you did a wonderful job. It was right up there with the time back when I was in seventh grade and you came in as Booker T. Washington's great-grandson. That was cool. You must've had to do a lot of research on that guy."

Sonny Pearman pointed his bat at my chin. He said, "There ain't but a few of us left in Forty-Five who have any hope for the future of our community, Mendal. You need to know this. Me and some other men and your father know that it could all go away unless there's some smart leadership. And smart leadership don't happen with a man who makes fun of the retarded or the Christian."

It probably didn't start with a boy who would turn around and urinate right onto the front-yard boxwoods, either, but that's what I did at this particular moment instead of peeing my pants. I said, "I couldn't hold on anymore. Excuse me."

"You our little Dalai Lama, Mendal Dawes. You go on and pee where you want. Nothing's enough for you, bubba. Nothing's enough."

I said, "The Dalai Lama is *picked*, I know. But who's the *old* Dalai Lama of Forty-Five? Are you the current Dalai Lama, Mr. Pearman?"

Sonny Pearman tapped his boot heels with the bat. He threw back his head and laughed. "You know I ain't that wise. And if you're the next one, you should know already."

I said, "I'm getting out of Forty-Five, though. I'm going off in a few years to a real college."

Sonny Pearman put on his Shakespearean-actor voice. He was being either Lear or Richard III. He said, "And then please come back." Or maybe Desdemona. "A man must experience life in order to offer life experience."

He tapped the bat against his boots some more, then took a stance as if a knuckleballer stood sixty feet, six inches away. Mr. Pearman swung at the imaginary ball. He looked at a point forty-five degrees on the horizon, as if he'd hit one out of the park, out of town, out of South Carolina. I zipped up my pants and followed his gaze. I saw exactly nothing— not even a cloud. Across the woods I heard Shirley Ebo's father's donkeys call out. Mr. Pearman didn't look over in that direction, past the cement truck, but I knew that he, too, could tell that their two-syllable cries sounded like "Men-dal, Men-dal. Men-dal, Mendal." If we'd've had a travel agent in town, I would've booked a plane to Mississippi, or any of those other states where I could get lynched quickly and without notice—just so I could flat-out *die* without much fanfare. I looked back to that imaginary spot in the sky and thought about how my mother should've been around to witness this spectacle.

I thought, Joke, joke, joke, joke, joke, joke, joke. That's it.

I didn't nod, or shake my head, or shrug. I didn't shake his hand. Mr. Pearman said, "You don't even have to think about it. There's nothing to think about. It's predestined. Like a dog that has no choice but to chase cars, you know. They're pretty much predestined to get run over."

He left, swinging his bat. He walked up Deadfall Road, not in the direction of the orphanage. I looked back up at the sky but saw nothing different to note later on. Dogs bayed off in the distance, mournful, not urgent.

I walked down the road to Marvin Childress's church. I sat on the stoop there, hoping that some power would come down and offer me solutions. Evidently Marvin Childress had spilled much of his honey on the porch. An inordinate number of flies thrived there, two feet from God's front door.

MUFFLERS

If my father had had a friend in the parole and probation office or working with the district attorney, I might have been fitted for a monitoring device around my ankle. But whatever spy gadgetry might have existed in 1974 South Carolina, it would not make it to the town of Forty-Five until decades later.

When I got my driver's license legally, at the age of fifteen, there were still party lines for all of our residents, and I'm pretty sure that some neighbors wired up tin butter-bean cans with string between their houses. *Gone with the* fucking *Wind* didn't make it to our sad drive-in movie theater until the late sixties, and it wasn't until then, when word of that movie and the South's loss spread, that a large portion of our black population felt free to move on. Men still trapped animals by digging deep holes and covering them with thin reeds and pine straw, and most mornings, thirty minutes before school began, the cries of woods-living children yelling "Help" could be heard. The CB radio, a fad that had trickled down from truck drivers to regular citizens in other towns, seemed too extravagant for the residents of Forty-Five. My biology teacher owned and operated a ham radio set, but communicated only with another biology teacher in France.

Hell, I remember when Lanky Jenkins walked into class one day all excited from learning that some French guy had figured out how to make milk last longer.

Oh, sure, I exaggerate somewhat. But I would bet that if a pollster came down to Forty-Five and asked about man landing on the moon, half of the population wouldn't know about it, and the other half would pronounce "Mojave" as two syllables.

So, because of the lack of technology and my father's basic parental understanding that teenagers needed constant supervision, the first car I bought with money I'd saved from a variety of tragic and misguided part-time jobs lost its muffler before I had put five miles on the odometer. This was a giant, baby blue, slanted-upward Ford Galaxie that—*with* its muffler—could be heard all the way over in tiny, reckless downtown Forty-Five, and probably all the way out to Gruel. "We're taking off the muffler so I'll always know where you are," my father said. "In case I need some help and have to come get you." He got beneath the Galaxie's carriage with a couple channel locks and ten minutes later said, "Start this thing up, Mendal."

I stood in the gravel driveway leading up to our cement-block house. I only wanted to go pick up my friend Compton, drive out to the Sunken Gardens Lounge, and buy an eight-pack of Miller ponies from one of the tray-twirling black kids who took orders in the parking lot. I said, "Dad, I don't want *no* muffler. How am I going to hear anything? It'll be embarrassing when I go out on a date or something."

My father emerged from beneath the car. He stood up and held the muffler with one hand. "A date?" He laughed and laughed and laughed. "I don't want to bust your sacred cow none, boy, but you ain't going out on dates with these girls around here. Unless I save up some money and have your tongue removed. They've heard you talk. Forty-Five girls don't like smart boys." He tossed the muffler into the yard. It clanged against a metal staircase he'd picked up somewhere and left in the sparse grass going nowhere. "Why you think your momma left me?"

I didn't say the usual, but I thought it: because she felt the need to improve her station in life; because she feared catfish at the yearly Catfish Feastival; because—even without the use of CB radios—she heard the voice of God calling her west, to Nashville. I said, "What if I tell you exactly where I'll be and come back exactly when I say. Then if I mess up, we'll take off the muffler. The very first time I'm a second late."

He spit on the trunk and wiped off an imaginary smudge with his shirtsleeve. "I know that trick," he said. "It don't take much time to change every clock in a house. Like mother, like son."

IF THERE'D BEEN any kind of seismic recorder in Forty-Five, it would've registered six point something on the Richter scale every morning when I warmed up the Galaxie, each afternoon when I drove home from school, and almost every night when I drove around aimlessly. My father added WINDOW REPAIR and SOUNDPROOFER to the sign he kept in our front yard on Deadfall Road, beneath HOUSE PAINTER, ELECTRICIAN, FLOOR REFINISHER, AUTO BODY REPAIR, ROOFER, LANDSCAPER, PREDICTER, and so on. He should've had SCAM ARTIST on top of them all, I figured out way too late in life.

I drove my Galaxie around town, out to Lake Between, over through the mill villages, and slowly past Libby Belcher's house. My father caught up with me in all these places, too, especially if I made it nearly twenty miles away. He said things like, "I need you to help me clean out the gutters," or "Come look at this stray dog that showed up on our front porch," or "Goddamnit, Mendal, I'm trying to sleep. How do you expect me to get up in the morning when your car's making so much noise?" If the party line wasn't being used, he'd call Mr. Ebo, or Mr. Lane, or Mr. Flack— knowing that I was approaching their houses—and ask them to go outside, flag me down, and send me homeward.

One time Comp and I were careening down Bucklevel

Road drinking, when I saw my father in the rearview. Buck-level Road split through no real property; it cut across Gray-wood County with a protected national forest on both sides. Comp scrambled over the bench seat to hide our cooler. I pulled over. My father said, "Compton's on the telephone back home. He says he really needs to talk to you." My friend knew to stay crouched on the ample, spacious floorboard in back. My father said, "What're you doing all the way out here. Hotdamn, gas doesn't grow in trees."

I didn't say how, actually, carbon dioxide was a gas that plants emitted once they decomposed, et cetera. I said, "I was looking for you, of all things."

In the backseat—and a family of four can live in the back of a Ford Galaxie—Compton was curled up under a wool blanket I kept. I didn't know if the missing muffler was what caused my heater to quit running, but it had. Or hadn't. My father said, "Bullshit, boy. You can't bullshit an old bull-shitter. I've been home all night."

I opened the car door, confident that no inside light worked. I stood up the best I could, bloated as I was. "Comp and I heard there was a KKK meeting out here tonight." I opened the back door. "Come on out of there, Comp. It's not a grand wizard or anything. It's Dad." Comp sat up. He kept our cooler covered, suavely. I said, "We were going to park nearby in the woods and rev the engine. You know how it sounds like a machine gun?"

"That's right, sir," Compton said. "That's what we were going to do. If we came across the KKK meeting."

Both of our fathers had gone to great pains to disrupt KKK meetings in the past. They had invested in Roman candles more than once and dug supposed deer traps all over the place on land they didn't own when they caught wind of where a meeting would take place. Mr. Lane once spent an entire year trying to corner the white sheet and hood market, or so he said.

"Good boys," my father said. "I thought y'all might be out smoking dope. Good. Good." He put his hands in his grease-stained pockets and nodded that homemade burr haircut like it was a stand of summer goldenrod.

I said, "You kind of blew our cover, Dad. We haven't found the meeting yet. If they're nearby, I bet they hear us now."

Compton walked past my father and stretched out on the berm. He said, "Man, look at the stars. Man, what if the sky only has holes in it, and we're all wrong? What if stars are really holes—kind of like hotel-door peepholes—looking into other galaxies, and then those galaxies have holes to look into other galaxies? Man. Cool."

I got back into the car and stepped on the accelerator. It sounded like six thousand soldiers were marching atop hollow logs simultaneously. My friend stood up as if a hypnotist had directed him toward the near-paisley front-seat fabric on which we normally sat. My father said, "Y'all go on back home. I'll drive around, see where these dumb sons-abitches burn crosses, peckerheads."

My rumble home reverberated against loblolly pines and hillsides and homes of people who probably wondered how their precious suppers had given them such horrific gas, for all I knew. Comp stuck his foot out of the passenger window and said, "Can you imagine ever living in a more stupid town? Nothing against your daddy." He said, "Mine's the same since my own mom left."

At our twenty-fifth reunion Compton brought all of this up, and I said, "What? What?" like that. "What galaxy are you talking about, buddy?"

I'M NOT ONE to believe in hidden-early-childhood-trauma syndrome, but I knew for a fact that my mufflerless Galaxie did erase a good summer out of my life. When all of Forty-Five's parents understood that I was nothing more than a trick junebug on a string, they, too, removed their teenaged sons' and daughters' mufflers. I'm talking the Midas guy in town went out of business. But the doctor who fit people for earplugs ended up buying a vacation house in Myrtle Beach.

I remember that much.

Anyway, a Friday night in Forty-Five sounded like the first lap of the Southern 500 nonstop coupled with endless freight trains, sporadic sonic booms, and haphazard thunderstorms. This was a time between real Cold War fears and terrorist attacks. The people of Forty-Five saw a need for corralling their kids, and without an official vote, they enacted mandatory law.

It wasn't good. For a while, word was that the teenaged women of Forty-Five had been touched by God and convulsed into speaking tongues, until someone realized it had happened only during the rhythmic bounce inside nonmufflered cars. No girls had resorted to sitting on half-filled washing machines or dryers back home when their parents were gone, is what I'm saying.

"I wish I could get a patent on this idea," my father said almost every night between getting off work unbuilding old heart-pine barns and my leaving for parts unknown. "I've started something that might take the nation by storm. Man. Nixon could've used me for figuring out how to beat them Vietnamites."

I always said, "What? I can't hear you. What?" I really meant it, seeing as I'd just come in from school.

"There's got to be a way to make money off my idea," my dad would say. "If you come up with a notion, let me in on it. I'll split the money with you."

It took me some time, but I finally answered him with, "Gas. Sleeping pills. Carbon-monoxide-level device. Invest in Texaco, seeing as every parent drives around trying to figure out which car is his kid's car. Invest in sleeping pills, seeing as no one can sleep right, what with all the noise. And somebody's going to die, what with the fumes coming through the floorboard."

My father leaned the metal staircase against the side of our house for no reason I could tell. He said, "Lanky Jenkins says that there's a woman in France who's done some amazing things with radioactivity. Maybe we can get her to come over and help us."

I stared at my father. "Madame Curie?" I said.

In the distance, my peers revved and idled with everything they had. I owned some imagination back then and convinced myself that these other cars—Pintos and Mavericks and El Caminos—*called* to my own Galaxie, that unbeknownst to whatever human being was tapping his respective accelerator, his car called out to mine, "Come on out and join us, Galaxie." I lived in a bland, bland, dull town. What else could I fantasize about?

My father said, "Sometimes I don't believe everything Lanky Jenkins says, but I don't let on. Don't you tell him that I know."

I said, "What? I can't hear you. What?"

ALTHOUGH HE SWORE that he'd foreseen the whole thing, my father thought one of the other boys would end up shot, not me. There wasn't but one other Galaxie in all of Graywood County, and that was owned by Boland Bobo and driven by his eldest son, Bo. Bo Bobo quit going to Forty-Five Junior High in the eighth grade when he turned fifteen years old, and he matriculated two years later to the vocational school on Old Bus Road, where welding, advanced woodworking, and engine repair got taught by men who couldn't take the pressures of small-business ownership. Bo Bobo's Galaxie looked nothing like mine: he had detailed his for free every Monday through Friday, at taxpayers' expense. Bo Bobo's blue Galaxie experienced no rust and shone like a glacial lake. His chrome, when the sun hit it right, could've been used for laser surgery. Unfortunately, perfect and imperfect Galaxies pretty much looked the same at night in a town that had no need for streetlights.

I drove around one Saturday night not smoking dope nor drinking. I rode alone, my Galaxie louder than a California motorcycle rally. Compton had gone camping with his father up in North Carolina. Any girl who might've been interested in dating me was sitting at home in the den with her parents, watching *The Lawrence Welk Show* and playing charades, eating homemade Rice Krispie Treats, and clapping her hands when the accordion guy started up.

I didn't know that Bo Bobo's daddy had put his son on restriction for stealing an acetylene torch from the vocational school. There was no way that I could've known that Bo Bobo should've been home at ten o'clock, that his Galaxie had thrown a rod way over on the McCormick Highway, that he was sitting on his hood waiting for help to drive by, seeing as this was a time before cell phones.

Me, I putt-putted around Forty-Five's perimeter, giving the

left-hand-index-finger wave to other mufflerless members of the Forty-Five High Speed Fire Ant community. I tried not to think about how none of us had anywhere to go later.

And then, in my rearview mirror, I saw what ended up being Mr. Bobo's sad Fairlane approaching me, right before I hit the boundary of Leroy Cannon's Baptist Orphanage where, I had heard, runaway girls could get picked up for drives all the way over to the Georgia border. I didn't hear a rumble louder than mine and figured it was only a poor traveling salesman having to take back roads between Columbia and Atlanta. When Bo Bobo's daddy shot out my left rear tire, too, I only thought I'd had a flat. When I pulled over, got out of my own Galaxie, and Mr. Bobo shot me in the right knee, all I could think was how I needed to drive around with a tin can, a long string, and a responsible friend waiting on the other end.

That's what I thought, by God.

"I tode you ten o'fucking clock it's ten-fitty I been hearing you riding circles thowing it in my face, boy," Mr. Bobo said. He had turned his headlights off but pulled in behind me on a wide spot parallel to the orphans' chapel building. I might not've been the smartest boy in the world but I knew enough to limp my way to the front of my Galaxie.

I didn't recognize Mr. Bobo's voice. I said, "Ow, ow, I've been shot." If anything, he sounded like any one of my teachers at Forty-Five High. I said, "This is Mendal Dawes. I think you got the wrong man."

Mr. Bobo stopped walking toward me in his John Wayne swagger. He said, "Shit. Got-dang."

I said, "Uh-huh." I covered my face with one hand and held my knee with the other. At the time, I didn't know that it wasn't anything but a couple shotgun pellets that had penetrated my blue jeans.

He hobbled back to his car and turned on the headlights. One of the housemothers came running over from Leroy Cannon's Baptist Orphanage's dorms. She evaluated the situation and started reciting one of those Psalms, the one about God being a rock, buckler, and horn. At the time, I foresaw amputation. I thought about rock, paper, scissors, dynamite—as I always did when I couldn't figure out what to do.

My Galaxie quivered on the side of the road, reverberated, waited for me to take it home, shivered and shook like a big, wet, long-haired stray dog.

MAYBE MY FATHER'S back acres were so filled with used heart-pine lumber and odd architectural elements that I never noticed the mufflers. After all the fathers had taken their sons' and daughters' mufflers off in order to keep tabs on them, my father went around collecting—as was his lot in life—that which had been discarded. He awoke early and drove around town, seeing who had thrown a muffler down at the end of a driveway for Mikey Adams's Trash Service to pick up in his dump truck with LET'S TALK TRASH hand-printed on the doors. My father gathered mufflers and made a note as to whose was whose. Then he waited for someone to get shot accidentally, though—as he told me at least twice a day until I left Forty-Five within a couple years for what I thought was for good—he didn't think *I* would be a part of the near disaster.

Boland Bobo took me to Self Memorial Hospital, driving his Fairlane so fast it outran its own headlight beams. The housemother came with us. She didn't even go back to the dorm to tell her orphans she'd be gone, and I knew that some of my friends and acquaintances would wonder which God had come down to offer them so many runaway teenaged girls wanting to hit Augusta before the bars closed there. " 'They shall fear thee as long as the sun and moon endure, throughout all generations,' " she said from the backseat. " 'He shall come down like rain upon the mown grass: as showers that water the earth.' "

Mr. Bobo took a curve too fast and said, "Would you please shut the hell up, please? I mean it. I thought you wanted to come along to rip sheets and apply pressure on this boy's leg."

I said, "I think I'm not bleeding anymore. You can slow down." Of course we came up on Bo Bobo pulled off on the side of the road.

Mr. Bobo slowed, and asked me to roll down my window. "Boy, what's wrong with you out here?"

Bo Bobo stood up from his hood. "I'm thinking I thowed a rod," he said. "The engine blowed."

"Get in," Mr. Bobo said. "We got to get to the 'mergency room." Bo Bobo slid in beside the housemother.

I said, "It only stings a little now. This isn't life-threatening or anything."

Bo Bobo in the backseat said, "My Galaxie looks better than your Galaxie, Cuz. I seen your Galaxie. It's a 'sixty-five? You oughter be ashamed of your Galaxie."

Mr. Bobo turned on Highway 25, a few miles from the hospital, where later a resident straight from med school would take special tweezers and pull shot from my knee. The housemother—we all learned later that her name was Martha Bang, though everyone at the orphanage called her Sister Bang, like she was some kind of incestuous porn star—mumbled about Job, Job, and Job. I said, "Well, I'd rather have a Galaxie with a flat tire over one with a blowed motor."

We pulled into the emergency-room entrance. When an orderly of sorts opened my door, the housemother jumped out from her perch and said, "I'm Sister Bang from Leroy Cannon's Baptist Orphanage, and I would like to bring the spirit of Jesus into the operating room."

I said, "I promise I'm fine. I don't even need a wheel-chair," and walked toward the wide sliding-glass door. "Someone probably needs to call my father, seeing as he won't hear my car going anywhere."

Sister Bang took me by the arm. Mr. Bobo stood up out of his car and bellowed out how it was only an accident, how he hoped I wouldn't press charges, how he only meant to shoot his own son. I said I understood completely, and for some reason I did.

THE MAN TOOK out my buckshot. He gave me prescriptions for infection and pain. Bo Bobo said he'd give me a dollar for every painkiller I didn't want. Sister Bang called her orphanage from the emergency room's pay phone and explained the situation to Sonny Pearman, who watched orphans in a different dorm. Mr. Bobo called my father and said he owed us a left rear tire.

When my dad showed up at the emergency room he didn't ask about my condition right away. And for some reason he wore a paper hat, like a corporal, like a Waffle House cook, like a waiter at the Rendezvous in Memphis, like an old-timey ice-cream vendor. My father bolted into the E.R. and from behind my curtain I heard him say, "Okay. All right. This proves it's time to get the mufflers back on. Okay. All right." He went on and on before pulling back the scrim that kept me shielded from a poor kid undergoing epileptic seizures. "You okay, Mendal?"

My pants leg was pulled up above the knee, sliced up the inseam like in a real-life documentary. "Mr. Bobo shot me because he thought I was Bo driving loose."

My father shook his head. "I've been working on a barbecue sauce that I think'll take hold. It's vinegar- , ketchup- , and mustard-based, all in one." He didn't need to add anything about how he needed to invent something in order to get us out of town forever.

I said, "Well that should just about suit everyone," as I remember.

"The mufflers must go back on," my father yelled back toward Mr. Bobo. To me he said, "I guess I got to give you a percentage of the proceeds, you know. I mean, I'll take out for gas and time, but I guess you deserve some of the profit. Hell, you can use the money for college."

Maybe my first Percodan kicked in and that's why I said, "You're fucking crazy, Dad." Maybe whatever local anesthetic the doctor-to-be shot in my leg caused me to say, "Mom left us because men's plans aren't ever enough. I read that in 'Dear Abby.' The tap-dancing black guy's more talented than the white accordionist. I'm pretty sure we have black blood running through our veins. Look at my wide nose! I might ask the doctor if I'm prone to sickle-cell anemia. Where's the camera, I can't find the camera, how do you expect me to act when I don't know where I'm supposed to focus?" and so on.

My father lit a Camel and stuck it in my mouth. Later on I realized that *he* realized—since he'd started me drinking at something like the age of nine—nothing mattered. I understood that my father followed the notions of Schopenhauer, how all of us were either in pain or boredom, with nothing in between there in Forty-Five. Sometimes I thought it even affected the strays near our house—that they chased cars only due to pain or boredom. I coughed and coughed and forgot about my leg.

Boland Bobo came in to my semi-semi-private room. "He ain't coughing 'cause we let him get cold, Lee. Don't go saying I caused him to get the pneumonia."

My father broke the man's jaw with one great right-cross punch.

And then everything was even, in a numerical town. No one pressed charges. The local newspaper ran nothing about the entire incident. Every second-car-owning father decided to remuffler his kid's automobile, and my father—since there was no Midas man left in town—obliged everybody for something like twenty-five bucks each, parts and labor. If I'd not gotten a pity-scholarship for college, my daddy's muffler ruse would've taken care of me for four years.

But what mattered is Sister Bang. From what I understand, she prayed and prayed. I came out fine, which must've made her feel better about herself. Bo Bobo went off to live a life of burglary, larceny, and arson. He got interviewed in prison one time years later and said he invented the rattail, and he expected some compensation.

My Galaxie stood on the side of Highway 10 for two days before my dad and I attended to it with a jack that worked. I looked over at the orphanage and saw little parentless children skipping around outside their dorms. Sister Bang's redbrick house stood silent.

My father said, "I'll follow you. Bobo's gun might've hit more than tire."

I drove twenty miles an hour home. I looked in the mirror at my father. He seemed to drive with his face uncomfortably close to the windshield.

Not that I had any kind of ESP, but it was at this point that I knew Sister Bang would leave her post, that she'd end up on the televised traveling-evangelist circuits, and that I would end up being the anecdote she told as to why she left an orphanage for a life on the byways of America. She would remember my name and everything. She would remember Bo Bobo, and say his name as if she stuttered. Whenever I saw her on Channel 16, she was telling her story, then singing a song. Sister Bang would hold her palm in the air and praise Jesus. And although I had no faith whatsoever, I would watch, and smile, and wonder what else my father might've collected off the side of the road.

My knee, later on, looked like the beginning of a crude tattoo, like two eyeballs punctured in. When people asked about it, though—when I wore shorts—I told them it was my birthmark, nothing else. Or I said I'd stood too close to a bed of vipers as a child—that there was nothing but beds of vipers all over my hometown—and I'd gotten struck repeatedly.

Tired of Old Tricks

During my father's convalescence, I counted splinters. I'd never kept a real diary or journal like our one new English teacher at Forty-Five High said I should do over the summer—like she did—so I could lug it in to a psychotherapist years later and trace backwards my mental, spiritual, and moral demise. Here was my marbled Mead composition book: "Monday, 6 splinters in right hand; Tuesday, 3 in index finger, 1 in left palm; Wednesday— working with cedar—about 150 in both hands; Thursday, drank six-pack of Schlitz, took powdered aspirin for the first time, cussed Dad; Friday, 1 splinter in forehead, which felt good to extract; Saturday, 5 in hand; Sunday, didn't go to church for the 844th straight time."

My father had rolled his pickup truck out on roughly paved Dixie Drive, halfway between Graywood and Hodges. He told the cops he'd swerved from a deer. He told me it was a pack of dogs en route to the tree farm across from our house. It didn't matter the truth—he'd been flat-out drunk and driving with Herbert Coleman, a man who sometimes helped Dad with heavy loads and otherwise played guitar at the Sunken Gardens Lounge when he wasn't on first or second shift over at Forty-Five Cotton. I imagined that they sang songs about women they didn't have, or women that they'd had but couldn't take anymore. Sometimes Herbert Coleman showed up at our house unannounced to ask my father personal questions about my momma's leaving, for he knew he would find a good hook or chorus there somewhere along the line. Herbert had sworn off marriage. He liked to say, "I'm of the firm belief that marriage is the number one cause of unhappy separations in America." He thought he was some kind of Einstein or Svengali or Dr. Joyce Brothers.

If Mr. Coleman had ever had the money to buy a bus ticket to Hollywood, and if he'd found his way to that famous drugstore where stars got discovered, he could've been the next Marlon Brando/Clark Gable/Humphrey Bogart. He stood six-one, had curly black hair and blue eyes, owned a physique that any Olympic swimmer would've wanted. But he didn't have bus fare. He worked as a doffer, or a spinner, or a picker, or whatever it was that men did inside Forty-Five Cotton for working-poor wages.

Anyway, that night Herbert Coleman got thrown from the pickup and bounced his head across the berm until he landed upside-down against a fence post that kept Frank Godfrey's prizewinning Angus caged.

My dad had remained in the truck's cab and only bounced

around like so many beans inside a burbling crockpot. He broke those floating ribs, a knee, and half the bones in his right hand and wrist. He also suffered a circular burn on his forehead, which meant that he'd pushed in the cigarette lighter about ten seconds before losing control, that it had popped out unexpectedly, and so on. I figured that much out, all by myself.

Herbert Coleman would never sing again, really, though he didn't get killed. He went from coma to half-wit in a matter of weeks.

All of this occurred the summer my father bought land once owned by men who'd needed sharecroppers some sixty to eighty years earlier. We went in and disboarded the outbuildings, the houses, and the barns. Later, we sold the land outright to land developers and the state. If my father wasn't in a wheelchair, then he stood on crutches. When crutches didn't support his upright body, then he leaned on a nearby tree or unfolded his body onto a stump and waved his arm for what I should do next. I pried and pried at two-by-twelves, then stacked them up to the side for later transport to our own yard.

At night we went to the hospital and sat in Herbert Coleman's room. My father smoked cigarettes there next to the crank-up bed as Mr. Coleman — who liked to introduce himself to strangers at Herbert "Tarleton" Coleman — only barely breathed. He wore an IV "like the tapeworm I used to keep for a pet when I was a poor kid," my father said nightly.

I would've written all of this in my notebook, had I been thinking of anything outside of splinters. I sat in the hospital room not looking at handsome Herbert Coleman half-dead. I pulled splinters out of my flesh and notched the numbers in a binder filled with lined sheets. I didn't care about the new English teacher at Forty-Five High School, though I knew I'd be taking a course with her in the fall. Her name was Ms. Shaw. Her daddy sold insurance and was best friends with our state senator. My father said she couldn't have gotten a job picking lint from a navel without those connections. Like always, I figured that she was just another woman who'd rebuffed my father's advances, until he told me that she once held the title of Miss Graywood County, and that when she didn't make the top ten in the Miss South Carolina pageant her father tried to prove collusion between judges and the mayor of Myrtle Beach. Her talent involved juggling on roller skates.

On this particular night I wrote down "Tuesday, 4 splinters in right hand. 3 in left hand. Crown of thorns." It was at this point that I knew how I would show Ms. Shaw my supposed journal. I would hand it in on August 20 or thereabouts, and nod, and say I couldn't wait to read some Charles Dickens, Nathaniel Hawthorne, those Brontës, and/or any of those other writers' books any sane high-school student views as very boring, melodramatic writing.

• • •

WHEN IT LOOKED like Herbert Coleman would survive his head trauma and at least get to the point of singing the first verse of "Amazing Grace" in a language that resembled English, my father let me take off from hospital duty. He continued to go up there to Self Memorial Hospital in order to poke lit cigarettes into Herbert's face, filter-end first. He'd either wheel or gimp himself up there and stay long after visiting hours should've ended. Most nights I stayed at home and wrote in my little notebook however many splinters I'd eased out with a needle or knife. On one late-June Friday, though, my friend Compton and I got invited, miraculously, to a pre-debutante-ball party, held at the Forty-Five Country Club, which was really nothing more than one tennis court, a nine-hole golf course, a swimming pool without a real diving board, and a one-room clubhouse lined with mirrors. The Forty-Five debs wouldn't be presented until a week before Christmas, but their parents, sponsors, and escorts held bimonthly parties leading up to the big event.

Let me make sure that you understand the entire debutante process: in places like Birmingham, Atlanta, Charleston, and Richmond, eighteen-year-old female college freshmen who attended colleges like Hollins, Vassar, Smith, Wellesley, Bryn Mawr, Agnes Scott, and Randolph-Macon came back home to be presented to society in a way similar to that of royalty. These were the young daughters of tycoons and barons, people who vacationed in the Hamptons, Cape Cod, and the Riviera. In Forty-Five—and every tiny crossroads in South Carolina, at least—a girl with all of her teeth and the mental capacity to potentially complete a two-year technical college with a degree in secretary science could pretty much undergo the debutante process, complete with gowns, elbow-length gloves, and cheap tiaras.

Compton called me up on a Wednesday night and said, "Hey, man, did you get an invitation to Libby Belcher's coming-out thing? Goddamn."

I said, "I thought it was a joke. They must be worried no one will show up."

Comp said, "Oh, we're going, amigo. You better find a way to get your daddy a babysitter for Mr. Coleman."

I didn't tell him how Herbert Coleman had rounded the bend, so to speak. I said, "Do we have to get dressed up?" I didn't own a suit, seeing as my father wouldn't allow me to attend church services, and no one I knew had died yet.

Compton said, "It's going to be a spectacle, buddy. It'll be an event. You can wear my other suit. You can wear my other tie."

I don't want to come across as a mystic, or the kind of person who can comprehend scenes long before they happen, but I could tell that Comp had something in mind that would embarrass not only the future debutantes, but their escorts, sponsors, and family members alike. These debutantes' boyfriends—who would all know only one woman in their lives—were the sons of cotton mill superintendents,

or mill accountants, or lawyers whose only task was to de-
fend the mill, or doctors who spent most of their time sewing
fingers back on. Compton and I hated these smug, stupid
boys, for the most part, and only hoped that—as my father
liked to say—"showing off good-looking poontang at a
high-school reunion twenty-five years down the road is the
best revenge."

But between the ages of birth and seventeen we were
helpless and hopeless, and we knew our place in Forty-Five
society. I said, "You going to spike the punch?" to Compton
over the telephone. So much for my vivid and overactive
imagination.

"Idiot," he said. "We won't have to do that. Armistead
will spike the punch. Or Calhoun. Hell, I won't even drink
that stuff. We'll be bringing our own flasks in, comrade."

I didn't goad him to let me in on his plan. I sat in the den
with the telephone to my head, daydreaming about Libby
Belcher's mother and me making out in the middle of a sand
trap, near a water hazard, while inside the clubhouse people
danced to whatever bad music droned out from a portable
record player.

I PUT ON Compton's other suit a week later and
drove us to the Forty-Five Country Club an hour before
dusk. Libby Belcher and I had been mortal enemies since the
third grade, so I wondered why we got invited, and if it had
anything to do with how we were the only boys at the pre-

deb party without real dates. There were single girls there—
last year's debutantes on summer vacation from Greenville
Technical College, Central Northwest South Carolina Bible
College, Andersonville College, and a variety of schools of
cosmetology. And there were the debutantes' younger sisters, all excited about their chance to undergo this same
process in due time. Drunken fathers wearing plaid coats
stood around with bourbon and Cokes, and mothers drank
chilled red wine. Maybe it was my imagination, but when
Compton and I walked in, it seemed like all conversation
stopped and every person in attendance stared at us.

"Well, it's Mendal and Comp," Libby said. She approached
us as if she was wearing ball bearings on her spangly gold
shoes. "I really didn't think y'all would come, but I'm glad
you did." She didn't shake our hands or offer us a shallow
hug. She turned to her escort, Jimmy Wingard, and said,
"Jimmy, would you go get Comp and Mendal some punch,
s'il vous plaît?" Then she took us to a table covered with
typed name tags. Compton's read COMPTON. Whoever made
these pin-backed things mistyped my name. It came out
MENIAL.

Either Earth, Wind, and Fire or the Commodores blared
from the record player. This was my idea of Hades, of
course. "Whatever you do, don't drink the punch, Menial,"
Compton said out of the side of his mouth. "This is a little
like Mexico—pretend that you're drinking it, but don't.
These people are not our allies, and you know it. Don't be

tricked. Never drink with the enemy." It sounded like he'd rehearsed his little monologue; it sounded like something I'd heard a gangster say once in a 1940s movie that maybe had played in Forty-Five a couple years earlier.

Jimmy Wingard was a halfback on the Forty-Five High Speed Fire Ant football team, and once ran a kickoff back almost ten yards. He didn't weigh more than 140 pounds and could've played offensive tackle—those lower-ranking mill boys weren't much bigger—had his father, the mayor, not threatened Coach Pinky Dabbs. Jimmy walked to us and said, "Drink up, boys. We gone have fun tonight." He also tried to cheat off of my test papers in every class.

At this point I still didn't know about Compton's plan, though later on in life he told me he had had about a thousand ideas. He and I milled around the outskirts of the dance floor, pouring our punch into various potted fake palmetto trees. We reached into our respective coat breast pockets and pulled out rum we'd poured earlier, Compton into an old cough medicine bottle, and me into a Welch's grape jelly jar with a pop-top lid of sorts.

This party went on and on. People danced. Mr. Belcher made a toast between about every second song and progressively slurred his way through them. As the night went on—and as Jimmy Wingard, Bingham Bradham, Wingard McGaha, McGaha Scurry, Scurry Wimmer, and Wimmer Bingham brought us more and more punch—I began to realize that they had devised some kind of drink that only we lap. Compton got out Jimmy's thing, took the other end of the Chinese handcuffs, and slipped it on.

"This will end up the best thing that's ever happened in the history of Forty-Five, South Carolina," Comp whispered. He got up and walked to the record player. He set the stylus on a particular song. "You need to stand guard by the door. Let me know when everyone comes back."

I pulled my jelly jar out and supped from its contents. I didn't want my father knowing about all of this at first, but then realized how proud he'd be of my unsettling two privileged, safe boys' lives. Here we go:

Mr. and Mrs. Belcher led the group of parents and teenagers back to the clubhouse. They had their arms around each other, and any anthropologist would've noticed how nothing but Love and Hope and Peaceful Existence and Confidence shown on their faces. Near-debutantes and their escorts followed, then other debutantes' parents who would be throwing parties presently. Invited guests who would either be debutantes or escorts later on in life brought up the procession's rear. Although I didn't know what Compton would do in a matter of seconds, I knew that there was something wrong with this entire situation. That "Ignorance is bliss" cliché almost came to mind.

It didn't, but it almost did. Me, I thought, "Disabled workers of the world, unite," because it was the last thing my father had said to me before he went off to blow smoke in Herbert Coleman's face.

supposedly would partake of, a purgative that should've sent us straight to the men's room off to the side of the sad pro shop.

Were they dipping cups into a punch bowl set off to the side, designated for us only? No. I watched closely. Had they dipped already spiked punch, then squirted a little Visine into our allotments? Yes. I said to Comp, "I know what they're doing. They're putting eyedrops in our drinks, hoping we'll get the squirts. I read all about this little trick one time. Some guy working at an airport bar flipped out and put Visine in everybody's Bloody Marys, then told them to have a pleasant flight."

Compton said, "Uh-huh. Keep pretending to drink. They think we're just two poor boys who can't keep up. This couldn't've worked out any better if I'd found the right God and prayed, Menial."

I said, "If you call me that again I'm going to kill you."

How many goddamn songs had Earth, Wind, and Fire put out? I wanted to go back to my Jeep, back it straight into the clubhouse, and play a Frank Zappa, Blue Öyster Cult, Wishbone Ash, Allman Brothers, or Grateful Dead eight-track. I said, "Let's go. Let's blow this Popsicle stand. I want out of here. I'm out of rum, and the more people here see my name tag, the better the chances they'll call me Menial for the rest of my life." The part about being out of rum wasn't true, because the rest of the quart of Captain Morgan was way beneath the passenger seat of the Jeep.

"Come on, man. This is stupid." I might've said I needed to go study for the SAT.

Compton looked at his watch. It wasn't eleven o'clock yet. The dance floor thinned, and more and more people either took to love seats, chairs, and couches that lined the room, or plain left to skinny-dip in the over-chlorinated, aboveground pool. Libby Belcher came up and said, "Have y'all been drinking the punch?" She whispered, "We spiked it, you know. You don't feel it?" Her left breast hung out to show a crescent of nipple.

I said, "We're drinking, we're drinking. What did you spike it with, though? Nothing will affect me unless it's peach-bounce moonshine."

Compton said, "Me and Menial were at a party last week down in Atlanta where the punch was spiked with LSD. Man, this ain't nothing."

One of Libby Belcher's eyes went west, but she smiled like an everyday temptress. She leaned my way and said, "I kind of wish I was with you instead of Jimmy. Later on I'mo be sorry that I didn't marry a man who went to a real college, I know. And it don't matter to me that you've been with a black girl none."

I didn't break. Libby had referred to Shirley Ebo. I looked down Libby's dress front and said, "Congratulations on your coming out."

. . .

COMPTON HAD THOUGHT to bring gloves him to the pre-debutante party. And let me make it that he was the one who put them on, that he was the who shoved Jimmy Wingard's little thin pecker into one of the Chinese handcuffs. "This was worth the goddamn dollars it took me to win these things playing ring toss a fair last year," Compton said.

We had pretended to go out on a golf-course walk everybody else, then circled around. Wingard and Bingh Bradham had passed out side by side thirty minutes ear on a love seat that looked like the one I'd sat on in Shi Ebo's parents' house more than a few times. My job only to gently get Bingham's right hand and stick one end the Chinese handcuffs on his index finger. Compton zipped Jimmy's pants, pulled out his sorry pecker, and tached the other end of the handcuffs halfway down. I those of you unfamiliar with the intricacies of Chine handcuffs, these devices are made from a raffia-like mater that, when pulled lengthwise, can only tighten. They're li eight inches of chitlins, and to release oneself from Chine handcuffs—which are normally attached to one finger one hand and one finger of the other hand—one must n become impatient and excitable and thus pull harder. takes a cool, logical head, the ability to relax one's finger and to twist clockwise properly.

I got the end of the Chinese handcuffs that held Bing ham's finger and slowly directed it onto Jimmy Wingard

I said, "Here they come, man."

Comp nodded and smiled. He said, "I'm going to blast this music, and then you and I have to run out the back door there. We'll come up from behind like we were out with everybody all along. And that's what we'll say."

I said, "Okay." Bingham Bradham still slept with his finger attached like an umbilical cord to Jimmy Wingard's little penis.

Compton pushed the On switch, and we took off. The singer screamed out, "*I was a lonely man,*" just as we made our way out of the clubhouse.

We ran. We took off. Compton and I skirted the exterior of the clubhouse like two field rats running from a flashlight's beam. We giggled like little debutantes ourselves. And when we entered the front of the Forty-Five Country Club clubhouse, Comp stood taller than he'd ever stood, for his trick had worked. We watched as Jimmy Wingard and Bingham Bradham danced the waltz of conjoined twins, hunched over, chaotic, and helpless.

Compton slid through the crowd to get a better view. Me, I stood back. Libby Belcher stared, knowing I had had something to do with it. When she came up and slapped my face, I could only say, "Hey. Teach you to call me Menial." I said, "Shirley Ebo never hit me like that. And she's going to a real college year after next, too."

Libby said, "You're behind all of this, ain't you?" She became the district superintendent of schools twenty years later, which I love to point out now. Libby put her fists on her evening gown and said, "Somehow you turned it all around so's they drank the enema."

I shrugged. I looked at her daddy, who—and I'll give him this, lawyer or not—laughed at the two boys' awkward dance on the linoleum. I said, "Man. You should learn how to control who you invite to parties. I'm a little unnerved." Word for word—that's what I said. I wish I'd had a tape recorder to prove myself.

Dr. Scurry Bingham, who once told me I had gas when in actuality I had ripped a ligament in my side while lugging heart-pine lumber from point A to point B, said, "You boys just settle down. I'll call an ambulance." He looked at the people surrounding him and said, "I got connections, I got connections."

Jimmy Wingard tried to run and hide from everyone. Bingham Bradham tagged along right at his side, all hunkered down and sideways. No one realized that it would've only took someone with a steady hand and a sharp knife to release these two fuckups. I would've volunteered if I'd've had the gloves in my possession.

MY FATHER SAT up in his worn, green, pathetic cloth chair. After Compton and I left the pre-debutante party we drove around—as we were wont to do anyway—laughing about our little prank, as if it were the best thing this side of disposable lighters. Compton came inside with me to help me regale my father with our escapade.

We didn't get the homecoming we'd expected. After we told the story, my father sat up and said, "You should both be ashamed of yourselves. That's one of the worst things I've ever heard of."

In the previous dozen years or so I had witnessed my father gluing people's mailboxes so they wouldn't open, letting air out of their tires, placing fake auction notices in the newspaper so that strangers invaded an unsuspecting man's Saturday morning, and so on. I'd seen Comp's father do the same. My father had disguised his voice over the telephone daily one bleak winter and invited a hopeful cemetery-plot salesman over to all his enemies' houses.

I had sat in the den and listened back then: "Yeah, this is Gray Dunlap, and I'm wanting to talk to someone about getting an entire crypt for my family." My father would give the address of Mr. Dunlap's house, hang up, then look at me and say, "I wish I could be a sweat bee flying around when that guy shows up and says, 'Mr. Dunlap, I understand that you've finally come to grips with the inevitable.'"

My father knew the grave-plot seller's speech because one Saturday a year earlier—and for all I knew maybe Comp's father had sent the guy over as a practical joke—my father had listened to the pitch.

I pulled the Welch's jelly jar from Compton's borrowed coat pocket and said, "You want some rum, Daddy?"

He took it from me and set it on the end table. "You might be drinking too much. How're you going to concentrate in college, boy?" He looked at Compton. "Either one of you.

They ain't gone be booze at every corner of the dorm when y'all go off to college. Maybe y'all should try to wean your-selves over this next-to-last summer. Those smart college boys ain't gonna be too keen on your silly hoaxes. They won't fall for them, and they'll get even."

I'll give myself this: I never contradicted my father when I learned that he really didn't know about college. I never pointed out that, first off, there *was* booze at every corner of the dorm, and that supposedly smart college boys—especially the ones from up north—did indeed fall for such pranks.

Compton said to my father, "Maybe you're not getting a true visual of this situation. One end of the Chinese hand-cuffs was on Bingham Bradham's index finger, and the other was on Jimmy Wingard's tallywhacker, Mr. Dawes. They kept pulling and pulling it tighter."

My father struggled up, grabbed his cane, took my jelly jar, and drank what was left. He said, "How would you like it if those boys did that to you? Y'all would be scarred for life. You'd never be able to come back to Forty-Five for the rest of your days."

I didn't say, "I have no intention of coming back here again anyway." I didn't say how they typed up MENIAL for my name tag. I said, "I'm sorry. I thought you'd think this was funny."

"Well, maybe I would think it was funny if I could laugh without it killing my goddamn diaphragm." He held his floating ribs.

I looked at Comp. I'm not one of those people who says later on that he saw a death mask on someone else's face a day before that person died. But I foresaw the wrinkles and worry on Compton's face—though I couldn't know that he would eventually become a good veterinarian driven out of business down in Montgomery, Alabama, by a group of rabid right-to-life pinheads opposed to spaying God's creatures—and knew that he would end up in Forty-Five sad, puzzled, and alone. In that moment, too, I understood that I would be bringing a smart wife back home to Forty-Five, that she wouldn't be happy whatsoever, and that we would spend a year in my father's cement-block house trying to sell off what leftover heart-pine wood, what sunken signs, my father had made me gather and store, that she and I would dig holes forever to uncover those things my progenitor understood, rightly, as valuable.

I never foresaw the wild local curs giving up and settling down.

My father limped to the phone, dialed up the hospital, and directed his call to Herbert Coleman's room. I assume that Mr. Coleman answered, for my father said, "I got back home all right, and I remembered something I meant to tell you earlier." Then he began singing "I'll Fly Away."

I threw my car keys to Compton and told him to drive himself home, then come back and get me in the morning. I told him I would pay him cash money to help me take a slave cabin down the next day on the old, old, old Latham land my father'd bought up thirty days beforehand. Compton shrugged okay.

My father continued singing. I went back to my bedroom and pulled out the journal. I wrote down what splinters I'd pulled out before putting on my borrowed suit. And then, without knowing that I'd do it, I began writing about what had happened at the party, and everything—and I mean everything—that had led to that day, empty or not.

The fire-retarded, triple-lined, steel-enforced Maxi-Cure safe stood inside a square false ammo box, inside a false cupboard, beneath a fake floor, behind a faux closet behind my father's empty rifle cabinet in the hallway. I had looked in there before, when I felt sure that he would be gone for more than six hours. There were skeleton keys with which to deal, then regular keys, then suitcase keys. The safe's combination was "left to 36, right to 24, left to 34"—what my missing mother's measurements supposedly were. My father had never divulged these numbers, but it didn't take but a few times of my looking on the backs of picture frames, family photos, book jackets, and beneath brown eggs in the refrigerator's dairy section to figure out why that series meant so much to him. Normally I only found a bunch of papers that dealt with land transactions. Sometimes I found a lucky acorn or arrowhead, a thick piece of quartz, maybe a buffalo nickel.

"I want you to go into the hallway and move the gun cabinet off to the right," my father called to say one Saturday afternoon.

I had answered with, "Hey, Shirley, sweetie, what you want to do this fine day?" like an idiot, because my father had left a note saying he'd be gone until past supper, and Shirley Ebo had sent me a note during class the day before saying she wanted to either have me sit still for a couple hours so she could paint me for her art class, or go see a crazy, white, traveling tent-revival evangelist who could make people fall down at will.

My father said, "Well I might have the wrong number, son."

I about hung up. I should've hung up, and when he called back I could've said, "I've been here all day. I didn't just pick up the phone," et cetera. I said, "Hey, Dad. I thought you were going to be Shirley. I was playing."

"Listen. This is important." I heard cars or trucks driving by. "A while back I got a call saying my twenty acres over here in Slabtown is some kind of fire hazard. I want you to go to the safe and find what that old boy's name was wrote me that letter."

I still tried to think of excuses as to why I had called Shirley "sweetie." I said, "I'll have to put the phone down."

My father said, "Shirley Ebo your official girlfriend finally? I don't know what the people of Forty-Five will say about your white ass having a black girlfriend. But I ain't surprised in you, boy. Plums are good, but bruised plums make for better pudding."

I set the phone down. I could hear my father laughing,

then heard him say, "Hey, hey, hey! You got to listen to me on how to get here."

I picked up the phone. "She's not my girlfriend. We're taking that sociology course together. We got teamed up together and are supposed to act like husband and wife." This had actually happened. "We're supposed to act in ways that'll keep one of us from leaving the other, out of the blue." I knew that my father would change the subject when the notion of monogamy cropped up, or his mismanaged attempt toward it some decade earlier.

"You got to go beneath the house and get a crowbar, then crack open this place that looks like it got plain sealed up for good in the wall."

I didn't say that I knew already. I didn't say how I'd learned to patch drywall all by myself because of cracking— then resealing—his hidden, hidden, hidden, hidden safe. I listened like the good son. I went "Yessir" when he was done.

My father said, "It might take you thirty minutes." He went through where all of his odd keys hung. "The paper I want will say something about a fire hazard, and Slabtown. It should be near the top of the pile. The first four to ten envelopes is what I'm saying. I'll call back."

"Where are you now?"

My father said to someone walking by, "Hey, is it true that this is still a dry county?" To me, he said, "I'm here. Don't worry about where the hell I am. You worry about finding that fellow's number before I stick another dime plus more in this telephone."

I said, "Okay then," and hung up.

It didn't take the beneath-the-house-crowbar to open up the drywall seams, let me say right now. I had a flathead screwdriver I'd been using since about the age of twelve, plus the sharp edge of a putty knife. I pulled the gun cabinet aside and slit the drywall tape, pulled the door open, and so on. I got to the safe, opened it, and noticed a mesh bag of handmade marbles that moved when I pulled the door my way. I started opening envelopes, and more envelopes. I went four-to-ten-envelopes down.

When I found what my daddy wanted, I set it aside. What other documents did he hide? I wondered. Oh, I found all kinds of IOUs from Compton Lane's father, and Glenn Flack's, and Libby Belcher's, and even Forty-Five's ex-mayor Dash Mozingo. They ranged from two hundred to two thousand dollars, and were dated from before my birth in 1958 right on up until 1975. I found something like two dozen four-leaf clovers, all laminated singly. My father had saved cocktail napkins from far-off places like Charlotte, Charleston, Atlanta, and a joint called the Wicked Witch in Greenville, up sixty miles north on Highway 25. He had an Esso map of the eastern United States with a thick pen mark showing the closest routes between Forty-Five and Nashville, and Memphis, and New Orleans. I found what I thought were my old dog's toenails in an envelope, what I thought were my baby teeth in an amber druggist's vial, and a rubber change purse with what I understood to be two gold fillings that had once resided in the mouth of a man my father punched out, seeing as Dad had written, "I guess this makes us even" on the outside.

There may have been other little gimcracks and trinkets, I don't remember. I dove my hand down six inches and pulled out one thin sheet of paper. It happened to be my birth certificate. I looked and saw my mother's name, that I was twenty-two inches long, that I weighed an amazing nine pounds and fourteen ounces. The doctor's name was Wilson.

My father, the document read, was unknown.

When the telephone rang and I picked it up in the den, my father said, "Did you find that letter?"

I said, "Oh I got it, man. I got it."

He said, "Have you been drinking?"

I heard more cars driving by on his end of the line. "No sir."

"Hey, is there any way you can bring that over here? I might need the pickup in case I have to haul something away. Do you know where I am in Slabtown? I'm at the intersection, you know. We've been here before. In front of the Slabtown Diner on the corner of 86 and 135. It might take you an hour."

I said, "What? I don't know, Dad. Shirley's supposed to come over here because the time's right for us to make a baby. What? What?" Then I laughed and laughed, and thought about my father's brown eyes, a face that wasn't close to mine, his nonchin. My mother had been gone so long that I didn't even remember what she looked like. I said, "I can drive your pickup."

Again my father asked somebody near his pay phone if it was a dry county, like he didn't already know every inch of South Carolina's Blue Laws, from Myrtle Beach to Caesar's Head. I'd seen him ask this question a thousand times before, and realized that he was only waiting for some stranger to tell him where a bootlegger lived.

I left the secret door to the secret cabinet to the secret safe in the false floor wide open, though I folded my birth certificate in half and shoved it into my back pocket. I took Highway 25 north toward Slabtown, driving with my right wrist draped across the steering wheel in the manner of my father—I even thought about how he drove thusly, how it must've been genetic. I didn't stop at Rufus Price's Goat Wagon for an eight-pack of Miller ponies or a mason jar of homemade peach bounce, should my father never learn Slabtown's local laws. I drove the speed limit, veered from potholes, and tried to find a radio station that didn't play country music.

"We have a prayer request for a nearsighted husband who keeps missing things by about two inches," this radio preacher said on one of the AM stations. "We have a prayer request for a sister who has too much love. We have a request for a son who takes to the drink." The background music wasn't any different from that played during a viewing. "We have a request for a boy who don't treat his parents right."

The letter from one volunteer fire chief, William G. Franklin, set opened on the bench seat. My birth certificate about burned a hole in my pocket. I sat up, pulled it from my backside, and reread, "Father Unknown." How could I bring this question up to my father? Would I? Did it matter whatsoever that I might not know my own people?

"We have a request to pray for a man who has cancer of the eye. We have a request for a man who has cancer of the foot." The background organ seemed stuck. "A good daughter has asked that we pray for her father's missing fingers after a chain-saw accident. We have a prayer request from a wife who can no longer tell taste. She asks the Lord to let her know the difference between salt and pepper."

I turned the radio off. My father's pickup truck hummed and hummed up the road. I found myself singing Merle Haggard songs, though I didn't like or understand him at the time, though I wasn't quite sure about the true lyrics.

I PULLED INTO the Slabtown Diner's gravel parking lot and, as a joke, gunned the truck toward my father. He leaned hard against our old Ford Galaxie's hood, and didn't move even when it looked like I meant business. I screeched to a halt, got out, and went for my father's neck, half-joking. My father didn't move. Had he known that I would find my birth certificate? Was this his way of letting me understand how maybe I wasn't as smart as I thought?

"It ain't a dry county, or a dry township," he said. "In case you were wondering. Hey, did you bring that letter?"

I pointed my thumb toward the pickup. My father reached behind himself and grabbed a pint of Jim Beam. "You want you a swig? You old enough still."

I shook my head no. "Come on," I said.

He tensed his lips, then said, "I'll leave the car here. Hand me the keys. I think I remember where this land I bought might be."

"Hadn't you better call this William G. Franklin man? There's not going to be a pay phone out in the middle of nowhere, likely."

My father pointed at me and raised his eyebrows. He smiled. "I knew there was a reason why I wanted to have you as a son. You're pretty smart. One time this old boy said you smelled, and I said, 'Like shit he does.'"

"That joke's getting old, Dad."

My father took the keys from my right hand. He got in the pickup, I got in the passenger side, and he said, "You want an old joke, call up your mother."

Here's the law in South Carolina: If someone's squatting on your land, and if said person has planted a crop, nothing can be done about it if the crop stands half-past harvesting. If someone takes over land you own and sets out corn, and the corn gets to three feet high, then the true owner of the land can't do anything about it. If he does go back and, say, burns down the crop, then he can be sued by the squatter. It goes all the way back to Civil War times. It goes back to Job, or at least when some Mormons traipsed through the region on their way to Utah, my father said.

This all came into play when my father and I met William G. Franklin at some mostly useless flat acreage somewhere between the Chattahoochee and Savannah rivers, a place that—in my later life—my father would sell for something like a million-times profit to California land developers who planned and built a townhouse and golf course retirement community that also had its own airstrip. Dad shook Mr. Franklin's hand, pointed to the middle of his plot, and said, "That ain't my snail-back trailer," which stood amid pole beans, tomatoes, and watermelons. Marigolds appeared to be planted randomly.

Mr. Franklin stood tall. He wore both plaid pants and shirt, plus red suspenders. His hair stood straight up in what would later on be a good punk style. Although he didn't chew tobacco at the time, he owned two good juice gutters that framed his pointed chin. Mr. Franklin stared at me as if I had something to do with the situation. "I've seen this once before," he said. He leaned one hand on his own truck, a Chevy.

I said, "Well. My name's Mendal. I'm his son." My father looked out at the trailer. There seemed to be no sign of life there. Whoever owned the place didn't have a car parked in the middle of the field, and there were no tire tracks going that way. The three of us stood on the berm looking west, the sun in our eyes.

Mr. Franklin scratched his crotch. "Them fields seem more'n half-past ready."

"How and why is this a fire hazard?" my father asked. "There's something wrong going on here, but I don't see the fire hazard. Fire hazard's when you got a big old tank of kerosene next to an open fire."

I kind of wanted to pull the pint of bourbon from my father's back pocket. I kind of wanted to drive back to the Slabtown Diner, get on the pay phone, and ask Shirley Ebo to meet me at the tent revival. "Let's go down there and knock on the door, y'all," I said. It didn't seem like brain surgery.

Mr. Franklin pulled a pistol out of his boot. He said, "I think it's the only thing we can do." He looked at me, but spoke to my father. "If some shooting goes on, can we count on the boy to keep quiet?"

Dad looked at the snail-back. "Can you keep quiet? You got it in you to be quiet should something bad happen?"

I said, "Me? I wouldn't wonder about me. Do you?" I thought about taking my birth certificate out of my pocket, and would have done so hadn't Mr. William G. Franklin stood there all staring down at me. I said, "I'll be quiet. In case we have to kill a man and stuff him in a freezer or something, bury him out in the front yard."

"We won't have none of that," Mr. Franklin said. "But I might have to call Larry for some help. He's another volunteer fireman. He's a good one. And to be honest, sometimes he's a little more rational than I am. Larry. Larry."

We walked down through tomato plants that had recently sprung green fruit no larger than jawbreakers. There were an inordinate number of spiderwebs connecting these plants. We passed the tomatoes, then the newly tendriled watermelons, then the pole beans. Mr. Franklin held his pistol in his right hand, knocked with his left a good hard five times. All of us heard a woman singsong out, "Hold on one second," and then the trailer's small aluminum door swung open.

"Oh, hey! It's about time," this wondrous woman said. She wore a sundress with spaghetti straps. Her black hair flowed in curls that seemed to spell out "beauty/beauty/beauty" in cursive. I had never seen such a vision, and I knew that my father and Mr. Franklin hadn't either, seeing as my dad's knees actually buckled, and William G. Franklin dropped his pistol right there in the dirt. "I take it y'all are from the extension service."

My father smiled and shook his head sideways. "Do you want some bourbon?" He spoke so slowly that it sounded like a 45-rpm record set on 33.

The woman stepped down the twelve inches from her trailer. "I'm afraid there won't be room for all of us inside. My name's Eva Laws. Come on this way and I'll show you what I'm talking about." For a second I thought she introduced herself as "Evil Laws," for what it's worth.

She jumped down from her trailer and didn't turn around. Mr. Franklin reached down and picked up his pistol. Eva yelled over her shoulder, "In all my years working experimental crops, I've seen nothing like this." She swished her rear end in a perfectly natural manner.

Some years later I would think that the only fire hazard present on my dad's property might have been him, the volunteer fireman, or me spontaneously combusting from Evil Laws.

About a hundred yards into the walk with Eva I noticed how writing spiders took up most of the space between the tomatoes. I'd learned early on that if you found your name in a writing spider's web, death was on its way down from above. The chances of a spider spinning out "Mendal" were pretty slim, but I swore I saw "Lee"—my father's name— more than once.

Eva stopped finally, and William G. Franklin said, "I think you have us confused with some other people. I'm the fire chief in Slabtown. This here's the man who owns the land. I sent him a letter a while back saying he had a fire hazard."

I said, "I'm his son!" like that, all excited, idiotic. My voice actually cracked in the middle of yelling out. I didn't think about my fake sociological marriage to Shirley Ebo, or how I couldn't tell whether my biological father was a madman or saint.

Eva turned and said, "Oh. Oh, I'm sorry. I thought y'all were from the extension service. I think I've come across an as-yet-to-be-discovered insect, and I wanted to bring some-one down here. It looks like a praying mantis and a wolf spi-der got together somehow."

"Like I was saying, we come out here for the hazard," the fire chief said.

I couldn't stop staring at this Eva woman. I daydreamed about moving into the trailer with her, about fixing her break-fast each morning, about going out at daybreak to pick fruits and vegetables. She said, "My area of expertise is organic gardening. I don't use pesticides."

I said, "That's good. I've been reading up on that lately." My father grabbed my shoulder and pulled me behind him, out of the woman's view.

"WHAT HAPPENED WAS this," Mr. William G. Franklin said. "I happened by one afternoon, and the sun beat down on your silver trailer, and a big glare shot off that way." He pointed with a wave of his hand toward the pole beans. "I figured that it might be like holding a magnifying glass down toward dry grass, you know. That they was a chance the hot glare reflection could catch a leaf on fire, and then the whole place would go up."

We stood in front of Eva's abode. My father said, "That ain't gone happen, Franklin. What are the chances of that happening?"

I couldn't help but stare at the woman. She said, "If I'd've known about that, I would've pitched a tent out here. And the whole reason why I'm here is because my professor told me that this land was owned by the university. I'm sorry. I'll be leaving tomorrow."

I said, "No, no, no," as if I were in control. My father looked at me, but the fire chief didn't.

"You put a tarp on top your trailer, I think we'll be fine," the fire chief said.

"Yeah," my father said. "I got a couple extras back home. I'll bring them over tomorrow. What, again, are you doing here, though?"

Eva went into some long-winded discouse about how she planted her crops and marigolds in purposeful patterns. She said something about how tomatoes attract aphids, that aphids attract praying mantises, and that any spider with a mantis in its web is a contented spider. Eva said that if we viewed the field from above, we would see that she had tomatoes encircled by pole beans, encircled by watermelons. We would see other areas where marigolds stood in the center, followed by watermelons, then pole beans, then tomatoes. Oh, she went through every possible configuration, and I thought about this woman later on in college when I was forced to take a mathematics course involving statistics and probability. She finished up with, "You fellows want any coffee, or some iced tea? I feel badly that you came all the way out here."

My father reached in his back pocket and pulled out his half-gone pint. He said, "I don't reckon."

William G. Franklin said, "No ma'am. I guess we're done here if you promise to cover your shiny edges with them tarps." He backed up, then turned toward the road. "I need to get back to my real job. This is done business. If anyone needs some cabinet work, come see me. That's what I try to do when I ain't out looking for glares."

I would later know that my father wanted me out of there, that he wanted to talk to this Eva Laws scientist all alone. But at the time I could only say, "I've always had a fascination with scientists. With science. I might go study up on some science when I go to college. I'm thinking about being a vegetarian."

My father could say nothing. He looked at Eva, and then she said, "I came from a whole series of scientists, in their own ways. My mother dropped out of college to marry my father back in Chicago. My father's father was a carpenter, and my father ended up working for General Motors. But my mother always concocted home cold remedies and household cleaning products. My mother's brother ended up working in the nuclear power industry, and my father's sister and her husband raised milk cows up in Wisconsin. I have a cousin who invented a better milking machine. They send me cheese hoops every Christmas, and I send them canned vegetables."

Here's what my father got out: "So you're not from

around here, are you?" And it was at this point that I understood how my mother, more than likely, got knocked up by some stranger, that I got born, and then my father married Mom out of pity, duty, or some kind of unresolved guilt.

Eva pulled her head back and laughed. "I've been down south now for six years. I guess if I live to be a hundred I still won't be from around here."

I wanted to belt out, "Me either!" and take my birth certificate out, maybe explain how my biological father might've been a northern salesman, or a midwestern soldier. I said, "What's your last name again?"

"It's Laws. I'm legal." She laughed.

Again I thought, Evil Laws. My father said, "Well, we better be going. I'll drop by tomorrow with the tarps. Maybe I can work out some kind of lease agreement with your people at the university for next year, you know. I hope you find out what you want to learn, whatever it is you want to learn."

Eva Laws said, "I do, too. I'm small-time, but in the long run I'm thinking what experiments I'm doing might help us all be healthier."

My father took the back of my neck and led us to the truck.

At the Slabtown Diner I opened the passenger-side door and got out before my father had stopped completely. He put the truck in neutral and got out. "I'll meet you at home," he said. "Maybe tonight we can go down to Forty-Five Barbecue and get us some ribs."

I said, "Okay," though I really wanted Shirley Ebo to come over so I could show her my birth certificate.

"All right. I'll be right behind you."

I took off before checking if my father had accidentally left his lights on, or his door open, if his battery had worn down. But I didn't burn rubber out of the gravel parking lot. There was a straightaway down Highway 135, enough for me to look in the rearview mirror and see my father turn the other way, back toward Eva Laws's snail-back trailer.

I swerved into a pebbled asphalt entrance and turned around. I thought about going back to my father's land, but pulled into the diner's lot and went inside. This joint had about a dozen booths, maybe four six-top tables, and a counter overlooking the parking lot. I looked eighteen, I knew, even though I wasn't but seventeen and a half. I said, "I'll have a PBR, please," to a woman who might've been twenty or forty.

"You look like the kind of man who wants to run a tab."

I looked around the room. "How in the world did this place get called Slabtown? Is there a cement factory nearby?" Oh, I was as worldly as they come. I was weary, too. I had my birth certificate in my back pocket. It would've been a good time to bring either Nietzsche or Schopenhauer up in conversation, I thought. "My father owns some land down the road that way," I said pointing. "Some crazy woman's squatting on his land."

The waitress slid my beer bottle six inches my way. "I don't know how it got named," she said. "It's Slabtown. I guess whoever got here first thought it looked like a big old slab. It ain't that flat, though. Maybe from above it looked like a slab of bacon."

I drank from my beer and looked out the window. "I just met that woman, and she said I needed to look at the land from above."

"That might be the only way to look at things," the waitress said. "I've been stuck here all my life and only seen things ground level."

My father didn't drive by within the hour. The waitress's name was Betty. She came around and sat beside me between my first and second beer. Betty asked if I drove an eighteen-wheeler. I started to lie, but could tell that she wanted a ride out of Slabtown. I shook my head no. She asked if I'd like a sandwich, on the house.

"Sooner or later this area will be worth some money," I said. "Don't ask how I know, but I know. Sooner or later these land developers will come through here and make it a regular paradise. You'll be sitting pretty. If there's any way for you to buy up some land, do so now. I can't give you the details."

Betty put her arm through mine and leaned in. She said,

"I don't live far from here. What's your name again? I'm glad I found you before any of the other girls did."

I don't want to sound like I was cool, that I wasn't scared. I said, "I need to wait to find out what my father might or might not do."

Betty said, "Oh, *now* I know that woman you're talking about. She's raising praying mantises. You know what a female praying mantis does to its mate, don't you?" Betty held her drawn-on eyebrows high, as if she'd explained one of the wonders of the world. She took her arm out of mine, said, "That'll be two dollars on your beers," and got up. She went back around the counter. Betty shook her fanny not unlike Eva Laws. "I take it you ain't man enough to want anything else."

I pulled out three one-dollar bills and set them on the counter. I pulled my birth certificate out and set it down beside the money, all melodramatic, I realized much later. Betty didn't say, "Thanks." She went over to another man wearing all plaid. I unfolded the certificate, took some sugar packets off the counter, and arranged them so only "Father Unknown" showed.

My daddy drove by at eighty miles an hour soon thereafter. Or at least the Galaxie went by. I assumed that he was bending down for a cigarette on the floorboard, or his bottle. I didn't see his head or shoulders anywhere near the steering column. I watched his Galaxie fly by and wondered what that scientist woman Eva Laws had said to him that would make him drive by so quickly. Did she remind him that he had a boy back home to tend? Did she rebuff him in such a way that caused a guilt he had not felt since marrying my mother? Or was she in that front bench seat, too, splayed out, dreaming of what symbiotic affairs might occur outside of aphids, mantises, and spiders?

I knew that I'd get home after my father. I would lie and say how I had stopped by Shirley Ebo's house, that we had homework. I would say that her own father had cleared the dining room table so we could spread our papers around, so that we could have space in order to find ways to tell our teacher how much our fake marriage worked. I would tell my father how Shirley and I made up some things involving gardening, and how important it was for us to know what seeds we planted came up healthy and unaffected by outside influences or troubles beyond our control.

Even Curs Hate Fruitcake

Whenever I retreat to wonderment at how my life turned to one of hoardment and obsession, I stop at the memory of a muggy June night. I found myself inside a smoke- and curse-filled beer joint on Highway 301 near the Fruitcake Capital of the World. I bent over to pick up a fallen blue cube of Silver Cup cue-stick chalk, reached over to set it on one of two pool tables, then became startled by an overall-wearing mountain man—his gray beard as windblown as John Brown's—who yelled at me, pointed toward my hand, and asked if I got Stonewall Jackson or John the Baptist. That particular night, not two weeks after I'd graduated from high school, I ran through every reason to make my answer one man of history or the other.

"Don't rub it up, goddamn. *Look* at it. Whichen is it?" the man said. He leaned on a house cue stick so warped it could've been used as a bow. I saw a knife blade *spack* glare from his other hand.

I said, "I don't know." I looked down to see a perfectly

carved visage on one side of the chalk. "Yeah, it's one or the other. But I'm not so sure I'd know Stonewall Jackson or John the Baptist if they both walked in the door."

This old man jerked his head once and held out the hand with his knife in it. I handed over the chalk. Two men from a fruitcake company—they wore work shirts with various candied ingredients sewn above their pockets—started a game of eight ball. The one who broke barely made the rack move, as if he was challenging Newton's action and reaction theory.

"It's one or the other, I believe, but I can't remember. And I carved the son-bitch," the man said. "Goddamn it to hell, I'mo have to get my book out again and see who this looks like. I got a book I keep at home. It's got famous people's pictures in it. Everything I carve ends up looking like somebody, somewhere." He handed the miniature near-bust back. "You figure it out and let me know."

Then he walked out. When he got to the door, without turning around, he yelled out, "If Stonewall Jackson and John the Baptist came in this bar alive and you couldn't tell the difference, I feel sorry for you, boy. One would be a-rolling and one would be a-strolling."

I had my back to the two pool players. One of them said, "I bet Brother Macon's on his way to the schoolhouse. They already told him he couldn't steal they chalk no more."

I went over to the four-stool bar and ordered a beer from a woman who wore the expression of a Rose of Sharon bud about to blossom. "You a buyer?" she asked me.

I said, "No, ma'am. My last name's Dawes."

"Huh," she said. "That's not what I ast you, but that's aw-ight."

MY NEW BOSS, Marcel Parsell, suggested that I start in Claxton, move my way north to Tallulah Falls, Georgia, then drive east to Chimney Rock, North Carolina, south to Denmark, South Carolina, then back west. He said I could then go inward, always traveling clockwise in a smaller and smaller circle. This was my first real, not-gotten-by-my-father job. I was working for a disgruntled ex-editor of Fodor's travel guides who wanted to put out a book about places in the United States to avoid completely. From what I had gathered, from this year onward he would hire fifty or sixty new high-school graduates every June to write sarcastic thousand-words-or-less articles about towns that offered no real cultural, artistic, or dining experiences. It was supposed to look like we'd gotten a scholarship, I guess. "A book like this will make everyone in bigger cities feel better about themselves and their lives. Plus, this idea has trade paperback best-seller written all over it, from here on out."

I had answered an ad that read, "Like to travel for money?" Imagine that. How come my high-school counselor never veered me toward a class in economics or ethics or logic, or ever took one herself?

I said to the bartendress, "I'm here because I'm writing a book on little-known places you might want to visit." I didn't want to end up being lynched for making fun of whatever slight populace inhabited places like Claxton, Georgia. And, since I hadn't taken that ethics course at Forty-Five High, I felt no remorse about lying outright.

Marcel Parsell—who had studied both geography and culinary arts—told my new colleagues and me that, just as it was okay to exaggerate how wonderful a city might appear, it was all right to exaggerate its limitations. "A local roadside diner that brags on its pork-flavored ice cream isn't a bad thing for our purposes," he said. I took notes.

"That man gave you piece chalk ain't like our regular people around here," the barmaid said. "Don't judge Claxton or its peoples from crazy Brother Macon. He says God told him to carve what he could into people God blessed before. He chose chalk 'cause it's made down in Macon. He seen a reason and connection."

I said, "I won't judge y'all by one man's vision."

"Hey!" she yelled. "This boy here's writing a book about us!"

At first I thought I'd've been better off only skimming the outskirts of all my tiny prearranged towns, that I should've been objective while detailing odd Catfish or Bucktooth festivals. Marcel Parsell handed all of us a ten-point dos-and-don'ts bulletin that included not falling in love with a local and not believing mayors.

I got paid fifty dollars for every article that made it into a book that ended up being called *Wish You Weren't Here*.

I got paid five bucks for the towns Marcel Parsell decided against. This was 1976. I had no clue about money and saw myself getting about three grand over a two-month period, then moving on to work for the South American, European, and Australian versions of the same book, working college summers. It didn't occur to me that if fifty travel writers each got fifty thousand-word essays published, the book might be a little on the thick side. I didn't realize that staying in twelve-dollar-a-night motels went way beyond extravagant, that maybe I should've considered KOA campgrounds or the backseat of my old Jeep at roadside rest areas.

I never got the chance. What I learned immediately in Claxton—the Fruitcake Capital of the World—was that there were citizens who would pay decent money to have their place sound utopian, and just as many people who would offer favors to keep strangers away.

"Oh, I'll tell you all you fucking want to know about a place people elsewhere think we make fruitcakes for doorstops," one of the pool players said.

"No, no," said his opponent. "This is a good place to raise children. Come talk to me about here."

Not that this has anything to do with my story, but over the years I've learned that any human who brags about his or her town being a good place to raise kids only says so because that particular town has no art museum that kids might beg their parents to visit. There's no theater without the word LITTLE on the sign. The horrendous school system doesn't offer after-school field trips and activities outside of dollar-admission sporting events. Nothing dangerous exists that might cause parents to *think* and *act* in these places. I was brought up in the town of Forty-Five, South Carolina, by God—the Raise Children Here Capital of the World.

Maybe my future background in anthropology jaded me, though.

I stood in the Rack Me roadhouse bar and fingered my carved cube of chalk. I didn't mention how I wasn't really writing a book solely on the Fruitcake Capital but tried to emit an air that, at any moment, I might change my mind and load up the Jeep, find some people to talk to in the Pecan Roll Capital of the World.

The barmaid opened a drawer beneath the cash register and handed me a dozen carved blue pieces of Brother Macon's chalk. The best one looked like Mount Rushmore on all sides and the bottom. The worst might've been one of those famous pirates, or a Cyclops, or James Joyce.

LOOKIT: THE AD WENT, "Do you want to make money and travel?" Then there was a non-1-800 number to call for a preliminary interview. For all I know, everyone who called made it through the first hurdle. I was asked to send a biographical essay, a descriptive essay about my hometown, an argumentative essay concerning my views on cats versus dogs, and a comparison/contrast essay about any two fast-food chains. I almost told the truth about myself, Forty-Five, and dogs because I got kind of tired of the whole process. My final essay went, "I only know diners and home-cooked meals built over a fire out back. I'm from a town called Forty-Five, named after a piece of vinyl that revolves second-fastest." The stuff about my place of training wasn't all true, of course, but I feel certain now that it got me the job.

I didn't tell Marcel Parsell any of the other theories, of course, dealing with community theaters and art museums or the lack thereof. He called me, went over the payment situation, and said I could start immediately. He sent his ten dos and don'ts—my favorite, rule number nine, went, "Never let them see you spit out food"—and I drove to Claxton with a suitcase, some Mead composition notebooks, a cheap handheld tape recorder, and a camera.

I returned from Rack Me to my motel outside Claxton, a little L-shaped place called the Fall Inn. It advertised free TV, radio, and telephone. The dozen doors to the place were each painted a different pastel shade, which I learned later was symbolic of the different colored candies in a five-pound fruitcake.

I wasn't in the room five minutes on my first night when the phone rang. I expected my dad, or my imaginary girlfriend checking up on me, or Marcel Parsell wanting to offer congratulations on my first day at *Wish You Weren't Here*. I cleared my throat and said, "Mendal Dawes," all professional, like I had seen Frank Sinatra do in a 1950s movie that showed up at the Forty-Five Drive-In Theatre in 1972 or thereabouts.

It was the desk clerk. She said, "I'm calling to see if there's anything you need, hon."

When I checked in, she'd not spoken at all, just taken my cash money and handed me a crude flyer explaining check-out time and how I shouldn't leave lights or the TV on unnecessarily. The woman looked to be my age, and held her face in a way that told me she didn't hold fruitcake-working people in the highest regard. I said, "I'm fine."

"This is Cammie at the front desk."

I said, "Yeah."

"You sure you don't need anything? It's free. Soap, towels, a big old bucket of ice." She paused and lowered her voice. "You know. Anything you want."

It's hard to be a man and admit that I didn't recognize nuance at the age of eighteen. I said, "I wouldn't mind a beer, I guess, but y'all don't sell them in the Coke machine and the only store I've seen out this way won't open until morning." I took all of Brother Macon's carved cue chalks out of my pants pockets and lined them up around the rotary telephone. One of them looked exactly like Cammie—at least how I remembered her, all slack-jawed and blank-faced at check-in time. It might not have been carved at all, I thought. Or maybe Brother Macon had carved a *Night of the Living Dead* character, I don't know.

Cammie said in a drawl that could come only out of a southern, southern woman with a mouth full of honey, "Beer. Well, at least that's a start," and hung up.

The television received two channels. One showed the local news. Before I finished watching a piece with Claxton's mayor explaining why the jail needed two more cells added on, Cammie let herself in with a passkey. She carried two quart bottles of Schlitz under one arm, and held an ice bucket. I said, "Okay. All right. Come on in. Make yourself at home and tell me all about your lovely hometown."

She set everything down on a chair. "So word is you're the famous man come down here to write about all us. Call me patriotic, but I want you to know what a friendly place we got." She took out a church key and opened one bottle. "Don't think we're only fruitcakes here. They's much more to offer for fun."

I got off the bed and found two wax-paper-wrapped drinking glasses from the bathroom. I called out, "Oh, I know that. I'm only supposed to find places like this that're misunderstood."

I don't want to come across as crude or insensitive—and I need to make a point that I didn't instigate what occurred soon thereafter. The only other thing I remember Cammie telling me was, "We have field days all the time down at the rec center. It's a great place to raise children. I won the sack race one time. Back then I still went by my given name, Camellia. My momma let me change it when I turned old enough."

I'm pretty sure that's what she announced. I wanted to call up my father and tell him what I went through on my first real job. I wanted to say a bunch of things concerning the life of an artiste.

I focused on the television, though. The local weatherman said it would be another hot and humid day.

MAYBE 1976 CLAXTON ran similarly to those backwards southern TV-sitcom towns where everyone eavesdrops on party lines, I don't know. But on my second day of full-time work I drove into town and hadn't gotten even close to the chamber of commerce office before I was stopped by people from all walks of life eager to exaggerate their hometown's worth and/or drawbacks. I couldn't figure it out, unless when Cammie left my motel room by midnight she'd called her best friend or mother and had her information stolen by half of the population. A woman at the drugstore, where I went to buy batteries for the tape recorder and headache powders for my hangover, said, "I can tell you that we have the clearest water between the Mississippi River and Richmond, Virginia, at least."

Out on the sidewalk, a Lion's Club member selling straw brooms said, "I've lived all over the place: Savannah, Atlanta, Chattanooga, Talladega. Not one of my neighbors in any of those cities ever asked me and the wife over for a barbecue supper. Here in Claxton, it happens almost every night. You got any children, son?"

I smiled and shook hands with complete strangers and nodded. A woman from Claxton Flowers ran out of her shop and gave me a boutonniere. A man from Claxton Gulf went out of his way to offer a free oil change and tire rotation. A cop came out of nowhere and handed me two complimentary tickets to the Claxton Policeman's Ball, which turned out to be a square dance held at the VFW.

I got stopped by a man and woman in front of what appeared to be a vacant theater of sorts. Both of them wore Bobby Jones alpaca golf sweaters, and they shifted their weights from leg to leg. I slowed down. "We want you to know that people have come out of here and done good for themselves," the woman said.

"Grainger Koon's in the movies. He's got a list of credits longer than our telephone directory. He played Crazy Customer in one movie," the woman said. "He's played Man at Bar, Man on Bench, Man without Glasses, and Man with Goat—all in the same year. I forget what movies, though. What were some of the titles, LaFoy?"

"I don't recall either," LaFoy said to me. "But you'd know him if you saw him. He's got a good face. He played Man Who Falls off Dock in one of those teen movies. Me and Peggy here, we both taught him singing and dancing lessons. At the rec center. Grainger was in a *Munsters* episode, too."

"It's a good place to raise children," Peggy said.

"That's what I understand," I said, but didn't go into my theory about people who make such claims.

I walked and waved like a returning hero, or at least like a celebrity who had returned home after appearing as Scary Man in Park. I picked litter off of the sidewalk and carried it down Main Street until I found a receptacle. The hardware-store man came outside and handed me two complimentary yardsticks, and a beautician offered me a haircut. I could only wonder what these people would do should a rock star or visiting dignitary happen by. I kind of stood in front of the local bank, waiting for a teller to come out with a bag of unmarked currency.

And it was in front of the bank that a woman pulled her 1976 Pinto into a parking space and wiggled her finger for me to heed. I leaned down to the closed passenger window and heard her say, "Get in."

I did, what the hell.

Her name was Lulinda. She worked at the fruitcake factory, but her husband drove an eighteen-wheeler coast-to-coast. "I heard that you were in town, and I thought you might want to know what most people down here won't offer up."

I said, "Okay. I appreciate that." What could I say? She wore a polka-dotted cotton dress, the hem of which might've come down to her knees had she not hiked it up past midthigh.

She introduced herself and drove in the direction of my motel room. That's where I figured we were going. I kind of wished that I had more than one old high-school friend to tell all of these stories about Claxton women.

"We won't keep you long, but we wanted to make sure you knew why no one should visit here, among other things."

I caught the "we." I tried to remember if, in the movies, hostages opened a moving vehicle's passenger door and tried to run, or if they covered their heads and rolled like crazy. I said, "I can't be gone too long. The mayor's expecting me. And the police chief," which wasn't true. I wondered what I should do with the yardsticks I had leaned against my right side. I glanced over at Lulinda's panties more than once.

We passed the Fall Inn and ended up at Rack Me. The parking lot was full. Lulinda said, "They ain't nothing to worry about. You ain't gone get hurt none," and smiled. She parked a distance from any of the pickup trucks and said, "I don't want anyone backing up into my car and exploding it."

I carried the yardsticks inside but left the boutonniere on Lulinda's cracked dashboard. I went over kung-fu moves in my mind, how to deflect pool cues with my own two weapons. At the door of Rack Me the only thing I thought about was how difficult it would be to keep my Claxton, Georgia—Fruitcake Capital of the World—essay down to a thousand words.

Brother Macon stood at the bar, across from the barmaid I'd met the night before. The same two pool players were there, too, along with a group of a half-dozen men wearing blue jean jackets. Brother Macon tossed me a cue-stick chalk and said, "This is for you, son. It's Marco Polo. He traveled around writing about places, too."

"It ain't too early for you to join us in a beer, is it?" one man said. He reached over the counter and pulled a can of PBR from the cooler. "My name's Gerald. Just like our president."

I said, "No sir."

Lulinda went back to the door and locked it. I could feel my knees shaking, just like any other normal cartoon character. My palms sweat so badly I went ahead and leaned the yardsticks against a barstool.

"You can't write no story about us, saying how Claxton would be a perfect place to bring the family on summertime vacations," another man said. He took the can of beer, opened the pop-top, and handed it to me. "We'd rather not go into detail, so let's just leave it at that."

Lulinda said, "It has to do with things changing, and things staying the same, and things changing. And then staying the same."

I put Marco Polo in my shirt pocket. Brother Macon said, "To be honest, I want people showing up to buy my carved works of God. But these old boys talked me into it, too. I got to go with the flow, you know. It's a democracy."

"Here." Gerald reached back into the cooler and pulled out a grocery bag. "You take this as a gift from us, and go off to somewhere else and forget that you ever come here." Gerald's hair stood up two perfect inches. One of his eyes seemed misplaced.

"Oh, you'll forget," someone said, and everyone started laughing.

I opened the top of the bag to find a good four or five pounds of thick buds I'd only seen on the national news. Brother Macon, already carving another piece of blue chalk, said, "They's certain parks and public properties we don't need people discovering, or trampling all over, you know what I mean. The way things are now, we ain't got nobody bothering us. Everybody thinks we just simple fruitcake-baking peoples. And they can keep that thought."

"It's not easy paying bills on what the fruitcake company pays out. All of us had to find other measures," Gerald said. "Now, if you'd prefer not to drive around with an illegal substance in your Jeep, Lulinda here has permission from her husband to buy it all back. We normally get thirty dollars an ounce for this stuff. Shit, it's so good we got people down in Mexico and South America buying from *us*."

I'd never heard of marijuana going for more than five dollars a nickel bag. This was a time before sinsemilla, or whatever cross-pollinations got developed out in northern California. I said, "Well. Hmm. Is there any way I could maybe keep a couple ounces, you know, and sell some of this back to y'all?"

The barmaid—wearing a bowling shirt this morning, but I doubted that her name was Cecil—said, "Let me tell him about the fingers, let me tell him about the fingers."

Gerald said, "I'm figuring there's two grand in that bag. You keep you a handful, and we'll still give you two grand. And then you leave us alone. Leave us out of the book. We'll run you down and find you, otherwise." He got off his barstool, pulled out his thick wallet, and extracted twenty hundred-dollar bills.

"Hey," Cecil yelled from her spot behind the bar. "Somewhere in America they's fruitcakes on the shelf with human fingers stuck inside from when LeRoy McDowell had his accident."

"There's worse than fingers," someone else said. "Don't forget about when Lulinda's brother's sister-in-law took that knife to her sleeping husband. Oh, she went into work that next morning and they never did find that old boy's manhood."

The jukebox came on without anyone that I saw putting in a quarter. Merle Haggard sang. I yelled out the only thing that seemed proper at the time, namely, "Drinks on me!" like a pardoned fool.

To be honest, I don't remember my return to the Fall Inn. I awoke in darkness, though, because Cammie banged on my door. I looked through the peephole to see her sporting a tiara and sash that read LITTLE MISS FRUIT-CAKE 1970. She was holding a baton.

I opened the door and said, "Hey," wondering if she could smell what pot still hung in my clothes.

"It's your lucky day!" she singsonged out in a drawl. "You're officially our only lodger left. Are you hungry?"

I stepped back to let her in. "It looks like I won't be staying here much longer, either. I might be leaving in the morning."

Cammie didn't enter. She looked to the side, waved her arm, and the same woman who had offered me a free haircut pushed a hand truck of boxed fruitcakes my way. "Mendal's cool," Cammie said.

The beautician said, "I still owe you the haircut if you want one and got the time. Or a full-body massage."

I had put my hush money in every single page of Revelation in the Gideon Bible. I remembered that much. Cammie said, "Open up your fruitcakes, open up your fruitcakes. My talent's baton twirling, but I can't do much with a low ceiling."

I said, "Oh, your talent might be something else," all wink-wink, as if the beautician weren't present.

"I'm Frankie," said the other woman. "Like in the song."

"Hey, Frankie," I said. "I remember you."

"Open the fruitcake like Cammie said." Cammie walked toward the sink and shimmied up on it. "It's from the Small Business Owners Association. I'm part of them."

I had no option but to believe in a God who looked down upon and cared about me. I pulled open the first box to find a fifty-dollar bill sitting atop the fruitcake. Subsequent boxes held twenties, tens, more fifties, and a roll of silver dollars. "What're you people doing?" I asked. This was a half-town of people willing to bribe me to leave them alone and another half-town bribing me to exaggerate their wonderful environs.

"You the money man," Frankie said. "The Christmas dessert and money man." She walked past me and stretched out on the bed. "I wish they was a good movie on tonight. Anyway, the association only asks that you let the world know how great Claxton is. Then people will indeed come visit. And it'll be nothing but an economic boom for the community as a whole."

All told, I got forty-eight free fruitcakes and another thousand-plus dollars. "Well y'all might win Friendliest Town in the South," I said. I foresaw a fine life of driving from one small forgotten place to the next garnering illicit payoffs, each town's populace evenly divided between hopeful do-gooders and ne'er-do-well outlaws. I said, "Do y'all want any of this money from the shopkeepers? I mean, did y'all come here to trade off some work, or what?"

Cammie said, "I got to get back to the front desk."

Frankie got up off the bed, looked at herself in the mirror, and fingered her hair upwards. She squeegeed her teeth and popped gum I'd not noticed before. "I hope you're not talking about what I think you're talking about, as cool as you are or not. Anyway. If the mayor or anybody comes by and asks tomorrow, don't forget to tell them we brought over the gifts."

That night I didn't call Marcel Parsell to tell him I'd be mailing Claxton in presently before moving on to Egypt, or

Canoochee, or Kibbee, or Emmalane. I didn't call my father to say how I'd succeeded in finding a satisfying job, regardless of what I might go on to study. I thought about calling Shirley Ebo, my imaginary black girlfriend who worked the summer as a counselor at a camp for children with missing extremities. Shirley taught knitting, somehow.

I didn't telephone my lost and wayward mother in St. Louis, Nashville, New Orleans, or Las Vegas. Compton Lane—my best friend since birth—didn't get a call.

I had three thousand dollars in my room, in a town of a thousand people, during an economic recession.

I took my leftover marijuana and pressed it in the Bible, like an autumn leaf. Don't think I left money in there stupidly so the chambermaid could change her station in life. Then I called Rack Me. When Cecil answered I announced myself and asked if anyone was playing pool, then told her I'd come bring tip money in the morning if she would direct the receiver toward the pool table. I said something about how I'd unexpectedly needed to hear the crack of one sphere hitting the other, that I needed to prove to myself that at least one law of physics was working somewhere. She covered the mouthpiece, but I heard her laugh right before she hung up altogether.

I packed and made a point to fold my sparse collection of clean clothes neatly. It seemed important to place my money everywhere possible—in my shoes, in the glove compartment, between two opened fruitcakes shoved together. It would take another twenty years for me to understand what little value all of these bribes had, and how fortunate I was to—even if it was only a joke at the time—stick a carved cue chalk of either Henry Ford or William Tecumseh Sherman on my dashboard as I left for another hopeless group of citizens two hours away. My remaining collection of Brother Macon miniatures vibrated atop the passenger seat in an awkward and mysterious historical orgy, the participants of which would one day attract both friends and strangers to my door. Everyone in my later life would remark how great it was that I could line up these chalk busts and offer little lectures at tiny libraries to kids wishing for a place worthy of their rearing.

Better Fire Hydrants, Shorter Trees,
More Holes to Dig

My deceased father's ex-stray cur Scarface dug another perfect six-by-six-by-three-foot-deep hole in the backyard I'd inherited along with him. I figured he'd been taught such a trick, so I moved—board by board—the pallets of heart-pine lumber that covered areas where Scarface needed to dig. I'm talking I cleared the land and reset all that salvaged lumber in the front of the house, for I knew that the dog had been helping my father by doing my old job since I left Forty-Five for college.

I stacked thousands of feet properly, then got out the shovel and pickax and metal detector and, starting at the back edge of my new acreage, uncovered caches of old, stolen, tin service-station signs: Gulf, Sinclair, Esso, Texaco, Mobil, all wrapped in newspaper and bed sheets. They were laid out horizontally, and in better than fair condition.

It proved to me that indeed my own father hadn't died unexpectedly without preparing some kind of last will and testament, that he had gone to his own odd lengths to take care of his only son. I went back inside the cement-block house of my youth to tell my confused, skeptical wife, Lyla, my theory—now confirmed—of how my father had spent most of his life.

Lyla followed me outside. Scarface sat erect next to his latest hole, as if expecting a bone. I said, "Good boy. You can retire. Go chase a car if you want."

After that I dug up ten thousand advertising yardsticks wrapped in a conglomeration of plastic and wax to prevent termites, and understood that my father had requested them at every hardware, appliance, and home-furnishing store, every car dealership, hospital, and sporting goods outlet in a three-state area, that he had foreseen the demise of a metric-converted America, that he'd journeyed to building supply conventions and extravaganzas in Charlotte, Atlanta, Columbia, and Asheville.

After Lyla clinked into a giant hole full of ashtrays, International House of Pancake syrup containers, and old automobile hubcaps and car lighters, she said, "It's like a yard sale for the dead in Hell, Mendal."

I couldn't respond. I myself had come across a stash of fishing lures, railroad spikes, and old oilcans. When I unearthed mounds of both clear and green telephone-pole insulators, I tried not to undergo flashbacks of my father waking me up early weekend mornings to walk the roadsides of Forty-Five armed with burlap bags in search of such treasures.

I lined those insulators up all the way to the back door

twice, to make a sidewalk for Lyla and me to follow. In another hole I found a group of metal church signs, Lion's Club signs, Rotary Club signs, Shriners signs, and town-limit signs. My wife found six lockers filled with stolen first-edition books. I uncovered the bones of my boyhood dogs, Peewot and Gypsy, strays that had shown up, received attention, and never chased cars to their deaths. Or at least the bones looked big enough to be dog bones and too small to be the mother who supposedly ran away in the early 1960s.

All in all, Lyla and I dug up an old john boat, two airplane propellers, a section of the Forty-Five High School football stands, twenty-two old oak school desks with ink-well holders, enough car bumpers to refield a demolition derby, enough restaurant salt shakers to kill all the slugs in the Southeast, enough free-pour sugar containers to sweeten Republicans into understanding the plight of unemployed workers in need of health insurance. I thought it might be good either to rent out a Quonset hut somewhere or start cataloging these things for sale on an Internet auction site. There was a filled hole of unopened Billy Beer cans and rotary telephones. Another hole held nothing but rubber Quikoin change purses made in Akron, silver church-key can openers, and wall calendars—all advertising give-aways—everything wrapped in plastic garbage bags. Lyla accidentally scooped out what must've been a refuse heap from a hundred years earlier, when an antebellum house had perhaps stood nearby in the middle of something like two thousand acres of cotton, corn, beans, and tobacco. She found old, old cobalt blue bottles and what appeared to be the remnants of a still. After I dredged up one last set of buried yardsticks, I wheelbarrowed off the last of the excess of red clay to the front yard's property lines. By then—and it took more than a week—I had built a wall not dissimilar to those that surrounded Old Testament cities.

After I found enough black-and-yellow tin NO TRESPASS-ING signs, red-and-white KEEP OUT, and regular posted signs, I understood my father's belief that the entire globe should be traversed easily by all persons, regardless of land ownership. He never locked his door, in keeping. After my wife and I had disemboweled the backyard of my upbring-ing, we stood three-to-six feet below original ground level and looked at everything my father had amassed, the great junk and precious, rare items. I thought Lyla, an archaeol-ogist by both trade and nature, an antique-hunting freak by avocation, would've been overjoyed with our newfound Americana. After she said, "You'd think he could've buried a few mayonnaise jars filled with silver quarters; you'd think we'd've come across some liberty dimes jammed into Ball or mason jars," I figured our marriage was back in trouble.

"There's a million dollars' worth of stuff here," I said.

Here's what Lyla said to that: "A million dollars that'll take two million to move, store, advertise, and sell. Add in your time and the years you'll have to spend with a chiro-practor, and you'll wish he'd only buried coins in the ground like every other paranoid schizophrenic does if they haven't been committed." Lyla leaned on her adze. She wore one bandanna around her neck like a cattle rustler and another over her scalp hoodlum-style. If it had been pollen season, she would've worn a third one across her face like a post–Civil War Texas bank robber.

We'd been married long enough for me to see a side of her personality that might've suggested cold-blooded accusations and a thin heart.

Lyla said, "I'm sorry I said that about your daddy," looking at the dug-up Frisch's Big Boy statue as she spoke. Scarface limped off to the side of the house and lifted his leg on one of the Golden Arches.

WHILE I WAS growing up there weren't but ten houses along the entire three-mile length of Deadfall Road. A hundred years before, I would imagine, there'd been only one. By the time my father died near the end of the century, nearly every landowner's inheritors had sold off acreage to developers who built nearly identical ranch house subdivisions, or nearly identical two-story brick pseudo-Tudor homes, or rented out nearly identical mobile homes with phony stone underpinning. The original ten houses from my childhood stood surrounded by a horseshoe of "homes," the inhabitants of which all worked at foreign-owned industries between ten and sixty miles away: Fuji, Michelin, BMW. Their children sat in front of televisions all day long and showed no curiosity about the graves, bullets, and arrowheads that lay beneath their canned homesteads. The homeowners invested in garage door openers, commuted to and from work alone, and never saw their neighbors on either side. Occasionally Lyla and I drove through the anemic development behind my father's house and watched men ride their lawn tractors as if competing in a synchronized swimming competition, with a yard always in between them. The residents of, say, 101, 105, and 109 Chaucer Court would be up and out to cut their front yards by ten A.M. on Saturday mornings while the men of 103, 107, and 111 did their backyards. Index fingers poking through venetian blinds meant these people feared conversation, that waving at one another two doors over satisfied their intentions to be neighborly. Did similar dances occur out of my view, all along the perfect arterial U of Shakespeare Lane and its veins and capillaries: Marlowe Street, Walter Raleigh Court, Dickens Circle? The whole dopey neighborhood together was called Sherwood Forest, which made me wonder what kind of grades land developers in America had made in their English 102 classes. The subdivision that ran behind Compton Lane's father's house had streets named—get this—Marlin, Sailfish, Dolphin, and Barracuda, but it was called Freshwater Acres.

Some days I hated life altogether.

A week after my wife and I had, we figured, excavated the entire back acreage of my dead father's soil, Lyla walked into the kitchen and headed straight for the blender. She pulled it forward, turned to the refrigerator for ice, then reached below the sink for a bottle of tequila. "I'm making margaritas," she said. "When we have had about two each I'll talk again."

I'd been on the Internet and telephone all day dickering with woodplanks.com, heartpine.com, pineplank.com, heartwood.com, and woodheart.com. I e-mailed them all, requesting prices for what I knew I owned out in the front yard. Then I called them back, said my aim was to see what a middleman like I should receive for his product, and so on. Because I knew that I had enough ancient lumber to make me wealthy no matter—and my father had sold off at least this much twenty years earlier, but that's a whole other story—I didn't make anyone stew for days like a regular bastard businessman might. I sold the unfinished and rough ex–barn wood to a man named Terrell Smoot for two bucks a foot on seven-to-ten-inch widths in full knowledge that his people got upwards of twenty dollars per square foot. We made a gentlemen's agreement, and he promised to drive up from his home base in Goose Creek the following morning, a couple of semis behind him.

Lyla poured her drink into a plastic Tupperware tumbler and finished it off. I said, "What's up with you? Where've you been all day? I kind of have some good news."

My wife had taken a job as a substitute teacher at Forty-Five High while she puzzled out what we would end up doing and where we'd go after I settled my father's strange and cumbersome affairs. Lyla also volunteered for the literacy program and taught the teachers of Forty-Five Middle School and Forty-Five Elementary on Tuesday and Thursday nights. In January she would sign on to teach Intro to Archaeology down the road at this place called Anders College and would come home every night saying she'd discovered another Cro-Magnon alive and walking the campus. "Lookee here what was in our mailbox." She pulled a recklessly folded sheet of typing paper from her shirt pocket.

I read aloud, " 'Last year the Sherwood Forest Homeowners Association voted unanimously that your father's house and property was an eyesore to the surrounding community. Since then, we have never heard from your father. We invited him to clean up his yard, put siding on the house, and join us—even though the house isn't even close to our three-thousand-square-foot requirement. We are hopeful that you will be more flexible and understanding in our concerns. You wouldn't want a KOA campground surrounding your property, would you?' " It was signed, "The Concerned Residents of Sherwood Forest."

I said, "Concerned residents. Well, I better walk out back and hunt down Friar Tuck or Robin Hood and see what this is all about."

Lyla said, "I'll stay here for the rest of our lives out of spite, Mendal. I will! These idiots obviously haven't ever tangled with an archaeologist with minors in anthropology and art."

I stood up and stretched my aching back, ruined from backyard excavation and Internet retrieval. I didn't say anything about how I knew my father well enough to know that he'd managed to ruin these people's lives without knowing them. "I sold all the heart pine today."

Lyla turned from the kitchen window as if I'd zapped her with a cattle prod. "No. No, no, no. If you sell that wood, they'll think they've won. If we sell anything—anything we spent all that time digging up—these hammerheads will see it as a victory for their little club."

I shook my head no. I raised my palms. Lyla stormed around the house, put Southern Culture on the Skids in the CD player, and worked one speaker out of the den window, aimed toward Sherwood Forest. It was too loud for me to tell her how, when I wasn't but maybe five, my father had foreseen this day and made me help him with a gross of fifty-five-gallon drums, that I even had a picture in my yearbook as part of a Before-and-After extravaganza.

COMPTON LANE, MY best friend growing up, found his way out of Forty-Five, South Carolina. He became a veterinarian and then quit his profession altogether when a strange group of people threatened his life daily for fixing AKC bitch dogs after they'd hooked up accidentally with nonpurebreds. At least that's what he told me over the telephone once, right before his crazy father died in a tragic, fluke incident involving a gust of wind and a less-than-stable

Duke Power electrical line. Comp took a job in Montgomery, Alabama, straight out of vet school and spent a decade as an upstanding member of the George Wallace–loving community until somebody decided that God didn't cotton to abortions of any type if said animal had once lived in the Garden of Eden. According to Comp, a pregnant snake was held in more esteem in Montgomery than anyone knowing post-1865 history. He came back home after demonstrators regularly held FICKSING IS BAD and NEUTER IS A GEAR, NOT A LIFESTYLE signs outside of his clinic. It made the national news, and about three years later—just as the Forty-Five town council voted that a cable television company could open up—there was a front-page item in the local paper about Compton's woes. He lived quietly in his old house, intent on writing something better than all those other writing veterinarians.

"Now you know what it's like," he said to me the day after Lyla got our ultimatum in the mail. "It'll get worse. My first anonymous letter back in Montgomery went something like, 'It's okay to litter.' And there was a Xerox of an X ray. That's how it started."

Compton got started on veterinary science because Forty-Five's only vet had found an odd Christian Science God in the middle of his career, and whenever anyone took a rabid, wormy, or car-struck hound to him, Dr. Wimmer just said, "Let's have a little prayer," or "If God wants Gypsy to get better, Gypsy will get better." Then he charged five dollars for the visit.

COMPTON AND I sat in my father's kitchen, drinking beer and bourbon at ten o'clock in the morning. Lyla was off subbing for forty dollars a day. Although Comp and I hadn't stayed in touch very well over the years—I'd seen him only once, at my daddy's viewing and funeral, since I'd returned home—we fell right back into our old ways as childhood friends fall, no awkwardness evident. I said, "I can't remember if you were in on this, man, but do you remember when I found out how my father bought all those fifty-five-gallon drums? Did I let you in on that?"

Comp turned a jigger upside down and chased it. He said, "This is just like those times we cut school in seventh grade. And eighth, ninth, tenth . . . " Although he still had a boyish face, his eyes showed the strain the people of Montgomery had forced upon him. He said, "Kind of. I remember your dad and mine always up to something, trying to teach some do-gooder a lesson. I remember the bait-shack scam."

"That Before-and-After picture of me in the yearbook was from this particular episode in Dad's life. He went and got ahold of a bunch of steel drums and he buried them for some reason. I was too young to recall the incident. It's kind of like a dream now, but then again most of the time I feel like that when I go back to ages three through eighteen. My father got these big drums from somewhere, and we buried them because he had a plan of sorts. He painted TOXIC MATERIAL on each one and buried them over there at Sherwood Forest, I believe. I don't think I'm dreaming all of this up. I don't think he told me a lie, either." I got up and looked out the window. "This is weird, but when Dad told me all about what he did, he kept telling me that I wasn't listening to him—which I probably wasn't—but that I'd thank him one day. He even said that my wife and I would thank him."

Compton stood up and looked out the window into my excavated yard. He nodded his head to *Workingman's Dead* blaring out of my father's console stereo in the den, an album I'd not listened to since 1976 or thereabouts, a band that in Forty-Five, South Carolina, only Comp and I knew. He said, "Toxic. Yeah. You told me. We were stoned, or trying to get stoned. Or we were selling Lipton's tea to those two teachers. Later on my father told me how he had some of those metal stencils you piece together and spray paint over. Your father borrowed them and sprayed TOXIC WASTE on those drums. Dad helped him bury a couple right back there." He pointed to what used to be good farmland, toward the subdivision. "I kind of remember the Before-and-After picture, but I have to admit I haven't looked at our old yearbook. There are people around here we went to school with who keep theirs on the coffee table. It's the only book they own."

I poured two more shots and said, "This old boy named Terrell Smoot is showing up later to pick up all the leftover heart pine. I ain't figured it out yet but I'm thinking I'll get a few hundred thousand dollars for Dad's big collection. Who'd've known he knew what he was doing all those years saving torn down barns."

"My dad said that your dad pissed in those fifty-five-gallon drums before burying them. The time my father helped, they drank beer and peed a bunch, and from what I heard, your father kept saying, 'This'll get 'em good,' every time he dropped one into the ground."

Comp and I sat there like deaf-mutes for a half-hour before he finally asked if I got the Animal Planet network on cable. Then he moved to the den and watched a documentary on North American burrowers.

MR. SMOOT BROUGHT his two semis, five men, and a number of tape measures. He said, of course, "I got to tell you. A lot of this wood is worthless. A lot of these boards have too many nail holes and splits in them."

Lyla had come home from sub teaching early. Comp sat in the den staring at the Animal Planet channel. I walked in once to get beer for the workers and felt pretty sure that Compton had been crying. On the TV they were showing emergency surgery on a dog that had fallen off a cliff trying to get to its buddy that fell off first.

"Oh. I'm sorry to've wasted your time," I said to Smoot.

"Hell, I thought you could use this. Let me let y'all go, and I'll get back in touch with plankpine.com, or one of those others."

His workers—Jose, Jorge, Pedro, and Senor Jorge— continued to measure out lengths and yell "ten!" "twelve!" or "sixteen!" which a short man, who looked like Pepino on *The Real McCoys,* wrote down on a legal pad. I knew that they'd probably slipped a couple hundred feet into the trucks without my noticing, but it didn't matter. Smoot said, "I'm not saying we won't take your wood. I'm only saying we've gotten better lumber over the years."

"Don't let me go down in history as saying I offered up the worst wood," I said. "Come on. Y'all take that lumber out of the truck and I'll write you out a check for the gas money it cost y'all to come up here." I pulled my arms in the international sign for unloading the loaded and said, "And let me go inside and make some barbecue sandwiches for your drive back home. Doggone, I'll have bad dreams about this the rest of my nights."

The Mexicans stopped for about two seconds in my front yard, then continued calling off lengths and stacking wood. Smoot said, "We're good. You and me, we'll be all right," and he laughed.

Lyla came out of the house and said, "Hey, Mendal, I don't want the homeowners association thinking that we've caved in. I ordered a bunch of plastic pink flamingoes over the phone, if you don't mind. I'm going to get some lawn jockeys, too, and paint their faces white. I'm going to buy some cement birdbaths."

I said, "Where's Compton? Is he okay in there?"

"There's got to be a junkyard around here. I want to get some old cars to park around the yard. I wish we had a big oak tree to string up an engine in."

Smoot said, "Oh, I'm gonna buy this heart pine. But the lengths you had resting on the naked ground are ruined."

"Yeah, yeah, yeah," I said. I slapped his back. "Tell it to the idiots you sell this stuff to for twenty dollars a square foot in New Mexico and Connecticut. My father's first batch of this wood pretty much decorates the insides of some of the first Cracker Barrels. You ever eaten there, on the interstate exits? They didn't seem to complain." I knew, also, that even though Lyla and I had uncovered all of those signs, my father had sold just as many more to these same Cracker Barrel–type, old-timey restaurants.

And then, as if a shaft of daylight beamed down from the heavens, it came back to me. I doubt it would've been clearer if my father had come back to life in front of the cement-block house, the Smoot operation taking place in his midst. I saw my father talking on a black, black clunky rotary-dial telephone and actually heard his voice say, "Oh yeah, in time, buddy. If it ain't in our lifetime it'll be in our boys' time." He said, "Forty-Five's going to grow. It'll double. Where else will people have to move? You can't build houses on water or asphalt, but by God you sure can set one down in a cow pasture." I could hear the clink-clink-clink in his glass.

Lyla said, "What else? What else? There has to be something else that'll make those homeowners association people so mad they won't know whether to zip their pants or scratch their ass."

I looked at her eyes. The Mexicans shuffled lumber in such a way that it sounded like emery boards over snagged fingernails. I said, "What? What're you on, honey?"

She looked like she was just a shell filled with throbbing adrenaline. Her feet danced in eight directions. "Oh, I'm just mad. You know I get this way."

"We're fine," I said and put my arm on her jittery shoulder. "You and I are fine. I'm kind of worried about old Comp, though."

At dusk Terrell Smoot handed me a check. He said I could cash it immediately. "I'm kind of surprised you didn't use that good wood to side your own house," he said. "God-damn, you don't see too many houses like yours anymore. Does it sweat real bad on the inside?" He pulled at his balls. "I'm betting you can tear down this place and make more money off the lot, what with what's surrounding you. All these big houses."

I didn't punch him in the nose. I said, "I grew up this way. I grew up here." I didn't say anything about how it was hard enough selling what my father stole, buried, and stored for thirty years. When Smoot backed out onto Deadfall Road I yelled out, "If you see any stray dogs trying to chase your wheels, stop and pick them up. They're only trying to get out of here, like the rest of us."

I DON'T WANT to cast aspersions on the people of my hometown, really, but exactly nobody had that star-69 feature on his or her telephone, either, because it cost some money or because of the number's connotation. I know this: a week after Lyla pulled that homeowners association letter out of our mailbox, and a day after she stuck pink flamingoes and whirligigs in the front, side, and backyards, plus the roof, she called the Department of Health and Environmental Control to say in a disguised, overly southern dialect what I had written down on a piece of yellow notepad, namely, "Nuclear waste been dumped down in Sherwood Forest." My wife drawled, "I don't want to reveal myself none—and I don't want to alarm the neighbors— but I went out to bury the cat and dug up a drum called TOXIC. I'm feared they's all over the place."

Oh, we watched. We got out the binoculars and telescope. We set up and pointed toward the subdivision, and we watched as DHEC officials ran their specialized detectors aboveground.

"You ought to go ahead and fashion a letter about how you don't appreciate a nuclear dumping ground behind the house," Lyla said. "Listen." She stuck her hand to her left ear. "Can you hear the sound of falling property values?"

WITHIN THE WEEK they had pulled my father's fake toxic drums out of half the lots. It made the front page of the newspapers all over the state. NO ONE KNOWS, ran the headline up in Greenville. In Columbia, the investigative reporter wrote a series on the history of illegal toxic dumping in the state. Our hometown paper, the *Forty-Five Platter,* in a bigger font than for V-Day, ran SHERWOOD FOREST CALLED A DUMP. At this point no one had tested the barrels' contents only to find an inch or two of human urine, if indeed it hadn't seeped through or evaporated.

Lyla and I walked over there once the yellow plastic DO NOT CROSS lines went up. I couldn't help but wonder, How did my father know this would happen? How did he know to plant drums in what would one day be nouveau riche people's front yards?

This was seven o'clock in the evening. No one was sitting on front porches, or cutting grass, or washing an SUV in the driveway. Lyla and I walked down the middle of Desdemona Lane without threat of traffic. Brown free-tailed Mexican bats flitted barely above us. A few children peeked out from their parents' living room windows. I said, "This is nothing but cool."

Lyla said, "It might be the meanest thing I've ever witnessed."

I tried to not consider how the scams I had connived during my lifetime emanated directly from the small town that spawned me. I said, "Yeah. Who'd've thought that my dad would've seen this far ahead? Damn his time."

But what a great trick! I tried not to giggle or jump up and click my heels three times. Lyla and I walked through Sherwood Forest holding hands. It was as if we were the only living human inhabitants in the middle of a disaster zone. No dogs ran out toward us baring teeth. No person stood stupid with a rake in his hand, staring. "From above, I bet it looks like giant groundhogs came through here," Lyla said. She ran her hand through the air, gesturing at heaps of red clay piled beside the holes.

"My father kind of had a Sisyphus complex. Instead of rolling boulders to nowhere he just dug holes, it appears. Who in Greek mythology kept digging holes for nothing?"

Lyla said, "I bet it was Diogenes. The dog philosopher. So, not a myth—a real person."

I let go of Lyla and stepped over someone's caution tape. The man of the house opened his kitchen door and yelled, "Don't do that, man. Get away from that hole unless you're from the nuclear facility."

I looked at him and ambled across his once perfectly manicured patch of Bermuda grass. I said, "I live over there," and pointed to the back of my property. "Are you one with your homeowners association?"

He closed his storm door and watched me through the glass. I walked toward him and slid my hand across his Jeep Grand Cherokee, parked—I assumed not in his garage so he could make a better getaway—in the side yard. "Yes," he said.

"Tell your people that my wife and I don't appreciate how y'all's yards are bringing down our property value. We can't get anyone to look at the cement-block house, seeing as prospective buyers fear all of y'all's open holes."

From the driveway Lyla waved like a float-riding beauty queen. At first I thought she was taunting this poor man—a fellow named Klauber, I learned later, who commuted all the way to Columbia daily in order to talk state legislators into backing prayer in schools, Confederate flags on public buildings, no lotteries, no Sunday sales of booze, no abortions, and so on. He was a pathetic Conservative lobbyist concerned with holding people back from their inalienable rights unless they had to do with firearms. But as Lyla and I trekked home, I realized that she had waved to me, too. Was she saying good-bye? Was she practicing one of those yoga poses?

I said something about how I would confess to my father's trick, how I would use our heart-pine money to clean up what yards lay behind us. After I interpreted my wife's face I knew that it wouldn't matter, that she'd shifted her views from victimizer to victim. After I volunteered to side our house with yardsticks—thus making it easier to figure out its overall square footage—my wife, I felt certain that night, would apply to a university somewhere far away in order to take additional courses in anthropology before going on with her life, either emptied or fulfilled.

I came home from my new job as a professional fundraiser—my first account was to stir up some money for a new wing at the Greenville County Museum of Art—to find my small house ransacked. In fact, I walked in during the act of plundering, heard the bedroom chest-of-drawers squeaking out, the mattress flopping back down. On the kitchen table stood a stack of disposable razors, an electric AM-FM radio, two cardboard boxes of Gem safety blades, a plug-in hair dryer, one length of rope, all of our Venetian blind pulls, and the extension cord. Paring and butcher knives were scattered there, too. Our dog Dooley wagged his tail and half-barked. He seemed to be missing his choke collar.

"Please tell me that you're in the bedroom, honey, so I don't come in there ready to kill an intruder." I opened the pantry to find my bourbon missing.

"Just a second," Lyla yelled back. She entered the kitchen holding a can of Dran-o and the sharpest scissors we possessed. "Hey. How was work?"

I wondered if Lyla needed medical and/or psychological attention. For a slight, slight moment I thought that she'd gotten pregnant and wanted a head start on child-proofing the place. But I knew better. Lyla took something like eighteen birth control pills per day in order that she never be blamed for aiding a baby in this world with my odd and calamitous genes involved. I said, "Work's fine. I came up with a great ploy. I'll tell you all about it once you go first."

Lyla set the Dran-o and scissors beside her pile. She reached behind my neck and pulled me closer to her face. Right before I kissed her, though, she said, "I want you to look me in the eye and tell me if there's a gun in the house. A pistol or rifle. A shotgun of any type. Fuck, a blowgun or potato gun."

I couldn't believe her question. "There's a squirt gun I use to trick Dooley some nights when he passes out too early. There's that thing. You know I can't keep a gun in the house. I'd kill myself, no offense."

Lyla let go. She grinned and raised her eyebrows. "Can you think of anything we might have in our house that could be used as a weapon of personal destruction? Other than what I've already uncovered?"

I didn't say, "Your experimental quiches, soups, pizzas, and breads." I said, "Where's my bourbon?"

When Lyla started off her answer with, "It'll only be one day. Between one day and three days. Three days at the most," I understood that a possibly tragic and dreadful set of activities would stand between my everyday uneventful existence and any realm where comfort reigned. "You won't even be here days. It's the nights I'm worried about."

Dooley barked for me to go outside and play ball. "Please tell me you're not hosting a group of non-toxic wayward archeologists over here for an impromptu conference. Or a sleepover thing." About once a year Lyla invited people over—men and women alike—to watch unending documentaries on the effects of aerosol spray on dead mastodons, et cetera.

"No, no," Lyla said. "You'll like her, probably. You've *met* her once."

There was a missing segue in the conversation, I understood.

"Who is 'her'?"

"Well, back when *I* knew her—and even when *you* met her—she went by her given name. Brianna-May Slesh." It sounded like a complete sentence to me, a subject and verb phrase. I couldn't place meeting Brianna-May Slesh.

"Where'd I meet her?'

Lyla said, "Up in Knoxville. She worked part-time as a waitress and part-time at a bookstore. The one who told you how she concentrated full-time on poetry."

I said, "Oh yeah. I remember." The woman had a body not unlike an isosceles triangle balanced on its long tip. Her measurements went something like 36DD-24-16. That day I pretended to be absorbed in the Science Section with a book about magnetic fields, but I listened to Lyla's friend spell out how her poems evolved out of trace amounts of breast milk that still circled inside her celestial orb, or some such crap. I said, "She's coming to our *house?*"

"She goes by May-Brianna now. And she's the Tennessee poetry slam champion. The regional finals are being held in Asheville. So she's staying with us, and some of her friends might be coming over one of those nights, I don't know."

I wondered how, over the last few years, Lyla kept her correspondence with May-Brianna from me. "You're hiding all the sharp objects so I won't kill myself. The radio so I won't play it in the bathtub."

My wife said, "I can see how come they hired you on as a fundraiser."

THE GREENVILLE COUNTY MUSEUM OF ART prided itself on a dozen Andrew Wyeth rejects bought up at auction by a millionaire South Carolina local textile baron of sorts. There were early versions of "Christina's World" where, off in the background, surrounded by acres of waving grain, a small child stood alone popping one of those fly-back paddle balls in the air. In another pre-"Christina's World" the same girl stood on her head, wearing no underwear. The rest of the museum held, in its personal collection, works by Jasper Johns, Roy Lichtenstein, Willem de Kooning, and Andy Warhol. This is the late 1980s. The most conservative members of the community saw "Christina's Upside Down World" as pornography, and the paddle ball piece as a sign of further economic downfall due to non-productive past times. Liberals who underwent unfortunate job transfers into the area saw the most experimental twentieth century pieces as near-realism. And I got hired on to get donations from both sides.

"I'm going to some of the Christian pinheads to say our new wing will hold nothing but Norman Rockwell illustrations and first century photographs of the crucifixion. They won't know. To the liberals—there's a list of union organizers and democrats that the Christians all keep—I'll say that Christo's coming over to wrap the entire goddamn Bob Jones University campus." Lyla and I sat in the den watching *Jeopardy!*. We waited for May-Brianna to drive up.

"Isn't that illegal? What'll happen when the addition's built and the museum director fills it with whatever?"

The director looked like Howdy-Doody and bought work from local women who would screw him. The museum, somewhere in its innards, held a vast collection of pinestraw baskets, bad watercolors, and fiber art that wasn't much more than bedspreads-on-walls. I said, "That's his problem. By then we'll be out of here. Hell, by then I'll be fundraising for a big, big museum—like up in Brooklyn—a place that won't ever have controversy."

I could've gone on and on about my future dreams—none of which would turn out due to death threats from someone involved in the 2000 presidential campaign when I faked being an avid and supportive republican—but May-Brianna knocked on the door and tottered herself in. I just sat there, but Lyla kind of shrieked and giggled and held out her arms. May-Brianna said something like, "At dusk / when night birds call out my name / I succumb, and curl inward, and / drink from myself like a game. . . ."

I said, "Who is Jeannette Rankin," the correct answer on *Jeopardy!* for the first female congresswoman elected in the United States House of Representatives. Lyla took May-Brianna by the hand and led her toward me. May-Brianna said, "You haven't changed a bit since we met, Mendal. Lyla must be taking good care of you yet."

I said, "Hey." Understand that—especially as a fund-raiser—name recognition and firm handshakes meant almost everything, outside of telling lies and bullshitting with strangers. But I feared that I would transpose May-Brianna's name, or pronounce it in a way that might cause her to barricade herself in a bathroom to write and panto-mime out a series of male-bashing diatribes. I said, "Well. Yes. Lyla takes good care of me but I won't be shaving for a few days."

Lyla said, "Sit down and tell us all about your life. What's this poetry slam all about?"

May-Brianna got down on the floor and crossed her legs in a way that made yoga gurus look like they suffered from that ossified bone syndrome. She said, "I brought a bottle of white wine that's out in the car. Could you go get it, Mendal? And I guess my bags, too?"

I smiled and looked at *Jeopardy!*, thought, "Who is Eggbert, King of Wessex," and said, "I love white wine," though I didn't, ever.

May-Brianna said, "When the grape turns itself / into a nectar corked / we must bless the hoe / and the corkscrew's cousin, the fork." She spread her hands all over the place, I think to represent the sun's rise and fall. She might've stolen her movements from the original production of *Hair.* I wanted the ghost of horrific Confederate poet laureate Sidney Lanier to plop down on my couch and recite anthems of massacre.

Lyla said, "You have a way with rhymes." I could tell that she, too, feared having sharp objects in our house. My wife's voice diminuendoed like a stock car going down a straightaway. May-Brianna said something about how it wasn't only A-B-A-B rhymes that the judges looked for, but facial expressions and enunciation. I think that's what she said. I walked out of my own small house trying to recite the periodic fucking table.

I WOKE UP AT MY NORMAL HOUR, namely four A.M., and walked into my kitchen to make coffee as always. This was a Friday morning. In the world of fundraising Friday might as well be Sunday, that's what I learned early on. I got my big quart bottle of Old Crow bourbon out from beneath my Jeep's passenger seat, brought it in, and poured some into a jelly jar while waiting. These were the times— I'm not ashamed or embarrassed or proud to let anyone know about my fundraising idea scheme routines—that the best thoughts appeared. I drank, and I thought. There had to be other professions wherein workers did the same, I didn't know.

May-Brianna sat at the round kitchen table, studying the surface. She stared down mesmerized. I'm talking May-Brianna looked like a geometry problem occurred between her pupils and some spot on the wood grain. I wore boxers. My wife's old college friend wore a sequiny thing that might've doubled for a NASA star chart. "Good morning," I said. "I didn't think anyone got up as early as me. As I."

May-Brianna said, "I've not slept in eight years. I'm not lying. This isn't an exaggeration." She sat there like Betty Boop reincarnate. May-Brianna's breasts stood an inch off the tabletop and half way over; her crossed ankles didn't take up the space of a matchbox.

I poured bourbon. I fixed the coffee and poured two bourbons, one for me and one for Lyla's pal. May-Brianna took the jelly jar and nodded thanks. She said, "So. Fund-raising. Like, do you go around selling those World Famous chocolate bars, and big M&M packs, and stick pens with special logos?" May-Brianna took from her morning shot-glass before I did.

"It's not like that," I said. "It's different. What I do—oh—there are all kinds of mailing lists and calculations to make. It ain't exactly Girl Scout cookies."

Normally at this hour I listened to AM radio news broadcasts. It gave me ideas. May-Brianna's nipples stuck out like knobs on a safe. Her peculiar wrists flapped around her glass like skittish vipers. "Big money," she said, slowly.

I detected a drawl for the first time. "Where did Lyla say you were from originally?"

She spread her arms out and jutted that chest forward. "Winston-Salem. Charleston. Macon. Some other places. Knoxville. Oxford, Mississippi. You know."

I could make out her nipples easily. I said, "Those are good towns. Those are fine towns."

"We come from small towns / we hail from large cities / I once saw a man / whom I tried not to pity," May-Brianna said. I tried not to think or say what I thought would rhyme with "cities."

The coffee maker chugged its first belch of steam. "So tonight's Round One in the poetry slam thing, huh? Are you scared or excited or both?" Why didn't I go back to the bedroom and put on some clothes? Why didn't I take up distance running for the first time in fifteen years, excuse myself, and try to undergo a self-induced heart attack some mile up the road?

May-Brianna stood up on her pencil-thin calves, pointed her wedge-shaped torso toward me, and whispered, "When does Lyla usually wake up?"

I whispered back, "I don't know. Why?" and got an immediate erection.

"I've always admired Lyla," May-Brianna said. "I mean, we're as different as the sun and an ashtray, you know—she studied that archeology and I literature—but that doesn't mean I have the right to move in on what she has worked so hard to achieve. Perhaps I knew that it would be taboo for me to invite myself here into y'all's home. Or maybe it was fate for us to find out if fate meant for us to find out."

Look, man, the coffee maker let out its final climactic exhalation. May-Brianna looked like a tapped-in old-fashioned cut nail steadied and readied to be hammered home. I stood with my back to the refrigerator, knowing that my wife hid every sharp object so that I wouldn't kill myself out of guilt after breaking those wedding vows. Yes, I underwent a pre-dawn realization that *Lyla brought a siren in to our home to test my faith.*

I said, "You want some coffee to go with that shot of bourbon?"

May-Brianna jerked her head sideways toward the kitchen counter. "Can I use that line in one of my poems?"

I MIGHT NOT BE ONE OF the most literate pecker-heads in America, but three "poets" into the National

Poetry Slam competition and I knew that real poets that I'd seen or heard before got nervous and read their good words too fast, but these bad, bad, horrible, pretentious slam poets could've sped up somewhat so as to take the audience members out of its extended misery. I'm talking there has to be another physical gesture outside of back-of-hand-to-head to express woe-is-me, man. There had to be a way to pronounce words like "tomb" or "doom" or "womb" in less than eighty-seven syllables.

Lyla got out of bed by eight o'clock that morning and came into the kitchen all wide-eyed. She said, "I hope I haven't missed anything. How long have y'all two been up?"

I said, "Not long."

May-Brianna said, at the same time—like in a sitcom— "Three hours."

I knew that, somewhere between the next hour and four decades my wife would bring this morning up again, say something like, "So what exactly were you and May-Brianna *doing* up so early together?" Not that I want to ever make broad, sweeping generalizations—and it's not like I have much experience with women besides my wife Lyla and this black girl named Shirley Ebo with whom I almost lost my virginity to in a cement mixer—but more than once, out of nowhere, a woman in my life has said something like, "Now explain to me why you were walking around the house with your pants around your ankles two minutes after you thought I went to the grocery store," a year or two after the fact, usually in the company of friends and/or relatives.

I didn't know about the conference opening at noon that day, or that I was supposed to attend. Asheville wasn't an hour from where we lived at the time—my trying out the new roving fundraiser job, and Lyla digging up ancient pre-Cherokee Indian artifacts. May-Brianna said, "Having a female and male friend together there will enhance my anima/animus strategem," or something like that. Me, I had out a notebook writing down notes as to how I would soon ask textile mill executives for money after lying to them that the new Greenville County Museum of Art two-story wing would hold works by Mississippi painters who only concentrated on cotton fields.

I said, "What?"

My wife said, "Come on, Mendal. This'll be fun. You can take a day off. Maybe you'll meet some art lovers full of money." Lyla'd changed into a long one-piece Blue Fish dress that looked more t-shirt than anything else. May-Brianna-the-Human-Top wore black leotards and a black shirt with shiny, shiny black lettering that read "Coal Mine Below."

It might've meant something. I didn't ask.

I drove. May-Brianna sat in back of the Jeep, reciting her poetry. I tried not to look at her full, full lips in the rearview mirror. As we pulled into the parking lot of a vegetarian food co-op where the contest was being held, Lyla turned back to her friend and said, "Do you want to smoke a number beforehand?"

I looked at my wife as if she'd sprouted horns and finally learned Tom Waits lyrics. She'd not smoked pot since we worked together one summer at Ghost Town in the Sky in Maggie Valley, between our sophomore and junior years at different colleges. I said, "I have a flask on me."

When we paid our dollar cover at the door the guy said, "Save your stub. If you're lucky you might get pulled to be one of three judges." When they called out the numbers later, I didn't look down.

May-Brianna waved her left palm like the sun's daily movement. She said, "I'm fine. I'm going to win. If I want something, then I deserve it. That's my motto. I want to win this poetry competition and share my words with the world, therefore I deserve it. You know that there's a two hundred dollar prize. If I win, I'll buy us a bottle of red wine and a loaf of stoneground homemade wheat crunch rosemary bread they make here. That'll still leave me enough money to pay one month's rent, all of the utility bills, and put some aside for another special fountain pen and parchment paper that I make from old leaves, dandelions, and dogwood blooms."

Inside, surrounded by men and women who didn't bathe often enough, I said, "Good God, Lyla, where can a person live off that little money? Is May-Brianna on some kind of work release? Is this her weekend off from the nuthouse, or what?"

My wife focused on the stage. A co-op waitress came to our table and asked if we'd like to order some kind of iced Zen tea or local micro brewed ale. Lyla said to me, "So when exactly was it when you remembered May-Brianna's name?"

Contestant Number One got up and yodeled. He was from Tennessee. This was a warm up exercise round. Contestant Number Two, from Alabama, did that "Rain in Spain falls mainly on the plain" thing. No one wanted to tip his or her hand on the bad poetry that would emanate presently, I figured out. May-Brianna stood with her legs apart in a way that made her body look like the letter X with the top half crayoned in. She looked above the ground and sang, "Mendal-Mendal bo-bendal banana-fanna-fo-fendal, me-my-mo-mendal, Mendal . . ."

I ORDERED AN ICE BUCKET of bottled beer brewed in a place called Pig Cliff, North Carolina. A free church key came with the purchase of a six-pack. Whoever made the stuff should've offered a door prize for anyone who could hold down the seventy-two ounces, kind of like steakhouses that give up meals for free when patrons polish off four-pound T-bones. And this particular prize should've consisted of a roll of Rolaids, some Pepto-Bismol, and a free trip to the rehab clinic. "Say," Lyla said. "Say. I guess

I should surmise that you and May-Brianna got to know each other pretty well while I stayed asleep in our bed. What time did you decide to get up, anyway? Did you set the alarm to go off? I didn't hear the alarm go off. Did you set your inner clock to go off?"

Lyla said all of this amid people snapping their fingers. There must've been a hundred spectators, most of whom wore beaded head- or armbands, jackets with fringe hanging off. They snapped their fingers at the end of each poet's performance, Beat-style, only twenty or thirty years behind the times. A few adventurous types said, "Yes!" about one-thousandth of a decibel above normal speaking.

I said to Lyla, "Here comes your ex-roommate," and pointed.

May-Brianna got up on stage and held her arms upward. She said, "Cigarettes and Pabst Blue Ribbon, regular baloney, white bread, canned Spam, Vienna sausages, liver pudding, quick minute grits, olive loaf, bacon, Penrose-brand hot sausages and pickled eggs, Armour potted meat, pork brains in milk gravy, and the latest *National Enquirer.*" Throughout this grocery list she melted down toward the floor. *"White trash grocery shopping!"* She completed her fall to the floor.

I snapped my fingers, but not loudly, and stopped long before Lyla.

May-Brianna got up to curtsey, of all things, then hopped off the stage and joined our table. She said, "Well.

All right. So. I think that had a little more socio-political statement than that man who wrote about his mother's collection of Coco Joe lava god statues, don't y'all?"

I said, "Indubitably."

Lyla said nothing at first. She looked at my bucket of beer. "You could've added cheap rubbers. They sell cheap rubbers at grocery stores these days. Non-lubricated, multi-colored, three-to-a-box rubbers. You should've mentioned those, too. What do you think about that idea, Mendal?"

I said, "Come on, Lyla. Ease up."

"Rubbers," May-Brianna said. "That's a great idea. Do white trash women use douches? What's the crummiest douche out there on the market?"

We watched the other eleven contestants read their melodramatic, didactic poems that concerned poverty, toxins, the government, childhood trauma, the beauty of pine trees, why intercollegiate sports should be abolished, and how there should be laws against non-contact rape.

The emcee came on stage. He wore silver and gold pants once owned by a bedouin, or gypsy man. This guy had a ponytail that sprouted from his crown and sideburns that looked like Italy. "As all of you know," he said, "the top three winners this afternoon will come back tomorrow night for the slam-off. And the overall winner will compete out in Taos, New Mexico in the nationals. I'm of the belief that our winner here will take nationals seeing as Asheville and Taos are on the same latitude. It's karma, y'all." May-Brianna's nipples stuck out like goddamn dowels, that's how excited she became. "I want all of our contestants to come up on stage with me here."

They all got up. Every one of the men wore pony-tails that couldn't be used for shoestrings, and they all furrowed their brows and slumped forward. May-Brianna kissed Lyla flat on the lips, then looked at me and said, "Wish me."

I won't go through the entire pathetic situation, but May-Brianna stood there in the final four. The emcee said all that shit about how if one of these quadruples couldn't appear the next night, et cetera. May-Brianna came in fourth. Before we left the food co-op, though, the second place winner—a man from West Virginia—said he needed to check himself into the nearest hospital.

I'd watched him earlier. He, too, had ordered a bucket of Pig Cliff beer.

It doesn't matter that my wife and I jumped out of our Jeep to see who could get back to the bedroom first. It doesn't matter that we both left May-Brianna alone in the driveway spouting off some new off-the-top-of-her-head epic poem about mountain shadows, ex-moonshiners, and Preparation H. I got to home base first and said, "You stay up with her tonight. She's your friend. I'll join y'all at four o'clock."

Lyla said, "I forgot how she plain exudes sex. I won't ask you again if y'all had a little fling if and only if you tell me right now that y'all didn't."

I stood flat behind the bedroom door, my right knee and shoulder pressed hard. Lyla's face poked in maybe two inches. I said, "We didn't." I said, "We drank some bourbon and I made your coffee and her nipples moved throughout the kitchen like sea anemones. Now you can't ask anymore."

It doesn't matter that I went to bed alone and dreamed the dreams of both underwater and pornographic film directors. No, it probably—in the long, long history of ex-roommate relations, or of a roommate meeting her ex-roommate's new mate—doesn't matter that I awoke pre-dawn as always, in mid-thought of how I should ask local upstate South Carolina businessmen for money to build art museum ells. I got up half-asleep and shuffled between mattress and linoleum floor to find May-Brianna and Lyla at the table, halfway into a pathetic, anti-misogynist game of Scrabble. What matters are these words: boar, bore, moron, fool, limp, noose, neuter, and nonsoul—which I didn't think was even a fucking word, by the way. Oh, right now I can't recall all of the juxtapositions, but those were the words, left and right, up and down. All of the Os seemed gone.

I said, like an idiot, "Are you girls having fun?" Who hasn't said that before? Who hasn't accidentally called women "girls?" Goddamn, I still dreamt of cotton mill owners and their fraudulent money. I wasn't a bad person then, or now. Plus, I didn't say "gals."

Lyla said, "How fitting," and placed down tiles to read "fucker."

I said, "You might want to save that U in case you get the Q." That's the way I was with my wife.

May-Brianna said, "Is there any place to take a walk around here? I want to take a walk. I need to walk. I need to." She stood up like a piece of upside down meringue.

It doesn't matter that Lyla drove to the co-op later on this particular day, that May-Brianna sat in the passenger seat, and that I took up the back. It doesn't matter that I couldn't get an ABABABAB ABABABABABAB rhyme out of my head.

Here: I paid my dollar, and thirty minutes later they called my number to be a judge. I could've sat there mute, but I said, "That's me," and then both Lyla and May-Brianna pointed. I tried to pocket my number, but they had me up by the elbows and pushed me in the direction of the judges' seats, front row. The two others chosen—and it seemed to be the highlights of their lives—were both women dressed in black-and-red checkered Pendleton flannel logging shirts, blue jeans, and wide leather belts with silver buckles. I stuck out my hand to shake but got no response. One woman nodded once in a perfectly misanthropic way and said her name was Dana. I might've misheard, but I thought for sure that the other went by either Howell or Howl.

We were given numbers to raise, just like in Olympic gymnastics or diving competitions, except ours started at 9.0 and ended with 10. It didn't take an ex-poet laureate to figure out that a 9.0 was about as good as a flat zero. I said, "This one woman coming up's a friend of my wife's, but I'm going to be objective. I'm going to call it like I see it. Or hear it."

Lumberjack woman Howell or Howl said to the other, "Well at least I ain't constipated like last night. But I tell you, whatever it is they sold me here come out more cob than corn, more husk than grit, more pone than mash." She turned up a bottle of Pig Cliff. "But I'm here, ain't I? Nothing can keep me away from true art, and you know I know art."

It was Howl, I decided.

This won't be good, I thought. I wondered what my old friends did at that particular moment as I learned the alimentary concerns of a woman prone to fermentable grain. Did my veterinarian buddy sit up all night with a birddog partial to fallen peaches? Did he diddle his veterinary assistant on a cold, silver, steel examination table? And what about my father?—I saw him sitting head-in-hands at the kitchen table, a baseball game playing over the portable radio, probably still wondering what my mother saw on the other side of the property line and well beyond. Had he given up a life of conjuring schemes yet?

I knew nothing. I had gotten nowhere. I shuffled through my judges' flashcards, kept most of the pile on my lap, held only the nine and ten in either hand. I would take my chances with each contestant, friend of the family or not.

Later that night I would spoon Lyla behind a locked door and try not to think of Yeats or Eliot, or even the public restroom stall poetry that my good wife's ex-roommate wrote between Asheville and Taos, on her way to a fame that would forever reach beyond most deserving citizens. I would not close my eyes, and worry about whether any vengeful losers, supporters, or judges followed us home in order to chant bad rhymes out in our front yard. I wondered if they would trouble themselves to pantomime simple words and obvious dictums, out there in the dark, dark midnight shadows.

THE EARTH ROTATES THIS WAY

I f forced to reflect on when my marriage might have started to fall apart, I began with how I'd told Lyla I once owned a significant collection of Houdini memorabilia that had simply vanished into thin air. We weren't even married yet—this was second-date material. It took me eighteen-plus years to understand the root of our problems. I'm talking I went backwards in time with the marriage counselor.

Lyla studied his wallpaper, as best as I could tell, while the counselor twisted hairs on his beard, on the left side of his lip like, I'm sure, he'd seen in movies. I said, "I was brought up believing that the whole process of death begins the moment you're born. Every day gone is a day of dying. Maybe it's the same in marriage. Like, as soon as vows are taken there in a Gatlinburg wedding chapel, the process of divorce kicks in. I'm a big-time believer that marriage is the number one cause of divorce in America, doctor. You *are* a doctor, right?"

The counselor pointed at three diplomas and a series of bona fide certificates. Lyla said, "I knew you wouldn't take this seriously, Mendal." To the counselor she said, "What did I tell you."

My wife and I sat together on a couch, and Dr. Boyce sat behind his desk. This was all the way up in Asheville, a three-hour drive away for us. Lyla'd seen Boyce do an interview concerning life choices, the alignment of planets, and carbohydrate intake on some ETV show. That's all she needed to be convinced.

"Yes, I am. I'm serious," I said to the psychologist. "Is there any way we could turn off those fake-waterfall machines over there? The sound of running water makes me want to pee."

Boyce got up and unplugged a miniature statue of urns, one tipping into another, and another, and another. He was wearing wool pants in summer, I noticed. "Y'all are what— early forties? Don't think you're alone in this situation. I'm always happy when patients come in without black eyes and slashed wrists. I think we can work this out." Then he reached into a drawer and said, "Who wants a Rice Krispie Treat?"

Lyla and I shook our heads no. He unwrapped his and started crunching away. I got up and turned one fake waterfall back on. Lyla said, "Control freak."

Dr. Boyce said, "You may be a confused water sign. Are you Pisces or Aquarius?"

You'd have to know me to understand how little I respect people who ride the pop-psychology/zodiac wave blindly toward rocky, oil-slicked shores. Anyway, I said, "Taurus."

"Aaah."

Lyla stood up for no apparent reason. I sat back down. She said, "First off, I want to say that I have a sense of humor. Take me to a comedy club and I'll be the first to slap my knee. But when nothing's funny, I'm not going to let out big fake belly laughs. I'm sorry. Mendal was brought up to believe he was dying every minute, and I was brought up thinking that what's not funny shouldn't be laughed at."

I laughed. Dr. Boyce looked at me in the same way that Mrs. Hawthorne used to back in high school when I thought Ethan Frome's sledding disaster was sidesplitting. Boyce said, "This may or may not have anything to do with your situation particularly, but how often do you two spend time apart from each other?"

We both said, "Never," simultaneously. It didn't take some kind of FBI voice-recognition expert to notice the edgy diminuendo in our responses.

From his desk, Dr. Boyce picked up a softball-sized beanbag with the continents sewn onto it and tossed it to me. "I want y'all to stand six feet apart. Mendal, I want you to gently throw the beanbag to Lyla, and while it's in midair quickly state something that bothers you. Lyla, after you catch the Earth, take a step back and do the same. You catch it, Mendal, take a step back, and so on."

The room was a good twenty-four-feet wide. I tossed the Earth in a high arc and said, "Thinks I'll cheat on her when I really only want to play poker on Monday nights with a couple buddies." Understand that I had to speak fast.

My wife caught the bag, stepped back, and underhanded me one. "Thinks my yoga class is stupid."

I nodded. I stepped back. "Thinks I'm forcing myself into her archaeological territory when in fact I'm only trying to make ends meet and give us a brighter financial future."

Lyla caught it, stepped back, and threw the Earth at me in a way that would've made any major-league pitching coach proud. "Self-absorbed."

Dr. Boyce said, "Wow. Good catch, Mendal."

I tossed the beanbag back to my wife and said, "Inferiority complex."

She stepped back and said, "Thinks he's smarter than anyone—which might be true in the hellhole town in which we live." Lyla threw another strike, Nolan Ryan style.

I caught it, stepped back, and said, "Can't admit when she's wrong."

This went on. Dr. Boyce said he'd never had clients make it all the way to his walls without dropping the beanbag. My wife and I kept our backs to the perimeter for six or eight more turns. Lyla threw another and said, "Still has a crush on Shirley Ebo, this woman who he loved from second grade on, or whatever."

I threw it back and said, "Doesn't like turnip greens."

"Scared of the dentist," Lyla said—that's how far we'd gotten.

I caught the Earth in my mouth.

I ENDED UP having to explain to the good doctor how I'd gotten it in my mind that I could be a buyer for the Cracker Barrel chain of interstate-exit country stores and restaurants, what with all the old signs I'd found buried in my dead father's yard. I told Boyce how everyone in my hometown of Forty-Five, South Carolina, probably—perhaps rightly—had deemed my blood crazy, seeing as my father, over a thirty-year period, had disassembled, saved, and stored every outbuilding, barn, and slave shack in a hundred-mile radius of our house. Dad had been forced to buy extra land just to stack twelve-by-twelve-by-twelve-foot pallets of lumber. It angered me that I—not my father—would be the person to gain financially.

"Y'all's problem has exactly zero to do with you finding old advertising signs," Dr. Boyce said to me. To Lyla he said, "And it's not about your *not* finding what's been buried. It's not about heart pine, or dead parents, or missed opportunities along the way, really. Are you happy, Lyla? Would you be happier if you got to teach again at some point in time?"

My wife said, "Yes," from the other side of the room.

"Are you jealous that Lyla wants a career, Mendal?"

I said, "Not at all."

Dr. Boyce spread out his arms. "You have both just spoken

the truth." He clapped his hands. Although no one would believe me later, he actually quivered back and forth like a baseball-player bobble-head doll. "I know the problem already, but let me tell you what both of you need to do."

At that juncture Boyce motioned for us to stand together in front of his desk. Lyla said, "On that show I saw you on, you said the colon was more important than the lungs. Is that true?"

I got a better look at his diplomas and certificates. I thought, I'll give him Duke, Vandy, and Chapel Hill, but scoffed at an Institute of the Spleen certification, framed next to one in glandular studies. I said, "I'm not an organ donor but I'm thinking about giving away my pituitary glands so some little person can grow. How about *that*?"

"The colon's very important," Dr. Boyce said to my wife. "I might've been exaggerating, though. The guy running everything told me to be somewhat controversial."

I said, "What's that other gland? I might die and donate that other gland so people can have a better life. I'm that way. So they can spit and such."

Boyce said, "I want y'all to hold hands now and close your eyes. I don't want you to move, or squeeze your palms. Just close your eyes and nod up and down for yes. Don't move for no."

I'm not embarrassed to admit that I wanted a drink. I wanted bourbon.

When my wife and I approached the therapist's desk there in his office on Trade Street I could tell by the look on her face that we weren't so hopeless as a couple. If Boyce had put a gun to my head, though, I wouldn't have been able to explain it.

Boyce said, "I'll close my eyes, too."

I took the beanbag Earth from my mouth and set it on the edge of his desk. Lyla and I held hands. I said, "How're you going to see us nod up and down or not if your eyes are closed?"

"Oh, yeah. I messed up. This is a new exercise I developed last week. Y'all are my first patients to try it on. Let's start over." Lyla squeezed my hand, even though it was against the rules. "I'll close my eyes and ask questions. Y'all answer out loud yes or no, and pretend I'm not here."

I said, "That's better. That's much better. It's kind of like having an invisible wizard in charge, or the voice of God." Then I worried that he'd think I meant it. "Let's get this thing going. Are you ready, Slick?"

Boyce turned his face toward the ceiling and closed his eyes. I let go of Lyla's hand, picked up the beanbag, and shoved it down the front of my pants. Boyce said, "Yes or no—I believe that it's better to be a good person as opposed to a bad person and that—although it's not written in stone, or in a philosopher's handbook—I have a pretty good idea what the difference is between good and bad. Yes or no.

Y'all can take your time before you answer." He spoke in a rhythm that would've been perfect for counseling turtles.

Lyla and I tiptoed to the door halfway through his speech. She turned the knob slowly, trying not to laugh. The door closed softly behind us as the doctor was saying, "Let me repeat it for y'all." I bet we had the car cranked before he realized that we were gone.

I said, "I feel bad, kind of. I'll send him a check for his time." The way I was sitting driving, beans were tumbling from one end of the Earth to the other.

Out on Highway 25 Lyla pointed to a service-station-turned-junk-shop with old gasoline memorabilia. The sign read I GOT GAS. She said, "Pull in here and let's check prices on the kinds of things you think you'll find more of below your daddy's soil."

I turned. "I'll send this Dr. Boyce guy fifty dollars. Fifty dollars an hour is more money than what anyone deserves." I unbuttoned my pants, pulled down the zipper, and extracted the world. "I gave better advice to dying men at Forty-Five Longterm Care when I wasn't but ten years old, working part-time after school for something like a buck-fifty an hour."

Lyla said, "I have a confession to make. I only wanted you to prove to me that you'd be willing to see an avant-garde therapist. Just by agreeing to go lets me know we're okay." She leaned over and kissed the side of my mouth. "You mean weirdo."

I said to Lyla, "I'd've gone to an acupuncturist with you, honey. I'd've gone to a rebirthologist who found a way to incorporate aromatherapy into her sessions."

A round white man with silver sideburns shaved into cowboy-boot silhouettes came out of the stucco filling station. He held his arms out to showcase his wares. I rolled down my window. "Evathang's thutty puhcent off!" he yelled out. "Take the price tag and mult-ply by point seven. That's thutty puhcent off."

Lyla stepped out of the car. She said, "Hey," and pointed at the Esso sign. "You get $175 for this?" she asked the man.

I got out and said, "Where'd you get your gasoline memorabilia? Have you been saving these things all along?" The man looked like a department-store Santa Claus who'd gotten bored with shaving and left the sharp-edged muttonchops. He looked like the Skipper on *Gilligan's Island,* like every other football coach/driver's ed teacher at South Carolina low-country schools, like that actor who played the warden in *Cool Hand Luke.*

"Oh, I *get* it," he said. He didn't make eye contact.

I looked at him harder and saw the same squint as my father's. This man had also seen the future and stolen these signs over the years faster than a man on second base peeping at the opposing team's catcher. Lyla said, "What's the best you can do on that sign?"

The parking area was plain flat brown dirt. My wife

stood with her hands on her hips, palms backwards, elbows out, like a domesticated turkey. She stood as erect as a soldier's dream. And although I had thought I loved Lyla most when we stole out of Dr. Boyce's office, it felt like Adrenalin got shot into my heart there at I GOT GAS.

Strother-Martin-with-sideburns said, "That's it. That's the best price I can do. One thing in America these days—people always pay good money to get a sign."

WE TOOK BACK roads to Forty-Five, as if there *were* any four-lanes between my old hometown and anywhere else. Lyla kept her feet propped up on the dashboard. "The problem is, nobody in Forty-Five would buy old advertising signs. We need to move to a place with more upwardly mobile people our age. But then the cost of living outside South Carolina will end up being too much, you know. Maybe we should just get a backhoe and see what else we can find."

"I'm not sure I want to know everything that my daddy put to rest on his land. Maybe he only *told* me that his only wife and my mother disengaged herself from our home when I was a child. Maybe my father was one of those men who accidentally shoved a woman's head onto a sharp countertop, then had no choice but to bury the body and claim abandonment before friends, neighbors, relatives, and co-workers could formulate other scenarios."

Lyla flipped her visor down and looked at herself in the mirror. "By the way, what's a rebirthologist?" she asked.

I said, "Listen. I don't know how to say this. You never knew my father very well. I mean, he acted pretty normal around you most of the time. But he wasn't normal. When he brought me up the best he could, he was flat-out nuts from the get-go. I'm just saying, I don't know if I want to know all that's buried back behind the house."

She flipped up the visor and squinted. "You started it, Mendal. You're the one who rented the metal detector and got everything in motion, not me. What're you talking about?"

"My mother didn't have a plate in her head. She had no fillings in her teeth. I'll dig, but no backhoe. Promise me no backhoe."

Lyla put her feet on the floorboard. She shifted in her seat. "We don't have to do anything, if you don't want. It's your house."

"*Our* house. You know that."

"Look, I'm happy. Sure, I wouldn't mind living in a town that could offer more than *The Sound of Music, The Music Man,* and *Oklahoma!* at its Little Theatre." We crossed into Graywood County. Lyla said something about my watching for stray dogs crossing the road unexpectedly. "Or that didn't have the audacity to call its old-timey drugstore and rifle collection The Museum. But that's all right. I'm fully optimistic that Forty-Five's just a tiny, tiny stepping-stone on our path to a better life."

I honked the horn and grinned and nodded like a trick

horse. I didn't tell Lyla how—after I'd gone off to college—
my father had gone through a suicidal phase, how he stacked
newspapers and kerosene-soaked rags in every room and
replaced the windows with magnifying glass.

I said, "I read somewhere about rebirthology. People go
through this thing when their lives are so messed up that the
only cause they can see has to do with their emergence into
this world. Like maybe a man's head came out cocked, or an
arm got stuck sideways too long. I read about it. I'm betting
that if one of us could disguise our voice, we could call up
Dr. Boyce and he'd be able to explain it better."

Lyla put her left hand on the gearshift, which always
made me nervous. She said, "People. What're they thinking?
You get cards from the dealer and you either play or fold.
There is no redealing in the five card draw of life."

I put my right hand on top of hers, on top of the gearshift, not wanting us—even by accident—to hit neutral or
reverse. Lyla pointed and said, "Watch out for that pack of
chows ahead. What's with people coming over the county
line to drop off their wild and unwanted strays?"

I didn't tell her my theory.

In mid-December it was still seventy degrees outside in Forty-Five. After Lyla and I resumed our lives I found
myself trying to list out everything I should do in order to
feel better as a citizen and husband, not necessarily in that
order. I thought, I could take in the stray dogs that roam my

county while waiting for the Earth's rotation to slow down so they can find their original owners—the people who opened a passenger-side door and shoved them out into a mysterious, sad, unfortunate, sterile place.

Lyla stood next to me outside. She'd fixed a pitcher of margaritas and we stood on our barren, barren soil. I don't want to sound New Age or anything, but I could hear what my father still had buried beneath; I heard his stolen signs and borrowed gimcracks sigh with what weight had encumbered them over the years. Across the way, Pete and Frank Godfrey's livestock bellowed away, as if they, too, understood what obstacles would no longer hinder the horizon. The cattle looked at Lyla and me as if they couldn't figure out if they should move or stay for the spectacle.

I looked at the nighttime sky. Six planes flew overhead, blinking lights. "We're small, small people. Not you and me, Lyla. I mean, you and I are small people, too. But good goddamn. I don't feel so great about myself here."

I'm not sure where my wife's gaze drifted, or what she really thought. Me, I tried to remember what my father had sold off already, what my grandfather had sold from *his* daddy. I wondered what my odd Irish ancestors held or foresaw as valuable outside of friendship and drink, truth and tradition. Lyla hummed a song I didn't know. No meteors showered across the sky, as would happen in a sentimental Hollywood production.

By midnight I would be asleep cross-legged on the ground

where I got trained. And I dreamed and dreamed and dreamed of Lyla and me living elsewhere without conscience, of my father explaining how he'd saved and buried yardsticks once all the talk of a metric system had emerged.

Lyla nudged me awake. She took me to what was once my parents' bedroom, told me she loved me, and held her hand on my forehead. "You were talking in your sleep outside," she said. " 'Shirley Ebo, Shirley Ebo.' Why don't you call up her daddy and see if she's living nearby still?"

"Shirley Ebo's not in Forty-Five," I said. "Before we were even in college she said she'd stay, and I said I'd be leaving forever. It's how things work out, always. Backwards."

Lyla rolled over in bed and told me that she'd once seen a documentary on educational television about the elongated grieving process between men and the women with whom they'd lost their virginities. It could be worse, she told me. But if indeed it got worse, we could always seek help again, to feel better, Lyla said. I'm not sure if I—always the pessimist—said something about Houdini again, or if I just thought about him before closing my eyes.

I met my in-laws-to-be only one month before Lyla and I ran off to Gatlinburg instead. At the time there was a regular, normal, planned church wedding complete with three bridesmaids and three groomsmen. Even my indignant, jaded father—a man who held organized religion on a lower rung only than the institution of marriage—agreed to stand beside me at the Churnville Holiness Church of God's Will's altar, right off highway 108 between Ruther-fordton and Spindale, North Carolina. Lyla had warned me of her kin, had said she couldn't stress enough how she had turned out different somehow. I took her tales of impending danger as mere hyperbole. Lyla's final college class dealt with the myths and legends of one of those Indo-nesian story-telling tribes. It affected her seriously. Some-times she would start off telling me something about going to buy eggs at the local farmer's market, then divert into a recital that involved dugout canoes and fruitbats the size of engine blocks. I found my fiancée both quaint and enter-taining, of course.

Lyla's father was second-generation statuary. My wife's grandfather had opened a roadside stand of cement bird-baths, turtles, frogs, and dwarves some time after he fought in World War II. This was before the interstate system, so northeners often found themselves lost on 108, half-way between New York and Miami. From what I gathered from Lyla, these misdirected travelers felt either forced or obligated to weigh down their trunks further after gaining proper instructions from the old man, drunk on moonshine and toting a sawed-off shotgun.

My father-in-law-to-be took that same spirit and per-suaded new nearby golf courses, condominiums, and moun-tain rental home developments to buy whatever he poured into molds. When Lyla and I drove up to Rutherfordton to meet her folks, they were right in the middle of a Department of Transportation bid he'd won that involved cement guardian angels with red reflector eyes, to be placed on secondary roads at every sharp curve. A team of guard-watched convicts came out every other day to pick up the angels and set them up at pre-arranged spots. From about Charlotte to the NC/GA/TN border there wasn't a quarter-mile stretch of asphalt on any of the state roads that didn't curl on itself like a copperhead balling up for cover.

"My father's going to ask you to help him perform some illegal activity," Lyla said somewhere between Tryon and Skyuka Mountain. "You have to promise me that you won't help him. You won't participate. He'll get you while Mom and I are out calling on the caterer about finger food and flowers. Trust me."

I said, "Look at that giant wooden horse," and pointed. Tryon was some kind of mixed mecca for steeplechasers and retirees. I said, "Please don't put unneeded pressure on me about your folks. I'm scared enough."

"I'm just saying," Lyla said. "He's going to test you. He's going to ask a lot of questions about you and about us. And then he'll try to get you to help him do something wrong-headed."

I didn't know my fiancée well enough to ask her about previous boyfriends and their episodes with her daddy. I wouldn't know my wife well enough to ask later on, either, even though we kind of took up the same space at an experimental college near Wally Preston Mountain for four years. I said, "I won't drink around him if he offers. I'll not smoke in front of your parents, either. I wish to God some scientist could invent a Band-aid filled with nicotine and tar to strap on your lungs or lips or wherever to take away the addiction."

That's what I said back then. If I'd've studied chemistry I could've bought Lyla and me a couple hundred vacation homes between El Paso and Antietam. Lyla said, "It's only the weekend. You'll have to sleep out in the pop-up. Don't take it the wrong way."

I tried to push the accelerator, but couldn't keep from going ten miles an hour out of sheer dread. I found myself calculating the advantages in falling in love with, and then marrying, an orphan. I said, "I guess my father would be about the same way," though he had no camper out back behind his poor house and I couldn't imagine his making Lyla camp out in one of the various holes he used to dig in the back yard. My father would've kept Lyla inside and sent me to sleep elsewhere.

"There's one more thing I need to tell you," Lyla said as I let the Jeep coast up an incline. "We're meeting at the church first. It's more of a community center than a church. You're going to have to meet about everyone from the valley right off."

Baptism by total immersion, I thought. I said, "Oh god-damn. Oh goddamn. I'm not going to be able to go through with this, Lyla." I turned off the road in order to pull the flask out of my suitcase.

She said, "Here we are."

She pointed. It took me a few seconds to make out the Churnville Holiness Church of God's Will. I said, "What?"

The place was camouflaged. I mean the wooden shot-gun shack-style church was actually painted in green/gray/brown/tan splotches that blended right in with the sur-rounding thick foliage. All of the pick-up trucks parked nearby were painted in like manner. I stared through the windshield as if at one of those Magic Eye tricks in the funny papers, as if I stood too close to a pointillist painting. Then I noticed motion, which happened to be the camou-flage-dressed church-goers pouring out to greet us in their Christian manner. I will never forget my father-in-law's first words to me: "Son, you're gone have to move your Jeep somewhere downwind where deer don't see it."

I said, "Hey," and stuck out my non-camouflaged hand to shake. "I'm Mendal. I'm Mendal Dawes."

Lyla's father stood thirty feet tall, it seemed. Later on I figured out that his own being merged with a hickory tree directly behind him.

THERE WAS A DWINDLING CONGREGATION, evi-dently, so the preacher talked the deacons into talking the six or ten parishioners into camouflaging the church. Then deer and turkey hunters would start hanging around —and they would bring their sons and daughters. Before long these killers and poachers would feel at home at the Church of God's Will, and feel reassured that God wanted both men and women to understand "survival of the fittest" even though Darwin's notion never entered the Holy Bible's tenets. It didn't hurt that Reverend Haulbrook parlayed plate money into salt licks and strategically-placed mounds of corn. The church became camouflaged, and the locals, indeed, flocked toward it. From what I learned, the Churnville Holiness Church of God's Will's outer walls supported hunters each fall and winter season, Monday through Saturday; they wandered slightly confused on days of worship.

When I came back from hiding my vehicle a couple curves down the road, Lyla's dad said, "Hey, Mendal," and hit me hard on my left shoulder. "You got to get inside fast as possible." To Lyla he said, "How come y'all didn't dress right, girl? You know better." Me, I had on blue jeans and a black sweater. My fiancée wore a teal dress.

Lyla said, "Hey, Dad."

I walked with her toward the building. Mr. Strites said, "I'm glad y'all're here. Do you hunt much? Well, if you don't, it don't matter. I could use someone gluing reflectors on the angels' eyes."

I said, "I'm happy to finally meet you."

"You can't put Mendal to work, Daddy. We're here for wedding business and relaxation only."

I said, "I eat red meat but I don't hunt. So I don't feel anything bad about people who kill deer and eat venison." Listen, I felt drunk walking toward a camouflaged church surrounded by men wearing camouflage coveralls. My first acquaintance with vertigo took place there at the hidden Churnville church, and even years later I believed I had an idea about the likely first symptoms of both Tourette's Syndrome and Parkinson's Disease.

Lyla's dad put his hammy left arm across my shoulders and walked. He said how he'd heard how I came up with ideas more than anything else. Lyla's father said how he never wanted his daughter to marry a manual laborer, unless that man couldn't provide for her in the ways that she deserved. He said, "We gone have a good time here, Mendal."

I said, "Yes sir," and hoped that he wouldn't hand me a four-ten shotgun.

Mr. Strites stopped at the church's stoop. He lit a short Lucky Strike and never offered me one. "They say that if you live in a big city breathing all those toxic fumes and car exhausts and smog it's the same as smoking five or six cigarettes a day. He in- and exhaled perfectly. I tried not to stick my hand out. "I like to think of myself living in a city the size of forty million."

I went ha-ha-ha. What else could I do?

"Come on inside and meet the wife," Mr. Strite said. He pressed his cigarette into the church's door frame and placed the butt in his front pocket. "She's the woman responsible for naming Lyla, you know."

We walked inside the church, where it looked almost normal. Outside, men took aim and *ka-powed* toward whatever game they wished dead. For the first time—and I'd known Lyla some few years—I thought of my future wife's full maiden name: Lyla Strites. With some pushing and shoving, "last rites" came out there toward the end. I said to Mr. Strites, "Well I'd certainly love to meet the woman who gave birth to, then named Lie-last-rites," like an idiot.

Lyla said, "I wasn't brought up in this church, I want you to understand. Mendal—when my parents told me to attend church, I declined."

I said, "Uh-huh." I wished that I'd worn green. To Mr. Strites I said, "So you're in the lawn jockey business. How's that going with all this be-polite-to-everyone's-feelings mindset? I guess people aren't buying three-foot black-faced statues as much."

We stopped walking down the aisle together toward a group of women staring at the organ. He said, "Yeah, I make lawn jockeys. What's that last thing you were talking about?"

My fiancée ran ahead of us to hug her flabby-armed mother. The organ women—all wearing powder green hats

—approached me, their collective lipstick smeared from here to there. I said, "I don't know. I don't know. I'm not thinking about anything."

He said, "You'll do fine here, son."

LYLA STRITES, THE WOMAN I loved even way back then, got brought up in a wooden house with about a dozen additions. There was a creek out back—water that her grandfather used for his still—and cement statues, mostly of angels, out front. The pop-up trailer squatted off to the side, next to a fake wishing well. After I met with a group of women named Betty or Gayle—all stuck inside the camouflaged church from their husbands named Tony or Tommy—we all came back to Lyla's parents' house, Lyla perched in the middle non-seat of Mr. Strites's pick-up truck and me trying to anticipate his curves from behind. Understand and believe me when I say that I thought of U-turning more than once. If I'd've known at that moment that Lyla and I would forego the traditional camouflaged church wedding I would've kept a toothy smile for her daddy to see in his rearview, certainly.

But I followed, scared. I lit three cigarettes and stuck them in the ashtray. At every curve I leaned over and inhaled mightily. When we pulled into the Strites's residence I made sure to park close enough to the road should I want to escape quietly, either that afternoon or in the middle of my first night. I kept ideas, sure.

"Y'all go on in and start the food," Mr. Strites said as I got out of my Jeep. "Mendal, let's you and me go for a little drive. Let's you and me go. Come on." He motioned for me to get in his pick-up. "Come on. I want to show you what I do."

Lyla said, "I'll get your suitcase out and hang up your shirts." I wanted one of those shotguns from back at the church. "Y'all have fun, but remember what I told you now, Dad."

"I'm only going to take your Mendal out to show him what I do up here, honey. Just a little ways up the road." Mr. Strites pointed at his wife. "*Honeys*. We'll be back in time for whatever happens later. Before *Hee-Haw*."

It wasn't but about one tire rotation out of the driveway when Mr. Strites reached beneath the bench seat and pulled out a ball peen hammer. He handed it to me handle-first.

I said, "What's this for?"

"You don't know how much money you've landed in, peckerhead," he said. "To be truthful I hoped that Lyla would fall in love and bring back a stupider boy. I guess not every father gets his wishes."

I held the hammer right. I thought about popping Mr. Strites up against the temple, then taking over the steering wheel and faking a veer down the mountain—wherein I'd jump out at the last second—just like in *Mannix* or *The Rockford Files*. "I'm not sure what you mean. And I'm sorry if you think I'm too smart." I didn't tell him that

I graduated with honors. I didn't tell him how I didn't graduate with highest honors because of an Ethics course. I said, "Buck Owens and Roy Clark can play some bluegrass together."

He drove with his left wrist only. Lyla's father draped his left wrist over the steering wheel as if it were a wet oak leaf. He took sharp curves without thinking until, finally, we approached a cement angel with big, big road red reflector eyes. Mr. Strites slowed down and pulled off onto the berm. He said, "It don't take nothing but one pop on the crown." He lit a cigarette. "Use the ball side. *Pop.*"

I'd never wanted a cigarette more. I said, "You want me to break the angel?"

"It's a state job, son. They pay me for these things. I make them, and they come pick them up. They place my angels where they see fit. They buy more when someone runs off the road anyways and hits them. Consider us running off the road."

Fuck, I reached out my window and *pinged* an angel. It fell in on itself. There was nothing left but cement dust and two red reflectors. "There you go," I said.

"Da-a-a-t's ri-i-i-ght," Mr. Strites drawled out. He drove on to the next one, not a quarter-mile up the road. "Let's see if we can do this without stopping. Boy, I wish I had a stopwatch. We could keep and break some kinds of records, you know what I mean."

At least that's what I thought he said. I hung out the window like a lucky dog from a leash, happy to be going anywhere.

I HAVE TO ADMIT THAT, sometime between about angels number fifteen and forty, way out nowhere on state roads 74 and 221, I saw myself moving Lyla and me to nearby Mill Springs or Bat Cove, learning the ins and outs of mixing cement and pouring it into various Snow-White-and-the-Seven-Dwarfs molds, and plodding along until our own children took over the operation. "That's enough for now," Mr. Strites said when we were halfway to Asheville. "I got to go work on the garden some before dusk. Then we'll eat us some supper and go on back out, if you want. It's easier at night. Them angels' eyes pull you right in toward them."

I stuck my torso back into the truck. My right wrist felt sprained, like I'd hit fifty baseballs wrong with a rebar bat. "How many angels have you made altogether, Mr. Strites? Good God. This could go on forever. You don't even have to make lawn jockeys anymore."

Lyla's father U-turned in the road. "There's always room for lawn jockeys, son. We can't forget what got us here, you know. I'm glad to see Americans becoming less racist. It ain't all black face anymore. I been selling a lot of Mexicans. And little eastern Indians wearing diapers and dots, for some reason."

I said, "I'll be damned."

We drove in silence. Mr. Strites smoked Lucky Strike after Lucky Strike. I wanted a drink. Hell, I wanted to shoot up some heroin for the first time. Mr. Strites finally said, "I know you're a college boy and all, but I'm betting you'll learn more from me in three days than you did studying whatever you studied. What did you study, by the way?"

I needed to lie. I didn't. "Anthropology."

Mr. Strites nodded. We might've passed the Churnville Holiness Church of God's Will. I didn't see it, of course, but either the pick-up backfired or one of the flock shot his thirty-ought-six toward a buck. When we turned into the driveway he said, "An-thro-pology. I ain't no spelling bee champ, but that word appears to have 'apology' inside it, boy. That's something to be sorry about."

Lyla came running out of the house, skipped over a series of cement Buddhas, and yelled, "Are you okay? Daddy, where the hell have y'all been all this time?"

I didn't kiss my fiancée. I said, "We're fine. We've been paying off your college tuition."

Lyla wore a pair of cut-off blue jeans and a plaid cotton shirt, not unlike any hillbilly girl in the movies.

I said, "Did you ever notice how 'anthropology' and 'apology' are closely related? Your dad did, right off."

I pointed toward him, but Mr. Strites walked away and opened the door to an outbuilding made of heart pine lumber. "Come over here, Mendal, and I'll teach you something that peoples from centuries ago knowed about."

Lyla said, "Y'all come on inside. It's late." She said, "Oh, Daddy," in a way that I would remember ten years later when we made love. "Mendal and I didn't come here for you to put us to work. Momma's already got me throwing out what canned beets y'all didn't eat over winter."

Mr. Strites stepped into the outbuilding—not much more than the size of a sno-cone hut in any town with a population over a thousand, a grocery store chain, and a parking lot—and handed me a rack of antlers minus the scalp. I peered past him and saw another fifty sets. I said, "Where'd you get all of these?"

Lyla said, "Hey, Mendal, I ordered the cake from the caterer while you were out. I ordered a special six-tiered red velvet cake with buttermilk icing."

Mr. Strites said, "Shed."

"I know you got them out of the shed. I'm here. I saw you open the door."

Lyla stomped her foot and said, "Listen to me. I will *not* end up in a marriage like what my mom and dad are stuck in. I will *not* end up just another little lady who no one listens to. To whom no one listens."

Mr. Strites handed me one side of a buck's proud decoration. He kept his eyes on his daughter, though. To me he said, "Not *the* shed, fur balls. Deer shed their antlers come once a year. They scrape them off on trees. Hickory. Elm.

Oak. I got me a walk I do that's on a regular deer run, and I gather them up."

Lyla shook her head. To her I said, "Red velvet." To her father I said, "Deer."

He said, "Sweetheart. Fool."

I followed him toward the creek. We approached a fallow spot of garden some thousand square feet. I said, "This would be a good place for a shade bed." I looked up at the trees' canopy. "This would be a nice place for an herb garden." What the hell—I had seen a documentary on rosemary, ginseng, basil, mint, and pilewort one time. I knew nothing about gardening at this age outside of how slugs drowned in thin pans of beer, like I did, too.

"Where do antlers point, boy?" Mr. Strites said. We stopped in the middle of his flat, flat tilled land. "I'll tell you. Toward the sun. All the time. And what does the sun hold for us more than anything else?"

I ran state capitals through my head. I thought about primary, secondary, and tertiary colors. I went backwards in regards to past presidents, starting with Reagan, then I did World Series winners. I said, "Light?"

"Energy. The sun provides us with energy. And if there's not enough sunlight in a certain spot of land—say right here—then it's extremely important to bring the energy there." Lyla's father clack-clack-clacked two deer racks together. "These here horns have nothing but sunlight inside them. Pure-tee energy, son."

He nodded his head and grinned as if he'd discovered oil beneath his feet. I said, "That makes sense. Maybe that's why longhorn bulls are so hot-headed. Ha." I knew that I sounded like a letter written from mother to daughter.

Mr. Strites got down on his knees. He dug into the soil, then reached out to me for an antler, then buried it. I mimicked him presently. We spaced the antlers out every three feet or thereabouts. He muttered, "Bringing Hell to earth, bringing Hell to earth," over and over.

THE POP-UP TRAILER HADN'T BEEN used since Nixon's first administration. I surmised this fact because there was a Myrtle Beach newspaper dated 1969 folded beneath the inch-thick pillow. At least Lyla didn't bring some boy home between the My Lai massacre and the boycotted Olympics, I thought. I pulled the musty sheet to my chin and wondered why the Strites ever left their home.

"Hey," Lyla whispered from outside. "You okay out here?"

The bed might've been all of five feet long. My legs were numb from the mid-calf on down, to match my right wrist. Mr. Strites and I didn't get to go out and demolish more angels, for Lyla and her mother thought we needed some time together in order to acquaint ourselves with one another. Mrs. Strites turned off their we-get-two-channels TV. Some kind of police and fire department scanner crackled and blurted at random from atop a side table. We played charades, old people versus newlyweds-to-be. They came up with *The Wizard of Oz,* which Lyla acted out by only tapping her heels. I got it immediately. I came up with *Jaws*—which I thought wouldn't be so hard to grasp seeing as it only took one index finger pointed toward the lower head—and Mr. and Mrs. Strites went on forever blowing apart brain cells until we finally quit.

"No, I'm not okay out here. And you better get back inside before your dad comes out here. Goddamn. I don't want to cast any aspersions, Lyla, but if we ever plan to have any kids we might want to do some DNA tests right about now to make sure things have filtered down and away from the family tree."

We had our mouths an inch apart with the gray, gray, mildewed screen between us. Lyla said, "Open up the door. Why do you have it locked? Once my parents go to sleep it's gone-time. What time is it now?"

I said, "Ten. Ten P.M." I got up and turned what frail clasp kept me from the outside world. I said, "This isn't going too well. Your father's nuts. He buries antlers. From his way of thinking, Indians should've planted scalps in order to grow their maize taller."

Lyla shimmied past me and sat down on the cot. She reached out and smoothed my hair back. "You shouldn't have picked *Jaws* for a movie. You should've picked something like *From Here to Eternity.* They like those movies.

I doubt they've ever heard of *Jaws* yet. They'll know it in about ten years, though."

I wondered how you could act out *The Lost Weekend*. It was impossible. And I would've said this, but out of nowhere Mr. Strites said, "Mendal, what did you make in high school algebra class?"

He'd rigged an intercom to the pop-up trailer. Wires ran through PVC pipe, buried in the side yard, through the house, and to wherever he stood. Lyla got up, but I held my palm out for her to remain quiet. I looked up over my bad pillow and yelled, "I made Bs in all of my math classes. If I'd've had an intensive education instead of Forty-Five High School I imagine I'd've done worse."

He paused. "What about all those anthro-apology courses, what'd you make?"

I told him straight As, which was true, but only because I had feared the overabundance of Young Republicans and Christian Coalition robots—a paranoia I had at the time—that permeated every place on campus except the library where I hid out. Studying was all there was to do there. Lyla tiptoed one step and turned the latch. I coughed loudly to cover up any creaking metallic sound.

"I guess in those classes it's important to find yourself, right? Isn't that what it's all about, finding yourself?"

I turned on my belly and faced where I figured the speaker to be. I said, "Not that I know of." I almost told

him how, during a winter term mini-course, I found myself
because I took a seminar in orienteering.

Mr. Strites said, "I got one more question, son. Did you
take a shop or woodworking class along the line?"

I said, "I sure did."

"And what did you make in there?"

I'd damn near failed that class for getting caught shooting nails up into the sky with a nail gun. I said, "Oh. I
probably made about a B."

"No, no, no. What did you *make*, Burr Balls. Like a
cabinet, or chest-of-drawers, or gun case."

I didn't laugh. I said, "Oh. I made a hope chest so your
daughter could keep some whatnots inside. Even back then
I figured a father like you wouldn't do so. Sir. A big old
hope chest. Maybe four feet long by three feet wide, and a
few feet deep. It was beautiful."

I heard Mr. Strites try to cover the intercom before he
said to his wife how they had a real smartass on their hands.
He said for a boy who didn't know about real energy I sure
did spend a lot of it coming up with worthless things to
think up and say. The final thing he blurted out made no
sense to me—I thought he said, "Thank you" in Japanese.

Lyla didn't kiss me good night. The look in her eyes,
though, told me that she foresaw years of irregular, tainted,
and disquieting in-law relationships. I whispered, "Well, I
couldn't tell him the truth. My shop teacher had some kind

of deal going with the county farm. We made cheap pine caskets for poor dead prisoners. I bet I made twelve coffins that semester, back in junior high."

Lyla let the screen door slam. She said, "My father didn't say 'origato.' He said, 'I got the gout-toe.'" Then Lyla said something about how she would try to get up earlier than everyone else, and make us some sandwiches for the road.

WE SLIPPED OUT IN THE JEEP right before dawn. Let me say that—although I never faulted Lyla—I was the one to mention how leaving one day early and unannounced would probably make one of those Top Ten things to never do in any etiquette book. I said, "Your dad and I might've started off on a misbeat, but this won't help. It's logically possible that in time we would've grown to understand one another." I pointed out one of the angels I had destroyed the day before. "If not even like each other."

Lyla drove. We had a sack of mixed meat sandwiches on white bread between us. We might've passed camouflaged Churnville Holiness Church of God's Will for all I knew, what with darkness, patchy fog, and paint job. I pointed at the next burst angel, its red reflector-eyes staring upward from the shards and powder.

Lyla said, "I used to know these roads. I feel guilty for no longer knowing the roads of my upbringing."

And then she fell silent. After about the twentieth murdered angel I quit pointing them out. When Lyla turned northwest toward higher mountains—the opposite direction from our home—I foresaw the entire future, minus, maybe, those times when she felt obligated to leave alone, to join various awkward and pointless archeological digs in the southeast when she believed that unearthing the remnants of vanished tribes and land mammals would help her understand those who both preceded and lived around her currently. I saw our elopement first, with a sideburned preacher in a shiny, shiny suit. I heard the tinny wedding march and felt my hand shake a witnessing stranger's.

It came to me that Lyla portended her parents' tragic sudden deaths—his from rifle shot because he wore a plain brown jumpsuit while picking ginseng near the camouflaged church, hers from falling beneath a rolling Oldsmobile in the driveway. Lyla had theorized that, had we gone through the church wedding and feigned in aspirations common with her parents, then we could only have returned to Churnville to run the statuary business. Neither of us would have been content, and both of us would have blamed the other. I would, more than likely, concoct X-rated cement lawn ornaments and get sentenced to a North Carolina prison or, worse, one of the numerous asylums of Morganton.

"I might try that trick with the antlers if we ever have a garden," I said to Lyla somewhere in the Smoky Mountains. "Maybe I could use bird feathers, though. Birds absorb the sun, I guess."

"I'm sorry," Lyla said. She put my Jeep in low. "For some reason I thought my dad would know how to change his social mask. The way he talks and acts in Churnville's fine. It's everybody, there. And my mother's just flat sad for getting stuck."

"You're making too much of this. It's nothing. And you and I will be fine either way, I'm betting." I flipped up the passenger-side visor. This was a time before mirrors.

Driving through a pass with dynamite-made alluvial granite embankments we got behind a slow-moving gravel truck. I thought of how mountaintop pebbles might hold energy, how radio antennae might, TV satellite dishes, pieces of space debris, and desert tortoise shells. As we crossed into the Gatlinburg, Tennessee city limits, home to some of the earliest wedding chapels east of the Mississippi River, Lyla said, "I'm going to say 'I do' and mean it, Mendal. But I have a couple problems with the whole vow thing. 'To have' bugs me. It sounds too much like 'to halve,' for one. And it's too much about possession."

I couldn't disagree with her. The gravel truck still urged forward. A sign on its tailgate cautioned us to stay back a safe distance, to expect both wide turns and frequent stops.

I slumped in my seat. Another sign warned us about not being able to see rearview mirrors. I worked my foot into the floorboard. The rear wheel flaps fluttered as if waving goodbye.

I MET MY FIRST REAL GIRLFRIEND and subsequent wife-to-be while standing in a registration line at Wally Preston College in western North Carolina. This was an experimental school founded by do-gooder Unitarians and, in keeping with some kind of mission, the board of trustees and admissions officer accepted one of everyone in each new incoming class: one Mexican American, one African-American, one Native American, one Buddhist, one Catholic, one atheist, one ex-jock who could've gone to Penn State. There was one quadriplegic, one paraplegic, one lesbian, one gay man, one person from Maine whose father was a lobster fisherman. This was a nearly-free college. There was tuition to pay, but room and board cost nothing seeing as all students worked the fields, pasture, greenhouses, and cafeteria. There was no janitorial staff because we all swept, mopped, and took out the garbage. There was no maintenance staff seeing as the admissions officer was smart enough to accept one son-of-an-electrician. On my first day, mesmerized by Lyla Strites's backside three freshmen ahead—and I planned on eavesdropping to see what classes she would choose so I could get in the same ones—I knew that I'd have "Michael Row Your Boat Ashore," "Kum-Ba-Ya," and every other horrific campfire song going through my head for four years.

"Hey, Mendal, you gone take that basket weaving class, or that one in quilting?" I heard from way behind me in line.

I stood between a young eastern Indian girl with a dot on her forehead, and my roommate Paul Michael Mathew Mark O'Malley—I got the Irish Catholic—from Sarasota, Florida, who planned to study theatre arts. When PMMM and I first met in our granite dormitory he said to me, "I went to Italy this past summer and when I saw the David, I *wept*." He might've been the token gay, instead of the Catholic.

I had said, "I went to Mexico. I saw a statue of the Virgin Mary and *she* wept." He didn't get it. PMMM pulled out a suitcase filled with show tune music scores.

I turned around to find Shirley Ebo, from Forty-Five High School—the girl with whom I may or may not have lost my virginity to—waving her registration forms. I yelled back, "I don't know," felt my face redden, and turned back to stare at Lyla Strites. In front of Lyla stood another black woman, so I wondered what Shirley Ebo could possibly be at Wally Preston College. I'd known Shirley since about the second grade. She'd been the editor of the Forty-Five Fire Ant yearbook. She'd helped her daddy harvest corn.

Shirley showed me an old slave graveyard near her parents' land where my own forever-missing mother may or may not have been buried with a memory jug for a headstone.

The line moved onward. I heard Lyla Strites say, "Archeology 101, Pottery 101, Literature of the Absurd, Laurel and Hardy and Schopenhauer, The History of Hell."

Shirley Ebo yelled back to me, "Don't act like you don't know me, Mendal Dawes. You know me. Hey, remember that time we crawled in your daddy's cement truck? Remember that time you tried to sell Senora Schulze tea for marijuana?"

I thought, Maybe Shirley Ebo was the one loudmouth Wally Preston College let in. I nodded my head and raised my hand, but didn't turn to look at her. When I got to the registrar I named off the same things that Lyla Strites said, but asked, "That History of Hell class—will there be any field trips?"

SHIRLEY EBO SETTLED ACROSS FROM me at the Post-Registration Picnic, on the edge of Lake Wally Preston. The residential advisors and argonauts had come in a week early in order to cook meals and proctor about a hundred get-to-know-each-other sessions. Shirley said, "I been knowing I'd be here since about April, Mendal, but I wanted to surprise you."

Lyla Strites sat on a boulder with her roommate, a young white girl from Augusta, Georgia who was the only debutante. I said to Shirley, "What're you doing here, Shirley Ebo? Goddamn. The last time I talked to you, you made a big point about how I'd be leaving Forty-Five for good, and you'd be staying there for the rest of your life."

She said, "I decided not to take basket weaving. I took Whittling 101 instead. I'm thinking about making a big old totem pole and giving it to your daddy. I'm thinking he probably misses wood."

I turned away from Lyla Strites and looked at Shirley. I said, "My father has something to do with you being here, doesn't he."

"He sold off a bunch of those boards in y'all'ses front yard and gave my father the money. I'm supposed to be here to watch you. To make sure you don't do anything stupid."

I turned to watch Lyla get up and brush sand from the back of her culottes. She wore a halter top, and from twenty yards away I could tell that she wasn't wearing a brassiere, something I'd never seen in Forty-Five. Most of my former female classmates wore two bras, and high-necked blouses. I said to Shirley, "Why are you here? I mean—I know you're smart, Shirley—but which different person are you? You ain't the black girl, 'cause I've already met Mauricetta."

"Who are *you?* I see more than a few white boys here," Shirley said. She picked up her lettuce, tomato, and cucumber sandwich on pita bread. "Maybe I'm here to introduce these people to pork, Cuz. I don't know if I can eat this stuff for four years."

Why was I here? I wondered. Was I the token drunk? Was I the agnostic, the smart-ass, the buffoon? When asked, as part of my application to Wally Preston, to write an essay about myself I'd sent in a thousand word lie about how I admired nothing more than snake charmers, cosmonauts, and alligator wrestlers. Was I the liar? Was I the communist herpetologist?

I said, "We sure did have some good times in Forty-Five, didn't we? I'm glad to be out of there, though."

Shirley looked at me as if I'd spoken Sanskrit. "No we didn't, and yes I am." She turned to see what I'd been watching over her shoulder. Shirley said, "That's Lyla Strites. She lives on my hall. And between the two of us, I'm the only one's seen her naked. I guess, for the right amount of money from you, I can tell your daddy that you're picking the right girlfriend. Otherwise I might tell him you messing up."

I said to Shirley, "Ha ha," but couldn't keep my eyes off Lyla. I said, "How much money?"

Shirley Ebo took a slice of cucumber out of her sandwich and threw it in the direction of PMMM, who sat with a blind guy from Texas who, in one of those get-to-know-you sessions, bragged about there being no dress code at his school for the blind back in Dallas or wherever.

Shirley said, "She's the one genius. At least right now. I guess they'll kick her out, though, when she picks you for a boyfriend."

I CERTAINLY WASN'T PICKED as one of a hundred incoming freshmen to Wally Preston College because I had a future in espionage. Lyla Strites wasn't in my first Monday-Wednesday-Friday Archeology 101 class, or my Laurel and Hardy and Schopenhauer class, or my History of Hell class. On Tuesday I found out she wasn't in my Pottery 101 or Literature of the Absurd class. Nope. She had the same classes, but backwards of mine. I had a semester of the History of Hell on Monday/Wednesday/Friday, while she only had it on Tuesday/Thursday. And so on. I went to the registrar to have all of my classes turned around thusly, but she said that it couldn't be done unless someone dropped, or changed, et cetera.

I knew right away that if it occurred, it would be only because Lyla changed classes, and then I'd still not be able to sit behind or beside her. PMMM O'Malley said to me, "Why don't you just start up a study group? Start up five different study groups, and then you'll see her. That's what my old headmaster used to do at St. Joseph's Prep. He had one-on-one study groups so he could meet with all of us, all of the time, every night." I bet he did. "You won't believe how much difference that made in my acting class—I can cry on cue, as long as someone stands behind me."

I bet he could.

Shirley Ebo lounged around the common area below my dorm for the first few weeks of school, and finally said, "Lyla wants to meet you, too. I've been meaning to tell you." I was on my way out to stand guard at the hen house, my first detail at Wally Preston College. There had been coyotes, or cougars, or wild dogs coming around, according to the Dean of Student Affairs and Poultry.

I said, "What do you mean you've been meaning to tell me? How long have you known?"

"I thought as smart as you were, you'd finally ask me to hook y'all up. Your daddy told me to make you come up with all the good ideas. In one of our three-a-day hall meetings we went over who we might want to see. Lyla mentioned you. She mentioned me, too, but she mentioned you first."

I thought, I need to call my father and have a talk with him when he's sober. I thought, I need to call my father at dawn. "We're talking about Lyla, right? Don't go playing any trick on me, Shirley Ebo."

"Lyla's working the after-hours information line for the next week. Why don't you call her up and pretend to need a telephone number. They's a payphone outside the chicken coops. Call her up and talk to her. Tell her what you did before taking that course in Hell, or something. Tell her everything you did after. Bring up nothing, man."

She turned a page in her Intro to Gastronomy text-book, which most people would call a plain cookbook. I ran upstairs to my room, emptied my piggy bank, and extracted all of the silver in case I needed to call Lyla more than once. Then I said to PMMM, "Hey. I want you to call up the after-hours number and keep asking for Mendal Dawes. Do it about five times. Then I'm going to call up and ask if there're any messages for me."

PMMM said, "Where are you from, again? Do you want me to call up the store down the mountain and ask if they got Prince Albert in a can, or if their refrigerator's running?"

I said, "Come on. If you'll do this for me, I'll let you play those Liza Minnelli and Barbra Streisand albums all you want until mid-terms and I won't make noise or faces."

"You're on!" PMMM said. He kicked off his high heels.

So I CALLED UP, AND LYLA STRITES answered the telephone with, "Wally Preston College Information," and I stalled like a fool, and she said, "Is this Mendal Dawes?"

I said, "How did you know?"

"I can hear the chickens clucking. You work at the coops, don't you?"

I actually held my palm out to the hens, as if they'd shut up.

I said, "Have I had any messages?"

Lyla said, "What are you, Mendal? There's one of everyone here. Please tell me you're not filling up the psycho killer quota. Please tell me that Wally Preston didn't let you in here only because they didn't have any other stalkers apply."

It's impossible to know how much noise a henhouse of chickens makes until you call someone from there. I said "No. No. I'm here as the lone existentialist." What the hell. "Hey, you wouldn't be interested in going out on Friday night to a little comedy club in Asheville that specializes in German food served on earthenware plates similar to those dug up in Central America, would you?" I tried to get everything in. I couldn't figure out Literature of the Absurd.

Lyla paused for a moment. She said, "This Friday? I can't this Friday. I've promised an old friend of mine from high school to go to the annual Moonshiner's Convention. On Friday. Then on Saturday I'm supposed to go to a storytellers' convention in the morning, and a snake handler's show in the afternoon. I won't be going to church on Sunday because I never do, but then I'm going to see these buffoons and smart-asses down in Tryon at some kind of Renaissance Fair."

I said, "You're kidding! Are you making fun of me? I'm a lying drunk snake-handling smart-ass buffoon from way back. I should be going to all of those events. I should *star* in them."

I couldn't tell if Lyla laughed or if I only heard the *bawk-bawk-bawk-bawk-bawk* of the chickens in my midst. She said, "I would ask you to escort me but PMMM told me how you promised to sit around with him and listen to famous musicales. Shirley Ebo told me, too."

Maybe those chickens went *balk, balk, balk, balk, balk.* I said, "Shirley Ebo is only here in college to tell a bunch of lies about me. My father paid her. It's a long story. I never slept with her inside the drum of a cement truck parked in my front yard. I never ran around the woods across from where I lived until we finally had to jump scary Forty-Five Creek where all the half-amphibians live."

Oh, I went on and on. I confessed everything that I'd ever done in eighteen years of life. I confessed so much that, later on when I told my roommate, PMMM said I might want to call up his Father Lance or whatever his name was. I mentioned stuff about all the old people I almost killed at a nursing home when I worked at Forty-Five Longterm Care, and how I got a man fired from coaching; I went into detail about how my friend Compton Lane and I stuck Chinese handcuffs on one passed-out boy's member, attached to another unconscious boy's index finger.

Lyla said, "I have another call, I believe." She said, "Listen, Mendal, I'll talk to you later. I promise. I'll call you back."

She wouldn't, I knew. I hung up the receiver, and listened to my hens clucking at a time when they should've slept. I thought, Lyla Strites isn't good enough for me—because that's what all young white boys think when they've been rebuffed rightly. I tried to convince myself, I know what I am here at Wally Preston College—I'm the Cool Guy, the Stud, the Winner, the Most-Likely-to-Succeed. I'm the Opposite of Everyone Else. I'm the Other. I'm either Everything, or Nothing.

But I knew why they put me with the chickens, really. And I knew that I would drop out of everything that first semester, except the History of Hell. During those hours when I should've been taking classes that I had no interest in whatsoever, I would not sleep, though. I would sit at my desk, and contrive ways to get myself as far from this world as possible, without anyone tagging along to remind me of what could never happen.